ICE COLD

Taylor Caley

I0677191

Taylor Caley

Copyright © 2018 Taylor Caley

All rights reserved.

ISBN: 0692124977
ISBN-13: 978-0692124970

CONTENTS

Log 0001

24 June, 2039

Following the account of

The Last Disciple:

"I am recording this for the log: In the year 1989, the 28th day of the 2nd month marked the beginning of the preliminary exordium into the new Age of Faith; after a long-standing relationship between the New York state government and the autonomous ménages of the Adirondack mountains was ended, by requisition of the mountain polity. The years following proved to be the most devastating and trying events of the lives of the mountain people. It is unknown exactly how many were able to escape the cataclysm, or if the tragedy was even noticed by the Outside State. But of this I am certain: the convictions of one boy can change the course of the future for many generations."

PART ONE

THE DARK ZONE

PROLOGUE

Summer, 2008

The Adirondacks, New York

The Dark Zone

One does not navigate through the Appalachian Mountains with ease if he does not belong there, especially in the dead of night. The glow of a single propane lantern is hardly enough to provide sight in the darkness while surrounded by the great cluster of tall trees.

In the immense dark of night, a group of young men slowly made their way through the woods. Two of them were leading the way; one holding a small propane lantern in front of him while the other stood by his side, wielding a rough blacksmith short sword. Following just behind them, a third man was carrying a wounded figure around his shoulders. At the rear of the group a second swordsman was standing guard. They had been hiking throughout the wooded mountain range for a couple of miles, but it was not for their own amusement. The light emitted from the lantern slightly illuminated the holder's face, revealing a large, dark bruise mark on his temple. Similar marks were shared among the entire group, for only hours before they had been assaulted while resting by unseen intruders. The attackers swooped in so fast and so stealthily that none of them had known what had hit them until long after it was over. They had all been knocked unconscious by blunt objects and some of them awoke to find their old, battered clothes covered in dried blood. But the factor that concerned the man holding the lantern the most was the fact that before the attack there were twelve of them. Now there was only five, and the most unfortunate of them was lying slumped over the shoulders of his comrade.

The man leading the group suddenly stopped and raised his hand to signal the others to be still. He set the lantern down and vigilantly scoped around the dark woods for a brief minute before leaning over toward his blade-wielding compeer.

"Go check it out." He said, pointing in the forward direction. Without hesitation, the young tyro cautiously walked forth toward the dark-engulfed tree line. As he watched his guard disappear, the man hazily pondered the reason they were even out here in this dreary, wooded desolation, and the events that had led up to their very involvement. Unfortunately, little was known to him about the people above him and their convictions that continued to leave him and his comrades isolated deep in the woods of the mountains for months on end. Despite what he sometimes thought of his leaders, everyone knew they had no choice but to trust them, unless any of them saw more fit to be left for dead in the middle of the cold wilderness.

In the midst of his deep thoughts, the man was disturbed by a sudden, awful moaning sound. Perturbed, he turned around to see his cohort setting the wounded figure on the ground as he writhed slowly and painfully, and constantly letting out a loud, anguished groan. The man leading the group held his lantern over toward his unsettling party. The maimed character continued to moan and gripe in pain.

The man shook his head in annoyance.

"Would you shut him up?" he growled under his breath.

The one who had been carrying him glared back at him hazily. "What the hell do want me to do, knock him out?" The injured wretch hissed in discomfort, his veins bulged in his hands as he twisted and turned on the ground to blot out the pain.

The rear guard turned his attention to the group and planted his foot lightly on the disturbed figure's head. He stopped squirming instantly.

"Keep quiet! They're still out there." He whispered loudly. He looked up at the trees and glanced around aimlessly but cautiously. "They could be watching us right now. Waiting. Waiting to swoop down from the trees and deliver the final blow." Feeling himself slowly begin to panic, he grasped his stone blade with both hands and held it in front of him.

The leader of the group flicked his hand to signal the panicking rear guard to back off of the wounded victim.

"Calm yourself," he hissed at his comrade. "If they wanted to kill us they would have done it already."

The paranoid man lifted his foot off of the poor victim and took a step back. He took a quick glance up into the darkness of the wooded canopy and then turned back to glare at their ringleader with a huff.

"I'm tired of this." he growled, pointing his finger. "I'm tired of putting my life and everything I have in the hands of that homeless son of a bitch and sleeping out here night after night, just waiting to be slaughtered, while he lounges around in the safety of his own confines!"

"What do you mean everything you have?" his other companion scoffed. "What kind of living did you think you were making out in the real world?"

The rear sentinel suddenly shifted his attention to his jeerer and clenched his fists.

"Don't make me put a steel-toe up your ass. My patience has serious limits right now."

"Don't you threaten me! You had nothing and you know it. That's the way of the world, my friend. That's the only reason you came out here in the first place: because you're nothing and you'll always be nothing!"

Upon hearing that final sentiment the man holding the backward guard felt himself lose his cool and lunged toward his comrade. The other reached for the short sword sheathed on his belt but before either of them could make a decisive move their leader had swiftly drawn his own blade and thrust it between their paths.

"Both of you stay where you are!" he commanded out loud. "Any more incompetence and this pitiful infighting will do those ruthless animals out there a favor."

The rear guard growled at his comrade and backed away in conformity, as the other relieved his grip on his sheathed sword and exhaled loudly. Though they both knew that their ringleader was right. It had been many months since anyone had heard wind of any news regarding their primary leader. As far as was previously known he had been keeping himself secluded in a small fortress camp he had set up in a valley trough somewhere in the southern territories of these Adirondack mountain ranges. The name of this mysterious inciter, though it was rarely spoken unless necessary, was Ramon Moreno.

Only years before, while he was a young vicenarian, he and his younger brother, Robert, had led an expedition into the heart of the Adirondack mountains; a territory the surrounding locals referred to as the 'Dark Zone.' It was a large, enclosed area of tall hills and small valleys completely perimetered by miles of Appalachian mountain ranges. The area received its nickname by the citizens who resided in and near the base of the woods and the mountains for one primary reason: nobody who ventured in ever came out.

Most people simply accepted the territory as dangerous and thought nothing else of it, preferring not to dwell on the vast rumors that emerged from the dark enclave. However, there were others who found the Dark Zone highly interesting and constantly spoke of the rumors and whispers regarding its hazard. Some believed the area to simply be a natural labyrinth of trees and creeks and hills so confounding and difficult to navigate that those who dared to enter its borders would become lost forever. Despite that most popular belief, no one, not even any trained rescue teams, would dare to cross into this perilous, off-the-grid territory.

So some others figured that the area was completely populated by untamed wild animals. One of the craziest rumors was that there was some sort of secret government organization somewhere in the center regions of the Dark Zone who did not want anyone stumbling upon what they might be working on.

Whatever the reasons this much was clear; the Dark Zone was literally 'dark.' If one searched its coordinates through a satellite its image was intentionally blurred at all times. Commercial airlines and other aircraft always avoided flying too close to its boundaries. Even the domestic animals of the residences nearest to its borders stayed away, for sense that there was something uninviting about it. But as the rumors behind the Dark Zone's mysteries began to grow and spread, more and more variations started rising as the media unhesitantly took hold of the intriguing story. Some people, very few, but some who lived closest to the shadows of the mountains spoke softly of a mysterious warrior race; some sort of hidden, secret society dwelling in the vast territories of the Dark Zone.

In the early months of 2005, despite any and all warnings and rumors surrounding the mystery of the redoubtable territories, word was spread throughout the Adirondacks of a young vagabond by the name of Ramon Moreno gathering a sizable following and leading them straight into the eastern borders of the Dark Zone. No one ever knew of his exact intentions or what kind of nerve he had managed to muster, but for three watchful years never was there a sign of anybody among the expedition coming out of the Dark Zone. Although with every month that passed more and more forlorn characters were seen traveling into the inscrutable mountains, always never to come back out. And so even to this day the Dark Zone remains ever mysterious and avoided by the citizens who thrived in its innocuous shadow.

The man leading the small, distressed party had heard all of the tales and horror stories about the mountains but little was known even to him about Ramon Moreno's business in these parts, for they were not a part of the original expedition. They each travelled to the Dark Zone about two years prior to this night when they had heard of Moreno's vague intentions, but the majority of their involvement was spent performing reconnaissance hikes in the wilderness for weeks, sometimes even months at a time. Who or what it was they were dealing with out here, or even why, remained as much of a question of interest to them as the cloud that surrounded their leader.

As the head of the small group began to withdraw his blade, a sudden rustling in the trees behind them caused him to jerk around quickly. Before he could brace himself for the worst, his comrade whom he had sent to scout ahead only moments earlier emerged from the darkness, much to his relief. He let out a soft exhale and released his grip on his stone sword. Then he looked at his returned partner as if waiting for him to provide news of some sort. Instead, he just nodded and gestured slightly to the dark path behind him.

That was all the man needed to know that a safe haven of some kind was just ahead of them. He turned to his other compatriots.

"Let's move," he ordered, then pointed down at the wounded slump still lying on the ground. "Grab him. Let's get out of here."

Without hesitation, the one who had been carrying the half-conscious unfortunate picked him back up and slung him over his shoulders. The rear guard produced his sword again and resumed his position, while the leader of the party grabbed the old lantern sitting on the ground and adjusted the rusty vents on it to enlarge the small flame. Once they all recovered their positions for their seemingly perilous hike through the dark of the night, they continued forward through the dense woods. They moved with more haste now, anxious to get to safety and away from the eyes and ears and claws of what was deemed to be the enemy territory.

Fortunately for the uneasy group, as was hoped, the

second part of their night journey was much shorter than the first. In only a few minutes of winding through the trees a faint light could be seen in the near distance. As they approached it, the dark outline of human figures emerged slowly and prepared to greet them. The man of the pack raised his lantern and one of the aphotic figures stepped forward into the light. He was not much different from all of the other individuals there; he was dressed in clothes dirty, torn and battered due to countless nights at a time stuck in the wilderness. Not far behind him, in a clearing amongst the trees, was a small cluster of shabby tents pitched roughly in a circle. The light they had followed came from a weak fire which had a much larger group of people crowded around it, all dressed and armed similarly. The party stopped in their tracks and the man sent to recognize them only glared curiously at the one leading them.

The two of them exchanged looks of contempt for a moment until at last the man from the disgraceful campsite spoke.

"What are you doing back here?" he asked bluntly. He looked around at his poor company.

The man holding the lantern instantly grew impatient and angry.

"I'm not talking to you." he replied, raising his finger at his confronter. "You tell that idiot Ramirez to stop hiding behind his tent flap and come out here and face the truth for himself."

His greeter opened his mouth to respond but he was suddenly interrupted by a hard, stern voice behind him.

"Face the truth for myself?" With that comment, the man from the crummy safe haven lowered his head slightly and stepped to the side. Just behind him, another figure stood up from the crowd surrounding the fire and ambled toward them. He was significantly taller and older than most of them, but no better dressed. Unlike anyone else, he was displaying a slight but rather arrogant smile as he approached the entourage. "Morales, my young acquaintance, I don't believe we're expecting your group back for another two days." he stated, outstretching his arms carelessly. "If everyone under my lead were just as sad and pitiful as you then how do you think that would reflect on my position?"

Feeling enraged, the man leading the group, called Morales, released his hold on the lantern and let it drop to the ground with a loud clang.

"This is bull crap! How many more of us have to die out there before Moreno sees reason?" he spat at the one called Ramirez.

"Do not speak like that about Ramon Moreno!" the man who first greeted them interjected angrily.

Instantly, Ramirez put his hand out to silence his companion.

"It's alright, let him speak his mind. You spend as much time out in such a desolation as him and you'd likely also feel the delirium begin to take over, don't you think?" The man nodded his head and stepped back.

Morales was still feeling the heat of his outrage fill him up.

"You listen to me now, and you listen well; twelve of us you sent out there last week, Ramirez, twelve!" He rounded his arm in front of the rest of his party. "Five of us came back this time. We cannot keep performing these senseless patrols blindly through the mountains like this, it's madness!"

Before he even finished speaking Ramirez raised his hand and rolled his eyes.

"You know what, Morales? It's the same thing every time from you: I send you out on typical recon like I do all of the others, but you're the only one who comes back with nothing but excuses. 'Someone attacked us on the paths'," he mocked. "'They don't want us out here anymore, Ramirez'. I certainly don't hear any of these justifications from anyone else."

"You don't send any of the other groups out into the

heart of those animals' territory!" Morales fired back. "And in case you failed to notice, once again, we are missing more than half of our entire recon party! Care to explain that?"

Ramirez looked at the men standing behind his subject and hissed quietly as he tried to sum up the situation.

"You claim it's 'them' who keep assaulting your men and stalking you in the middle of the night but tell me, dear friend, have you ever seen them? Ever caught them in the act?"

Morales' eyes widened. He was taken aback by the question. Sure it was true he had never properly seen who or what it was that kept disturbing them on their routine mission in the darkness of the mountain woods, but he simply could not understand what more he needed to say to convince Ramirez and everyone else that something needed to be done immediately.

"How can you still be so ignorant?" he said, frustrated. "Why can you not face the facts!?"

"Because, boy," his superior replied sternly. "This is hostile territory, you should know that. This is what you signed up for and God only knows what kind of animals are out there or how many there might be. Your predicaments, as far as I'm concerned, are nothing more than nighttime animal raids due to your clearly inept ability to take proper precautions when performing a simple scouting routine through the God-forsaken mountains!"

At the sound of his loud sentiment, the slumped figure hanging over Morales' comrade's shoulders began to groan and writhe again in discomfort. Feeling weary of lugging him around, the man carrying him set him down on the ground in front of him, where he continued to squirm.

Ramirez glanced past his secondary at the unfortunate wretch.

"What's wrong with him?" he asked, gesturing toward the fifth member of the disgruntled party.

At this point, Morales was not exactly sure what to think about this guy anymore. He stepped over to stand by the side of Ramirez and spoke softly into his ear.

"They left us a message." He whispered. Ramirez's eyebrow raised in curiosity as Morales then turned and signaled for his comrade to show him what he was referring to. The man settling their derelict peer sighed as he repositioned him so that he was sitting with his back facing the two of them. Then he reached over and brought the lantern closer as he pulled his smudged top up to reveal the flesh of his back.

Upon seeing the revolting horror underneath Ramirez gasped out loud and the crowd behind him at the camp fire began murmuring anxiously amongst themselves. Even his seemingly iron willed companion beside him winced in trepid disgust at the sight that marred the man's flesh. Gathering his nerves, Ramirez kneeled down to get a closer look at the major wound. In the faint light of the propane lantern it was shown in his eyes that he was beginning to feel fear for Moreno's imprecise cause. Of all of the uncertainties that were hanging over their heads lately, one thing was clear to him now; these were no animals.

"Certainly a sight to behold, isn't it?" Morales interrupted his disturbed thoughts.

Ramirez stood back up and turned toward him. "What does it mean?"

Morales laughed.

"You're asking me? I'm not the superior hand-chosen by Moreno himself, my friend," he scoffed. Then, turning serious, he continued, "Alright look, this is the only clue we have. Either we were out cold in sleep or knocked out, I don't know, but when we woke up the others were gone, taken, and we found this one hanging unconscious by his overshirt on a low tree branch. It wasn't long until we discovered the surprise they left for us."

Ramirez only looked down at the terrifying sight in dread. His mind was racing as he tried to sort out the situation at hand. Whatever would he tell his own superiors who reported directly to Moreno? That after three years his own worst fears were suddenly coming into fruition? Maybe Morales was right. Maybe it was time something be done about whatever mindless savages were out there, watching their every move.

"Ramirez," his comrade stepped forward impatiently. "What do we do? Should we send out a warning to Moreno's camp?"

Ramirez pondered all of his few options for a moment. He let out a rough sigh of compliance and then turned to his companion.

"No," he responded, placing his hand lightly on his shoulder. "Not yet. Inform Caine at the Iron Furnace that our enemies might still be out there. We need to know our next best option. He'll know how to handle this. Go, quickly." His comrade nodded in approval and darted off into the startled crowd behind them. "At least I hope so, or we might be in big trouble." Ramirez reached up and wiped the sweat from his forehead as he stared one more time down at the large, chirographed lacerations carved into the wounded man's back which read in bloody, roughly cut writing:

"Ravenna will be avenged!"

CHAPTER ONE

April, 2010

North Elba, New York

"Lake Placid"

To be young is as bitter and difficult as it is the most opportune chapter in any person's life. The road is full of challenges waiting to strike, and there are many trials to engage, countless choices to make, both easy and hard, some regarding honor and conviction. There are lessons to be learned that teach of the hardships of sacrifice and judgment. And whether you're up high in the mountains of pride and noble idealism, or down in the valleys of trials and temptations, you must always remember all of the loved ones who welcome you into the arms of all their faith in you.

It was barely six in the morning and the reddish spring sun struggled to cast its light through the young boy's bedroom window. The early sunlight that magnified through the glass would be enough to awaken anyone's sleep, but the boy was already awake. He was sitting on the edge of his bed with his back to the sun, fully clothed and fully groomed, as if he had been up before the break of dawn. He was wearing a light, gray-striped DC hoodie and a pair of blue jeans defaced by holes in the material of various sizes. His dark hair was long and ragged, reaching halfway down the back of his neck and almost over his eyebrows, and his expression was one of bitterness and exhaustion. Not exhaustion due to lack of sleep, but fatigue of the mind. To him the weight of typical life pressing down on him every day was taxing and burdensome, and he would see himself confined to his room for long hours each day, as it was his only way to seek privacy for himself. This boy's name was Alex Lee.

Clutched in his hand was a black, steel-tipped throwing dart. He stared down at it for a moment, twiddling it around in his hand, as if admiring or disparaging the thin, metal point of the dart. The silver surface glistened faintly as the morning light barely reflected off of it. He looked up ahead of him at his bedroom door. There was a dark-red target spray-painted on the white wood. All over the target and its surrounding area were dozens of tiny puncture marks, as throwing darts against his door was an activity that he would do aimlessly most mornings upon waking up, sometimes for hours on end. In a way it helped him clear his mind. Whatever it was that he ever needed to break away from, this was how he did it. Without any effort, Alex quickly repositioned the dart in his hand, wound up and whipped it at the door. The dart instantly drilled its sharp point into red center of the painted target. Alex brought his hand up and rubbed his head lightly as he let out a drained sigh of self-misery.

In the next room over from his own, a young girl was lying awake in her bed. As the light of the new morning sun also brightened her room, she too had been awake before dawn. Her name was Nickole Lee. She was Alex's 12-year-old sister, and she was awoken this morning, as she was every morning, by the sound of her brother piercing his door with darts. Strangely enough, the early disturbance was neither irritating nor soothing to her. Rather, it filled her with concern. The only solace it gave her was that Alex always seemed to be better than ever as long as he did not stray from his miserable, morning routine. But with every day that passed, Nickole could sense the cold wretch that was her brother slipping further and further into the shadows, and she feared that one day he would go so deep that he might never return.

As each dart dug its way into Alex's targeted door, the sharp sound made Nickole's mind wander. Her thoughts traveled deep into the far reaches of her mind in search of the better memories of her brother. She could recall a time long ago when the two of them were much closer. They never knew their father, for he had left when they were both very young. Alex never spoke of him, but every time Nickole would ask their mother about him, she would never give a proper answer. All of their friends were convinced that he simply turned out to be a typical dirtbag that ultimately wanted nothing to do with family. But somehow, Nickole did not get that sense from her mother. She was the only one in the household who really knew what kind of person their father was, and though she rarely ever talked about him herself, she never showed any sort of contempt or anger toward him. Was she just trying to ignore him and move on? Or was there something she knew that she did not want Alex or Nickole to know of?

Whatever the reasons, Nickole somehow doubted that Alex's radical decline in spirit was due to the disappearance of his father. She could vaguely remember when Alex was not the gloomy, emotionless boy she knew now. His darkened hair was once much lighter and his gray, somber eyes used to show off a rather elegant, cool form of blue; the shade of ice cold blue whose gaze would temper one's exhaustion in the summer and fill one with peace and amity in the dead of winter. But the one thing she missed most was his smile. It was a short smile that warmed people up inside, the kind of smile that showed aspiration for life and for the lives around him. Yet for all that was once good and pure in his heart, Nickole would wake up every day to see more and more of her bygone brother sinking further away.

Her thoughts were suddenly interrupted by a rapid knock on her door. Nickole's eyes jerked back open and she turned toward the door as a woman's voice traveled through the wood barrier. "Get up, Nickole. You two will be late."

Nickole rubbed her eyes gently and sat up in her bed.

"Coming, Mom." She replied tiredly. She stood up and lumbered over to her dresser and glanced into the mirror that stood on top of it. Looking at her drowsy reflection, Nickole casually recovered her tangled, blonde hair from the night of unconscious tossing and turning. Soon she began to notice also that the darts in her brother's room had stopped flying.

At the sound of their mother waking Nickole, Alex tossed his last darts at his door and allowed himself to fall back down onto his bed. Instead of coming next to knock on his door, Alex's mother walked past it and proceeded down the stairs at the end of the hallway. Every morning she would wake her daughter as she did but knew that her son was always already awake and disturbing his quiet mood was the last thing he wanted, so she saw no choice but to leave him alone until he picked himself up. For several years everybody watched the boy slowly decline into discord with the world he had grown up in, and everyone knew it was having an effect on his small family, even though they did their best not to show it.

After dressing for the morning, and still feeling the ragged effect of sleep, Nickole applied a small amount of makeup to cover the slight dark circles under her eyes. It was the only amount of makeup her mother allowed her to use. She was extremely perceptive about the concept of makeup and, unlike their father, always made sure she was close so as to ensure that her daughter would not grow to become the kind of reckless adolescent who felt the need to drown her true self beneath the wall of a false image. Setting down her makeup, Nickole smiled as she understood her mother's tacit notion of, "You are beautiful just the way you are." She walked over to her closet and pulled out a light, sky-blue jacket and put it on. She opened her bedroom door and started to walk down the hallway, but before she passed the door of her brother's room it opened up immediately. Nickole halted suddenly as her dismal brother emerged quickly from his den of solitude. He stopped in his tracks as well and directed his attention to Nickole. The two abruptly locked eyes. It was something that they rarely found themselves doing much anymore, and from his taller stature she felt like Alex was glowering down at her with his dim, gray eyes. Trying to show no expression, Nickole waited for her brother to say something, anything. Instead, Alex just nodded to her ever so slightly, as if he wanted to say good morning but found himself holding it back. He then turned and continued down the hall to the stairs. Nickole exhaled with some disenchantment, and proceeded to follow him downstairs.

As soon as Nickole descended the stairs the savory scent of buttermilk pancakes enveloped her. It was her mother's knack for homemade pancakes that had the influence to sedate her thoughts and welcome her to a brief state of bliss. Sometimes it was just what she needed to fully awaken from the lingering dreams of the night. Nickole walked into the kitchen where her mother was stacking fresh pancakes onto a square ceramic dish.

"Morning, Mom," She greeted cheerily.

"Good morning, sweetheart," her mother responded as she proceeded to cut up an apricot.

Nickole opened the refrigerator and pulled out a 59 ounce bottle of Tropicana and walked over to the counter to retrieve a small glass.

"That smells really good!" She said, inhaling the warm scent of the breakfast.

"Thank you, Nicki," Her mother smiled and placed the dish of pancakes on the island counter in the center of the kitchen. Right beside the pancakes she placed a small dish of sliced sections of the apricots she had been cutting.

Nickole poured herself glass of orange juice and turned to examine with a smile the enticing breakfast her mother had prepared. What was amazing to her was that, despite all of the years that had passed since their father had left, her mother hardly ever seemed to decline in mood. She always seemed to be cheery and loving. She did everything to make sure her children felt welcome and taken care of. However, Nickole still often wondered why then she seemed to give her more attention than Alex, although she always assumed her mother had her reasons. Nickole could not read minds, but she was smart enough to understand that their mother loved neither of them more than the other. Yet there was something perpetually positive about her, almost as if some sort of virtuous energy was constantly coursing through her.

"Nickole, where's your brother?"

Suddenly disturbed from her brief, captivating daydream, Nickole quickly straightened up.

"What?"

Her mother laughed lightly.

"Where's Alex? Is he still in his room?"

Nickole shook her head.

"No." She replied. "He came down just in front of me."

"Hm, I must not have noticed." Her mother responded. "Do me a favor? Take these to the dining room table." She said, pointing to the pancakes and fruits as she turned around to wipe off the counters. Nickole set her glass down and picked up the breakfast dishes and carefully walked them through the small kitchen archway and into next room. In the dining room there was a small, circular wooden table. Nickole set the plates down in the center of the table. Just as she was about to return to the kitchen to retrieve her drink, she saw Alex appear from around the corner and approach the dining room table. She figured he must have lounged himself in the family room while their breakfast was being prepared. He sat himself down in a chair and kicked back slightly so that the back of the chair was propped up against the wall. Then he withdrew his cellphone from his pocket and centered his attention away from his surroundings.

"Well, breakfast is ready." Their mother's voice suddenly spoke up. Nickole turned to see her carrying in the bottle of Tropicana and a gallon jug of 2% milk. She placed them down on the table next to the dish of pancakes. "Oh, Alex, would you please not do that with the chair?" Alex glanced up from his phone. He exhaled briefly and set the chair back on all four legs. "Thank you." His mother sighed in relief. "I don't like it when you do that, it's such a precarious position."

Alex turned and looked back at the wall just behind him. "Sorry. I wouldn't want to fall right through the wall." he said with arrogance.

Nickole giggled as she reached for a pancake. Her mother shook her head at his joke.

"Ha-ha," she scoffed. She sat down at the table only to jump right back up again. "Oh, good Lord," she exclaimed. "I make pancakes and I forget to bring out the syrup of all things." Laughing at herself, she quickly retreated back into the kitchen.

"You're not perfect, Mom," Nickole called after her, humorously.

"Thank you, honey, eat your breakfast!" Her mother joked back. As Nickole laughed, Alex looked up a little from his phone and shook his head. To him, it seemed like his younger sister took some sort amusement in playing the role of the mother's cub, but he did not want to delve too far into the thought. He did not care. Why should he care? The small amount of time he spent in the same daily activities as the rest of his family was as much as he preferred, and not because he disliked them. Rather, he knew it was becoming in his nature to have the desire to simply be left alone. It was the time in his life when he felt that he just needed to survive the morning breakfast routine until he could get to school and regroup with his friends. It seemed easy for him to accept that, at least for now, the days of childhood cheer were done. As he looked toward his sister, who was happily savoring the apricot slice in her hand, he mused to himself, 'you're going to be here next.'

Just then, their mother reappeared from the kitchen with a brand new bottle of maple syrup. Nickole reached for it and opened the cap, peeled off the seal, and began to pour it down onto her pancakes.

"Easy on the syrup, Nicki," her mother commented. "That's way too much sugar." She sat down and grabbed a pancake and a few fruit slices for herself. She saw that her son was still buried in his cell phone, swiping the screen consistently. "Alex," she sighed. "Come on, put the phone away and please eat something." Alex hesitated, but reluctantly returned his phone to his pocket and removed a single pancake from the stack and dropped on his plate. He poured a small amount of syrup on top of it and ate a piece of it, but seemed to forget how to enjoy it. "What, you don't want any fruit?"

Alex looked back up at the breakfast selection. He swallowed his pancake fragment.

"I really don't care." He returned to his small breakfast with as much solitude as he could make for himself.

Nickole looked to her mother and waited for her response, but there hardly was one. She had heard it all and she was not so surprised.

"Well, whatever gets you up in the morning, I guess." Nickole muttered.

Her troubled brother just ignored her and continued to finish his breakfast.

"Ok, Nickole, maybe that's a little far for now." Their mother rebuked.

Nickole laughed to herself as she continued to feed on her drowned pancake. As she was cutting up pieces a sudden thought hit her. Her happy morning was disturbed by invading thoughts once again about their father. Looking at her mother, she could simply not understand how and why she seemed to remain so unaffected by his absence. She almost felt the urge to ask yet again about their father, but suddenly she remembered something she had heard her mother mumble in her sleep one night, and without thinking, she blurted it out with a stammer,

"Mom, what is- aeon?"

Her mother jumped in her seat and dropped her fork on her plate. It made a sharp clang as it landed which caught

Alex's attention as well. He was looking around the two of them anxiously, waiting for one of them to say something. Their mother caught her breath and looked roughly toward her curious daughter.

"What did you say?" she asked firmly.

Nickole did not expect such a harsh reaction to the question, but her curiosity got the best of her, so she continued to speak.

"I got up to get a drink the other night and I heard you say it in your sleep, like several times."

Her mother's eyebrows raised.

"What all did you hear?" She muttered.

Nickole tried to remember exactly what all she might have heard that came out muffled through the bedroom door, but she was so tired that night that she hardly even took notice of it.

"I don't know," she answered. "I just thought I heard you say something like that. I'm sorry, I was just a little curious."

Alex had no idea what was going on. Whenever this happened he must have been completely out of it because he had no recollection of their mother talking in her sleep. Not like he cared anyway.

There was a silent pause. Their mother swallowed nervously. Trying to forget the conversation quickly she looked up at the clock on the wall.

"Oh wow, it's getting late already." She broke the silence. Nickole glanced up at the clock and then turned around to look at the window. The sun was already far over the tree line. "Finish up," she said, standing up. "So I can get you both to school before you're late."

Alex stood up as well and carried his plate out of the dining room. Nickole was suddenly feeling a little slow. The weight of the question she just asked seemed to be holding her down. Her mother had never reacted so startled whenever she asked about their father. So why over such a seemingly insignificant topic was she so shocked? Considering it to be simply insignificant and meaningless, Nickole shrugged it off as much as she could and stood up, grabbed her dish, and followed her family from the dining room.

CHAPTER TWO

30 miles south of the

Borders of the Dark Zone

Three nights earlier

"GHUAHH!"

The man forced his head above the surface of the river and sucked in a massive intake of air. The current of the stream had carried him for nearly a mile but now it was finally starting to weaken. The man's feet were slipping on the rocky floor of the river as it continued to pull him along. He inhaled a deep breath and dove under the surface, scrambling around the creek bed for a handhold of some sort, but the rocks were just too slick.

In the middle of attempting to grab onto something to resist the current, it suddenly caused him to strike his head against a higher rock. The man gasped underwater and returned above surface to catch his breath. He brought his hand to his temple and felt a small amount of blood seeping out of a wound. His vision was blurred briefly, but just up ahead he saw a low hanging tree branch jutting out from the wooded shoreline. He struggled to work his way over toward the riverbank and, using the current for momentum, he launched himself upward to reach for the branch. He outstretched his right hand to grab the branch but missed by a hair. Quickly, he braced himself to be plunged back into the flowing stream but in a split-second reaction he snatched the branch with his left hand. He tensed his muscles, trying to prevent himself from accidentally falling back into the water. The branch shook and creaked, but it proved to be stable enough to support him. The man let out a sigh of relief and used the tree limb to climb his way to the bank. Once he reached the end of the limb he released it and fell down to the damp ground, taking in several deep breaths. He then rolled himself over onto his back and took a long look at his surroundings.

The man was somewhere in the woods, no doubt, of the Appalachian Mountains. Most likely farther north, where the mountain peaks rose up high and stretched for many miles. They were heavily forested, that much was clear. There were an abundance of sounds of numerous animals so it was unlikely any settlements were nearby. The man was in his early forties. He was over six feet in height but quite thin and lanky due to months of wandering and hiding in the wilderness with limited food. His hair was dark and dirty and hung low, and his face was covered with roughly shaved stubble. He looked up past the tree line and toward the sky. The stars were creeping out as the sky was faintly illuminated by the last dimming rays of the setting sun. It made him suddenly realize that he was shivering from the cold of the water, and that very soon it would grow even colder. He had to move on and seek out shelter for the night.

But wait...where was it?

The man suddenly panicked and reached his hands around to his back. He had been wearing a small leather harness on his upper back supported by his shoulders. On the harness was what appeared to be part of scabbard which seemed as if it could support a large blade of some sort. But there was no blade or weapon there. He must have lost it in the river.

Trying to hold himself together, the man scoped up and down the riverbank to find his lost possession, but it was just too dark to see properly. He gathered his thoughts, and then kneeled down and placed his hand on the ground as if trying to feel something's presence.

The man breathed steadily.

"Where are you?" He called under his breath. He was glancing around slowly, and seemed to wait for something to respond, but nothing happened. "Come on," he continued to whisper. "I know you're close. Guide me." The man stood up and cautiously began to walk downstream. "I hear you calling. Show me the way."

The sound of the flowing river to his right and the noises of birds and insects on his left made for a soothing yet agitating stride through the trees as the drenched man seemed to follow some intangible force. However, at last he spotted up ahead a small rock ledge in the river. Sticking up from in between a couple of rocks was...

"There you are!" The man gasped. He ran down the bank to the end of the ragged ledge. The sun was completely down now, but he did not need the light to tell that there was a large sword of some kind lodged in between the rocks. It looked precariously positioned against the flow of water, as if one wrong shift in force could set it off balance and send it travelling farther downriver. The man shook his head in disbelief, and then gently set his foot down on the first rock. As expected, the hard surface was slippery and made it difficult for him to keep his balance. This was impossible, but he had to reach that sword. He outstretched his arms to hold his stability and stepped onto the next rock in the haphazard natural dam. Each step out into the rushing stream was even more perilous than the last, but when he finally got close enough to the sword-like object the man got down on his knees to get a better grip of his rock, and then reached out to grab the sword. Unfortunately, it was a little too far away to touch, but he was already as close as he could get. The rock that held the sword in place was too small for him to step on without disturbing its position.

"Come on," The man hissed quietly. He reached out as far as he could. He was so close that he could almost touch it. As he attempted to adjust his own position he felt himself lose his footing and nearly slip from the damp, rocky surface. He dropped down and clutched the rock, catching his breath and regained his balance. He reached for the sword again, but still it was just too far away. "Come on," he growled again. The man could feel himself becoming heated with frustration. He clenched his teeth and tensed his arm muscles. "Did you not hear me?" He retracted his arm slightly, and then launched back out to reach again. "I said...COME!"

Just then, the sword instantly tilted in its clamped position toward the man's hand, and he quickly grabbed hold of the handle. He slowly stood up and pulled the large weapon out of the rock ledge. Letting out a sigh of relief, he turned and made his way back to shore.

This was certainly not the future he had envisioned for himself, but it was not like his past had given him any certainty of a halcyon life ahead of him. Twenty years ago he found himself engulfed in an incident that changed his life forever, as well as the lives of one of his best friends and eventually the only love of his life. During this event he came in possession of the sword-like weapon he was carrying. It was certainly no iron-forged blade, rather it was very large and broad, made not of any kind of common forgery metal. Instead of being straight, the blade consisted of several smaller blade-like beams that intertwined upward from the large hilt to form a vague shape of a blade. As for the material, it gleamed faintly with a shade of bronze. Despite travelling with the man for two decades, the gold-bronze metal of the blade had not dulled or begun to deteriorate. It was no material he had ever seen before, but the man had more than enough reason to believe that it was made of orichalcum.

The exhausted man plopped himself down against a tree and set the sword down beside him. His wet predicament did not seem to bother him in the least, as drenched clothing had been the least of his worries for many years. His mind was constantly racing with thoughts and ideas of what he should do next or where he should go.

"Home." He mumbled to himself. "Home to peace and

good comfort once again. Oh, that would be the day." The man just stared out into the dark sky above him, most likely fantasizing about returning to the life he had so long ago forsaken. He then shifted his attention down to the sword at his side as if it were trying to tell him something. "No," he continued to mutter. "You know I can't go back, not with all of that heat on my ass. I would be endangering them all if I did."

He paused again, not taking his eyes off of his weapon. "For the time being, we are still wanderers."

... ...

"No. I am not vagabond. I'm not homeless, I'm simply a traveler now, a Ranger."

... ...

"Exile. It was the only thing I could do, in order to protect those whom I call my family."

... ...

"Yes, I would do anything to protect my family, to keep them out of harm's way." The man, who referred to himself as Ranger, leaned his head back against the tree, closed his eyes and let out a sigh of exhaustion. "Even if it means never seeing them again. Never seeing my wife again, never being able to watch my children grow. But I would still sacrifice all of that, all of it..." He placed his hand down on the sword's handle. "...to keep you safe, my friend."

... ...

"It is essential beyond reckoning that I protect you from those on our tails. If your power or your secrets were to fall into the hands of my enemies, God only knows what kind of disasters would follow simply as a result of humanity's selfish desire for more power. It's a risk I cannot, and will not, take. I would spend the rest of my aging life alone in the desolate hills of the Dark Zone if I have to."

... ...

In his mind, Ranger would always be right about the actions he was taking. It was for a noble cause. Twenty years ago, when he came to claim possession of the sword-like weapon, he found himself set by fate on an unforeseen quest. Traveling alongside him was his beloved wife, before he had taken her hand in marriage, an old friend of his from all of his childhood, and two other companions who joined them to aid their quest. Ranger had spent years trying desperately to wipe the memory of these events from his mind, for he had lost his friend before it was over. He felt as though it was his fault, as he knew it was he who sparked the quest.

When he was only 21, Ranger was helping his parents to clear their attic space of all of his personal belongings while he was preparing to move into a place of his own. It was in one of many large boxes he was moving that he found an old copy of a children's book that his mother had once used to read to him. The very next day he approached his two friends with the old storybook and proposed a plan to search for the author of the book, as he believed that the author had left a puzzle of some sort in the book which he became obsessed with solving. However, upon learning that the author had been deceased for some time, the small group picked up two more travelling companions and found the abandoned house of the book's late writer, and it was here that they discovered something that would change all of their lives forever.

In a hidden chamber of the abandoned home, they found a small collection of strange objects that appeared to be some sort of relics, one of which each of them took as their prize. It was the large sword in his hands that Ranger chose, and he had kept it close to him ever since. Unfortunately, the quest came to a sudden shift of events when the five of them realized that they had been journeying into the clutches of a hellish nightmare. It was truly a trying and traumatizing experience for all of them, but that is a story for another time.

Soon after the quest had finally ended, and Ranger's best friend had fallen, the remainder of his companions destroyed their relic prizes, for fear of the wrong hands claiming possession of the secrets the items held. But it was that very fear that peaked the fascination of Ranger, and he could not bring himself to destroy this sword, even though he knew very well that it would have been his only chance to do so. Ranger kept the sword and returned to his life back at his home in New York, where he married his girlfriend who had so bravely accompanied him on their journey and finally settled down. He planned to make it a life's ambition to thoroughly study the secrets within the sword relic. For several years his obsession fueled his fascination, and at times it threatened to drive his family apart. But through all of it, Ranger could never allow such petty obsessions to distract him from the life and family he had strived to build.

Unfortunately, the days of peace were not to last. It was not long before Ranger soon began to discover the kind of power that his relic had confined within itself. And not only him, but his wife began to feel it as well. When a couple of men, dressed in black suits and claiming to be federal agents came to his doorstep requesting repossession of the sword, Ranger knew instantly that his worst fears had been realized; that other, higher orders would eventually turn their eyes to his prize and try to claim it for their own manipulative purposes. When these men threatened to blackmail his family, Ranger took up the sword and struck them down in a fit of rage. It was then that he knew he would be forced to disappear, to be sent into exile in the wilderness, as the officials of the government would now be after him. There was no time for any long goodbyes, so he gave his beloved wife one short farewell, and then vanished from her life.

Ten years had passed since he had made the difficult decision to leave his life behind. He had been chased into the flowing river trying to escape from his enemies once again. He was tired and battered, constantly running and hiding. Forced to live off of the land, hunting his food, whether legally or not. He lived and wandered anywhere his instincts took him, and he slept wherever he saw fit to rest. The laws and regulations of the world no longer mattered, for the world as once knew it was gone. But perhaps he had finally found the perfect place for such a ragged life.

The night was filled with the yipping and howling of a pack of coyotes in the distance. It was late, the sun had long set and the temperature was still dropping. Ranger pulled himself to his feet. It was time to move and find shelter. He held the sword up in front of him and gripped it tight in his hand. He squinted as if thinking hard about something, and then the sword's intertwining blade structure suddenly seemed to transform, instantly retracting down into itself. In no more than a second, the blade had shrunk down to the hilt until it only stuck about eight inches outward. Ranger then reached back and slipped the minimized relic weapon into the harness on he was wearing, where it fit perfectly in place. Giving his dark surroundings a quick look around, Ranger set off from the riverbank and up into the mountains.

The hills were steep and the darkness of the dusk sky made the venture extremely difficult. And not to mention quite terrifying to be out navigating the wilderness alone at night. Ranger, however, was hardly concerned about the many nocturnal eyes that were surely observing him. He was armed and knew that he was more than capable of fending off any wild foes, it was the sentient inhabitants for which he had himself on alert. He knew exactly where he was, there could be no doubt, but he was not exactly a convincing denizen. If anything, he would be most content if he could simply blend himself into the environment for as long as he needed to plan out the next stage of his future.

Ranger had been hiking up the immense mountainside for what felt like hours, crisscrossing through mountain laurel and thorn bushes. It was dark and cold, and he was growing increasingly tired. He was not sure what it was, but something about the mountains seemed enchanting. He could feel his eyes growing heavy with every moment that passed, and almost felt like he could lie down and drift into a comfortable sleep.

What was he thinking? Ranger shook the thought away. It

had been many years since he had been able to fall into a good night's sleep that he had all but forgotten what it felt like. This was not the time to hallucinate, but Ranger could not deny that the hike was beginning to wear him down. He made his way to over to a tree and leaned against it, catching his breath. It was not just a sense of comfort that seemed to cloud around him, but also a feeling of coming down, as if gravity was pressing on him and pushing him further into exhaustion. He supposed it was not the strangest thing he had ever felt during his long exile.

Speaking of hallucinations...

You know what they say; the trees have eyes. Large, eerie yellow eyes peering at you from the darkness. The hairs on Ranger's arms suddenly stood up followed by a wave of goosebumps. Feeling his jaw muscles clench from sudden anxiety, Ranger slowly shift his attention to his left. There, appearing suspended a few feet above the ground in the darkness, were a pair of eyes staring right back at him. They were large eyes that gave off a faint, yellowish glow as they reflected the dim starlight. Ranger felt another wave of goosebumps travel up his spine. He could feel himself growing nauseous due to fear, yet he could not bring himself to move or reach for his sword.

As the eyes continued to stare him down, they seemed to let out a quiet but menacing growl. Ranger knew by the sound of the growl that he was in the presence of a wolf. A great wolf at that; he could hardly make out any more than the eyes, but judging by how high from the ground they were, he knew it was a wolf of large stature and possibly incredible strength. But strangely enough, that was not the sense that came over him.

It was neither fear nor despair that gripped him. The great creature continued to growl under breath, but Ranger soon felt his goose bumps start to fade. He relaxed his jaw and his tense muscles, and he turned and began to walk ever so slowly toward the mysterious animal, which remained still as ever, not taking its eyes off of him. Ranger continued to approach the floating eyes. He was completely calm, in fact he was feeling a strange sense of tranquility. It was a kind of tranquility that might make a person feel protected. But that same person would be stricken with utter fear and panic if they were to witness Ranger's actions. He walked right up to the wolf and kneeled down directly in front of it. He was no more than two feet away from its eyes. At this point, he could vaguely make out the figure of the strange animal. From what he could see it was indeed a massive wolf-like creature. He could see no farther than its broad shoulder bones. It was as if the dark of night was shrouding the creature, yet its eyes still glowed. The wolf never moved, and Ranger stared right into its fell eyes. No. Not fell. Rather there was something almost spiritual about them, angelic even.

Ranger tilted his head.

"You wield such terror for a simple beast," He whispered softly, remaining calm as ever. The beast which he spoke to was still motionless, but had ceased its growling. "Or maybe...not so much a beast at all." At this point, Ranger did the most incredibly irrational thing imaginable. He reached out ever so gently to touch the creature that stood before him. Though he really could not see it, the fur of the animal's face seemed to hang out and wave very lightly in the cool, nighttime breeze. It felt rather endearing, and it caused Ranger to spur a grin. "I feel like you know something, like you know that everything is going to be okay. Or maybe I am just going crazy, but I am exhausted. I'm tired of running and hiding. Hiding, when I could be fighting. I should be fighting." There was no reaction from the creature. It only continued to peer into Ranger's soul, but his composure never ceased. "I would do anything to protect the ones I love. I am ready to do anything."

In a sudden shift of atmosphere, the great wolf's eyes blinked for the first time. For such a small action, it seemed to send a wave of energy through Ranger's body. The wolf then turned and walked off into the darkness of the woods.

For such a massive beast, its feet barely made a sound on the forest floor. When Ranger was certain it was gone, he stood up. As he rose to his feet he realized he was standing with a newfound confidence. He felt something inside him like a surge of motivation to move on. Perhaps it was because he had stared death in the face. But the creature that he locked gazes with did not ultimately strike him as an omen of death. Maybe it meant that, for once in ten long years, circumstances would finally stand in his favor.

But not tonight. Tonight, Ranger was faced with a new chapter of his exile. The eminent borders of the Dark Zone were before him. Within the territory he would be safe from those were pursuing him. However, something told him that a new destiny awaited him in the Dark Zone. It was time for him to keep moving.

Before he did, Ranger pondered on a thought that his experience in the great wolf's presence flowed into his head. Ranger reached back and removed his sword from its harness. Gripping it in his hand as he did before, the blade re-extended to its original length. He held the relic directly in front of him, grasping it tightly with both hands and closing his eyes.

"Eira," he breathed the words forth. "My love. This may be the last time I can speak to you. With your relic gone I don't know if you can hear me, but I want you to know that I have not given up. The Heart within my relic is what keeps me on my feet. And though you may not know it, even though you destroyed your prize the will of the Heart is still with you. It's what protects you from our enemies as it has protected me all these years. But I promise you, I will find a way to set things straight once and for all, and I will return to you once I do." His thoughts were suddenly interrupted by a loud wolf's howl in the distance. Ranger stared out toward the source of the cry. "I have to go now." He began his brief farewell. "I love you, and Aeon protect you."

The sword quickly shrunk back into its portable state and Ranger stuck it back into its harness, and he returned to his long journey into the Dark Zone. As he walked, he continued to muse the final words of his message.

'*Aeon protect you.*'

CHAPTER THREE

Alex spent the entire car ride with his head leaned back against the headrest and staring aimlessly out the window. It was still early in the morning but by now the sun had the sky illuminated and the neighborhoods of North Elba were active with the life of a new day. People were pulling out of their driveways heading to work or wherever the day would take them. The springtime dew on the blades of grass glistened in the early sunlight as did the serene, blue water of the Mirror Lake and the morning clouds cast a series of shadows all along the vast mountainsides. It was one of the many beautiful sights of the great Adirondacks, but none of it swayed Alex's mind to any sort of fascination, as it was such a sight he had seen all his young life.

Nickole, on the other hand, always found herself interested in the sights of her home. She and her older brother had spent their entire lives in the village of Lake Placid, rarely travelling very far outside of the county, and she would often stare out at the mountains and wonder what life was like in the places beyond their hilly borders, just as she had been doing from the back seat of her mother's silver Subaru Legacy.

The entire ride was little more than five minutes, but the silent atmosphere of the Subaru's confined cabin always made it seem like a journey. Before long, several yellow buses could be seen merging into one area as they drew closer to the school zone. Each bus began piling behind one another in front of the school and dozens of children emptied out and scattered into the building and all over the school grounds. Within minutes the entire area was crowded with students and attendants, as well as countless vehicles pulling into the parking lots and alongside the curbs while parents dropped off their children.

Alex made his first movement of the short ride as his mother veered off the main road and approached an open spot beside the curb, by reaching over to undo his seatbelt. His mother discreetly glared at him from the corner of her vision. She always hated it when he removed his seatbelt before she parked the car, no matter how slow she was going. Unfortunately, like everything else she did not bother to fight with him about it. She always knew what things were best to argue with her son over because, despite his slow descent in mood and lack of care, Alex never did anything to recklessly endanger himself or his family in any way. Therefore, unless the time came to consult any form of parenting skills, she sat back and allowed him to be himself.

As soon as the car was put in park, Nickole snapped out of her daydream staring out toward the mountain ranges, grabbed her backpack and hopped out of the car. Alex moved much more sluggishly as he exited the passenger side. He reached into the back seat of the car for his own backpack and slung it over his shoulder. As he turned to walk away his mother rolled down the passenger window.

"Alex." She called to him.

Alex stopped in his tracks and grumbled to himself as he turned around. His mother leaned down to look at him through the open window and smiled.

"Have a nice day," she said, trying aimlessly to lift his mood. Without making the slightest gesture Alex turned back around and walked toward the school building. "I love you, too," she mumbled as her son lumbered way. Feeling the awkward vibe, Nickole looked over and waved to her mother before catching up with Alex.

Some would describe the two siblings as total opposites. Where Alex grew increasingly distant and downcast with every day passing, Nickole had always been secure and held her head high for the life that each morning would bring. Of course, everyone knew it was not always that way. Those days when Alex was the happy and energetic one, his little sister was too young and helpless to know anything of the way of the world. He was always there beside her to offer a helping hand, yet for reasons unknown he still continued to sink farther away, as if he had grown weary of his energy. The most interesting thing was that no matter how careless and moody he became, never was there doubt that his caring for his sister held strong. Although he would look at her with the gloomy expression he constantly displayed, many believed his ice cold heart was still warm enough to protect her. And Nickole knew this too. She must have. Alex had developed an uncanny tendency to fill the atmosphere with a dreary and pitiful vibe. So as one of the only two people to live with him, how could she still maintain her own constant, positive energy? It was almost as if the two had a connection with each other deeper than simply brother and sister. It was as if, despite what everyone else now thought of Alex, she could still feel her brother's love.

Nickole walked beside Alex, who was already fiddling with his cell phone, as they made their way through the large crowd of students and into the school building. This was the time of day when they truly separated. Their small family was a stagnant family. The two of them had grown up spending nearly all of their days together, and school hours were the most time each day in which they were apart from each other. Not like Alex cared, as far as everyone imagined. Upon entering the school, Alex would always hang around the cafeteria a couple of his friends, and everyday Nickole would follow and stay with them until the bell rang. Nickole had friends of her own, and they would often question why she bothered to spend her time before school hours with her melancholy brother and his older social clan. They would talk about their own lives and interests while she sat beside Alex and hardly spoke to them at all.

Alex was glancing at his phone during the majority of

their navigation through the hordes of students. It was not difficult since they would walk this same path every morning for five days a week. Each daily routine was always the same. When they reached the edge of the crowds Alex and Nickole went to lean up against the wall. At this time Alex finally looked up from his phone, and at the same time he heard someone call his name.

"Alex!" A young male voice called out over the noise of the crowds of students. To his right, Alex saw one of his friends approach him. The boy's name was Seth. He was slightly taller than Alex with short fair hair and glasses. The two of them had been friends since elementary school and would always find themselves hanging out in the same spot by the cafeteria just before school hours began.

As he approached, Alex slipped his phone into his pocket and firmly grasped Seth's hand briefly.

"What's up, man?" Alex greeted him in the typical, casual teenage lingo. Nickole just leaned back against the wall and watched the two friends converse.

"Nothing much," Seth responded as he removed his backpack and set on the floor beside him. "Just gotta get through today and then the weekend is finally here. How you doing, Nicki?" He said, glancing past Alex toward his sister.

Nickole looked up quickly at Seth.

"I'm good, thanks," she replied in a somewhat mellow tone.

"Ok then," Seth nodded slightly.

Alex seemed to ignore their exchange and continued his conversation with his friend

"You're going over to Saranac Lake tomorrow, right?"

"Yeah," Seth answered excitedly. "To my uncle's lake house. We're gonna be there till next Wednesday. Haven't been there in forever."

"Lucky you." Alex laughed to himself. "I'd be damned if I ever managed to get away from this quiet slum."

Hearing his remark, Nickole looked up at her brother in shock.

"Slum?" She repeated under her breath. She could not understand why he had such adverse conceptions about their home town. Lake Placid was no slum, at least not to her. It was definitely not quiet most of the time as well, especially in the winter time when the skiers and winter sports enthusiasts would stop in town while heading up to Whiteface Mountain, which was about thirteen miles northeast of Lake Placid. In fact, their home town was a popular local tourist attraction all seasons of the year. It was one of the few traits which Nickole resented in her brother.

Alex either disregarded Nickole's quiet comment or simply did not hear it, but he started looking around at the crowds in front of them.

"Hey, speaking of which, where's Danny?" He asked, referring to another of their good friends who would often meet them there at the wall.

"Out sick, I think," Seth replied. "He sent me a text earlier saying that he probably wasn't going to be coming in today. Either that or he probably woke up drunk again. That freakin' redneck!" He laughed out loud. "Did he text you at all?"

Alex did not recall seeing any messages this morning. He shuffled into his pocket for his phone.

"I don't think so, let me check." He flipped the phone open. There were no notifications on the screen to inform him that he had any messages, but he opened up his message folder anyway and sure enough there was a text from his friend Danny. "Huh, how did I miss that?" He said, looking over the text.

It was simply a short message which read, *'Yo, I ain't gonna be in school today. Had a rough morning lol.'* Alex snickered as he read his hick friend's text. "That was kind of an unearned 'lol.' He mumbled as he put his phone away.

"Well hey, you doing anything after school?" Seth asked he reached down to pick has backpack up and throw it back over his shoulder.

Alex just looked at him with a teasing glare.

"Yes, Seth, you know I'm completely booked with my lame full-time job and that war going on overseas, I barely have time to breath." He responded highly sarcastically. "No, you know I never have anything going on."

Seth laughed and shook his head.

"Well anyway, I heard from Danny that his brother Hetrick got his old truck fixed up and running again and we're probably gonna take it out mudding at the old quad path on the mountain."

Of course it was true that Alex never did have anything going on in his stagnant life there at home, so he was always excited when he and his friends would go out to the mountain paths for stupid redneck thrills like mudding up a truck.

"Yeah I'd definitely be up for that!" He nodded in approval.

"But Alex, isn't it supposed to storm tonight?" Nickole interjected with concern.

Her brother just rolled his eyes arrogantly.

"Well Nickole, part of the idea of mudding is that you get a little bit of rain to produce mud on the dirt roads."

Nickole narrowed her eyes, feeling herself getting a little angry.

"I know what mudding is." She huffed. "But you know what Mom says about being out driving around when it storms. She doesn't even like your friends to begin with!" Realizing what she said, she glanced over at Alex's friend beside him. "No offense, Seth." Seth waved his hand to signal that none was taken.

Alex was getting as annoyed as his sister was.

"That's none of your concern, Nickole." He scolded her. "When you're old enough to start making your own decisions maybe you'll understand. What you and Mom do is entirely your business, and what I do with my friends is mine and mine only. When are you going to learn that? I don't need you watching my back."

It was exactly that sort of attitude rising in Alex that had the potential to bring Nickole on the verge of tears. It made it much more difficult for to see through his moods and know if her old brother was still alive and well or not. A lot of times there were mixed thoughts rushing through her head making her wonder what to say next.

Her racing thoughts were suddenly interrupted by the reverberating sound of the school's bell going off. Hardly more than a second later everyone amongst the crowds quickly shifted their attention and moved to wherever their day's schedule sent them. Alex and Seth situated their backpacks and went to fall into the moving hordes of students, with Nickole just behind them.

As they shuffled their way through the halls Seth continued talking to Alex.

"So you remember the quad path, right? You remember the branch that splits off and heads down toward Roger Brook?"

Alex had to think back for a brief moment.

"Yeah, I remember. That shaky, rocky path that sits on the edge of the mountains. That's about as far as we've ever gone, isn't it?"

"Yeah, that's it." Seth replied. "Hetrick says he might have found the remains of an old express road that's supposed to cut right through the mountains and he wants to try to get a closer look at it."

"Really?" Alex responded with interest. "What do you mean an old express road?"

Seth shook his head.

"I don't know. Apparently it was closed and blocked off some twenty years ago or something like that. But Hetrick says it's supposed to be completely abandoned and that he thinks he's found an entry that could lead to it. Danny told me that's where he wants to go later today when they take the truck out."

Alex took a quick glance back at his sister. Nickole had not been listening to their conversation as they walked. She had fallen back a little bit, and it seemed as though she was a little bit more distracted today than usual. But Alex did not care. He preferred it if Nickole did not butt into the social life of he and his friends. He was not worried, though. Alex had gone out driving around with his friends in that area just off the mountains lots of times and Nickole knew it, but he also knew that Nickole could never bring herself to rat him out to their mother.

However, there was definitely some reason as to why their mother did not approve of him going driving around with friends on the borders of the mountains. Alex did not know what reasons she may have had because she never told him. As his parent, she should not have to explain her reasons to her son, but to Alex that only made him ever defiant. The path which he and his friends were planning to drive on was one of a series of small dirt roads which skirted the mountainside just west of the village of Lake Placid, some of which stretched out for miles. They had been primarily used recreationally as tracks for four-wheelers and dirt bikes, but over the past few years the novelty had worn off and the tracks were all but abandoned. Every time Alex's friend's older brother took his truck out on the paths he would track further and further out, almost like he was mapping it for some reason.

Of course, if what Seth said was true, about Hetrick wanting to go as far as near Roger Brook, then it would be the farthest Alex had ever gone outside of home on his own, so naturally he was a bit excited. Roger Brook was a small creek about seven miles out from his home that extended down from Oseetah Lake and flowed into the Adirondacks. It was hardly more than trees and rough paths out there, so what exactly were they expecting to find?

As Alex and Seth were nearing the hall that led to their own classes, he turned around to face his sister, who still seemed a bit distracted.

"Nickole," he called out to grab her attention. Nickole stopped in her tracks. Alex pointed toward one of the staircases leading to the next floor where many of the younger students were separating from the crowd. "That's where you're going." Nickole followed his attention to the staircase and then she glanced back at him one last time before she headed off on her separate path for the day. Alex watched her go until she disappeared up the stairs amongst the rest of her peers.

"Is she alright?" Seth spoke up, interrupting Alex's brief thoughts. "She seems kind of distracted lately."

Alex shook his head and turned to catch up with his friend.

"You have no idea." He muttered. "Every day it feels like she tries to get closer to me, it's almost like..." He was suddenly cut off when something bumped into him from the side and sent him stumbling toward Seth, who caught him and set him back onto his feet.

"Watch it!" A voice yelled out from just behind him.

Feeling annoyed and not thinking about it, Alex snapped back before he even turned around.

"You watch it!" he fired back with frustration.

"What did you say?" The same voice responded instantly.

As Alex gathered himself, he suddenly froze and his widened slightly, now realizing the severity of his situation. That "voice," which he unintentionally reacted aggressively to, belonged to one his old antagonists of his younger years. Alex exhaled anxiously and turned to face his confronter.

"Davis," he mumbled to himself.

The name of the boy standing before him was Drake Davis. He was your typical classroom bully. He was significantly taller than Alex, by about a head height. His hair was cut short and he was wearing a black tank top in an unnecessary effort to sport his juvenile muscles. They had known each other all of their school years, but never on any good terms. In Alex's mind, he was not exactly afraid of Davis as much as he was simply annoyed by him. He definitely imposed an intimidating stature as the two of them glared at each other, but Alex still waited for the day when someone would just knock Davis off of his feet once and for all, as it seemed as though it was long overdue.

"What are doing, Lee?" Davis began menacingly.

Alex tried to tread carefully, but instead responded before he could think.

"Going to class, what the hell do you think I'm doing?" That was the wrong move and he knew it. Alex winced as soon as he said it and cursed himself in his head. Davis dropped his own backpack on the ground and inched closer to Alex, staring him down.

Sensing the impending battle, Seth suddenly threw himself into the middle of it. He grabbed hold of Alex's shoulder and pulled him back a little, putting his hand up in front of Davis' path.

"Come on, Davis, let's not do this," he said, hoping to be a peacemaker. Davis turned his contempt toward Seth. At this point, Alex felt like he was watching an animal trainer attempt to calm a wild wolf. Several students were now stopped and huddled around in silence, most likely thinking the same thing. Seth continued to sweet talk their aggressor. "Are you having a good morning, Davis?" he joked. "We're having a good morning, and we'd prefer it if the janitor didn't have to wipe blood off the floor today, okay?" Seth laughed at his own joke, hoping to calm the atmosphere a little. Alex was certainly not in the mood for any fight to break out, but it was obvious that the audience around them was itching to see a little bit of action.

Usually, everyone knew Davis had the tendency to be stubborn as a mule when it came to picking fights. It had been that way for as long as Alex knew him, and many times he had to learn that the hard way. However, to his surprise Davis took a deep breath, picked his backpack off of the floor and backed away. Seth lowered his arm in relief.

Davis only scowled at Alex.

"It's pretty convenient having someone else do your fighting for you, isn't it Lee?" Davis mocked. "You just remember that the next time you wanna try to act tough." His final sentiment was short before he turned and walked off in frustration. At the same time the small circle of students dispersed, clearly disappointed.

Seth looked at Alex and shook his head in a teasing manner.

"He's right, you know," he joked with him. "Why did I have to be one to end that?" Alex disregarded his comment and they continued to follow their peers down the hall. "It's okay, I hate him as much as you do." Seth added.

"I don't hate him," Alex responded. Seth looked him with a confused glance. A short grin briefly came across Alex's face. "I'd just like to kill him, to be a little more accurate."

He and Seth laughed at the jest following their near-brutal experience with their old Elementary School wrecking ball.

"Yeah, don't do that," Seth said with a sheepish smile. "I'd rather not bury you." As he came to the door of his first class of the day, Seth held his fist up in front of his friend. "Alright, see you lunch I guess."

Alex brought his hand up and bumped Seth's fist and nodded to him.

"See you after school then, too." Seth turned and headed into his own class. Alex continued down the hall toward his own destination. This where all of his days began and as far as he was concerned, he would simply have to suck it up and get through it like everyone else. He was no different.

CHAPTER FOUR

As the day pressed on, the spring sun began to penetrate the tree canopies of the vast Adirondacks. At night the Dark Zone had the proclivity to live up to its name by appearing to be a very dark and dreary wilder land with a hostile vibe intent on instilling fear in the hearts of those who wandered near its borders. To some, however, such ideas were deeply misunderstood. When the sun was high and the woods were illuminated, the Dark Zone could be seen as a very beautiful and peaceful land of valleys and forests full of life. But with its enormous reputation, what sort of people could possible think highly of the mysterious Dark Zone?

Along the shadowy floor of the mountainous woods a young girl wandered. She was no simple or average city girl lost in the mountains. Though she looked slightly older, the girl was quite young, about fourteen years old. She had long, black hair that hung down her back and over her shoulders. Her clothes were poor; stitched primarily from leather and fur. Her face carried an expression of boldness and gallantry, yet also a sense of compassion and love for home. Her home was not located on any site on the side of the mountains. It was here, in the very midst of the Dark Zone itself. In fact, home was merely an understatement, for like some who had never seen the mountains, she had never wandered beyond these territories. This was all she had, all she needed. But unfortunately, for several years times were difficult for her and her people. So difficult that even the woods that she had walked all of her life had become dangerous. Such dangers, however, may have ravaged the girl's home, but not her heart.

She hiked ever so stealthily through the light morning woods. In her left hand she carried a short, carven bow and slung on her back was a quiver which held about a dozen arrows. Aside from that she was also carrying a small handmade knife tucked into a sheath on her back just above her waist. It was no secret that she was out hunting for something. She woke up at the first light of the morning sun and crept out of her home for the sport. It was not something she was able to do every day because her older brother did not always allow it, but she hunted whenever she could.

Suddenly, she halted in her tracks and began glancing around, as if she heard something inaudible catch her attention. The girl looked down at the ground in front of her. She kneeled down and examined the dirt of the forest floor for tracks. And sure enough, there were signs of deer tracks. Judging by the size she figured they probably belonged to a single juvenile host. They were fresh tracks, possibly a few hours old. With this information, she consulted her knowledge of the mountains and the terrain of her home. She knew, in her location, that just a few miles north the mountain would split into a narrow, rocky trough. More to her interest, however, is that a small creek fed out from the trough and met with many others to form a pond on the edge of a valley. If there was a herd of deer nearby then the pond is where they were mostly likely headed. The girl stood back up with a confident posture and ran silently off deeper into the woods toward the mountain trough.

It was about a two mile journey through the trees and hills but the girl traversed the rough terrain quickly and very quietly, as she had done so for years. When born and raised in the heart of the mountains one learns to memorize their environment, to know every rock and leaf and stream that rushes down the mountainsides. It takes strength, passion and an excessive amount of willpower to call the mountains home. For many generations the girl's people were dwellers of these lands. They were self-governing, minding their own business and cared little for the dealings of the Outside world.

The girl's name was Rowan. A skilled hunter from a young age, her every breath and fiber she dedicated to the well-being of her home in the Dark Zone, or at least that is what she wanted. For a long time her people were farmers and hunters in these mountain territories. Now, for five years they had been turned into warriors and survivalists, pushed from their homes in the valleys of the mountains. Not by famine or wild animals, that much they could handle themselves. Invaders, however, were an entirely different situation. Five years ago, the mountains were entered by an enormous group of outsiders in the middle of a winter's night. Driven by malicious intent, they attacked and drove Rowan's people out into the deeper territories of what became known as the Dark Zone.

At last, Rowan found herself coming to a break in the dense woods. She was getting close to the trough and the pond which she predicted she might find the deer. The sunlight grew brighter, and before long Rowan stopped near the edge of the tree lines. She could now see through the trees; the edge of the woods was looked down at a pond sitting in the middle of a small valley at the edge of the rocky mountainside. As she scanned the area, sure enough she could see a single small deer with its tail turned toward her as it drank from the water of the pond. It was completely oblivious to her proximity.

Rowan crouched down and pulled an arrow from her quiver. Not blinking, and keeping all her focus on the target, she slowly positioned the arrow and pulled the string back. She lined her sight up perfectly along the arrow. One simple release of her fingers and the arrow would fly with blinding speed at her prey. She inhaled and held her breath to hold steady, but suddenly the deer stopped drinking and looked up. Rowan froze, waiting to see if the deer would make another movement. Luckily, it did not see her, rather it was looking off into the distance at the mountains. At this point

Rowan got a better look at the unknowing animal. Small as it was, she realized that it was not a juvenile fawn, but an adult doe. Its head was smooth where a male's antlers would have grown. As the Dark Zone was a territory that sat off the grid of the Outside governments, there were no open seasons or game restrictions when it came to hunting. Instead, Rowan simply could not bring herself to knowingly slaughter a female animal while hunting. Releasing her breath, she began to lower her bow.

Just then, the doe down by the pond took notice to her presence at the edge of the woods. It stared at her with wide, dark eyes and did not move a muscle. Rowan just stared right back, with a look of compassion now instead of the look of a predator she had before. The doe stared for a moment and then shifted its attention slightly to its right. Rowan followed its gaze and slowly looked over toward her left. There, about thirty yards away, a second animal walked out of the tree line as if it were also headed toward the pond. Rowan examined the new arrival. It was buck, a large, adult buck. Its antlers were grown but just a bit small, telling Rowan that this buck may have just transcended into adulthood. Unlike the doe at the water, this buck remained unaware of her presence. Rowan regained her position to kill, pulling the arrow back and getting steady. As she did so, the buck now froze too and looked directly at her. *"Etime're."* She whispered under her breath in the tongue of her people, which translated most closely to "Forgive me." Without hesitation, she released the string of her bow.

The arrow soared out of the tree line in the blink of an eye and hit the buck in the side just behind the socket of its front leg. The buck let out a brief cry of pain and toppled over onto the ground. Rowan smiled with a sense of success, and she stood up and ran over to her kill. The doe had already taken off and was out of sight now. The buck, on the other hand, was still alive and writhing on the ground in pain. As sad as it was, Rowan knew what she had to do. She knelt down beside the dying deer and pulled her knife from the leather scabbard on around her waist. She pinned the buck's head down on the ground and swiftly forced the blade into its heart. The poor animal gasped briefly for air and then in seconds it was dead.

Rowan took a deep breath. She brought her right fist up and placed it gently against her forehead, and then lowered it down to rest against her heart. To her people it was a gesture of respect, acknowledged by the heart and the soul, and she used it now as if she were thanking the deer for its sacrifice. She then pried the arrow from the deer's flesh. She pulled a small canteen from her belt and dropped a little bit of water down onto the head to clean the blood from it, and then she placed it back in her quiver amongst the rest.

The next step of her hunting session was the tougher part. She knew she could not carry the entire carcass back to her home by herself, for it would be a several mile hike through the mountains. So she would come back later with the means to haul it. She did it all the time.

Rowan withdrew her knife and then dragged the buck back into the dense woods. In there it would be safer from bears and crows and other scavenging animals. She found the tightest cluster of trees she could, and then she reached down to her belt. On the right side she was carrying a pouch containing a rope which she planned to use for this very purpose. She pulled the rope from the pouch. It had been folded and wrapped together in itself to make it easy to carry, but she unraveled it to reveal that it would extend out to be very long. One of the ends of the rope was tied to a small metal loop, which she would use to help anchor it. Rowan took the rope searched for an open branch high enough from the ground. When she found one, Rowan wound up and threw the rope with the looped metal end into the air. With perfect accuracy, the rope travelled over the branch and fell back to the ground. She retrieved both ends of the rope, and then one end of it firmly around the dead buck's hind legs. After testing the stability of the rope and the branch it hung on, Rowan grabbed the other end of the rope and began hauling up the deer carcass.

Expectedly, the load was quite heavy. Rowan pulled on the rope with all of her strength. She lifted the deer up slowly but steadily. As it rose higher she had to move further back and keep choking up on the rope, until at last she found it to be high enough. Holding on tight to the rope, Rowan quickly wrapped it around a large nearby tree. She wrapped the rope around its base several times, and then she slipped the metal looped end under the other layers and hooked the loop onto a knot sticking out of the trunk. She checked the security of the metal loop and then made sure the rope leading up to the high branch was tight. She flicked the rope-line a few times, tight as a drum. It was definitely one of her best jobs. That game high above her was going nowhere until she returned.

Rowan took a few steps back, staring up at her kill. By now it was just after midday. It was still early, but it was time for her to head back to her home. Her brother no doubt knew she was gone by now.

"Rowan?" A male voice suddenly called out from the woods just behind her.

Rowan turned swiftly around. Out of the trees, a young man stepped forth. He was about six feet tall dressed similarly to Rowan, but instead of a bow, he carried a stone sword in a sheath on his back. On the belt around his own waist he carried a small knife like Rowan's on one side and a tomahawk on the other. He had long, brown hair, not nearly as long as Rowan's, but it hung down against the back of his neck. On each side of his head he had a section of his hair tied into a tail that hung down the side of his face. He approached Rowan and nodded slightly as a greeting, and she nodded back to him.

"Matheus," she greeted him.

The man called Matheus stopped in front of her and spoke in the same language that she had previously used.

"You should not be out here," he said to her. *"It's dangerous, you know that."*

Rowan wanted to shrug his words off, but she knew that he was right. She knew what kind of dangers now existed near their wooded boundaries. Not animals, but their heartless invaders who constantly had their eyes watching in their directions. She was simply tired of her brother trying to keep her contained in safety, even though she knew very well that he was doing it for her safety.

"Yes, I was on my way back," she replied fluently. *"Delmar does not control me, you know."* Rowan remarked, referring to her older brother.

Before she could say anything else, Matheus put his hand up to interrupt.

"He loves you, Rowan," he rebuked her. Rowan's brother Delmar assumed the role as leader of their people's society five years ago when their lives were thrown upside-down. He was a good man, loved and well-respected by everyone. When there was nobody else, when there were no other options, he was the one who stepped up to protect his people and his family. Now he had devoted all of his time and resources to providing home and safety for their lives. Rowan knew what Matheus was saying was true. She sighed and nodded her head. Matheus continued to speak. *"There's a storm coming in."* Suddenly switching to English, he said, "Delmar wants you to return to the Citadel immediately."

What they referred to as the Citadel, it was where Rowan came from in the morning on her hunting routine. When she and her family were forced from their home in the valleys her brother, Delmar, led the construction of a safe-haven in the deep southern territories of the Dark Zone. They scaled to the top of a small plateau amidst a range of rough and rocky mountains, and for the five years since they had placed all of their time and resources into fortifying the plateau into an armed and well-protected fortress where they could keep the remnants of their society safe. The Citadel was seen and known only by its builders and its citizens. There was only one way in or out of the fortress's vicinity, and that was over the narrow head of a slope which acted as a natural bridge between the plateau and the surrounding mountain range.

Although Rowan never spoke of it, in her mind she knew that she was afraid of their enemies. She had never actually encountered them, but she had heard the horror stories from many of her people who had escaped the initial invasion. Her worst memory, however, was that she was there in her valley home the night it was attacked. Despite how much she had grown, she was only a small child at the time. She remembered being woken by her mother in the middle of the night and rushed out of her home. She watched Delmar hurry to meet their attackers with their father, wielding nothing but a hatchet and a hunting knife. Those who could not fight followed Rowan and her mother to a wooded path leading up into the mountains. Under the highly unlikely possibility that such a horrifying event should take place, they knew to take refuge in a series of abandoned clay mines running throughout the mountains' underground. They had always kept supplies and weapons available in the mines in case of emergency, and it was there that they remained until the fight was over.

By dawn that day, only two men made it out of the fight and to the mine refuge. Delmar had been wounded, but when the fight was over he was helped away by his loyal friend, Malachai. They had spent a week hiding underground in the tunnels of the clay mines. To Rowan's horror, Delmar had suffered a sickening slash to the left side of his face. When he was rested and his wound was fixed, he revealed that their father had fallen in the fight and their home in the valley was burned and destroyed.

A seemingly endless period of grief followed as Rowan's people were brought to their knees in one night. She watched in helplessness as her mother succumbed to the grief, leaving Rowan, a nine-year-old child, to be raised by her young adult brother while they faced the trials ahead alone and looked after what was left of their people.

As their people began to scatter and fend for themselves, Delmar, a well-respected youth, took it upon himself to step up and keep their long-preserved civilization together. At first the load proved nearly too much for him to bear alone. He saw it all his responsibility to pull his people back onto their feet, start over from scratch and find them a new home while trying desperately to keep his sister, the only family he had left, safe from the harm he had experienced. By the summer of that year Delmar and his most trusted companions found the plateau in the south of the Dark Zone where, over the years following, they constructed the Citadel and drew all remnants of their society into its boundaries.

Delmar found himself becoming somewhat distant from Rowan, mainly due to the obligations that he had been working for years to maintain. His duties included keeping track of the workloads throughout the Citadel, regulating who could or could not leave their fortress and, most stressful of all, making sure the people had hope for the future, no matter how dim that hope may have been. Delmar constantly restricted Rowan's activities around the Citadel. She has young and it was his fear that she might become too reckless. He rarely allowed her to leave the safety of the plateau and would always demand that someone accompany her. Most of the time when she wanted to leave the Citadel she had to sneak out. Delmar kept a close eye on her but he was not able to stay by her side all of the time, so he always had someone standing by to go after her when she snuck out into the wilderness.

That is why Matheus was there now. He was a close friend to Delmar and the minute they realized Rowan had gone again Matheus armed himself and set out to bring her back. It took him a few hours but he was more adept than Rowan when it came to tracking, and he caught up to her faster than she had found her deer.

As Rowan knew her brief time to herself had come to an end for the day, she withdrew her weapons. Looking back up at the buck that hung from the tree above them she said, "I must return for my kill. I cannot leave it overnight."

Matheus smiled and raised his hand to calm her, looking

up to observe the impressive prey.

"I'll see to it that it is retrieved in one piece, Rowan, don't worry." He stepped forward and placed a hand on her shoulder.

Reluctantly, she nodded in agreement.

"And do me a favor? Lay down the repellent so the vermin don't get to it?" She did not say another word, but she looked at Matheus one last time, almost as if she wanted to thank him for coming after her, and then she walked past him and off into the woods toward the Citadel. Matheus watched until she was out of sight. He knew her well enough to know that Delmar's fear would eventually be realized. Rowan was indeed a reckless girl. Ironically, considering what kind of life they were forced to live, it felt like there was something else missing from her life. She had not been allowed to grow up with a free and happy childhood, their enemies made sure of that. Did she want revenge? Did she desire a chance to prove her strength and courage to her brother and avenge their fallen blood? A proficient hunter she may have been, she was still not a warrior. She had never seen conflict with their antagonists, but Matheus had, and it was no laughing matter. It would be selfish of her to recklessly endanger herself like that after everything Delmar had done to protect her, but as young as she was Matheus knew that it was not her intent. She simply needed someone to look after her, at least until this conflict was over. If it would ever end at all.

CHAPTER FIVE

The school day came to end for Alex as it always did; with dozens of students filling the hallways in crowded clusters as they had been in the morning. Alex walked out from his last class of the day and pulled his cellphone from his pocket as soon as he entered the hall. With school hours over, Alex planned to meet up with his friend Seth out in front of the school building, where ordinarily he and Nickole would be picked up by their mother. And so he flipped his phone open and typed a text message to Seth, *"Hey Seth I'll meet you out front."*

He made his way quickly to the nearest staircase where he would make his way down to the first floor. The doors to the stairwell were being held open by the groups of students all heading down. Alex pushed his way through the hordes and down the stairs. Once at the bottom he felt his phone vibrate. He opened it up to see a response text from Seth which read, *"Alright, already there."*

As he finally passed through the front doors of the school the sunlight was bright and the grounds were once again packed with students boarding school buses. Alex looked around for his friend. What caught his eye was what sat on the side of the road near the end of the school ground, a large, black Ford F-250. He recognized it as the truck belonging to his friend Danny's brother. It was a 1998 F-250. Hetrick had been working on it for the past several months, fixing what needed to be repaired and adding a few new features to it. Standing by the truck, Alex saw Seth there talking to Danny. Seth looked out and waved for Alex to come over. He quickly headed over to join them. The low roar of the truck's engine filled his ears as he approached it.

"Hey, there you are," Seth called out as Alex walked over to stand beside him. He brought his hand up and Alex grasped it as a greeting.

Alex looked over at Danny, who was leaning against the passenger side door of the F-250. He was wearing a Mossy Oak camo hat and a black tank top, perhaps a bit too light for April, but he never cared. In fact, it was the sort of outfit he seemed to wear all year round. He was Alex's friend, but Alex could never figure out if the cold simply did not bother him or if he was just a redneck idiot, and his older brother was the same way.

"Where've you been today?" Alex asked Danny.

Danny just rested himself against the truck door casually with his hands hanging in his pockets. There was no way he had been sick earlier.

"Oh you know," He began with a grin. "Couldn't afford to go to school today."

Alex just glanced over at Seth, who was not sure what to say.

"Couldn't afford to go to school?" Alex laughed as he repeated his words. "Never heard that one before. What were you doing this time?"

"I had to help Hetrick." Danny replied. "He had a tow job to take care of over near Wilmington and his friend had to cancel on him, so I went along with this morning. Had to help my brother so we could make time to take the truck back out on the old paths today. That's important, isn't it?"

Just then, the driver's side door opened and Danny's brother Hetrick got out and walked around the front of the truck. Basically, he looked like a bigger, older version of Danny. He wore a similar camo hat and a red *"America"* with the sleeves cut off. He leaned against the hood of the truck and pulled a can of Copenhagen chewing tobacco from his pocket. He twisted the cap off and placed a pinch of it into his mouth.

"What do you guys think?" He said with a deeper voice

than his brother's, gesturing to his F-250. "Got the last of the leaks fixed up this week so we can take her back out right now."

Seth nodded in approval. "You said you wanted to go out near Roger Brook, right?"

"Yeah, Danny told you, I guess?" Hetrick responded. "I want to see if I can find where that rocky road goes to that we found last year."

Alex was about to say something, but suddenly another voice spoke up behind him.

"Alex, Mom's waiting for us." He turned around to see Nickole stop in front of him. He was sort of hoping to slip away without her seeing him.

"Just tell her I'm going over to Danny's for a while." He instructed her. "I'll be back later."

Nickole just stared back at him with a serious look.

"Well that would be fine with her, Alex," She said back. "But then that means I have to go home with her, and I know where you guys are really planning on going. So do I tell her the truth, or do I tell her your truth?"

Alex raised his eyebrows. Was it him or did Nickole just give him an ultimatum? It was certainly a tactic he had never seen her use before. Regardless of the reasons, Alex knew what it was she wanted. He sighed and rolled his eyes.

"Do you wanna come with, Nickole?" he reluctantly asked.

"I'd love to! Thanks for asking." She smiled.

Alex ignored her sarcasm.

"Just tell mom..."

"I got it." Nickole interrupted him. She turned and quickly headed back over to their mother's car.

He turned toward his friends and shook his head. Danny looked a little confused.

"What is it?" He asked curiously. "Your mom doesn't let you drive around with us?"

"She's too restrictive," Alex answered him. "I'd never be able to go out with you guys again if she knew what it is we do or how far we've gone. So you don't mind if she tags along with us?" He asked, looking at Danny's brother.

Hetrick shook his head.

"Not at all," He replied. "I don't recommend it, though. It gets pretty rough out there and I can't keep my eye on her."

"I'll keep an eye on her." Alex said. "She'll be fine. I don't need her telling her mom where we're going."

Just then, Nickole came back to Alex's side. Alex noticed she no longer had her backpack with her. She didn't say a word, rather she looked eager to leave with them.

Alex waited for her to speak.

"Well?" he asked. "What's the word? What did you tell her?"

"She's fine with me going with you." Nickole replied briefly.

"Wait, she's letting you come mudding with us?" Seth asked, surprised.

"No," Nickole said back. "I told her you were going to drop me off at a friend's house and then you guys were going back to Danny and Hetrick's place. I also told her you guys would pick me up later and drop Alex and I off at home."

There was an awkward silence among the small group as they seemed to be impressed with how fluently Nickole lied to her mother, Alex most of all because she was never one to lie about anything. He did not think she had it in her.

Hetrick just shrugged it off.

"Ok," He began, breaking the silence. "Let's go then, everybody in." He turned and headed back to the driver's seat. Danny jumped into the passenger side and the other three of them all piled into the back row of the truck. Watching out for the dozens of other students crossing the street, Hetrick put the truck in gear and slowly pulled out to the main road.

It was about a twenty minute drive out of the Lake Placid area as they headed toward the edge of the Adirondack mountain ranges. In the back of the truck Nickole was sitting in between Seth and her brother. She remained quiet the entire time, listening to the four boys yammering on about their own interests; cars, girls and other teenage topics which Nickole had absolutely no interest in. Several times she found herself wondering why she was even there. Nickole began to analyze the choice she had made. Her relationship with Alex was becoming distant, their mother was not fond of his friends and frankly neither was she. Come to think of it, Nickole hardly had any interest in driving around with them at all as well. So why did she risk lying to their mother for Alex? Maybe she thought of it as her chance to try to strengthen her relationship with her brother, by taking part in his own interests. Plus, going out with he and his friends also meant a chance for her to see more of the mountains, even if they were only going to the edge of ranges. Regardless, it would be the farthest away from home she would have been in a long time. Though she was ashamed to admit it, she was excited to be doing something active for once and, overall, glad that she lied to her mother about it.

After heading off of the main road and onto more narrow, winding roads they began to approach the base of the mountains. The paths became rougher and more unpaved the deeper they traveled along the side of the ranges. The tremendous stature of Hetrick's F-250 was built to endure rocky mountain roads, but that did not negate the shaking of the truck's cabin. Though, Nickole hardly took notice of it. She found herself glancing past the boys on either side of her and glancing out the windows when she could. She was trying to view the splendor of the wilderness that traveled past her, at least splendor was the way she saw it. But the trees and hills only began to move by faster as they continued to pick up speed.

As they reached ever deeper into the old path, Hetrick slowed the truck down before bringing it to a stop. They had gone far enough into the hills that everywhere Nickole looked she could not see beyond the trees. Hetrick turned off the truck and suddenly everything went deathly quiet as the roar of the F-250's engine was silenced. At once, everyone opened the doors of the truck and stepped outside. Nickole followed Alex out the left side of the truck. She could instantly feel the soothing touch of the mountains' warm, spring air as it brushed across her flesh in the form of a soft breeze. The atmosphere was filled with the sounds of the birds all around them and the smell of pine surrounded Nickole. She was only several miles from home and yet it was as if she had crossed over into a whole new world.

Alex might have felt the same kind of warm fascination as his younger sister were it not for his heart which grew ever colder. All he cared about right now was his time alone with his friends, away from his sheltered life at home. Looking around, they could see that they had come to an end in the dirt path they had been travelling. There was nothing but trees, trees, and more trees surrounding them on all remaining sides. Alex was under the impression that they were heading for what was once a main road stretching through the mountains.

"Where are we?" He asked out loud. "Is this it? Where's the road?"

Hetrick walked around to the bed of his truck. He grabbed an old, worn backpack and slung it around his shoulder. Closing the bed gate, he headed back over to the group.

"What's in that?" Seth asked Hetrick, pointing curiously to the bag on his back.

"Just a few things we might need." Hetrick replied casually. "Come on, follow me." He began heading uphill into the trees.

Alex was about to follow when his pocket suddenly vibrated. He quickly pulled his phone out to see a new message from his mother. Nothing serious, she simply reminded him to ensure Nickole was brought home later from her friend's house. It seemed Nickole's deception really had worked to perfection. Still, Alex shook his head in annoyance at the way their mother was constantly looking into their lives. Not wanting her to inadvertently spoil his afternoon, Alex dropped his phone into the truck through the open window, and then he caught up with his friends.

They were only walking through the woods for a minute before Alex was beginning to question what they were even doing.

"Hetrick," He called up to his friend's brother. "I thought you said you found a road that cuts through the mountains."

"No," was Hetrick's response as he stopped briefly and turned to look back at Alex. "I said I found what could be the remains of one."

Alex found himself confused.

"What does that mean?"

Hetrick continued hiking up the hill.

"You'll see. Come on." Alex and Seth exchanged glances, but decided not to question him just yet, and they followed Hetrick and Danny further with Nickole just behind them.

It was not much farther, but when the tree line began to break open the first thing they found themselves standing before was a small cliff that rose up in front of them, blocking their path. It was not exactly a cliff, rather it looked like the result of a landslide or something of the like. It towered about fifteen feet above them, with numerous tree and plant roots jetting out from its wall. Nickole's jaw dropped. Alex shook his head at the way she was so easily impressed by new sights. He, on the other hand, was more concerned now about how Hetrick and Danny seemed to be leaving them in the dark.

"What is this?" he said, a little aggravated. "Where's your 'remains?'"

Hetrick walked forth and placed his hand around a large tree root sticking out of the cliff.

"You're standing on it." He responded with a grin. Alex and the rest of them looked down simultaneously. Suddenly, he realized what Hetrick was talking about. As they stood before the dirt cliff, they found themselves standing on not the forest floor, but what appeared to be a disfigured formation of black, rugged rocks embedded in the ground. Some were flat and level with the ground around them while others pointed out as if they were dug into the ground. Alex looked behind and saw more of these stretching down the hill. Scanning the cliff once more, it was clear to him now that some time earlier the road where they stood had been destroyed, and they were now standing on its concrete remains. So it would be anyone's educated guess that the rest of the road lied above them. But why would anyone have wanted it destroyed?

"So this is it?" Seth spoke up.

Hetrick nodded in affirmation.

"Yeah, I found this last year while exploring the edge of the quad paths. I've just never taken the time to get up there, until now at least."

Seth shrugged as he glanced up and down the ravaged hillside before them.

"Well how hard could it be?" He said confidently. "It doesn't look like much of a climb." With that, he walked forth and grabbed hold of one of the roots embedded in the dirt.

"I wouldn't do that if I were you!" Hetrick shouted after him. As soon as Seth put pressure down on the root to pull himself up the loose dirt supporting it suddenly gave away. Seth fell onto his back as the cliff quickly began to disintegrate. Nickole laughed to herself and attempted to help him up. It was then that they realized just how unstable the cliff really was when a large, young tree sitting near the edge of the deteriorating ledge was brought down in the slide.

"Oh shit!" Seth exclaimed in shock. He scrambled off of his back to hurry out of the way of the collapsing tree. Alex rushed forward to grab Nickole and pull her out of the way. Danny and Hetrick stepped clear as the tree toppled over the edge with the flow of the small landslide and crashed onto the ground. After a few seconds the event was over and fortunately nobody had been harmed. Nickole shook Alex's hand off of her arm. Seth climbed back onto his feet and wiped the dirt off of himself. There was a brief silence but then everyone broke out into a laugh of relief.

"Is everyone okay?" Hetrick asked cautiously. He looked over at Seth and shook his head. "Now you know why I've never been up there yet." The laughter was then directed at Seth, but something suddenly caught Nickole's eye.

"What's that?" She said, pointing toward the remains of the fallen cliff. Everyone shifted their attention toward the dirt and debris. Hetrick inched forward and began digging away at the dirt around the roots of the downed tree. After clearing away a little bit of the debris they could make out what appeared to be an old-looking frame that formed the shape of a small doorway.

"Whoa," Hetrick gasped under his breath. The others walked over next to him to get a look at their discovery.

"What is it?" Nickole asked with growing interest.

Hetrick continued clearing away the surrounding dirt.

"It looks like the entrance to an old mine or something." He removed the bag from around his shoulder and set on the ground. Rifling through it, Hetrick pulled out three small flashlights. He handed one to his brother and the other remaining light he tossed to Alex. Turning them on, Hetrick shined his light toward the opening. The light revealed a tunnel heading into the hill. He could not tell if there was an end to it, but it was definitely a mine of some sort. Hetrick ducked his head and slowly crept his way into the tunnel, followed by Danny.

With the only other flashlight, Alex went to join them inside. As Nickole attempted to go in with him he reached his arm out to stop her.

"Stay here." he said in a commanding tone. Nickole gave him a look of disdain, believing if the mine was safe enough for him then it was safe enough for her. Alex looked over at Seth. "Could you keep an eye on her?"

Seth nodded. "Yeah, sure," He reluctantly replied.

Just inside, the tunnel was narrow and compacted. The

three of them inched their way through the darkness, shining their lights around as they went. In seconds, however, the tunnel began to open and become more spacious. They could now stand up straight and were able to take a better look around. The only other source of light came faintly from the way the entered. Alex guessed it must have been an air duct rather than an entrance. But who could tell? These mines must have been abandoned for many years.

Hetrick kneeled down by the wall of the tunnel and picked some of the materials from it. He shined his light on the dirt in his hand. It was a light brown color. It was soft but remained intact as he handled it.

"It's clay," he said, his voice echoing in the close quarters. "This is a clay mine!"

Hearing this, Danny felt around the walls a bit, realizing his brother was right. Alex walked a little further down the tunnel. Still he could not find an end to it as far as his light would travel.

"I didn't know there were any mines in these mountains." He said.

"This could be a single vein of a whole system." Hetrick replied. "Clay is pretty abundant in the Appalachians. There were a whole lot of mines like this back in the old days."

"Uh-huh," Alex mumbled. He looked over at a wooden frame stretching out on the ceiling of the mine. "You think that express road you were looking for had anything to do with these mines?"

Hetrick shrugged.

"Maybe," he muttered to himself. Getting back to his feet he said, "Let's get out of here. We'll come back another time when we're more prepared, and give this place a little look around." He and Danny turned to head back to the entrance.

Alex reached up and touched his hand to the wood beam over his head. Without any warning, the beam suddenly collapsed, and with it the fragile frame came crashing down. Alex dove out of the way as more debris continued to drop from the ceiling of the mine. Hetrick and Danny watched in horror as the tunnel's structure grew increasingly unstable.

"Get out of here!" He yelled, shoving Danny toward the opening. In one final effort, Hetrick attempted to rush over for Alex but the mine was caving in too rapidly. It was no use. Hetrick cursed and scrambled out of the tunnel with the cave in hot on his tail.

Outside the mine, Seth rushed forth to help Danny and Hetrick as the slipped out of the disaster. As soon as Hetrick got clear of the entrance the frame had caved in with the rest of the tunnel. They hurried to their feet, but it did not end there. After the entrance gave in, the remains of the previous landslide caused by Seth picked up again.

"Alex!" Nickole screamed as she recklessly rushed toward the sliding earth.

"Nickole, No!" Hetrick reached out and pulled her back. The whole cliff was now crumbling and quickly falling down the hill. "Get out of the way! Run!" He shouted, pushing the others to move away from the calamity. Hetrick dragged Nickole clear of the landslide's path.

At last, the action faded and ceased. The entire area of the hillside had been transformed by the mishap. Nobody said a word. Hetrick caught his breath, he couldn't find the strength to move just yet. Nickole was extremely shaken. She tried to remain as calm as she could, but her brother was now trapped on the other side, buried under the mountain. She could not maintain control of herself, and she cried out, "ALEX!"

CHAPTER SIX

Alex was revived from his black out by a throbbing pain in his temple. There was a sharp ringing sound in his ears as he struggled to open his eyes. He tried opening his eyes but could not tell the difference, the space around him was even darker than the closure of his eyelids. He was dazed and disoriented from the dramatic cave in.

The cave in!

Alex's eyes flew open and he hurried to his feet. As he tried to stand up he bashed his head off of a low beam. The incident had caused most of the mine's structure to cripple, but he could not see a thing in the intense darkness. Alex cried out and put a hand to his head as he fell back against the wall. He was breathing heavily and could feel himself begin to panic. He brought himself down on all fours and felt around the tunnel. His hand suddenly came upon a familiar object. Alex gasped as he found the flashlight Hetrick had given him. He scrambled to find the button to turn it on and a dim beam of light shot from the tool.

The light hardly illuminated much in the darkness of the decimated mine tunnel, but pointing it round Alex was finally able to distinguish the direction of the way in which they had originally entered. He knew which way it was because it was completely blocked off by dirt and broken supports. Alex quickly tried digging away at the new wall that cut him off from escaping this trap, but the debris was too tightly packed by the weight of the collapse. Becoming increasingly anxious, he put himself against the wall and began shouting for his friends to hear him.

"Hetrick!" He called out as loud as he could. There was no response. "Danny! Seth!" Nothing. It was deathly silent in the darkness. "NICKOLE!" He knew that they would not have just left with him trapped in here, but the cave in was so thick that there was not a chance they could hear him. He had to get a hold of them somehow. Alex quickly dug into his pocket for his cellphone. Feeling around, he froze suddenly, and a cold chill shot up his spine as he realized that his phone was not in his pocket. He remembered leaving in Hetrick's truck just before they hiked up toward the mine. That was it then, he had no way of reaching his friends.

What was he going to do? Surely they would try to fetch help to get him out. But the panic and impending sense of claustrophobia were starting to make him unwilling to wait. He could not dig his way out, so Alex turned and shined his flashlight deeper down the tunnel. As before, he could see no end to it, but it had to lead somewhere. He had to make a decision and go for it before his light died out. Alex shook his head in disbelief, inhaled a deep breath, and crept his way down the dark tunnel.

"Alex!" Nickole continued to scream. She rushed toward the great pile of disaster which now trapped her brother. "Alex!"

"Nickole!" Hetrick cried out to seize her attention. She was absolutely frantic and shaking from the sudden shock of it all. "You need to calm down, now!"

Nickole could not stand still for a second.

"I can't!" she cried. "We have to help him! We can't leave him stuck in there!"

Hetrick grabbed Nickole by the shoulders.

"NICKOLE!" he shouted out loud. Nickole suddenly went silent and cold, her eyes wide open as she stared back up at Hetrick. "Re-lax. Alex is going to be fine, but right now he needs you to remain calm, okay?" Nickole was still trembling, but she managed a slight nod. "Good." Hetrick released her.

"What happened in there?" Seth finally got a word in.

Hetrick took a deep breath.

"The mine structure was unstable. One touch and the roof of the mine came down."

Seth's jaw dropped.

"If the whole ceiling collapsed then how do we know Alex wasn't crushed...?" Hetrick quickly put a hand up to silence him, for fear of Nickole having another panic attack.

"He wasn't." Danny interjected and everyone looked to him. "He dove out of the way, I saw it. He's probably on the other side trying to dig his way out."

Hetrick looked around the group briefly. There's not much to do except get ahold of someone to come and help them, which was precisely his idea. Hetrick reached into his pocket and pulled his cell phone out.

"Who are you going to call?" Nickole asked anxiously.

Hetrick bit his lip as he thought deeply.

"I don't know yet."

"What do you mean you don't know?" Seth questioned. "Call one of your friends to get a truck up here or something!"

"And do what?" Hetrick rebuked him. "None of my friends have the means to move a whole pile of earth this far up the hill!" There was silence among them for a moment. Now they thought about it, their predicament was a serious one with very few options of a solution. He flipped open his phone and let out a sigh of disbelief. "It wouldn't matter anyway." He muttered.

Everyone else looked up suddenly.

"Why not?" Danny asked.

Hetrick faced his phone toward his brother.

"I have no service here."

Nickole moaned to herself. She was walking around on the edge of panic and worry. Danny walked over to take a look at the phone.

"We're going to have to get off the mountain to get a better signal."

Nickole halted and her eyes widened.

"You mean leave Alex here!?" she cried. "We can't do that!"

Hetrick put a hand up to calm her again.

"We're not going to," He responded lightly. He dropped his phone back into his pocket. "Danny, you and Seth stay here at the mine entrance. Under no circumstances should you go anywhere else, got it?"

The two exchanged glances of curiosity.

"Okay," Danny nodded sheepishly.

"I'm gonna run out and get help as fast as I can, and then I'll be back." He looked to Nickole and gestured for her to follow him. "Nickole, come with me."

"No!" Nickole shouted in refusal. "I want to stay here and help Alex!"

"No you're not." Hetrick replied. "You're coming with me to get help, and then I'm taking you to your friend's house. When Alex gets out we're all going to catch deep shit for this, and you're not going to be a part of that. Now come on."

Nickole was hesitant to move. She looked back and forth from Hetrick to the others. Her own decision was to stay by her brother's side when he needed help, but she recalled the lie she had told to her mother just to travel out into the mountains with Alex and his friends. What was more important to her now; her brother, or her status?

"Nickole, please," Hetrick urged her. The pressure was just too much for her. Reluctantly, she lowered her head and followed Hetrick down the hill and back to his truck.

This was insane! The tunnel never grew any lighter as far as Alex crept farther down, and the beam from his tiny flashlight hardly did him any justice. The air around him was cold and moist, he could feel it coming through his thin hoodie. Worst of all were the thoughts that kept gnawing at him; would he be able to find a way out of here at all?

No, that was morbid thinking. The tunnels could not possibly go on forever, and even if they did he knew where the entrance was, or what was left of it. Help would come as soon as possible.

However, the thought of currently being buried alive had a mind bending power of Alex, and he was simply not willing to wait for help to arrive. If this was a mine then surely there was another access point to the surface of the mountain, whether it was an air duct, an auxiliary entrance or the main entrance itself.

Alex was trying to keep the heart in his chest from exploding. He had to keep his cool that was more important now than anything. He waved his light all around the tunnel for any signs that might lead him to an escape route, but no other options revealed themselves except forward. Alex felt as though he had been walking through the dark tunnel forever, constantly stepping over and bending under disfigured and broken segments of the mine's structure. Panic was beginning well up inside him again as Alex cursing the seemingly endless underpass. Thoughts were racing in his head and he could feel it getting tougher to breath. Was it because he was starting to lose his mind, or was he only travelling deeper and deeper under the mountain? Surely he would have, had his alerted panic not saved him from his next step.

"JESUS!" Alex cursed out loud, his voice reverberating throughout the dark, crumbling corridor. Nearly falling forward, he managed to snatch hold of the small end of a tree root sticking out of the wall as he was almost taken over the edge of a massive hole in front of him. In the sudden jump scare, Alex accidentally dropped his flashlight into the chasm. As he regained his footing, he watched the faint beam of light spin as it continued to fall. Alex held his breath waiting for the flashlight to stop falling. After several seconds which felt like hours he heard the light hit the ground, but the beam itself was hardly visible at all. Alex's jaw dropped and he tightened his grip on the root. That was perhaps the luckiest thing to happen to him all day. If the fall itself had not killed him surely bashing his head off of the walls of the hole several times would have.

His brief thoughts of gratitude suddenly evaporated when he realized that now he was without a source of light and trapped underground in a highly unstable abandoned mine. Yet as he stared blankly down at his lost light, he was still able to faintly make out his surroundings, as if the light was somehow still illuminating the tunnel.

Without thinking, Alex quickly glanced up. To his great surprise, he found himself looking up into a vertical tunnel similar to the hole he had just dropped his flashlight into and saw the dim outline of what looked like a shaft leading above ground. Alex felt a smile instantly expand across his face, only to be swiftly wiped by one curious and rather confusing fact: the faint light which shone through the shaft revealed it to be nighttime outside.

Alex's eyes widened and he felt an intense wave of goosebumps travel along his arms. There was absolutely no way he had been trapped in the mine for that long. Of course, he admitted that was a little out of his senses with the fear and panic gripping him, but he could see the total dark of night through the vent above him, which would have meant that he had been wandering this tunnel for many hours. It was not logical!

To make matters worse, the state of panic combined with the new factor of confusing and curiosity was preventing Alex from calling out up through the mine shaft, in the hope that somebody might hear him. Something was just not right here. It was as if the world around him was going mad. Or maybe it was just him, for another inconceivable idea presented itself to Alex.

He bit his lip as he reached out and felt along the tip of the hole above him for some sort of hold to grab onto. The walls of the tunnel were completely ragged with chunks of dirt and roots and other forms of debris sticking out of them, so why should this one be any different. Still, even Nickole would find herself shaking her head at her brother's mindless efforts if she saw him now. Perhaps it was this whole freak incident that reminded Alex of one thing at this moment; his sister. He knew she had to have become absolutely frantic as soon as the mine's entrance collapsed, knowing that her older brother had been trapped in a matter of seconds. But the thought of escaping on his own and seeing her face light up with relief was what kept Alex going at this point. It was a shocking thought to him. He did not think his love for his sister, one of his only close family members, was still very much alive in him. Or was just the spur of the moment?

Alex shook his head to wake his sense up once again. At this point, he realized that he had managed to climb about halfway up the vertical tunnel. One of his hands was grasping another tree root in the wall, the other had hold of a rock which barely jutted far enough out to grip properly, and he had his feet dug into the dirt for as much support as he could make for himself. But coming to this realization, Alex gasped as his foot slipped out of its hold and he nearly lost all of his grip. He held and his breath tried desperately to regain his footing.

"You've gotta be kidding me!" Alex breathed through clenched teeth. One more slip and it was over, he just knew it. How did a simple afternoon out with friends suddenly turn into a sick game of survival? Alex took in a deep breath and slowly and very carefully heaved himself farther up, quickly scrambling about for more points to hold onto. As incredibly stressful as the effort was, at last Alex pulled himself high enough to reach the shaft vent. He carefully reached up and put hand against the vent and began applying pressure, hoping that, like the rest of the mine, it was old enough that he could push it right off without issue. Surprisingly, the vent cover would not budge, and Alex was beginning to feel it digging into his hand.

Finally giving up, Alex gasped and brought his hand back down to help support his precarious suspension. Now he just stared up at the sky through the mine shaft's vent. He could feel the warm outside air against his face. Instead of more panic gripping him, the thought of a single, metal obstacle standing between him and escaping this nightmare only made him increasingly angry. Not just frustrated by his inability to remove the vent, but so angry that was beginning to heat him up inside. So angry that he was not thinking straight anymore. His teeth were tightly clenched and he was breathing heavily and angrily. He felt the anger force his eyes shut and he was starting to feel a sharp pain around his forehead, and for a brief moment he thought he saw something strange in the darkness between his eyes and their closed lids; strange images like some sort of glyphs blurring around in his mind. Was that part of his insanity? Whatever it was that was happening to him at this heated moment, Alex felt a sudden, powerful urge that made him cry out and throw his fist up into the air.

The vent covering the mine shaft broke off as Alex's fist hit it with amazing force. Yet it was not pain in his knuckles that struck him, rather he instantly felt a wave of dizziness and shock emanating from his forehead. Hardly thinking at all, Alex forced himself up and climbed out of the shaft in the ground. Once he was clear of the dark chasm he rolled over and lied on his back for a moment to clear his mind.

The dizziness and the weird pulsing sensation in his head took a while to wear off. When he came to his senses, Alex found himself staring blankly up at the nighttime sky. The light of the stars tried to push through the clouds that covered a large portion of the sky. The muffled sound of thunder in the distance caught Alex's attention. It seemed the storm they had been expecting to pass over tonight had already occurred and long since ended. With that in mind, Alex realized how damp the ground upon which he lied was. He groaned in frustration as he pulled himself to his feet, feeling his wet clothes rub against his skin. Well that was just fantastic.

Calm down, Alex, he thought to himself. He managed to get himself out of the crumbling deathtrap of a mine, now he just had to his way back. But where was back exactly? It was nighttime already. That had to mean he had been wandering lost for hours, and he had serious doubts that his friends would still be on the other side of the tunnels waiting for him. In fact, by now they would have already sought out help and made an effort to clear the debris out from in front of the tunnel's entrance.

Still, if Alex had really been underground for so long, then he must have wandered a whole lot farther than it seemed. By the time he had stumbled upon the gaping hole in the tunnel he could have sworn he had been walking for no more than ten minutes at most. If it really had been hours then he would have to be at least a couple of miles into the mountains. None of what just happened to him made any sense! However, if Alex just turned and hiked back the direction from which he came he should eventually arrive back at the dirt path and the ruined mine entrance. That would at least be a start. So he took a deep breath and turned around to head back, but before he could take a step he suddenly froze in place as the new obstacle in his way made him go cold in shock.

Alex's jaw dropped down again as he gazed upon another cliff-like obstruction in his path, similar to the one they came to when they discovered the mine. But this one was different; it was much larger and rockier. It towered over Alex and extended outward at the top, making it appear to be a menacing, unscalable barrier. He looked to both sides and saw that this cliff also stretched out as far as he could see, as if it were meant to be a wall separating the mountains from their base, which meant that Alex was still cut off from his quickest route out of the dark hills. What more could possibly go wrong tonight?

Alex had to force himself to relax. With this malicious looking cliff standing in his way one of his few options was crossed off. What else could he do? If he hiked off into the hills or along the cliffside then he would surely encounter civilization at some point. After all it was the Adirondacks, not Middle-Earth.

Throughout this entire episode he could feel his sanity

slipping away. He was only fourteen, he should not have to be going through this. But he had to get out of this desolation somehow, even if it meant spending the rest of the night hiking and wandering the dark and eerie atmosphere of the Appalachian Mountains. So taking a few deep breaths and giving a slight head nod that said *'Screw it,'* Alex walked cautiously off into the woods of the mountains.

CHAPTER SEVEN

It was late into the night, but Rowan found no sleep. It was not often lately that she was able to relax behind the security of the Citadel. Many mixed thoughts would rush through her head as she sat awake with burning eyes in her small, torch lit abode. Her quarters was built mostly of wooden structure and the walls were hung with the hide of deer and bears to keep the space insulated and warm and the bed she was sitting on was nothing more than a roughly sewn mat on the floor,

In her hand, Rowan was fiddling around with a small, carven necklace. It was one of the last things handed down to her by her late grandmother and she never let it out of her sight. Sometimes, just like tonight, when she was alone in her Citadel quarters she would remove it from her neck just to grasp it in her hand. It helped her recall long lost days before her home was taken. Days when she would watch the first rays of the morning sun rise over the hills and cast its light upon the flowing rivers in the valleys and her entire world was a place of peace and unity.

Rowan glanced down at the necklace in her hand. Carved into the circular, wooden pendant was a basic image of what appeared to be a man holding a staff in one hand and in the other he held an object which Rowan was never quite able to make out. Outlined around the image was a series of hexagonal shapes. Rowan never understood the significance of the pendant, if there was any at all. The only thing that mattered to her was that she kept it on her person, for it was one of her last possessions since the world she knew was destroyed.

With these thoughts, Rowan leaned her head back against the wall and closed her eyes as she allowed her mind to wander back into the memories of her childhood.

Rowan often wondered if her memories were really as happy and tranquil as they were in her head. She remembered years before when she was only nine-years-old. Her home lied in a great valley surrounded by the mountain ranges of the Appalachians. Over the course of many generations her people had built a flourishing settlement in the valley. A great homeland established and passed down from their ancestors: Ravenna, as they so named it.

Rowan remembered running through the trees at the edges of the valley on the warm, summer days. She zigzagged happily around the trees and bushes, stopping only to catch her breath. The sounds of the birds and small animals rushing to and fro was a tone of absolute bliss. Deeper into the woods Rowan would race until the foot of the mountains would stop her.

The air that surrounded her was cool and refreshing thanks to the cluttered tree canopy. Rowan stopped suddenly and turned to look back the way she came. Quickly, she crouched down behind a patch of mountain laurel and held her breath as she peered through its branches, as if she were searching for something, but there was nothing to be seen or a sound to be heard save for the forest life surrounding her. Rowan scoped all around the woods, and then she leaped up and ran back into the trees.

She continued to glance back and forth hastily as she ran. At last she halted and found herself standing before a tree with branches low enough for her to grab hold of. Rowan jumped up and reached for the lowest branch, barely snatching it and pulling herself up. As she was just about to reach out for the next branch, something suddenly grabbed her by the ankle and began to pull her downward. Rowan gasped in shock and released her hold on the branches. She fell down out of the tree but was caught securely in the arms of her captor, who allowed himself to fall back onto the ground to ease Rowan's own fall.

"Got you again!" A young man's voice cried out from under her.

Rowan began to laugh.

"You got lucky, Delmar!" she said, pulling herself back onto her feet. "I almost got away that time."

Her older brother, Delmar, eighteen years of age at the time. On his feet he stood over six foot in height, his hair just as black as Rowan's with a single braided strand going around the back of his head. The way he towered over his young sister was almost menacing, but he smiled down and placed a hand on her shoulder.

"You'll never get past my tracking skills, Rowan," he laughed. "Leastwise not till you're about my age."

Rowan grinned back up at him.

"Well you're a good teacher!" She looked back out through the woods toward the valley. "When is Father ever going to teach me to hunt with him?"

Delmar turned and gestured for Rowan to walk with him back out of the woods.

"When you're old enough to handle a bow." He replied as they headed out. "I was a year older than you when he taught me, just be patient."

Rowan sighed to herself.

"I know." Everyone always knew Rowan wanted to be just like her brother, and understandably so. Delmar was held at much higher esteem than most others in Ravenna. Their father was the leader of their modest civilization, their Chief as the title was referred to. Although Rowan's home territory only spanned across of portion of the Adirondack mountain ranges, their culture had existed and thrived here for over two hundred years. The birth of her people came about shortly before the spark of the American Revolution when a band of colonial farmers, fearing an impending British assailment, aligned themselves with the remnants of a mysterious Native American tribe, known as the Seluitah, or the Light Walkers, and disappeared into the hills of the Appalachians. They had originally been under the belief that the Colonial resistance would have undoubtedly been suppressed when the British reinforcements arrived on the shores of the new world, and it was not until more than a decade after the end of the war that this hiding interracial tribe was found and told of an unanticipated Colonial victory. Yet despite their worst fears having been abated, the Colonial refugees stayed among the tribe in the Adirondacks and came to an accord with the newly formed American government to rule themselves and keep their interactions at a minimum, and it was not long until their civilization was built and all territories beyond their borders they simply referred to as the Outside.

The Dark Zone, however, was a name that did not arise until much later. Throughout the late 1900s relations between the people of Ravenna and the Outside quickly grew uneasy, and in 1989 Ravenna's chief, Rowan's grandfather at the time, bitterly requested to completely sever all connections with the Outside, in order to avoid any possible form of conflict. This request was granted by the Outside's governments on the condition that the people of Ravenna would be restricted from affiliation with the Outside, and the Outside would have no legal obligations to Ravenna. It was at the time of this event that the territories of the autonomous mountain society was named the Dark Zone, as a means of classifying the area as unconditionally off limits. And so the civilization of Ravenna was soon forgotten and the people surrounding the Dark Zone came to fear the territory as some sort of deadly wilder land.

Of course, having spent her entire life with the boundaries of her home, Rowan knew little to nothing of the Outside as well as their misconceptions regarding her people. However, if she did she would have known how incredibly misguided all of the stories were. Her people were certainly no warrior society. In fact, they were undeniably peaceful and compassionate. It was only when her home was invaded and stolen from them that her people were forced to become warriors just to survive.

Rowan's young life before her hardened years was defined by peace and happiness. As she and Delmar exited the wooded boundaries of the valley they walked alongside a stream which flowed toward rapidly downhill around the northern borders of Ravenna. The stream began pouring from the mountainside in several mouths and grew exponentially as it traveled in a deep, narrow ravine along the valley's edge. It was believed by the people of Ravenna that over the course of several hundred years the river had eroded away a prodigious clay deposit beneath the valley and formed an elongated canyon.

Nearly halfway down the length of the ravine a large oak tree stood defiantly on the edge of the cliff. Rowan's grandmother told her that it was the only a tree along the riverside that was not uprooted and taken away by the river's great erosion. Instead, the river seemed to flow around the tree and formed its foundation into a tiny peninsula jutting out from the rest of the cliffs. As they came near it, Rowan ran over to the tree.

"Rowan!" Delmar called out to his reckless sister. He did not like her going out onto the narrow cliff, as dangerous as it was. Rowan approached the tree and placed her hand upon its wearing bark. The tree did not have much meaning to everyone, but it had some to her. It was from the wood of this very tree that her late grandmother had made the pendant that she now wore around her neck. It was the last memory Rowan had of her.

Delmar came to her side and put his arm around her. Rowan simply looked on at the tree with emotion creeping up on her. She reached a shaky hand up and rested it against her chest where the pendant hung just beneath her rough, leather garb, and she remembered the morning only months before when she had awoken to find that her grandmother, whom she had been so close to, had not. Was there something now that she wanted to say? If there were any words to say, Rowan could not summon the strength speak them. So all she could do was just stare out toward the old tree in front of her that stood precariously on the eroded cliff.

Such a narrow point was not a place in which Delmar preferred to linger.

"Come on, now," he urged his young sister, pulling back lightly on her shoulder.

Rowan only resisted.

"Do you think she watches over us?" she spoke suddenly.

Delmar stopped at the sound of her words, and he tried to find the right thing to say.

"Of course she does, Rowan," he replied quietly. "She made that necklet for you so that you would always know that she is still here to protect you."

The powerful words made Rowan choke up a little as she tried to fight back the tears welling up in her eyes.

"I want to make something like it someday," she responded, stepping forward to place a hand on the peeling bark of the tree. "Something just as special to someone, and from the same wood."

Delmar smiled at his sister's amiable devotion.

"I believe you would," he said to himself. Looking up toward one of the tree's outstretched limbs, he replied, "I have always considered crafting a spear from that branch there." He mused at the thought for a moment, however he was still cringing as Rowan continued moving closer to the tree and to the edge of the cliff. "Rowan!" He called out with more authority, and she turned her attention to her brother. "Please come. I don't like you standing so near to the edge." It seemed a little harsh, but Rowan quickly complied and followed Delmar away from the tree.

As they walked, Rowan glanced back several times. All her nine years were spent in peace here in the valley, and she had grown to love everything about it; every blade of grass and every stone in the river, and all of the people she called her family and her friends. Such a love that one might ask themselves, 'Would they fight for it? Would they die for it?'

The two of them headed back to the outskirt of the village when they were suddenly greeted by a young man, about his teenage years, rushing up to them.

"Delmar!" he called out.

Delmar smiled as the boy stopped before them.

"Morning, Matheus," he replied casually.

The same Matheus whom Delmar would trust years later as one of his closest friends and allies. However, he was much younger at this time, about sixteen years of age, and he did not have his hair grown so long nor braided on either side of his head. He caught his breath as fast as he could before speaking again.

"Sorry to bother you," he said coyly. "I was looking for your father."

"He's out on a hunting excursion," Delmar responded. It was something his father did quite often in order to keep their food storages overstocked. "You remember Rowan, right?" He said, gesturing to her sister beside him.

Matheus nodded with a grin.

"Of course!" he replied heartily and turned his attention to the young Rowan. "You're growing every day, little one!"

Rowan grew a wide smile and nodded back to him. Delmar laughed to himself and then drew back Matheus' attention.

"What is it you need, my friend?"

"Nothing," Matheus answered seriously. "It's just a couple of Outsiders came down from over the mountains."

Delmar raised his eyebrows.

"Outsiders?" he responded with curiosity. "They found the valley?"

"That's right." Matheus continued. "They're waiting in the square now. They wanted to speak to someone so I told them to be patient while I fetched the Chief. That was when I ran into you."

"Who's with them now?" Delmar asked.

"Caine is entertaining them in the meantime."

Delmar looked out toward the mountainside. It was not yet midday and he knew his father would not be back until after dusk. So it was up to him to welcome their apparent visitors. He took a deep breath and began heading back toward their village.

"Matheus," he spoke to his young friend. "Keep an eye on Rowan for me, would you?"

"Yes, absolutely!" Matheus replied, as he and Rowan watched Delmar walk quickly across the field.

The valley village of Ravenna was settled in the center of the vast field between the river and the towering mountains. It was built of a series of a great many cabin-like structures, constructed from the never-ending supply of trees which surrounded them. Delmar entered amongst the cluster of cottages, which ranged mildly in size from one another; all large enough to house a typical family. Delmar passed through the quaint-looking community and a number of his fellow citizens here and there, many of whom waved and called out to him in respect, and he would nod his head back to them.

Near the center of the village the cottages and other structures broke apart and revealed a wide plaza. The paths and trails made throughout the village became stone-laden as they joined together in the middle to form the open courtyard which Matheus had referred to as the square. There was nothing too fancy about it. It was bordered on all sides by the homes and structures and the area was set with stone grounding, much of which Delmar had recently helped to replace. In the very center of the square stood a young tree, just like the one precariously grown at the edge of valley trough, but significantly smaller. It was planted years before at the time of their ultimate separation from the Outside.

Through the crowds of his people Delmar was able to spot the one Matheus had referred to as Caine. He was Delmar's age, and much like him in certain aspects, with the exception of his hair being much lighter and his eyes carrying a piercing expression about them. Delmar was well acquainted with Caine, as their fathers had worked together for years; not in the valley or the mountains, but in the Outside, working to maintain the relationships between their two worlds before their separation. They were the only ones . to ever go out beyond the borders of their territory, using a long stretch of road which cut straight through the surrounding mountain ranges. It was not the only way in or out, but it was certainly the easiest. Delmar had always thought it best to keep his focus at home where it belonged, with his people and his responsibilities, and he did not often ask his father about the Outside. Caine, on the other hand, quickly became fascinated with the world beyond his. He learned from his father all about the business he made with the Outside and, unlike nearly all of his people, Caine grew to be against severing their ties and would rather have preferred that their societies mingled together.

Predictably, Caine was quick to welcome their guests from the Outside when he learned of their arrival. Standing with him and deep in conversation were the two outsiders Matheus had reported. Two young men, no more than a few years older than Delmar himself, but much younger than he had thought. The older one stood with an impressive stature, standing even taller than Delmar. He had broad shoulders and a stern, rough-shaven face, but right now he appeared to be more excited than stern. The one next to him was about a head shorter and a little less built than his associate who towered over him. Just looking at them, Delmar guessed they must have been family in some way.

Caine shifted his attention to Delmar as he approached the three of them, and he bowed his head slightly as if to welcome him.

"Ah, Delmar!" he started with a grin. "You're looking well. But if I don't mind saying so, I was expecting the Chief?"

Delmar returned a fabricated smile.

"He's out, Caine," he replied. "You should know that, you're father is with him."

There was a brief silence as Caine let a slight laugh that sounded almost mischievous.

"Well then, I thought I would welcome our good strangers from the Outside."

Delmar nodded as he glanced over to their guests. "

Very good, Caine. If you don't mind, I'll take it from here."

Caine bowed his head again as slowly back away before turning and disappearing amongst the crowd. Delmar watched and waited until he was sure he was gone. He could not put his finger on it, but there was something about him that he was not sure he could trust.

"Pay no mind to him," Delmar began, turning his attention to the outsiders. "He's a good man. But he's a bit too inquisitive."

"I'll take your word for it." The larger of the two responded casually.

Delmar made a quick scan of his visitors.

"Welcome to Ravenna!" he said, trying to sound enthusiastic. "You can call me Delmar."

The same Outsider nodded to him.

"My name is Ramon." He replied with a grin. "Ramon Moreno. This is my brother, Robert." He put his hand over on his brother's shoulder.

Clapping his hands together, Delmar said,

"Well, to business I guess! What brings a couple of young outsiders to Ravenna?"

The two brothers exchanged quick looks before the one called Ramon spoke up.

"We were told about a society of people who live deep in the mountains. For some reason, they warned us not to go looking." He looked around at the village. "Now that I see this place, it's not really what I expected."

Delmar raised his eyebrows.

"Well, our worlds may not be the same, but we as people

are not so different from each other."

There was a bit of an awkward silence as neither one of them knew quite what to say next. Delmar and Ramon just stared blankly at each other. Robert was looking back and forth at the two of them, waiting for one of them to speak.

Delmar gestured toward one of the stone paths leading away from the square.

"Let's walk," he said, "and learn a little more about each other." He turned and walked slowly across the plaza with the Moreno brothers following just beside him.

They walked and turned at random through the bunch of cottages, with people looking up at the outsiders with growing curiosity. Along the trails, Delmar and Ramon began by exchanging small talk with each other, asking simple questions about their own worlds, while Robert was mostly silent.

"I am a bit curious," Delmar said as they turned a corner and headed slowly out into one of the open fields surrounding the village. "How did you manage to reach this valley? Surely not by navigating these immense mountain ranges?"

Ramon glanced over at his brother, who seemed to display a slight expression of apprehension about his eyes. Ramon looked back at Delmar and replied confidently, "Difficult to imagine, isn't it? The journey itself was even more challenging."

Delmar raised his brow in interest. He knew that the road which had been used by then to travel in and out of their territories was by far the easiest means of traversing the mountains, but when their separation was finalized his father saw to it that the road be destroyed at the point of their borders. This was more symbolic to their isolation than it was meant to hold much effect. Any other means of hiking through the mountains was still surely possible, just very difficult to manage.

This fascinating feat of theirs brought Delmar to at last address the main issue at hand.

"Well, you've certainly made great effort to come all this way to us. And since you have, what is it you're looking for?"

The three of them stopped in the tall grass of the valley, no more than thirty yards from the edge of the village. Ramon turned and scanned the entire area; the valley, the village and the people in it.

"Simply a place of our own," he muttered before returning to face Delmar.

The words caught Delmar a little bit off guard. Although, he was not sure what he was expecting to hear.

"One more time?" he responded quietly.

"We're nothing but drifters," Robert spoke up. "Derelicts. We've been on our own for years, ever since we lost our family."

It truly hit Delmar hard. This was not the sort of circumstance he was qualified to handle, even as the Chief's son. Part of him was uncertain, and wanted to know more about the history of these young outsiders, but he still found himself not desiring to know any more. His people had separated from the Outside for their own reasons, and he could not just simply welcome in anyone on their doorstep.

Before he could answer with anything, Ramon continued, "I know what you're thinking." He gave Delmar a serious look. "We've heard all the stories, we've done our own research. We're fully prepared to give you our services in exchange for nothing more than a place to stay." Delmar glanced down and around, trying to find the proper response. Ramon kept trying to persuade his thoughts. "We've tried everything we could to make a living out there," he said, pointing out beyond the mountains. "They never gave us a chance. That world is a cruel place. Surely, you're not the same. Not if you saw fit to isolate yourselves."

Delmar pulled himself together and straightened himself up.

"It's not that simple," he replied. Ramon seemed a bit taken aback. "It's not up to me to begin with. But even if it was, I'm not sure how what you expect me to say."

Ramon shook his head.

"What do you mean?"

Delmar sighed as he breathed out his next words.

"We, as our own culture, have our reputations to consider."

"Reputations?" Robert repeated in disbelief.

"It's nothing against you," Delmar put his hand out in an effort to cool the heated atmosphere. "I did not make the decisions that divided our two societies, and many here in Ravenna still don't agree with them, but what comes first and foremost is our faithfulness to our word. It's what truly defines us from the people of the Outside."

Ramon seemed offended at that statement. Even more astounded he was at the realization that these people would really turn their backs on them.

"Even after you just said that we are not so different?"

This was rapidly turning into a heated argument, Delmar could sense that much. He was trying to understand the struggle these two were living through. Were it his decision, Delmar saw no ultimate harm in helping a few outsiders in need. The only obstacle standing in front of him, and the greatest obstacle at that, was the contractual obligations made between Ravenna and the Outside; neither of them should cater to the other while the separation remains effective. If he crossed that now, even for the sake of two people, what kind of man would he be to his word?

"Listen," Delmar did his best to satisfy them. "You can wait here for the time being until our Chief returns at dusk, and then you can plead your proposal to him. He is the one and final say in this. But I would have to warn you, he is less patient and tranquil than I am. I would not hold your hopes on it."

Ramon turned around, putting his back to Delmar and facing out toward the rest of the vast land between the mountains. Robert saw him clenching the muscles in his hand, and felt his brother's anger beginning to take hold of him as well.

Delmar held his breath as he awaited an answer from his guest. He was feeling the pressure of the tension mixed with the heat of the midday summer sun. Ramon took a deep breath and lowered his head.

"You're right," he said under his breath. "You're not so different us. You're all the same."

Feeling the sense of guilt and betrayal heaped upon him, Delmar returned his final words to the outsiders.

"I'm sorry," he breathed roughly. "We will see you out then."

Ramon rotated his head to the side, peering at his host with contempt.

"We can see ourselves out." He gestured for Robert to follow him back toward the village, and he did so after casting one quick glare at Delmar.

Delmar knew he should have gone with them to ensure they made their way out into the mountains, but he desperately wanted to avoid the tension at this point. Still, he knew his people and his friends would be there waiting to see them off. From the start, there was something about the Moreno brothers that he did not trust, and the way Caine had taken so much interest in them only made him more uncomfortable. His first priority was to his home and to his people, and he could not help but feel that intermingling his world with any element of the Outside would bring their conflicts right back to their front door. So, musing on that defining thought, Delmar could only watch until the outsiders were finally out of sight. And he hoped it would be the last he saw of them.

Rowan hardly had any knowledge of what really transpired between Delmar and the Morenos. All she knew was what she trusted her brother to tell her, and it was simply that Delmar did what would have been right by her people and her father. She could not blame the fall and destruction of their lives on Delmar's decisions.

Sitting in her small quarters on that brisk spring night,

Rowan's mind kept going back through the devastating events of these past five years. Ramon's anger with her brother had led him to rely on sheer force to take what was denied him, and he did so by gathering people like him; wanderers, drifters, those who had nothing left and nowhere to go, until they were numerous enough to catch her people off guard in the middle of the night. Burning everything they had built. Destroying everything Rowan had come to know and love.

Her eyes were dry, all the tears had been shed over the years. Sometimes it made her feel like nothing more than an empty shell. A vessel that needed to be filled by something, but by what? Some kind of closure, maybe? Or Revenge? Rowan looked over at the wall where a long spear was supported. The very spear Delmar had crafted from the tree on the cliff. He had given it to her after everything else was taken from them. After her home was stolen and her people torn apart, like a blade thrust through the heart.

Rowan stared at the fine spear with narrow, vindictive eyes, and hoped to return the favor one day.

CHAPTER EIGHT

Miles away, it had also been a long and damn near sleepless night for Nickole. All of her mind was centered on the insanity of the previous day. She was a twelve-year-old girl who witnessed her brother vanish in seconds within the darkness of an unstable, abandoned mine. It was traumatizing, and no matter how many times Alex's friends tried to assure her that he was going to be fine, Nickole's irrational child's mindset caused her to visualize the most horrific outcomes.

The element of the accident that chewed Nickole up almost as much was the part she played in Alex's entrapment. For months all she wanted was to strengthen the old relationship she once had with her older brother. Their mother had been so protective and sheltering ever since their father had left, and while Alex was out with his friends for most of the afternoon she hardly had any time during the day to really spend with him, if he even to spend time with her at all. The one time she had stood up and told a seemingly harmless lie to her mother, just to go with Alex and his friends, and she watched him disappear right before her eyes.

Hetrick had driven a shaken Nickole off of the mountain and dropped her off at her friend's house, where she had told her mother she would be. Hetrick quickly informed her friend's parents of the incident at the clay mine but was careful to take Nickole out of the picture of it, after which he hurried back to his truck and sped off to get help.

Nickole barely spoke to her friend or her parents, the

shock was still gripping her. By the time her mother had picked her up Nickole had done her best to pull herself together. She was in such a stressful position between her lie and worrying about Alex. Her mother never asked about Alex for the rest of the afternoon, and all Nickole could do was wait out the remainder of the day until the bomb was finally dropped.

Her fears had begun to be realized in no time when her mother finally started asking where Alex was and why he had yet to come home. Nickole tried to play the part of knowing nothing about the incident, but found it difficult to remain calm as she was so full of worry. It was not long before the telephone started ringing as Nickole's mother answered it to hear the Lake Placid Fire Department informing her of the situation at hand; that there had been an accident at an abandoned clay mine on the side of the mountains which left her son trapped inside, and that they were working to get him out.

Feeling so welled up with fear and guilt, Nickole confined herself to her room for the rest of the day and did not come out, not even to eat. She woke up numerous times that night, sometimes because of discomfort and sometimes due to nightmares; irrational thoughts that she might never see her older brother again. Her mother was also quite shaken, but had told Nickole many times that he was going to be fine.

At the first light of morning Nickole just lied awake in her bed, her eyes burning from a poor night's sleep. With the sun's rays cutting weakly through the dense early fog, Nickole pulled herself up and sat on the edge of the bed, rubbing her eyes. It was much quieter without her brother in the next room throwing darts against the door.

The sound that did break the silence, however, was the sound of someone knocking on the front door. Nickole stood up from her bed and went over to look out the window. She could not see the door from her angle, but what she did see was a single Lake Placid Police cruiser parked along the side of the road in front of her house. A cold ripple went up her spine. There was only one reason she could think of that would bring the police to their door. Nickole heard the door open. She ran over and opened her own door a little to listen in to the impending conversation.

"Sorry to bother you, ma'am," came a low male voice, obviously belonging to the officer. "This is the Lee household?"

"Yes," Nickole heard her mother's brief response.

"And are you the head of the house, Mrs. Lee?" the officer asked.

"Please call me Eira," her mother answered coldly. "Yes I am."

There was something a short silence as Nickole anxiously waited for the conversation to continue.

"I wonder if we might come in?" the officer said at last. Nickole did not hear her mother say anything, but she soon heard the sound of footsteps walking through the house. Interested, she slipped just outside of her room and peered down the hall toward the stairs, where she could see her mother leading two uniformed officers to the dining room. They disappeared right around the corner and Nickole was once again reduced to listening.

"Just to recap," the first officer began upon sitting down. "We are dealing with a case of a fourteen-year-old boy missing as of yesterday afternoon. This boy, Alex Lee, is your son, correct?"

Eira nodded her head.

"Yes," she replied with a slightly shaky tone of voice. "Have you found him?"

The two officers exchanged looks.

"The report says that Alex and friends were exploring around the entrance to an old abandoned clay mine when the mine gave in and only Alex was trapped inside-"

Eira put her hand up.

"I know that already!" she said, getting annoyed. "What I want to know is if anyone found him!"

The officer sighed.

"The fire department was called up and helped to safely remove the obstruction. When they did they conducted a thorough search of the tunnels in the immediate vicinity. They found nothing there."

In the uncomfortable silence that followed, Eira found herself a bit confused.

"What does that mean?" She said, growing increasingly frustrated. "Where is my son?"

"Ma'am," the second officer spoke up to try to calm her down "It's most likely that your son found his own way out of the mine. The tunnels are very old and caved in at many places. If he were still in there they would have found him."

"But I still don't understand." Eira was still unsatisfied. "If he got out of the mine then that means he has to have been wandering around the mountains all night. Did nobody think to send a search party out to look for him?"

The first officer's eyes suddenly went down, as if he was trying to find the appropriate next words to say.

"Therein lies the problem, ma'am." He exchanged quick glances with his partner again before finally breaking the ice. "Our department fears that your son may have inadvertently wandered into the Dark Zone."

Eira did quite know how to respond. Her eyes widened at the officer's words, but she was more confused than anything. She did not know what he was talking about.

"What do you mean 'Dark Zone'? What is that?"

The officer swallowed nervously as he could see he was forced to deepen the wound.

"Y-you're not familiar with the term, ma'am?"

Eira shook her head impatiently.

"No, I'm not."

"Well," he began to explain. "There is a...district deep in the mountains, the borders of which stretch close to the area of your son's accident. It is an off the grid territory, labeled as off limits back in '89. It's out of our precinct. We are not permitted to go into the area for any reason."

Feeling a bit dumbfounded, Eira responded, "If it's off limits, how could my son get inside? Isn't it fenced off or something?"

"No, ma'am," the officer replied. "It is a desolate area, nobody goes back into it. The state did not issue the raising of a fence or a wall. To be completely honest, this is the first case our department has received about someone getting lost out there." He took a deep breath before continuing. "I'm afraid your son is on his own as long as he is on the other side. But until he finds his way out, we will keep our eyes open."

The atmosphere grew cold and dreary. Nickole felt the gust of the appalling news engulf her. She was speechless as she stood halfway out of her door. Despite that the odds were as great as her brother simply navigating his way out of the mountains, Nickole was very uneasy and welled up with the feeling of loss. Not knowing what to do, she just watched with watery eyes as her mother saw the officers out, and then she retreated into her room and shut the door.

Meanwhile, in the midst of the Dark Zone, a single figure was riding by horse through the trees in the faint morning light. The fog, though still very heavy, was slightly blocked by the woods of the mountains, and so even just after dawn it was quite dark at the ground level.

The rider travelled swiftly, zigzagging around the woods along a narrow dirt trail. He was young man, in his early twenties, and he was one of the people of the valley. He was wearing a ragged leather chest plate, on which he carried a large knife in a holster and a wooden longbow on his back. There was also a harness attached to the horse, one side of it held a quiver full of arrows and a stone sword in a scabbard on the other side. The man wore a brown hood over his head, and under which his face showed an expression of ceaseless hate and resent as well as a few old battle scars.

He rode for miles in the dark break of dawn. After nearly an hour he soon came upon a slight opening in the woods.

The fog that had been blocked by the tree canopy became denser as it settled low to the ground. Before long, the terrain to the left of the path began to rise up as to the right it began drop downward. The tree line had broken apart and within minutes the rider found himself coming out onto a much wider but still narrow path stretching straight outward, with a high cliff side directly to the left and a steep drop to the right. The path itself was only about thirty feet in width at its widest point. Beyond the cliff the rider could see Appalachian mountain ranges extending for miles. There were many hills and valleys to be seen as the fog began to dissipate, painted the light green color of the trees' spring blooming, and towering rocky mountains pointing ever upward.

Most of these areas belonged to the boundaries of the Dark Zone. Straight ahead, at the far end of the perilous cliff trail, the path suddenly fell and joined the drop off. Just on the other side of the drop was the border of a large plateau belonging to a separate section of the mountain ranges. The area was still cloudy as the fog continued to slowly rise, but the man on the horse could make out the interesting, natural structure of a bridge erode from the mountainside leading up to the plateau. He rode across the land bridge, which was quite sturdy and supportive as the horse galloped over it. Upon reaching the other side, the rider stopped and looked out the sight that stood before, a sight that would strike awe in the average person.

Lining around the edge of the plateau was a man-made wall, standing around twenty feet high. It was built primarily from countless amounts of stone piled evenly atop one another and held firmly together by a frame of wooden beams and posts. Another path was laid down to lead the rider up straight toward the wall, where it split into a gate-like opening. He rode into the wall's perimeter and then brought his horse to a quick halt. He set himself down on the ground, and as he did so two other men appeared to greet him.

The first man approached him.

"Welcome back, Malachai," he said, bring his hand up to touch his forehead and then back down to rest against his heart.

The horse rider, Malachai, nodded back to him.

"Am I the last back?" he asked.

"Yes," he replied, looking out through the entryway. "The last of the riders came in just before dawn."

Malachai looked inward to the plateau.

"Where is he?"

The man followed his gaze and pointed in that direction. Knowing whom Malachai was referring to, he replied, "In the map room. He's been there all day."

"Alright," Malachai nodded slightly. He reached over and patted his horse. "Take him down to the stable." He then turned and headed away into the plateau. As he did so the man at the gateway muttered something in their speech to the other with him and they led Malachai's horse away.

The Citadel; the last place of refuge for the people of Ravenna. It was here on the mountain plateau that Delmar led the remnants of his people to make camp, and over the years they had come to construct an imposing fortress atop the great upland. A quaint pathway extended from the gateway through which Malachai had entered and travelled just up a small rise. Malachai followed it up over the hill, and that was when he saw it.

The fortress called the Citadel was made of an immense structure which sat near the center of the flatland of the plateau. At its base a second stone wall encircled it, this one slightly shorter than the plateau's outer wall. There were several dozen people standing all along the top of the wall, looking out in every direction. Some just stared out into the distance, some looked down to see Malachai approaching, while others were just talking amongst each other. On the other side of the wall, the fortress rose upward with a great barrel-like structure. It was built in layers, each next tier smaller than one below it. The central structure consisted of four layers pointing up like an obelisk. Over Malachai's head, there were many long, bridge-like extensions stretching from the tower and connecting to the plateau's outer wall in several directions. It was a truly impressive construction of wood, stone, and clay.

Malachai passed through the opening in the wall, similar to the first one he had come to. There were many people within the walls; speaking with one another, some hauling materials in and out, wood, food and other resources. The fog was only just starting to lift completely and the keepers of the Citadel were already busy trying to maintain their new home. Looking up at the tower in the middle, there were several bridge-like walkways extended outward from it and connecting to the wall surrounding it. Through all of the morning activity, Malachai entered into the base level of the Citadel tower.

It was dimly lit on the inside, but Malachai and his people were well accustomed to the dark. The bottom level had a diameter of approximately thirty yards. The walls were covered all the way around by hundreds of hanging bows and quivers of arrows with each one. Throughout the rest of the large chamber were many rows of standing racks holding sheathed swords and other bladed weapons. It was obvious that this room was designed to be the Citadel's armory, where they kept their weapons in case of an ensuing conflict.

This is not where Malachai was headed, though. Just inside the chamber there was a staircase to the right of the entryway and an identical one on the other side. The stairways traveled up along the wall and disappeared about a quarter of the way around into the next layer of the tower. Malachai followed it up.

The next level was only a few yards smaller than the first. As the bottom layer was used as their massive weapons closet, this chamber appeared to be some sort of forge. At the walls adjacent to where the stairs entered there were clusters of stone blocks, similar to anvils, and furnaces sitting against the walls. The furnaces each had a large, metal pipe sticking out through the wall to vent the smoke outside of the structure. They were stone cold, however, as the people of the Citadel had all of their weapons made and, at this point, never had a reason to mass distribute them from the armory.

The stairs continued up around the wall. The two identical staircases met when they reached the third layer of the tower. This level was much different than the two below. It was much more brightly lit, and the chamber revealed a corridor in the middle running from the stairs' entry to the other end of the room. On either side of the hall were several rooms, the doorways of which were covered by a cloth-like curtain. Malachai knew this to be a medical chamber, intended for any who acquired a serious injury in the wilderness of the Dark Zone. Just like the armory and the forge, it was rarely used because such incidents almost never occurred over the past five years.

From one of the rooms on the left side a woman emerged into the corridor. She was an older woman, with aging gray hair put up in a bun. She wore a light coat of fur, and in her arms she carried what appeared to be a folded blanket. As she entered into the hallway she looked up to see Malachai, and smiled to him as he approached.

"Good to see you back, Malachai," she beamed.

Malachai nodded to her.

"Morning, Altha," he replied, stopping before her. "How have you been?"

At first she seemed to disregard Malachai as she headed over to another room along the corridor.

"Another long day out with the crusaders?" she then responded, reaching into one of the rooms and placing the blanket onto the ground in the corner.

Malachai grinned to himself.

"It was just reconnaissance, Altha," he replied. "We're not at war yet."

Altha reappeared into the hall and looked back at Malachai.

"And God willing," she said seriously. Of all the people inhabiting the mountains of the Dark Zone, Altha was one of the last of the people of Ravenna with ties to the Outside. Her grandparents had integrated into their communities many years before. Despite being raised all her life in the isolations of Ravenna, she was taught all about the outside world. Even when hell opened up and unleashed its wrath upon their people in the form of an unwarranted invasion, she remained as a calm and compassionate as ever, trying to understand the outsiders' true motives and the ongoing stress that must have caused them to turn so aggressive against her people. All in all, Altha always would have preferred any other possible solution to this conflict without Delmar seeing fit to strike back at their enemies. But they were running out of time, everyone knew it. More and more outsiders were still pouring into the Dark Zone every day under Ramon Moreno's influence. The game board was being set; one side was going to have to make a daring move sooner or later, peace was simply no longer an option.

Malachai glanced back toward the other end of the corridor. He breathed very heavily, "I'm ready to do whatever it is he needs," he said seriously to Altha, referring to Delmar. At first she seemed to give Malachai a look of disapproval, but then she smiled and nodded her head as if to say, 'All of Ravenna is behind you.' Malachai bowed his head slightly to her. "Take care, Altha." He turned and headed for the archway at the end of the hall which would take him to the zenith level of the tower.

He always found it somewhat uncomfortable when climbing these steps. For years his closest friend, Delmar, had been a much different person as he dwelled constantly on the devastating past and spent all of his time ensuring that his people had a future ahead of them. At the peak of the tower, the map room as they commonly referred to it, Delmar could be found most of the time, and there were times Malachai was worried that the stress was starting to go to his head.

Upon reaching the top of the final staircase, Malachai found himself staring out at an incredible view. The great stature of the tower provided a lookout point jutting outward from the structure and gave clear view over the entire plateau. The sun was now peeking through the tree canopies of the mountain ranges in the east, and below dozens of figures could be seen moving about all around the Citadel. To the right of the tower the plateau sloped downward where it cradled a small, clear-blue lake. The sight from this man-made vista always gave even Malachai a great sense of wonder, but he quickly remembered why he was up here and shook it all off. Just behind him, positioned up a few more steps was a large, curtained archway leading into the tip of the tower. Malachai climbed the steps and quietly move the cloth hanging over the doorframe aside, and slowly made his way in.

It was dimly lit inside, much like the rest of the great structure, with the exception of the light of the sun peering through the doorway. The room was quite small, and its walls were covered haphazardly with many roughly hand-drawn maps, each seeming to portray a different region of the Dark Zone, hence the room named as it was. In the center of the small chamber a single man was standing over a table, staring down at another large map laid out onto it. The map seemed to be unfinished in one of its corners, and the man was just gazing at it intently as if lost in deep thought. As Malachai approached him, he could see a strip of his hair grown down over the left side of his face. This he knew was meant to cover the scar he had received years ago when Ravenna was first attacked.

"Delmar?" Malachai stopped in his tracks and spoke out softly.

In response, Delmar shifted his glued attention right to Malachai who now stood before him. Looking just past him at the sunlight penetrating the archway, he said, "Malachai. What time is it?"

Malachai made a quick glance at the doorway behind him.

"After dawn," he replied. "Have you been up all night?"

Delmar just took a deep breath.

"No. Not exactly." He stood up and walked over to his friend. "You have anything to report?"

Shaking his head, Malachai answered, "It's been really quiet out there lately. A little too quiet." He gave Delmar a serious look in the eyes. "Listen, we can't hide behind these walls forever."

Delmar seemed like he wanted to ignore his comment. He turned and looked back at the map laying out behind him.

"We've been over this before, Malachai," he said, the intensity growing in the atmosphere. "It's not as simple as that, we're talking about starting a war within our borders. We're not soldiers," He looked harshly at Malachai. "And we have no support."

It was a quiet for a moment. Malachai just shook his head in disbelief.

"So how would you justify all that they've done to us? Are we just going to wait behind our walls until they overwhelm us?"

"We're not ready yet, Malachai," Delmar responded. "We're vastly outnumbered right now; much of our people are still scattered throughout the mountains in hiding. We can't risk revealing ourselves yet, my friend. I will not bring further harm upon us." He swallowed and lowered his head. "It's best for now that we all remain hidden."

"I'm not asking for open war, Delmar!" Malachai continued, moving closer. "Their scouting parties are starting to move deeper into our territories, eventually they'll find us here. I say we let them come just a little closer. We can attack them in the night like we did before, but with full force. Kill them all swiftly, and we'll inflict so much fear upon them that they won't come anywhere near this place again-"

"Or the opposite, Malachai!" Delmar cut him off. "If we show them absolute hostility then they'll unify and march right through us."

Malachai couldn't help but grin at his old friend's comment.

"They won't be able to penetrate the walls of the Citadel," he said confidently. "And besides, I was there with you when the valley was attacked, remember? We weren't prepared and they knew it. They took advantage of our weakness. Sure their numbers may be growing but we're much stronger now. If we don't do something then our people here and out there will forever lose hope. We're backed in the corner, Delmar." He looked him directly in the eyes. "We must fight!"

The map room suddenly went silent and tense. Malachai felt that he might have gone too far insisting that they march to war. He was prepared to apologize for his words, but Delmar began laughing under his breath. Malachai was taken aback.

"What's so funny?"

Delmar put a hand on his shoulder.

"Stick to your fighting skills, my friend." He replied. "There's more than one way to fight a war."

Malachai raised his eyebrows. This was a sudden shift in Delmar's attitude.

"You've already given commands?" He was starting to feel a tingle of excitement.

"Not exactly," Delmar said back. "But I sent Matheus back out into the mountains to take care of something for me."

Malachai could not help but feel a bit confused.

"What did you tell him to do? And why couldn't I be involved?"

Delmar put his hand up.

"For now I need you here, Malachai. The rest remains in the dark for now."

With that being said, Malachai was a little bit hurt that Delmar could not let his most trusted friend in on his plans. Nevertheless, Malachai knew better than to question him. Delmar had never let their people down yet. For now, however, Malachai was lost on what to do. Delmar seemed to have his mind made up. All that was left to do was wait patiently for his next command, if it ever came at all.

"Alright then," Malachai nodded in compliance. "I'll take my leave." He turned and headed back for the doorway.

"Where are you going?" Delmar called after him.

"Down to the arena," he replied a bit coldly. "I'd rather not grow too stale."

Delmar shook his head.

"Malachai, you should get some rest."

As he lifted the cloth curtain to exit the map room, Malachai looked back at his trusted friend.

"I'll rest when this is over." Then he was gone.

Delmar gave a soft sigh. His friend was right about one thing: time was running out. The enemy's numbers were always increasing and their tactics were getting bolder. If he did not do something to raise his people's hopes soon, he feared he would fail them all, and that was not on his agenda.

CHAPTER NINE

The day was beginning to wear on to midday and yet Alex found himself making no progress finding his way out of this impossible labyrinth in the Appalachian Mountains. He had followed the irregular ridge as far as he could, but when the terrain became too ragged and steep for him to continue he was forced to turn away. Now his aimless path had led him deeper and lower into the mountain ranges. He was exhausted and dehydrating fast. He was certain that as long as kept heading in one direction he would eventually come to the end of the mountains, or at least to some sort of refuge. But anyway he went he could be miles away from civilization, and there was no guarantee that the terrain would be traversable. How did this happen? How did Alex, in one day, manage to get himself into a terrible hole like this? Nothing about it made sense.

As the sun rose higher into the sky the soothing heat of spring shrouded the woods. Even in such a serious predicament Alex could not help but feel mesmerized, captivated even by the aura of this place. There was just something about it that was so tranquilizing, like all of his fears and worries could be swept away. However, it certainly did not relieve him of his exhaustion.

Throughout the morning and well into the afternoon Alex continued hiking straight as he could, zigzagging through trees and brush. The terrain soon began sloping uphill again. Alex groaned as he tried to catch his breath. How many times was he going to have to climb these God-forsaken mountains before some sign of life showed itself? Now he was practically praying that this hike would be his last and he could finally find his way back home.

With every bit of effort he could muster, Alex made his way through the trees and up the hill. It was a very tiresome trip, as it had been all night and all morning. Higher and higher he climbed, and the trees slowly began to recede. The woods became less dense and Alex almost found it easier to breathe and relax. The atmosphere felt soothing and fresh and was filled with was filled with the scent of the moist forest air. Alex inhaled it all deeply, and he could almost say he was rather enjoying himself. At least until he finally reached the top of the hill and saw what lied ahead of him.

Alex took in a deep breath but then his eyes widened and his jaw dropped as he scoped his broad surroundings. From where he stood the hilltop was green and sparsely populated with the same trees that dotted the mountains and the valleys below. As he looked around, however, there was nothing but a great series of mountain ranges surrounding him in all directions. As far as his eyes could see the hills of the Adirondacks stood high and low for miles outward. Feeling weak and light-legged, Alex dropped himself down against a tree and closed his eyes. The past night had been the worst of his life and everything was going wrong for him at every turn. He was completely lost in the wilderness now, as far as he knew nobody might have been looking for him and he no food or water at all. The only things he had with him were the clothes on his back and the small LED flashlight given to him by Hetrick which would probably only survive one more night on its battery, that is if he managed to survive one more night.

Alex was constantly enduring the pain in his stomach due to the lack sustenance all night. His mouth was so dry from dehydration. However, the very realization illuminated the light bulb in his head. Alex pulled himself to his feet and walked out to reexamine his surroundings. Surely there must have been a stream or a river somewhere flowing through these mountains, somewhere he could get water. The sun was cresting into noon and it was getting significantly warmer than at night, and this was only antagonizing Alex's thirst even more.

Sure enough, just a few miles to the south Alex could make out what appeared to be a small lake settled in a trough between the mountains. The terrain between him and the lake sloped ever downhill, meaning there might be a high chance that there would be a stream pouring forth from the hills and feeding into it. Alex shook his head as he could not believe how fast he had been reduced to the single instinct of survival, but he could belly-ache over that later. A source of water miles away was better than nothing, and for all he knew it might take him closer to some sort of sanctuary. One step further to getting out of this mess. He still had a bit of hike ahead of him, but Alex was just glad he at least had somewhere to go to. So he mustered what strength he still had and began his long walk down the hillside and toward the lake.

Unknowingly, of course, Alex had no idea how he alone he was not. All the while following the break of dawn the mysterious wanderer called Ranger had been following him stealthily through the mountains, not for any other purpose but to keep an eye on him.

Ever since Ranger himself had found himself wandering the mountains of this region he went wherever his instincts told him to go; and by instincts he meant the hulk of magic metal he carried on his back. However, what sounded like pure insanity to anyone was not the same to him. Whatever power was concealed within the sword on his back Ranger did his best not to question it, as it helped him to survive in the wild all of these years and kept him hidden from the prying eyes of his enemies. And just that night it told him news of a young boy entering into the northern borders of the Dark Zone. So Ranger hiked all night through the vast woods, following wherever his will directed him, and by the first rays of morning he spotted the boy struggling to navigate his way through the wilderness.

At the moment, Ranger had quietly perched himself in a high tree so as to observe the boy's movements as he came to the top of the hill. Upon seeing his fear and distress Ranger's heart was filled with pity. He knew deserved to be isolated out in the wilderness in such a manner but not this boy. He could see that he was desperate for water at this point, and he figured that was what he was now heading off in search for. It would have been easy for Ranger to simply reveal himself in order to offer his help, but something was holding him back. Something told him that for the time being he still had to restrain himself from making contact with anybody he came across, especially the boy.

Ranger leaned himself against the tree and allowed his legs to dangle off of the limb on which he sat. Long days still lied ahead of him, and now he had this young boy to keep an eye on, for reasons that were simply unknown to him.

"What am I doing now?" Ranger groaned, putting his hands over his face. "I feel like I'm losing my mind, and things are starting make less and less sense to me." He casually reached behind him and placed a hand on the cool, hard surface of the large sword hilt. It almost felt was though it was vibrating lightly. "I admit I'm growing impatient and tired of waiting for some sign of fate to show itself."

... ...

"I still don't understand. How could the boy possibly be significant?"

... ...

"What does he have that I need?"

... ...

"'Output?' What are you talking about? I don't understand!"

... ...

Ranger felt himself growing increasingly frustrated. He leaned his head against the tree and grasped his head as if it were in pain.

"I'm hearing your voice inside my head, but I still don't know what you mean. I'm trying to solve your riddles and it's driving me to the brink of insanity!"

... ...

"The boy - is the output? What does that mean?"

... ...

"The wakening...of the Heart..." Ranger's eyes suddenly flew open and he found himself absolutely speechless. He held his breath for a moment, but then shook his head in disbelief. "No." he muttered to himself. "No, that's not possible. I don't know exactly what kind of power lies dormant within you, but if what you're telling me is true then we're talking about infinite power; raw energy that could change the world forever. That's exactly what our pursuers are after, and why we're hiding here.

... ...

"The boy? No, it's just not possible. My wife and I alone could hardly withstand your own power, let alone more than twice the amount. Why should the boy be any different? Unless..." A sudden, chilling thought coursed through Ranger's head. He froze and his body went cold as he stared down at the distant figure of the lost boy heading down the mountainside. "My God," he breathed. "It cannot be!"

... ...

Ranger brought himself back to his sense.

"You're right." For the first time in years, a long lost feeling came over Ranger. It was an intense feeling of hope. He felt goosebumps come over him as a wide smile stretched across his face. Unfortunately, that smile was quickly extinguished by another sudden realization: For many years he had wandered almost aimlessly, but now things were truly about to change, he could feel it. But how that change would show itself, he did not know, and there was nothing he feared more than a cloudy future.

Nevertheless, Ranger set his mind to it. He knew what he had to do now. Regaining his poise, he grabbed hold of the tree limb and prepared to make his descent back to the ground.

"I can't let him out of my sight!"

Nearly a mile had been traversed since Alex had reached the bottom of the hill. Under the tree canopy it was still nice and cool even with the sun peering down through it, which was nearly upon the peak of its rise. Alex had no idea where he was headed, but stayed as straight as he could and hoped he would come across a water source soon, otherwise he was not sure how much longer he could last.

Although, Alex would be lying if, even despite all of this, he said that was not enjoying the scenery while he was stuck out here. He hardly ever travelled outside of his home in North Elba, New York, and this was certainly a sight he had never before experienced firsthand. The woods were quiet and peaceful and the views from the mountaintops were absolutely beautiful. Still, Alex never forgot how important it was that he find his way out of the mountains sooner than late. He could only imagine how much everyone back home must have been losing their minds worrying about him. Then again, Alex was not so sure. His time alone out here in the wilderness made him look back at the life he had lived thus far. Though he was still quite young and had much of his life still ahead of him, Alex admitted to himself that he was not exactly proud of his life so far. He thought particularly of his sister, Nickole. They had been such good friends as young children, and she always looked up to him more than anyone. Now he was starting to realize how much lately he was starting to ignore her; his only sister. When she looked at him every morning, Alex hardly ever took notice of it. Now he was starting to understand how she felt toward him, like she was losing him, and it made him feel like he was losing his own grip on the world.

As he was deep in thought, he was suddenly brought back to reality by something. Alex paused. He held his breath and listened intently. It took his ears a moment to adjust to the silence of the woods, but soon enough, just past the distant sounds of the birds and squirrels rushing around the ground, Alex could make out the faint sound of flowing water. From the sound of it, it might have been a small creek or stream, like a tributary to a larger body of water, and it may not be so far away.

"Thank God," Alex muttered under his breath as he licked his lips. Though he could not find the energy to run for it right now, he continued heading straight for the sound of the water. It was farther away than it seemed at first, but after about ten minutes of lumbering through the woods Alex came to the source of the sound.

It was indeed a small creek and it was running further down the mountainside. Alex knelt down next to the edge of it and dipped his hand down into the water. To his surprise, the water was freezing cold and Alex shuddered as it almost chilled him to the bone. However, looking past this Alex was more than thankful he had found it. He cupped his hands lifted a small amount of water up from the creek and drank what he could before the rest of it fell out through his fingers. Alex gasped in relief at the refreshing sensation. He then collected another handful of water and splashed it onto his face. The light shock of it definitely allowed him to forget about his exhaustion, and momentarily his grave situation as well. With the sense of hydration in him now, Alex eased himself down on his back alongside the creek and allowed his hand to float gently in the water. He just wanted to lie there for a little bit, close his eyes and breathe. Then he could return to the situation at hand and figure out his next move. If only he had any idea what that next move might be.

The approaching sound of footsteps did not register in his mind until it was too late.

"Hey you!"

Alex nearly jumped out of his skin. He gasped in panic and threw his hands upward. Catching his breath, Alex looked back toward the direction he came from. Someone was approaching from out of the trees. It appeared to be a man in his early or mid-twenties. He was very poorly dressed, as if he had been wearing the same clothes for months and his hair was ragged and grown out likewise. The most disturbing element of his person was what he held in his right hand: a large, sword made of stone. He stopped, however, as soon as he seemed to get a good look at Alex, narrowing his eyes at him.

"You're not one of them?" He said after a brief moment's pause. Alex was still quite taken aback, staring with wide eyes at his blade. "Who are you?" The man continued to ask. Alex was too shocked to say anything, or to even pull himself to his feet. He opened his mouth to speak but no words came out.

Just then, the stranger turned his head toward the woods and gave out a loud whistle. Alex struggled to sit himself upright, and as he did he saw many more men making their way out of the tree lines. None of them looked any better than the first; some of them holding swords of their own and some were not. One of them, Alex noticed, actually had a bow on his back.

"Morales," the man called to one of his new company. With that, the one Alex assumed to be called Morales stepped up to him. However, he stopped dead in his tracks as soon as he laid eyes on Alex.

"Is he one of them?" Morales asked, pointing toward him.

The first man shook his head.

"I don't think so, judging by his clothes." Alex took a quick glance down at his clothes. He was still wearing the same clothes and gray DC jacket he had yesterday, which were now darkened and mired from the stress of his long hike. He almost looked like he could have belonged with these people. But who was "them?"

Morales took a step forward to more closely examine Alex, but then they all suddenly shifted their attention off into the woods as the sound of another set of footsteps nearing. The sword bearers quickly braced themselves as if they were expecting to be attacked. Alex held his breath in anxiety and confusion.

Then from the trees another figure stepped. This one, however, was much different from the others. Though he also appeared to be a young man, he was dressed in an outfit combination of leather and fur, as if he was wandering the mountains long before Alex had. The other men lowered their weapons when they saw him.

"Caine!" Morales exclaimed when he saw him approach. "Is that you? What are you doing out here?"

The new arrival, called Caine, stopped before Morales with a hard expression about him.

"I've been keeping an eye on you for some time now," he responded harshly.

The rest of the men exchanged glances with each other. Morales raised his eyebrows.

"What do you mean? Have you been following us around?"

"Well, that 'trouble' you encountered two years ago certainly caught my attention. I was quite interested when I received the report instead of Moreno."

"We haven't had any other issues of the sort, if that's what you're trying to get at." Morales replied, annoyed.

Caine laughed to himself.

"Indeed," he muttered. "Things have gotten a bit quiet lately." He then shifted his attention to Alex, locking eyes with him. "And what is that?"

Morales looked back down at Alex, who was just watching and clearly had no notion of what was going on.

"I don't know," was Morales' answer. "We thought he belonged with them at first." There it was again: 'them.' "He's certainly not one of ours."

Caine lifted a brow in curiosity. He opened his mouth to respond but closed it suddenly and looked up and around at the woods. This gesture made everyone else on edge as they started doing the same, which made Alex begin looking around for what they seemed to be scoping for.

"What is it?" Morales said anxiously under his breath. Caine did not answer. Everyone was holding their breath as they seemed to wait for something to happen. One of the men walked slowly deeper into the woods and pulled his own sword from a sheath at his side. It was so quiet and Alex could literally hear the sound of their heavy breathing.

Like a silent bolt of lightning and with a quick whizzing sound followed by a disturbing groan, the man was thrown backward and onto the ground, revealing an arrow sticking up out of his body. Alex's jaw dropped at the sight of it and he could not help but jump to his feet. The rest of the party panicked and yelled out, holding their weapons out in front of them.

Just then, a second arrow came flying out of the trees from a slightly different angle. This one came from above, as if their attackers were up in the tree tops. It struck another sword bearer and he dropped right to the ground.

"Ravennites!" Morales shouted in shock. The remaining men were moving back and forth as if they were trying to dodge any more arrows that might rain down on them. Sure enough, a third arrow revealed itself from lower than the last and found its target in one of the men's heads, causing blood to fly in all directions. Alex dropped back down to the ground, he didn't know what to do except pray one of these ballistic killers did not strike him too. Morales was trying to keep his head low.

"Miller!" he called out to one of them. "Get your bow! Shoot them!" With that command, the man carrying the bow on his back produced it and armed it with an arrow. He rapidly scanned around for a target in the trees but none were to be found.

Suddenly, there was a movement high up on a branch a few trees back. Alex could not make out any materialized figure but it seemed to be good enough for the bowman as he released the string. The arrow soared up and drilled through the exact spot where the movement had occurred but only fell to the ground after grazing the tree. As if out of nowhere, yet another arrow was expelled from nearby the bowman's target area and planted itself into him.

Alex was too stunned to move anywhere, but just to lie low and watch in horror as the fourth man was dropped instantly. Counting Caine and Morales there were only half a dozen of them still standing. Caine began slipping away back toward the woods from where he came.

"Destroy them!" he declared and then turned and disappeared.

Morales was shocked that Caine just ran off now, but fortunately turned his head in time to duck out of the way of a fifth arrow which buzzed right over him. He was tempted to make a quick run for the fallen bowman's weapon but just then another disturbance rang up from the trees. This time, Alex watched in sheer awe as a single man came running low on a tree limb out from the cover of the leaves. He leaped off of the branch and snatched a thin vine wrapping loosely around another tree and he used it to quickly descend himself down onto the ground.

Within little more than a second he reached the bottom and threw himself over toward the nearest opponent, and what he did was like nothing Alex had ever seen before. The man from Morales' party was hardly prepared as the newly revealed assailant produced a dagger-like blade from his side like lightning and swiftly ran the knife across his abdomen. The poor bastard gasped horrifically and collapsed, but suddenly his attacker spun around, grabbed his own knife-blade held on his belt and whipped it like a tomahawk over at another target, striking him directly in the throat. Now only Morales and two others were left alive, as well Alex watching from the ground by the creek. The three remaining survivors regrouped together at the sight of their enemy. Now Alex took the time to get a good look at him.

He was dressed quite similarly to the one called Caine, and his hair appeared to be braided into a tail on either side of his face, almost in a Native American-like fashion. Alex could also spot a quiver of arrows on his back, so he must have been one of the archers. The only major difference between him and Caine: he was seriously pissed!

The man hissed under his breath as he poised himself for a fight; wielding his dagger in front of him with his left hand, he pulled a longer sword from his belt side and held it behind his head in a menacing manner. Glaring right at the others, he cried out, "Let's dance, Domineers!"

The three survivors exchanged looks briefly. They clearly registered their three-on-one odds, but Alex wondered if they forgot about any other archers in the trees. Without hesitating another second, they cried out and charged down their assailant. He did not move but just stood there still as a statue until they reached him. In a sudden, swift movement, one of the men prepared to strike a blow with his sword but he quickly deflected it with the sword held behind his head and forced the man to spin around, at which point he did the same and dug his knife into his back, letting out a battle cry as he did.

Morales jumped back as the mysterious attack made a swipe at his stomach with his sword and then turned to engage his last comrade standing. They were locked in combat for only a few seconds, which ended when Morales' partner attempted to bring his sword down on their attacker, but he blocked it with both his blades. Growling at him, the man from the trees kicked his opponent back and reached out with his sword and cut his throat, dropping him to the ground.

This left only Morales, who was sweating intensely and displayed a look of fear as the outcome was quite apparent to be the same for him as it was for the others. The two circled each other for a moment, and then Morales engaged by swinging his sword at him.

The other man dodged his swipes as if they were nothing. After only a few swings the two locked swords, but out of nowhere the strange man grabbed a small club-like weapon from the back side of his belt and whacked it across Morales' face, causing him to spin around in a daze. The man seized the opportunity, wound up his arm and thrust his sword through Morales' back. He grabbed hold of Morales' shoulder and used it as leverage to push the blade further. Alex could hear Morales' distorted groans and gasps, and it was quite sickening.

The man leaned in toward Morales' ear and whispered only, "Murderers." Before pulling the sword from his body and allowing him to fall haphazardly onto the ground. And with that, it was over.

Alex was half afraid to move a muscle, but something told him to ease his way on to his feet and take off into the woods. He began inching away as quietly as he could while the victor knelt down to wipe the blood from his stone blade. Alex was trying to hold his breath as much as he could, but suddenly the man spoke up without turning around.

"Stay right where you are!" He called in a cold tone. Alex felt the adrenaline rushing through him, and he could not help but turn and run for his life. "Hey!" He heard the man shouting after him. All Alex could think of was to run as fast and as far as he could, but before he could even make it a mere ten feet, something struck him.

Alex let out a short cry in shock and pain as something hard was thrown at the back of his head. Instantly, Alex felt his body go limp and eyes go dark, as he collapsed down to the ground and everything went black and silent.

CHAPTER TEN

The distant sounds of the clashing blades had died out quickly after Caine fled the scene of the brief assault. He stopped and looked back through the woods. He knew the fight would be over soon and it could have gone either way. Not likely, though. Caine knew just how ferocious the Ravennites could be. The Moreno brothers would have to be absolutely foolish to believe they could ever dominate these territories without fighting the good fight, and Caine knew that.

There was no time to waste, as there was a good chance the Ravennites would be swarming the area soon. He had to make his back to their base camp. Over the past few years since their arrival in the Dark Zone, the great number of outsiders under the influence and leadership Ramon Moreno and his brother, Robert, organized several large camping sites throughout eastern region in an effort to compose himself and his company and get the lay of the land, and with time and resources they were able to build these sites up to stand as outposts as they travelled deeper and deeper into the hostile territories. Eventually, the brothers decided to split up and cover more ground as they spread and their numbers continued to grow; Ramon began establishing camps in the southern areas of the Dark Zone, and Robert took to the north.

However, when Robert's teams began encountering subtle resistance attacks from the Ravennites they were forced to withhold from moving any further west into the region. That was around the time that Caine, whom had aligned himself with Ramon and helped him to navigate the mountains, was told to go and aid Robert in his struggle to keep up. Caine had a faint respect for Ramon but did not care for his brother in the least. Robert was a pitiful idealist with an overwhelming desire to be just as good, if not better, than Ramon. That was how Caine always viewed him, and he had a feeling that Robert's stubbornness would be his downfall. Caine did not care, though. He had no respect for this excuse for a young leader and constantly told Ramon that he was far more capable than Robert to lead their followers into the heart of the Dark Zone. Despite his reasoning, Ramon always ignored Caine's warnings, believing him to be nothing more than his navigator in an unknown territory. Still, Caine remained faithful to his duty; all he had to do was support Robert's parties against any possible threat of a Ravennite retaliation.

However, there were a couple of things Caine knew that the Morenos never took into account: he knew that the Ravennites, even under Delmar's leadership would never dare to launch a full-scale attack at them, the difference in numbers were too steep in favor of Ramon Moreno. At the same time, Caine knew his own people well enough to realize that they would never forsake their homes without putting up a fight, and so far they done just that in the form of hit and run raids in the middle of the night, nothing too devastating. But Caine's knowledge of the Dark Zone provided him an advantage to his own personal agenda. Although they still did not know where the remaining organized Ravennites had found refuge, eventually they would have them pushed into a corner which would result in two subsequent outcomes: if Robert, in all his prowess, were to ever believe he held a strategic advantage over their enemies then he would ignorantly attempt to step in for the kill, forcing the Ravennites to strike back in defense. The ensuing conflict would be the end of Robert, Caine knew that for sure, and when that day came he would seize Robert's former position and finish the job himself.

With all of this in mind, Caine did his best to remain silent and convince Robert that he was always on the right path to defeating these 'savage natives'. He pondered all of this as he traversed several miles through the Adirondack lowlands, until at last he came to his destination. The Iron Furnace, as it was once called by the ancestors of Caine's people. Here at the remains of an old stone-built furnace sitting near the mountainsides, Robert's companies had spent more than two years constructing an outpost around it. Cutting down many dozens of trees in the area they erected a wall around the area and built structures within, starting by surrounding the furnace itself and using it to mass produce their weapons for the wild. Caine approached the wall, where a large, wood gate stood keeping the area enclosed and secure. Caine did not stop, but continued to walk toward it, and eventually it was opened up when somebody recognized him.

Once on the inside the gate was immediately closed behind him. One of the men looking after the wall went over to greet Caine but was a bit taken aback wondering why he was alone.

"Where is the rest of the party?" the man asked curiously. "I thought you were heading out to retrieve them."

For a very brief moment, Caine wanted to simply ignore the question and walk away, but his desire to see Robert Moreno fall caused him to suddenly lash out and snatch the man by the throat. He grabbed hold of Caine's hand and tried to pry it off but Caine turned and shoved him against the wall. Caine brought himself close to his ear and whispered menacingly, "You listen here, not a word of this gets out to anyone or you'll have me to answer to. Understand?" He shook him by the neck and the man struggled to give a nodding gesture. "Good!" Caine then threw him down to the ground and he gasped as he caught his breath. He knew how serious Caine was and thought it best not to ask questions and let this whole situation disappear. With that taken care of, Caine headed off to blend into the outpost for the time being. He had a lot to think about; the Ravennites were starting to reveal themselves, and violent conflicts were imminent, that much was clear. He had to be ready for it.

Alex's head was imbued with the vexing sound of a high-pitched hum as he started coming to. He was still dazed and his eyes were weak and heavy. The spot on the back of his head where the hard object had hit him was throbbing with pain. Alex groaned quietly as he struggled to regain consciousness. He still could not open his eyes completely, but he could tell that wherever he was it was dark. He could make out a single faint source of light to his left. It was clear that he was no longer in the woods.

Wait, what!?

With the sudden shock of realization coursing through him, Alex's eyes flew wide open and he gasped out loud. After breathing rapidly upon waking up, Alex began glancing around to take in his surroundings. He was right, no longer was he lost in the mountains per se, but he found himself lying on a bed-like heap of leather and cloth. The room he was in was small and square like a cell, with a single doorway draped with a curtain. He had never seen something quite like this, but with the events leading up to him being knocked out starting to come back to him, it was his guess that he was still somewhere in the Adirondack mountains, but he had to know for sure.

He didn't even know who these people were, but judging from he had just witnessed something in his gut told him that they were not the friendliest. Alex pulled himself up from his mattress and onto his feet. His head continued to throb and he grabbed hold of the spot, moaning under his breath in pain. He took a deep breath and slowly moved the curtain away from the doorway and peered out. He was looking out into a dimly lit corridor lined with many small archways similar to his own. Looking down the hall there was no one in sight. He could not even hear anyone nearby. Maybe that was what he needed if he was going to try to get away.

Alex slipped into the corridor as quietly as he could. On either end there seemed to be entryway. To his left Alex could see the start of a staircase heading upward. Looking the other way a small opening in the floor indicated to him that there would be another flight of stairs going down. He looked back and forth a few times, ultimately deciding going down would probably be his best option, wherever down would lead to. Alex slowly and carefully started making his way over toward the end of the hall when suddenly someone entered the corridor from one of the rooms ahead of him. Alex froze and held his breath. It appeared to be an older woman, dressed no different than the man who attacked him earlier. He waiting anxiously for her to turn and take notice of him but she never did. Instead, she seemed to walk further down the hall and disappeared into a separate cell-like room.

Without thinking, Alex took this opportunity and to turn and make quickly for the stairs on the opposite side. The steps were old and ragged, but upon reaching them Alex did not hesitate to climb his way up. A few of them creaked a little bit as he stepped on them and Alex gritted his teeth, hoping that nobody else was going to stand in his way. He still had no idea where this path was going to take him, nor did he realize what sort of surprise he was in for at the top.

Upon coming to the top of the flight he was greeted intensely by the harsh light of the afternoon sun. Alex put his hand up to block the temporarily blinding light. When his eyes adjusted he looked out ahead of him, and what he saw took his breath away.

Alex's jaw dropped as he found himself staring out from the pinnacle of a man-made tower at the astonishing view of the Citadel. From the tower, just below, he could see a series of bridge-like structures stretching out from the tower and connecting to the wall at the edge of the plateau at many different angles. There were hundreds of people on the ground below and to his right he spotted the lake that sat cradled within the lone highland. The mountain ranges that surrounded were nothing compared to the beauty of this fortress. Alex never would have guessed what sort of activity was really going on in the regions so near to his home. It was absolutely mind blowing.

"Hey!" A sharp voice called out. Alex jumped and over to his right he saw that someone had taken notice to his presence. "What are you doing?" They yelled out at him. Alex was on the verge of panicking. There was no way he was going to deal with this again. He began looking around rapidly for somewhere to go. As high up as he was, jumping was in no way an option. Alex was hardly thinking right now, he let his nerves take over and turned around and ran to wherever he could. "Stop right there!" The man called after him, and Alex could hear the unnerving sound of a sword being removed from a scabbard.

He did not get very far around the outside of the tower before his path was suddenly blocked by two more guards, as it were, both bearing stone smith swords. Alex halted in his tracks and looked back to see his other pursuer right behind him. He glanced down to the side and spotted another platform about ten feet down the tower side from where he was standing. The three surrounding him all point their swords at him as they cautiously closed in.

Alex shook his head.

"You've gotta be kidding me!" he breathed. With no other thought he turned and jumped over the side and landed down on the lower platform, rolling onto his back as he did. It was a more shocking drop than he imagined. As he tried to recompose himself he watched as the guards chasing him prepared to take their own leaps down after him. Alex cursed under his breath and rolled onto his feet to keep running along the walkway. His chasers were quick to drop down and their landings were much smoother than his. Further down the walkway along the side of the tower something caught Alex's eye. There was a rope tied onto the wood rail of the platform and he could see that it descended much closer to the ground. There were ropes like this all around the tower and were mainly implemented when it had been under construction. Alex lifted himself over the rail and grabbed hold of the rope, just as he saw the other men pursuing him approach. As he unhesitantly descended down, a sudden, horrifying thought came to him: what if they saw fit to cut the rope loose with their swords? Alex had already started rappelling himself down, there was nothing he could do except get as far down as he could and hold his breath as he waited for them to do the worst.

Much to his surprise, however, the rope was never cut. The guards only took a quick look down at him and then hurried off, presumably to cut him off elsewhere. Alex felt somewhat relieved as he slid the rest of the way down. When he landed at the bottom, Alex grunted as his hands were scorched from the friction travelling down the rope, and he clasped them together to sooth the pain. Looking around, he saw that was now on another walkway, this one was bordered by walls on either side several feet high, sort of resembling a wide trench. A few yards down and he could see an opening in the wall on the left side. This must have led to one of the bridges jutting out to the wall at the far side of the plateau. He did not know where exactly he planned to go but as long as he could get outside of this seemingly hostile territory he would be satisfied. He headed straight for the opening and would make a break for it once on the bridge.

However, before he could even get through the opening an arrow suddenly buried its way into the wall frame about six inches in front of him. Alex cried out in astonishment and looked over toward the source of the fire. As he did, somebody jumped down from the opposite wall and approached him, arming another arrow on the string of their bow and pointing it right at him. Alex immediately put his hands up and backed against the wall, and it was now that he got a look at his captor.

Unlike all of the others he had encountered, it was no man who had him cornered. Rather, it was a girl, a young girl, hardly any older than Alex by her looks. She had long black hair that flowed down over her back and shoulders, and she stared right at Alex with the gaze of a hawk targeting its prey. Her green eyes were piercing, though there was something about them that gave Alex not the sense of hate and hostility, but rather a notion of fear and hopelessness.

At that same moment, the guards whom were previously chasing Alex down had found their way back to him. This time, they were accompanied by many more sword-wielding comrades. Alex looked around and painfully took in his current situation. Never before had he felt a stronger feeling of being unwelcome.

Just then, from behind, someone was heard making their way through the crowd of Alex's captors. He seemed to shouting something at them all but in some form of language Alex had never heard before. The voice sound familiar, though. He turned his head and to his horror he saw the same man that assaulted the company just by the creek. He must have brought him back here after knocking him unconscious.

At first, he locked eyes with Alex for a second, and then shifted his attention.

"Rowan!" he shouted at the girl armed with the bow, again in his strange speech. *"Stay that weapon!"* The girl gave him a quick look of compliance and lowered her bow. She then walked toward Alex, looking him dead in the eyes as she did. Alex did not move, but felt like his eyes were drawn to her gaze. She stood directly in front of him, and then firmly grabbed hold of her arrow stuck in the wall and pulled it out. Alex still could not bring himself to put his hands down. The girl then withdrew the two arrows back into her quiver and walked away through the crowd.

Before anyone else could make a next move, the man spearheading the crowd approached Alex.

"You," he said out loud in English, placing a firm hand on Alex's shoulder. He shuddered slightly at the thought of making physical contact with a man capable of killing. "You will come with me, now."

Alex was still speechless, but he had no choice but to do what he was told. As he turned to follow the direction the man pulled him in, Alex saw something out of the corner of his eye. It was something on the man's outfit, on his left arm. It looked like a patch of some sort, but Alex was not able to make out what was on it. He was ushered through the crowd and back within the tower's structure. Alex did not know where he might be leading him. He led him inside and to yet another staircase winding up the inner body of the tower, but before Alex got a chance to take a step, the man stopped him abruptly and turned him around to face him.

At first, he seemed to glare fiercely at Alex, but his tone suddenly shifted slightly to a weak smile.

"First of all," he began, not sounding as harsh as he spoke this time. "That was a rather impressive run." He seemed to be referring to Alex's attempted escape.

Alex narrowed his eyes in caution.

"Thanks." he responded curiously.

"Well then," the man continued, "allow me to introduce myself; my name is Matheus." He held out his hand as if he wanted Alex to shake it.

Still taken by surprise at Matheus' sudden change of attitude since his attack run, Alex was quite hesitant to take his hand. Though, he managed to find the will to simply reach up and shake his hand.

"Alex," was his response to his introduction.

Before any more could be said, Matheus released his hand and moved ahead of Alex to climb the staircase.

"Follow me, please," he said strictly. Even though he had just blatantly turned his back on him, Alex did not see fit to try to run away again, so he cursed himself in his head and followed Matheus up the steps. "Second thing," Matheus continued. "Sorry about the head." Alex was just then made to remember the throbbing ache in the back of his head from where he was hit, and he was guessing it was from the club which Matheus now had back on his belt. The pain had since all but dissipated now. "I can be a little overzealous in a fight."

Alex felt around the back of his head.

"You don't say," he whispered to himself.

The two of them climbed all flights of stairs they came to until they reached the peak of the tower again. All the while, Matheus seemed as though he was trying to get to know Alex.

"Many of the men believe you to be one of the enemy," he said, which only confused Alex even more. "I personally do not think that as of now, otherwise you understand I would have killed you too out there."

Alex raised his eyebrows, stunned.

"Well, that's cheerful news."

Matheus laughed to himself.

"Don't worry, if you were a Domineer then your escape attempt would have been a little more successful. But that's why I'm bringing you back up here."

"What?" Alex replied. "I don't understand." As they reached the top of the tower again, Alex recognized the same lookout point that he saw when tried to run. Matheus led him to the small set of steps leading to the map room of the tower. Just before they could enter however, someone quickly approached them from the other side.

"Matheus!" he called out. Alex observed this new arrival. He was significantly taller than Matheus himself, and he seemed much more sharp and punitive, especially when he laid eyes on Alex.

Matheus bowed his head ever so slightly as he approached. "Malachai," he greeted him.

The one called Malachai stopped right in front of him and pointed over at Alex.

"What is this one doing here, allowed to walk freely around the tower?" he said angrily in that same language.

Matheus glanced at Alex.

"He is not one of them, I am sure of it," he replied in defense. *"I am taking him to Delmar now."*

"To Delmar?" Malachai was surprised. *"You can't just bring an unknown outsider into Delmar's presence! We don't know who he is!"*

"I was instructed directly by Delmar." Matheus rebuked him. Malachai's eyes widened. He looked over at the archway

leading to the map room and stormed into it. *"Malachai!"* Matheus called after him. He turned his attention back to Alex, trying to think of what to do next. Trying to compose himself, Malachai said in English, "Do me a favor? Please just wait out here. And, for your sake, don't try to run again, because you're not going to get far." Before Alex could respond Matheus too disappeared in through the archway.

Alex let out a sigh of disbelief at everything that was going on lately. His future at this point was very uncertain, as he still had no idea where he even was. He had no choice but to do what Matheus said, so he examined his surroundings. Alex walked casually over to the adjacent lookout point. It was an incredible view and even now it had the power to take his breath away. He sat himself down and leaned against the pole next to the small flight of steps and just allowed himself to relax for a moment. Maybe now he had more time to think about his situation. If he was fortunate enough, it was possible these people might be able to help him get out of the mountains.

"Enjoying the view?" came the sudden sound of a female voice. Alex jumped again, this was happening far too often with people coming up to him while his mind was elsewhere. To his right, he saw the same girl that held him at bow point just earlier stepping out onto the lookout. Alex made a movement to stand himself up but the girl was quick to respond. "Relax," she said, putting her hand out to calm him. "Can I sit down?" She asked, hardly politely. Alex did not even have a chance to answer, she sat down next him anyway.

He had no idea what to say, especially to someone who damn near could have killed him. However, she was quick begin talking again.

"I was hoping you'd let me apologize for my threatening behavior toward you earlier."

Alex was not sure how exactly to respond.

"Uh, don't worry about it," he stuttered. "It wasn't the first time someone pointed a weapon at me today."

The girl laughed at his words, and for a moment Alex found himself laughing to himself as well. He glanced over at the girl beside him, and it was then that something caught his eye again; something that Matheus had been wearing that sparked his attention. Sewed onto the left sleeve of this girl's outfit was a patch similar to the one he had spotted earlier. This time Alex was able to get a much better look at it. It was as ragged as her outfit; on the patch was what appeared to be two medieval-style weapons, a stone sword and a hatchet, or a tomahawk. They were crossed together in an X-fashion and underlapping them appeared to be a green arch shape, sort of resembling a Greek Lambda.

The girl looked over at him and caught his gaze.

"What's your name?"

Alex looked right back. This time her eyes were not so spine-tingling to look at it. Instead, he saw the eyes of a truly kind and compassionate young woman. He felt much calmer now as he replied, "Alex." He was breathing much more smoothly. "Alex Lee."

The girl managed a smile, now they were getting somewhere.

"I'm Rowan," she said back.

After that brief introduction, Alex tried to find something else to say. He ended up saying the first thing that came to mine.

"You have a last name?" he had no idea what kind of question that was or why he asked it, but he was relieved when Rowan answered it.

"No," she answered, shaking her head. "I don't have a need for one, never have. We're not so much like your people in that sense."

His people. Alex had grown up in what he always believed to be a quite normal environment, mainly because that was all he had known. Now he was here, witnessing firsthand a very different kind of people. At this point there were so many questions he could ask.

"Who are you?" he asked very curiously. "What is this

place?"

Rowan opened her mouth to answer, but she was suddenly interrupted by the sound of someone exiting the map room just behind them. She immediately jumped to her feet as Malachai came out in a huff. Alex looked back at him. Whatever had been going on in there, it clearly did not go well for him. He just glared down at Alex very angrily and then stormed off.

Out of the archway, Malachai had been followed by Matheus. Now Alex stood to his feet as to await his next instructions. To his expectations, Matheus pointed to him.

"You, Alex," he said to him. Then he pointed over his shoulder toward the doorway. "You're next." Alex's eyebrows went up, as he was not sure what to expect upon going in there. He was hesitant at first, but then he reminded himself that it was best to comply at this time. He walked around to the steps and headed toward the draped archway.

"Good luck," Rowan said in a joking manner. Alex, on the other hand, was not exactly in the right mood to handle many jokes right now. Taking a deep breath, and preparing himself, Alex lifted the heavy curtain and entered into the map room.

CHAPTER ELEVEN

God only knew what these people were sending him in here to do. Upon entering into the room Alex found himself looking around at a small, round chamber lit only by a row of torches near the ceiling. There were hand drawn all along the walls, which Alex guessed all were intended to depict different areas of the mountains.

Alex's attention was quickly brought to the center of the room where he saw a man standing there with his back turned to him. As soon as Alex entered the room, however, the man turned his head and looked in his direction. Alex's first impression was that this was someone who had seen the world come to hell and be spat back out. His expression seemed to be that of a ragged mess, and one side of his long hair had grown down into a strip over the left side of his face. Alex felt a strange feeling come over as he looked into this man's eyes; it was no feeling that he could describe, but he could only just stand there and wait for anything to happen.

The man breathed heavily before he began to speak.

"So," he said in a deep, cold tone. "This is the outsider wandering freely around our territories?"

Alex suddenly felt quick to respond on the defensive.

"I wasn't trespassing, if that's what you're getting at." He said in an annoyed tone of voice.

The man put a hand up to silence Alex. There was a brief, silent pause.

"And what exactly do you intend to tell Ramon when you get out of here?"

This random question took Alex completely off guard. He had such a look of confusion about him. He stuttered briefly

Taylor Caley

as he tried to find the words to explain to this man that he had no idea what he was talking about.

Just then, the man turned all the way around to face him and, much to Alex's surprise, smiled lightly.

"Relax," he said with a calmer tone. "That was all I needed to hear."

Alex was still narrowing his eyes in confusion.

"What are you talking about?" he asked with growing frustration. "What do you want from me?"

"Nothing, really," the man replied. "I just needed to know that you weren't on our enemies' side."

"Y-your enemies?" Alex repeated in curiosity. He again recalled his encounter in the woods with the one called Matheus. There were at least a dozen other men who confronted Alex at the creek, and Matheus just swooped down from the trees and killed them all with relative ease. He turned the area into a bloodbath, and it was clear that there was good reason. There was no way this was mere territorial dispute between neighbors, and Alex was almost eager to learn more.

The man walked toward him.

"The name's Delmar," he introduced himself. Delmar placed a quick hand on Alex's shoulder and then moved over to the wall toward a cluster of maps hanging on it.

"Alex," was Alex's own anxious introduction for the third time today.

"Do you think you could tell me, Alex, where is it you come from? I'd like to know what you're doing in these parts." Delmar asked him, staring at the maps.

It was time for Alex to speak the truth and possibly get himself out of here once and for all.

"I don't know," Alex began, struggling to find the right words. Delmar glanced at him from the corner of his eye as if to question Alex's logic. "I mean," Alex continued, "I came from Lake Placid."

Delmar shook his head. "And where exactly is that?" he asked in a joking, yet somewhat condescending tone.

138

Alex raised his eyebrow. Do these people never come out of the mountains or something?

"It's just a few miles outside of the mountains. Haven't you ever heard of it?"

"The Outside world is not too welcoming of our kind, my friend," was Delmar's blunt response.

Alex was taken aback.

"Why is that?"

Delmar only seemed to ignore the question and moved on with his own.

"The other part of my question now," he began again, "what is it you are doing in these mountains?"

"I told you, I was not trespassing!" Alex defended himself.

"Who's implying that you were?" Delmar rebuked him.

Alex took a breath and tried to calm down.

"I just got lost, that's all," he said, remembering back to the unnerving events that led him all the way out here. "My friends and I found an abandoned mine on the mountainside. We were taking a look around it and the whole thing just collapsed and trapped me inside-"

"You were in the clay mines?" Delmar interjected with concern.

Alex nodded in affirmation.

"Yes. It was dark and I was trying to find a way out. When I did, I came up lost in the woods and I spent the whole night trying to get out and back home. I didn't even know anyone lived way out here, but if someone did I was hoping to find help to get me out of here."

Delmar was silent for a moment. He started pacing around the room slowly, as if he was trying to think of some solution to his problem.

"I don't think you understand the gravity of your situation," he said, grimly. "You don't know how fortunate you are that Matheus found you when he did. Don't you ever wonder why he didn't just kill you too?"

The conversations coming from these people were

growing increasingly disturbing by the minute.

"I still have no idea what is even going on right now," Alex admitted.

"Those men that you ran into out there," Delmar continued, pointing out at the blocked archway, "are not the sort of sanctuary you were hoping to find out here, and frankly neither are we." Now wearing a more serious expression, Delmar walked closer to Alex, staring him dead in the eyes. "Have you heard of the Dark Zone?" Alex was a bit lost on words, and he just shook his head silently. "I thought not. It's not a name that floats around with the wind.

"The long and short of the story is this: many years ago my people who live here in the heart of the mountains held a connection, a sort of allegiance, with the people of your world, what we call the Outside. However, that allegiance was declared broken by my father, who was the leader of our people at the time. All of our connections and relationships were severed and we remained quietly here in our own home, to live our lives free of the your ignorant, power hungry governments. Outsiders were not welcome to live among us just as we are not permitted to dwell among your kind.

"But five years ago, our home was savagely invaded by an army of men from the Outside. They attacked us first in the middle of a winter's night in my valley home. We were gravely outnumbered and unprepared. My father and I took up what arms we had and met our attackers head on. To this day I can hardly imagine the motives behind their actions, but mine are still simple: to protect my people and my family." Delmar found himself looking down in anguish. "My father was killed that night. And me, I barely escaped with only this to remember him by-" He then reached up and lifted the hair on the side of his face out of the way. Alex was stunned by what he saw. The mark of a large scar had defined the left side of this young man's face. A true sign of conflict.

Delmar laid his hair back down carefully over his ugly

battle scar.

"You understand, Alex? This is not the place in which you want to find yourself lost and alone."

"That's what I'm trying to say!" Alex responded. "I don't want to be lost in here, I'm trying to find my way out."

Delmar's eyes suddenly showed a sign of concern, and even pity, and he slowly shook his head.

"There is no way out."

Alex felt his body go cold, even in the soothing warmth of the spring air.

"What are you talking about?" he muttered quietly.

"You are wandering within an enclosed territory, Alex," Delmar explained. "Naturally enclosed. The hills bordering our lands are nearly unscalable, and the rivers that flow through them are treacherous. The only way one could simply walk out of here with ease is through an old path heading to the north of our territories. That would take you to our borders, but unfortunately, those areas are under the control of the Domineers.

Still feeling the slight shiver going down his spine, Alex shuddered as his curiosity continued to prod Delmar on.

"What- who are the Domineers?" he asked intently, even though he probably already knew the answer to that.

"I think you should know," Delmar answered, likewise to Alex's thoughts. "Most of them are on the brink of insanity from being exposed to our wilderlands for so long, they would most likely kill you as soon as look at you. I cannot, and will not, allow you to simply walk out there with your blood on my hands."

"I thought you said you don't house outsiders here," Alex replied, attempting to seize his chance to be let go. "All my life I've lived by the base of the mountains, I think I'm perfectly capable of keeping a low profile while making my way out, and then I'm off your hands for good."

"And yet here we are," Delmar mocked. "Nevertheless, it is no way as easy as that. Their numbers are growing constantly. That action you witnessed, eleven against one, that was the equivalent of what you would call a fair fight."

"Yeah, somehow I got the sense," Alex joked, remembering how easily Matheus had slaughtered them all. But his mood suddenly shifted when he understood the meaning behind Delmar's words.

"There's hundreds of them out there, Alex," Delmar seemed to read his mind. "Hundreds in the northern areas alone. It would be infeasible to sneak past any of them. For several years we've been on high vigilance for the actions of one another, and now your arrival is causing us to reveal ourselves even further."

Alex put his hands up in defense.

"Wait, you're blaming me for you issues?"

Before anything else could be spoken, Delmar made a quick glance up at the dark ceiling of the map room. Alex followed his eyes, not sure what it exactly he was looking at. However, the ceiling did seem to exerting a soft creaking sound as if something had been moving around above it.

Delmar raised a hand.

"We'll discuss this matter later," He said, shifting the conversation. "It was nice meeting you, Alex. Now if you wouldn't mind, I need you to return outside now."

Still failing to receive any valid answers to his predicament, Alex was reeling in frustration. He groaned under his breath and turned to walk back through the archway and out of the map room.

As soon as he was certain Alex was gone, Delmar and rolled his eyes and looked back up at the ceiling.

"What are you doing here, now?"

Once outside, Alex came right back to the scene just before he entered the map room; Matheus and Rowan were standing by the lookout as if they had been talking to one another all the while Alex was inside. As he exited, they both looked toward him. Alex was certainly feeling alienated as ever while he was forced to be held among these people. Despite everything he was going through, however, there was still something about them that gave Alex a strange feeling of, what were some of the words that were coming to his mind: tranquility, kindness, and for a moment he was almost starting to feel like he was at home, more at home than he had felt in years.

Matheus approached him.

"How did it go?" he asked, hardly sounding interested. Alex was about to mutter something before Matheus suddenly cut him off. "Don't answer, it's not my business to ask." he said with a clever grin about him.

Alex was feeling less and less in the mood to deal with anymore nonsense. He was entirely stressed out already, and now it would seem he was stuck here for God knows how long, wherever he even was. With every hour that passed he felt like his mind was growing more distant from his life outside these mountains.

"I do know, though," Matheus continued, breaking the silence, "that we are not permitted to let you leave these walls without Delmar's consent. I can also see that your mind is dealing with a lot of stress and frustration right now."

"Really?" Alex responded sarcastically. "What gave that away?"

Nothing really seemed to phase Matheus as an insult. Instead, he gave a brief laugh and continued.

"You need to get it out of your system. Why don't we show you around the Citadel? After all, it's clear that you're no threat to our people, and if you're not going anywhere then there's no sense in just sitting around and wallowing in anxiety, now is there?"

Alex looked past Matheus toward Rowan. She appeared to be in agreement with the idea.

"You're an outsider, Alex," she said to him. "I admit I'd be a bit interested to know more about your world."

There was much he was still not quite sure about these people. But surpassing all thoughts and suspicions about them, Alex was always met with a calm sense which told him he had absolutely nothing to worry about. With that, he managed a slight smile and stretched his arms out, signifying that he was ready to go.

"Well, in all truth," he began, "there's not much my world has to be proud of."

Matheus led the way as the three of them returned down the tower from the way they had come. Alex had not taken a chance to get a good look around at the incredible structure before, but he felt much calmer now that it would seem he was no longer being held as a prisoner. The sun, as it passed its peak, was leaking its light through and into the tower's interior and illuminated each level like a natural daytime light switch.

"It took years to build," Matheus said as they headed through another archway and out onto one of the many series of bridge walkways extended outward over the plateau. It was truly an incredible view from here. "It began as a refuge for our scattered civilization, and over the years we made it into an impenetrable safe haven. We call it the Citadel. The Domineers still do not know of its existence, and even if they did, they have no way of taking it from us."

Alex was truly fascinated by this amazing feat of architecture.

"How can you be sure they won't destroy this place if their numbers are as great as you tell me they are?"

Matheus stopped and pointed out toward the gate in the wall.

"You see that over there?" Alex followed his direction and saw that beyond the gate the plateau dropped away suddenly and formed a narrow land bridge connecting to the adjacent mountainsides. "There is only one way in and out of this fortress sanctuary, and it's over that path. The Domineers could try to attack our hold, but as long as we remain on the defensive all of those numbers they have will mean nothing on that narrow stretch of land."

Interesting. Alex felt as though he had heard of this tactic before.

"Sounds like you guys are taking after the Hot Gates." He

joked.

Clearly, the time and place were not right because Matheus just looked at him in total confusion.

"The what?" was his perplexed response.

Alex was surprised by yet another of the differences between these people and his own.

"You don't know the Hot Gates?" He looked over at Rowan, who just shook her head as she was just as lost as Matheus. "You've never heard of the 300 Spartans?"

Matheus looked as though he was thinking about it for a brief second.

"Can't say that I have," he answered. "We don't lecture ourselves here so much on the topics of the Outside world, Alex."

"I can see that," Alex muttered. This was truly a different world than his own, and yet it still sat so close to home. Alex could tell if these people were really dedicated to their solitude of if they were just plain ignorant of the world around them.

"What did they do?" Rowan suddenly asked as they continued to move on.

Alex was unprepared for the question.

"Who?"

"The Spartans," she clarified. "What did they do that compares us to them?"

Trying to find an appropriate answer, Alex struggled to think back about everything he ever learned about ancient history.

"If I remember right," he began, "300 Spartans defended a narrow pass they called the Hot Gates against enemies numbering in the tens of thousands."

Matheus froze and looked at Alex with wide eyes.

"By the moon!" he exclaimed. "Tens of thousands?"

Rowan felt the blood in her veins suddenly run cold.

"How did they do that?" she asked, full of fascination.

It did sound incredibly unbelievable. While still trying to recall what he knew of the story, Alex looked back out at the narrow passageway on the other side of the gate, and suddenly, the term he was searching for started coming back to him.

"It's called a phalanx," he muttered to himself. "They used their shields to form a wall across the gates, a tactic called a phalanx formation, and fought the enemy back wave by wave. They essentially eliminated their advantage of numbers. Well, at least until their enemies found a way to flank around and defeat them."

"Incredible!" Matheus said with interest. "We'll certainly keep that in mind should the circumstance ever call for it. I think I know someone who would be more than willing to take that opportunity if it was given to him."

"Who's that?" Alex asked.

Matheus looked down off the right side of the walkway and pointed.

"Him," was his reply.

Alex looked where he was pointing. Past the center of the plateau the terrain suddenly sloped down to meet the lake crater. Just before the slope, there was a large section of the area walled off and encircled. It appeared to be designed like an arena of some sort; Alex could spot several targets set up presumably used to practice archery. Though, it was easy to pick out what Matheus was pointing to; within the enclosed training area was a fenced off ring in which three figures could be seen wielding makeshift swords made from wood. Two of them were encircling the third figure like predators preparing to take down a target. As soon as they attacked, however, the man in the center reacted with incredible speed and force, knocking them back constantly and occasionally hitting one of their weapons clear out of their hands. It was an impressive display of physical prowess, and Alex did not need much of a closer look to know who it was.

"Malachai has always been one of our toughest fighters." Matheus explained. "He practically lives in that ring, honing his fighting skills and channeling his rage for when the time is right."

"Yeah," Alex was a bit mesmerized by Malachai's passion for violence. "Rage seems to make up the majority of his character."

Matheus shook his head.

"He wasn't always that way," he rebuked Alex. The bridge ended at the outer wall of the Citadel. Alex followed the other two along the wall and down a roughly built ladder on the side. From the ground the tower was astonishing to look at. There were dozens, if not hundreds, of people going about their businesses in all different directions. Many of them made quick glances at Alex, some with interest and some with utter contempt. Scattered around the plateau near the inner wall which surround the tower were many tent-like structures; their frames were made from the bodies of trees skinned of their bark and planted firmly within the earth, and large conjunctions of animal skins were used to insulate them. *Lovely*, Alex thought to himself, as they seemed to head over in the direction of one of them.

"We were all different at one time," Matheus continued to speak over Alex's admiration of the Citadel. "Peaceful, solitary, not bred for war like the Outsiders. It was not until we lost our homes to the greed of the Domineers that we were forced to embrace this way of life."

Despite everything he had heard so far, Alex was still very confused about the nature of their conflict with the outsiders they call the Domineers.

"Hold on," he began, "you're still very far ahead of me. I don't understand, why did these people even come after you in the first place? What did you do to provoke them?"

"We didn't do anything to them!" Rowan cut in. She almost seemed offended by the questions.

"But then why won't you seek help? The government can't just allow this to happen to you."

The conversation entered into an intense silence. Matheus and Rowan exchanged looks of grief.

"I'm not sure I'm the one to tell you that, Alex," was

Matheus' only response. With that being said, they came to one of the tents and stopped in front of it. "I'm sorry your path has led you to be stuck within our walls, my friend," he said, turning to face him. "But until Delmar feels it's safe to secure your leave, you might as well have a canvas to sleep under." He directed Alex's attention to the oversize tent that stood in front of him. It was completely covered with the exception of a single flap that was cut out to hang freely open on its side. "This one's completely vacant. We're constructing as many as we can in anticipation of finding and gathering the last remnants of our people scattered throughout the mountains."

Assuming he was meant to enter, Alex headed over to the tent and ducked in through the opening. The light of the sun, like it did in the tower, penetrated the tent and illuminated it, except it was much brighter in here than it was inside the tower. There was not much in it, actually there was virtually nothing in it at all with the exception of another small sewn together mattress, similar to the one he woken up on just hours before. He guessed Matheus was not joking when he said it was completely vacant. Still, Alex found himself quite content as long as these people were not showing him any sort of hostility.

Once Alex had entered into the tent, Rowan was quick to seek Matheus' attention.

"Matheus," she said in a quiet tone, "you don't really think Delmar would force Alex to leave, do you?"

The question seemed quite surprising coming from Rowan. He was not sure how to respond to it.

"Not while the Domineers still swarm all over the eastern regions, no. It's too dangerous and we can't risk Alex being taken by them after all he's seen here."

"But that's what I'm talking about," Rowan replied. "He's an "Outsider, Matheus."

"I know," Matheus said back, not sure of the point of Rowan's words. "I've met the boy. I know where he comes from."

"That's not what I mean," Rowan was becoming annoyed. "He's an outsider, and so are the Domineers. I'd be willing to bet he knows all about them."

"What exactly are you saying, Rowan?"

Rowan looked Matheus dead in the eyes with a look of straight seriousness.

"We should take advantage of this. Maybe Alex might know things about them that we don't; how they think, their mannerisms, maybe even their weaknesses. We could learn a lot from him!"

At first, Matheus was preparing to disregard Rowan's idea, by reminding her not to allow herself to become too entranced by this outsider, but he suddenly found himself lost for words and taken her suggestion into deeper thought. For five years they had sat back in their hold and watched vigilantly for the movements of the Domineers. For five years they had struggled to wage a silent war against their enemies to no lasting avail. All of a sudden, Matheus was beginning to realize the validity of Rowan's words. However, he knew it would not be as simple as that.

"Rowan," Matheus tried to keep himself in check, "not everyone here would be exactly thrilled by thought of adhering to the guidance of an outsider, especially after what their kind has done to us already."

"No one else has to know," Rowan replied. "Please, will you speak to Delmar about it? You want to reclaim our freedom just as much as I do, it would be a shame to let a perfect opportunity go to waste."

Matheus was not sure how go about with Rowan's idea. He sighed and then put a hand on her shoulder.

"I'll talk to him," he said calmly. "I can't assure you that I can sway his mind. Just," he looked around and then leaned into closer to her, "be careful around him. No matter how harmless he may seem, we can't let our guard down around anyone from the Outside."

Rowan gave a docile nod.

"I understand."

Just then, Matheus found himself looking at Rowan in a different light. In their home in the valley, he had always seen her as the playful, innocent little girl that she once was, and even over the past few years he continued to view her that way. Now he was starting to see that that was wrong. Looking down in her eyes now, Matheus saw how much she had grown while trapped in this perpetual nightmare. She was becoming a brave young woman with an undying passion for the wellbeing of her people. He wondered if her brother had seen that in her lately as well.

Matheus nodded in approval.

"I will talk to him." he repeated. Without saying another word, but simply exchanging one last look of hope with Rowan, he turned and headed back toward the tower.

CHAPTER TWELVE

"What are you doing here, now?" Delmar said as soon as Alex had left his presence. The ceiling of the map room had continued to creak quietly above him. It was as if something was moving around up there, and the creaking starting moving further to the end of the ceiling. Suddenly, shrouded by the dim light of the corner of the room, a dark figure dropped swiftly and stealthily down from a small, inconspicuous opening in the ceiling. The figure was tall and lanky, and even more ragged looking than each of Delmar's people themselves. On his back, a large sword hilt was held within a leather harness.

Ranger stepped forward from the darkness.

"You know what I'm about to tell you," he breathed in a low, serious tone. Delmar gave an aversive nod of affirmation. "First," Ranger continued, "the following conversation never occurred."

"As usual," Delmar acknowledged his terms.

Ranger allowed his attention to dart around briefly, as if he was trying to find the best way to speak his mind.

"You must also sense what I've come to suspect."

"Regarding the boy?" Delmar asked.

Nodding his head, Ranger continued to speak.

"I have experienced a few less than welcome perceptions of the near future recently."

Delmar glanced back at the map room's entrance to ensure that their conversation was indeed out of earshot. He moved closer to his battered visitor.

"What is it you know?"

"I'm not sure," Ranger shook his head. He looked Delmar in the eyes in an effort to ensure that they both realized the seriousness of his tone. "But you have to understand: this conflict, this war you're breeding with the enemies on your doorstep-"

"We did not start this war!" Delmar lashed out, pointing his finger at Ranger. "And I will not be held accountable for their actions or the choices of my ancestors!"

Ranger tried to calm Delmar, urging him to keep his voice down.

"I am not blaming you or any of your people for your problems. But this is a whole lot bigger than you, Delmar. Whether you want to accept it or not doesn't matter. I have been chased across the four corners of this nation by black ops government militants for ten years," Ranger reached back and pulled his relic from his back and held it in front of Delmar. "This thing has caused me more pain and anguish than you can possibly comprehend. I am reaping the consequences of my choices of the past and your people will suffer the same fate if you do not tread lightly."

Delmar was starting to feel a bit heated inside.

"Don't you dare threaten my people," he growled. "You are only here because you made a promise which I expect you to keep; I will listen to any advice you have to offer and allow you to hide yourself within our territories, and you will maintain your distance from our conflict with the Domineers. I don't know anything about your business with your magic, mystical toy there, and neither do I care. All that matters to me is the safety and security of my people and our way of life."

Ranger sighed to himself.

"I'm not here to try to convince you to follow me out on some fool's adventure, and believe me I would not condone it. I'm here to ask only one thing of you, and yes, it regards the boy."

Delmar began to cool himself down and was prepared to listen to whatever it was this wandering stranger had to say.

"Go on, then."

Composing himself as best he could, Ranger began to

speak.

"I have reason to believe that there is great significance, importance even, surrounding him. I didn't realize it until recently, and I count myself lucky that things didn't turn out for the worst for his fate. I fear that the same people who have me at large would turn their scrying eyes to him if they too started seeing a connection between us both."

"What connection could you possibly have to Alex?" Delmar interrupted, growing curious.

"It's far beyond your understanding," was Ranger's simple reply. "Likewise, all I'm asking of you is to oversee his safety. I heard your previous conversation with him just moments ago; you refuse to release him from the walls of your sanctuary because of the dangers that might await him out there. Well, now you have another reason to keep him safe here with you; my reasons."

"And what are your reasons, pray tell?"

Ranger was starting to look like he might completely lose his mind at any given moment.

"I wish I had the capacity to explain." He looked at Delmar with eyes that were beginning to go bloodshot from exhaustion. He took a step closer to him. "As the son of your society's leader, I'm sure you know all about the cultures and beliefs of your great ancestors?"

"Of course," Delmar replied.

"As well as the old deities and spirits embedded in the writings and legends of your Native American roots?" Ranger added. "Religion is a thing of the past. Lost, forgotten, and even dismissed by most people today but most people would be fools. Most people are ignorant and blind; blind to the incomprehensive reality that surrounds our world. In truth, people are afraid." Delmar was growing wary as this man continued to speak to him. All his time alone and running from the world must have been going right to his ravaged mind. Ranger never took his eyes off of Delmar. "What if I told you that I have seen more than you know? More than you can possibly imagine." He raised the hilt of his ancient relic once and again as if to draw Delmar's attention with it, and then he slipped back into place in its harness. "There are secrets in this world, Delmar. Ancient secrets that have been lost to the abyss for millennia, and they're coming back for us. I can't alter the future, but together we can help to assure that the pieces remain in position. I'm not here to lecture you on everything I went through to learn all of this, but I will make myself as clear as possible: Alex Lee must not come to harm. He does not yet know the part he's meant to play, but when his time comes, his life will change forever. The entire world is going to change forever."

Delmar put his hands over his face and tensed his muscles. He was nearing the breaking point every minute he was forced to listen to this man's twisted words. Still, somewhere in the back of his mind he believed he had an obligation to fulfill this one simple task.

"Fine then," Delmar groaned in compliance. "But just know this: you're placing this boy in a very volatile environment and asking for a lot if you think I can guarantee his safety. As an outsider, I can promise you that many of my kin are not going to take an immediate liking to him."

"Alex is making his own decisions," Ranger responded. He rubbed his forehead as if it were aching. "But something tells me Hell is about to open its mouth upon all of you soon. I can't do anything to help you. Just be warned: you are not warriors. Be careful how you envision the future. If push comes to shove then it won't be a war you're fighting, it will be a chaotic bloodbath."

"I don't need your lectures," Delmar retorted, maintaining his composure.

Ranger bowed his head to him. "Then I take my leave. Good luck to you all." Keeping quiet, Ranger turned and he lifted himself back up above the map room through the opening in which he first entered. Delmar did not know where he was off to, just so long as it was away from the Citadel. Though he did not much like the man, something about him still made Delmar believe he could trust him not to betray their position to the Domineers.

Delmar walked outside of the map room and looked out over the tower's over watch. As crazy as Ranger tended to be while they spoke, Delmar recognized the truth in his words every now and then. His people not warriors, and were never meant to be. But what choice did they have now? Delmar was far too young to be faced with these difficult decisions. One way or another this had to end, or there would be no future for the Ravennites. There would be no future for his sister.

Alex sat on the mattress with his back leaned against the corner post. In the brief time that he had alone in this tent Alex had fallen into deep thought. He rubbed his hands along his face. He was not sure what he was doing anymore. This whole place, there was something off about it; something unsettling as if in the air around him. He had felt this ever since he accidentally wandered into this mysterious territory. It was like walking into an alien world, as if this place had some sort of invisible dome shielding it from the eyes of the rest of the world.

His thoughts were suddenly interrupted by someone calling his name.

"Alex?" came Rowan's voice from just outside. She carefully lifted the opening flap out of the way. "Are you okay?" Alex did not move, but simply nodded his head tiredly. Rowan entered the tent and let the flap fall back into place behind her. "It's not much, I know," She said as she looked around. "But they gave you one of the larger shelters. Not sure what they were reserving it for."

"It's not that," Alex responded quietly. He looked up at Rowan, appearing somewhat exhausted. He was not sure what to say at first. Alex's mind started to go blank. There was something rather captivating about Rowan. After knowing her for no more than a few hours now he could that she, and all of her people, were very different from those whom he grew up around. As he gazed up into her green eyes, Alex was beginning to sense an attraction. Not an amorous attraction, it was...something else.

"I feel so lost," Alex exhaled.

"Lost?" Rowan responded. "I understand, this must be a strange place to you."

Alex shook his head.

"No, not that way. Not that way at all. I just don't know what I'm doing anymore." He put his head back into his hands.

Rowan looked on him with a great sense of pity. Though she was not sure what Alex was thinking inside, she felt another strange sense every time she saw him. She was not sure what it was; some sort of attraction?

"Walk with me," Rowan spoke up.

Alex glanced up at her.

"What?"

Rowan gestured toward the tent flap.

"You need some fresh air, Alex."

"I got more fresh air in the past 24 hours than I bargained for," Alex sarcastically replied.

Rowan laughed.

"Come on. I'd like to talk to you myself."

Alex was quite tired from all of the stress of the past night and the circumstances that continued to multiply. He did not know what to think about the rest of these people, so far some of them seemed to like him but others, such as Malachai, appeared quite hostile toward him. Yet, something about this girl gave him the assurance to be calm and relieved. He stood up and the two of them exited the tent.

He was still not too thrilled about walking among the people of this mountain fortress. For the time being they viewed him as an outsider, maybe even as an enemy. In his heart, Alex knew that he meant no harm to them. Actually, he was almost beginning to forget what he was even doing all the way out here. What concerned him the most was that his mind was starting to blur out the familiarity of his home back in Lake Placid. He felt as though if he was not careful this place would go right to his head.

"What is it like?" Rowan interrupted his thoughts again.

Alex jumped from his trance.

"What's what like?" This girl seemed to have a problem with asking the most vacant questions.

"The Outside," she replied. "The world you come from."

Alex was not sure how to go about explaining it to her.

"You guys talk like I come from another planet," he said somewhat disdainfully. "Have you really never been outside of these mountains?"

Rowan shook her head.

"This is where I belong," was her response. "Most of us have never set foot beyond our borders, except for my father, of course. He was the leader of our people."

"Really?" Alex replied with interest. He looked back up at the tower looming above them. "Then who was-"

"My brother," Rowan answered before he could finish. "I'm sorry if he gave you any trouble. He's just been stressed out for a long time trying to keep us all together."

"So if he is your leader," Alex said to himself. "What happened to your father?"

Just then, Rowan stopped in her tracks. Alex realized he had made a mistake asking that when she closed her eyes and lowered her head. Something was eating her up inside and Alex wasn't sure he wanted to know the backstory.

"I'm sorry," Alex said. He hesitated for a second but then he reached over and put a hand on her shoulder.

Rowan immediately looked up at him.

"It's alright." She rubbed her eye lightly with her thumb. "He died years ago."

Rowan's words sent a chill up Alex's spine. He knew exactly how it felt to go through life without a father. He was amazed by all the similarities he seemed to share with her.

"I know the feeling," Alex said, trying to relate to her.

Rowan looked over at him as they walked.

"Oh, I'm sorry. When did he die?"

"Oh, he didn't," Alex replied. "At least I don't think so. But he left when my sister and I were both very young."

Rowan raised her eyebrows.

"You have a sister?"

For a moment, Alex's mind had gone so blank that he had briefly forgotten about his own sister. What was happening to him?

"Yes," he answered, "my younger sister, Nickole." As soon as he spoke the words a sudden, shocking thought came about his mind. "She was there when I first got lost out here."

"Really?" Rowan responded curiously. "What exactly happened?"

Alex again began thinking back to the events of the previous afternoon. After everything that happened it all felt like an eternity had passed, and now he was here.

"My friends and I," he began, "we were exploring around one of the abandoned clay mines when it collapsed on us. My friends got out, but I was trapped inside. I can only imagine how hysterical Nickole must have been." Suddenly, he even started to wonder how his sister must have been dealing with his accident. She and their mother both may not have even known exactly where he was. Even Alex still had no idea what to make of his new environment.

As the two of them continued to walk, they found themselves heading away from the plateau's center and before long they came up to the lake which Alex had seen from above on the overlook. It was much larger in person. The water was clear and blue and gave off a cool, soothing vibe as its surface rippled in the light, spring breeze.

Rowan knelt down at the bank and placed a hand in the water.

"How old is your sister?"

Guessing they would stop here, Alex sat down by the edge of the water. "She's twelve," he answered her. "Two years younger than me."

Rowan continued moving her hand around in the water.

"I'm sure she's lovely."

Alex shrugged. That was something he had never really

taken the time to think about, especially regarding his sister. However, it still made him recall how many years he had spent practically ignoring her, so much that he never seemed to realize just how much she was growing. He almost wondered how he could ever show his face around her again.

"She is," Alex muttered to himself, hardly thinking. "You remind me of her a bit."

Alex was barely listening to himself, but Rowan was curious.

"I do?" she asked, looking back at him. "How?"

He tried searching his mind for something quick to say, but as soon as Alex locked eye contact with Rowan again he knew exactly what it was he meant to say.

"You're both very strong," he responded confidently. "My sister shares the same optimistic outlook on life that you do, no matter how difficult things seem to get. Although," he took a quick look around again, "I imagine you have it significantly harder."

Rowan managed a quiet laugh, but it quickly subsided as the memories returned to haunt her mind again; the memories of the devastating loss her people suffered. Yet, Alex's words did not fail to remind her how important it was that she remained strong for her people, and for her brother. How far she had come since only hours earlier when she first believed Alex to be a dangerous threat. Looking at him now, there was simply no way this boy was capable of harming anyone without cause. She still wondered how Alex would feel if they asked him to reveal the weaknesses of his Outside kind. She knew nothing of the culture of outsiders and did not know if it would be insensitive to ask him or not. Part of her even wanted to ask how far he would go for them, if he cared about them at all.

All these thoughts racing through Rowan's head were too much for her right now. She needed something to take her mind off of it all. Reaching up to her neck she pulled her grandmother's old, wooden charm from under her outfit and gazed at like she did during most sleepless nights. It was not long before Alex even took notice to it.

"What is that?" he asked, breaking her concentration.

"My grandmother made it for me," Rowan replied with deep emotion, "just before she died. She carved it from the wood of the oldest tree in our village."

"Your village?"

"Our old home in the valley," Rowan smiled faintly. "Ravenna, we called it. Much of our culture thrived there for years before it was destroyed. My grandmother made this for me so I'd remember her when she was gone." Rowan removed the necklace carefully and handed it to Alex. "You want to take a look at it?"

Alex was careful as he took it from Rowan's hand. It looked very old and darkened with age, but he could make out the markings on it very clearly. However, Alex narrowed his eyes as he stared down at it. It was not what he thought it would look like. The plain, carved image of a strange man made up the majority of the space in the small charm. He was almost a stick figure in appearance, but Alex's eyes were drawn to the object carried in his left hand. It possessed a vaguely cross-like shape; it almost appeared to be shaped similarly to an ankh.

Alex's eyes widened with much curiosity.

"Who is this man?" He muttered softly.

"I don't know," Rowan shook her head. "I could never figure out what my grandmother wanted to tell me when she made it. Why do you ask?"

Alex did not know any other way to explain his thoughts.

"Because it almost seems to resemble an Egyptian god."

There was an awkward silence between the two. Alex was very intrigued by the carving on the necklace, but Rowan still maintained a vacant expression.

"I don't know what you're talking about."

Her response was genuine enough, Alex could tell. It seemed, living in this environment, Rowan would never have learned much of anything about the cultures of the world beyond, ancient and present, as he had. It was true, this figure posed a striking resemblance to ancient Egyptian depiction but Alex was still not sure. It might have helped if knew Rowan's ancestors a little more, but unfortunately he never knew they even existed until this morning. What captivated his attention even more were the strange, hexagonal symbols carved around the edge of the charm. Each one was different from the next, and they seemed to encircle the man. Above the man's head was a symbol that was even stranger to Alex. It was much simpler than the others; two triangles side by side and pointing downward. In the space between their sloped sides was a full diamond shape. All three shapes of the symbol were tinted a deep red color.

A sharp pain suddenly struck Alex in his forehead. He grunted and placed a hand on his head.

Rowan looked at him, concerned.

"Are you okay?"

His head was throbbing faintly.

"Yes," Alex lied. Of course, he was more concerned about this pain in his head than he was before. It was not a natural headache; it felt like someone was attempting to push a pin out of his head from the inside. The last time he had felt it was just the previous night when he was lost in the mine.

He handed the necklace back to Rowan as the pain quickly dissipated completely.

"It's a nice necklace," he complimented, trying to forget the strange sensation that came over him.

"Thank you," Rowan replied with a smile.

"You know it's a locket, right?" Alex added.

Rowan seemed a bit confused.

"A locket?"

Alex directed her attention around the thick side of the charm.

"Right there," he said. Running around the side was a very thin line like a narrow opening. At the top, between where the leather strings attached to the charm was a small wooden hinge. "It's meant to open up. Haven't you noticed it before?"

"No," Rowan admitted. "What would be inside of it?"

Alex shook his head.

"I don't know. Usually it's just a photo of somebody."

For a second, Rowan seemed as though she would attempt to open it. However, the thought of desecrating her grandmother's necklace turned her away. It just did not feel right to her.

"If you don't mind my asking," Alex continued, "what do those symbols mean?"

Rowan looked around at the hexagonal symbols on the edge and shook her head.

"Just another thing I've never been able to figure out," she sighed to herself.

"Right," Alex nodded slightly. "What about that one?" he said, referring to the red symbol above the figure's head.

Rowan glanced back down at the charm's surface again, but her expression suddenly went blank as she stared.

"Which one do you mean?"

"That red symbol at the top, right above the man's head," Alex clarified.

"But there's-," Rowan began, scanning the area Alex was referring to. "There's nothing there." The charm appeared the same to her as it always had; the symbols lined around the edge of the image and were separated by a blank area at the top, but there was no other symbol that she could see.

Alex was beyond confused at this point. He was also looking at the necklace and the red, ternion shape was there, clear as day. Rowan's eyes appeared to be looking at the same thing, how could she not have seen it? Alex reached over and pointed directly at the spot where the symbol was carved into the surface.

"It's right there," he insisted. "You really don't see it?"

Rowan narrowed her eyes one last time.

"No," she responded bluntly. "It's just a blank space."

The blood in Alex's veins ran cold. He was still staring right at this mysterious symbol. It was unmistakable and more conspicuous than the rest of the markings, yet for some reason Rowan was insistent that she could not see it. Why would she say that? Was she desperately trying to hide something? Or was she telling the truth?

During the brief silence, Rowan slipped the locket back around her neck and tucked it away. Alex wanted to forget that whole situation ever happened. He felt a little sick inside after that second episode of pain in his head. Nothing about it felt natural, and that was not to mention it struck him as soon as he laid eyes on the symbol which appeared to be invisible to Rowan. Putting those thoughts in the back of his head, more relevant questions were returning to fuel Alex's curiosity.

"Rowan," he began, speaking her name for the first time. He hesitated to speak at first as she looked into his eyes again. "What exactly happened to your people?"

As Alex brought it up, Rowan's concentration seemed to fade, and he could have sworn he saw tears welling up in her eyes.

"I," she responded shakily. "I don't want to talk about it."

That was all he needed to understand that he made a mistake in asking. He was not trying to hurt her, but he still wanted more answers than he had already gotten around here. What did he know so far? He was told that these people had been chased out of their home some time ago, but by who? And more importantly, why? Alex had a feeling he was going to find out the answers to his questions soon enough. Right now, he hardly knew much of anything about their current situation, but it was clear to that they had exhausted every possible means of resolving it, save for one. Remembering how potentially hostile Malachai had acted toward him, the scowling looks many of the others had given when they saw him, and not to mention Malachai's fierce prowess he displayed in the training area, it was obvious they were preparing for the worst. They were preparing themselves for their enemies to assault them here; or to take the fight to them. Either way it went, Alex was breathing heavily as looked around at all his surroundings once more. Despite everything he saw before him, this was a very beautiful place, and he did not like to see such people so miserable, especially the one sitting next to him now. His head was swimming with strange thoughts that had never come over him before; powerful thoughts.

"Sometimes I lie awake at night," Rowan spoke up over his thoughts, "and wonder if there will ever be something we can do to reclaim our lives and our freedom. But it's been five years now and nothing has changed."

Alex did not know what sort of mind tricks these people were playing on him, or if he was in complete control of his own mind and simply insane at this point. Whatever the case, it still did not stop Alex from feeling an overwhelming sense of pity, condolence, and even anger. Despite any thoughts he had, he knew he had never been oppressed in his life, and now here he sat in the heart of the true meaning of oppression, and it was something nobody should ever be made to suffer through.

He looked back to Rowan, focused at the last thing she had said to him.

"Well, maybe now is your time," he said to her.

Rowan raised her eyebrows.

"What do you mean? We don't have an army."

"What have you been doing for the past five years?" Alex retorted, almost sounding critical. "I don't know what your culture was like before everything went to hell, but look around you. I see an entire society perfectly capable of taking back all that was stolen from you if you really wanted to. I mean, look at your friend, Matheus; he annihilated almost a dozen of them single handedly when he brought me here! That's a whole lot more than anyone I know could ever accomplish."

Rowan sighed.

"Even if that were true, it's not up to anyone else but Delmar to command our next move. And, despite what you might think, we've never been put through this before. No one knows what would happen if we went out there and took on the Domineers hand to hand."

"Maybe," Alex looked outward at the large wall surrounding them along the great plateau. His mind was so consumed right now that the words he spoke seemed to surpass his own thoughts "If only there was something I could do to help."

CHAPTER THIRTEEN

Not long after Ranger had left his presence, Delmar fell into deep thought. Things were difficult enough already within the walls of the Citadel as he tried to keep the remnants of the Ravennites in order through all the fear and doubt which clouded their future. It did not help knowing that a great many of his people were still in hiding all throughout the Dark Zone, helpless and exposed. Now there was this boy, the outsider: Alex Lee.

Ranger's behavior was changing, too. Delmar had no idea who he actually was nor did he care. He knew Ranger was not the man's true name, and that was the only clue Delmar needed to know that he was running from someone. Under normal circumstances Delmar would not have permitted any outsiders from seeking refuge within the borders of the Dark Zone, with or without his knowledge, after the Domineers' atrocious campaign against them under the influence of the Moreno brothers. The vast majority of the Ravennites would not be pleased with Alex remaining among them for the time being, and they would surely be shocked and outraged if they were ever to learn that their trusted leader was secretly sheltering another fugitive from the Outside. Chaos and disorder would almost certainly ensue as a result of the created distrust. Delmar could not allow that to happen in their darkest hour.

All of this was almost too much for Delmar to deal with. He needed air. Delmar lumbered tiredly outside of the dim map room. The day pressed on, as every day had, but he could sense the atmosphere drenched with concern and apprehension by the coming of this outsider. He felt as though he was divided by the thoughts of his people; part of him did not trust the boy in the least. However, another part of him sensed something that he had never felt before. Maybe it had something to do with what Ranger had been saying, or maybe this was truly a sign that things were about to change. Whether changing for the better or not was unclear.

Delmar looked out from the overlook all around the great refuge they had built. He would die before he saw those walls fall, and his people suffer. Of course, he knew that Malachai was right. They could not hide forever within the confines of the Citadel. Though Delmar told him that he had a plan in action, the truth was that Delmar's inexperience as a proper leader was constantly getting in his way. Sure, he knew the territories of the Dark Zone like the back of his own hand but to lead the Ravennites into a battle that they were never prepared to fight was so risky it almost made him sick to his stomach, and now he had the issue of the boy from the Outside on his hands. What was he to do with him? What would his brothers and his sisters have him do?

"Delmar," Matheus' voice spoke up. Delmar's attention was drawn to one of the several staircases opening up from below the peak level of the tower as Matheus approached him. "I need to speak to you."

Delmar sighed to himself.

"It's about the boy, isn't it?"

Matheus stopped and nodded his head casually.

"Yes," he replied. He was trying to choose his words carefully, as stressed as he knew Delmar already was. "I understand your feelings on the issue."

"Do you?" Delmar responded. "My thoughts have been so unclear for a while and I'm afraid this situation may be clouding my judgment even further."

"Yes, it's that which I understand," Matheus said. "I want to do right by our people too, you know that. But I think you should also know that we are running out of time. Those Domineers are growing bolder. They think we're too powerless to do anything; they think we are afraid."

"I know all of this," Delmar retorted.

"But maybe we are afraid," Matheus immediately added. "I mean, look at us, we know nothing about outsiders; what kind of people they are, how they think," He looked Delmar directly in the eyes as he repeated Rowan's previous words to him, "or what their weaknesses are."

Delmar narrowed his eyes at Matheus as he listened intently.

"What are you saying?"

"I'm saying that in all the time we've been stuck in this oppressive nightmare we've never learned a thing about our enemies from the Outside. Well, Delmar, now we have one."

Delmar suddenly stood up straight and looked around them as if to ensure that they were alone up here.

"You're suggesting we study him?" he said under his breath.

"No," Matheus shook his head. "I'm suggesting we employ him."

"Employ him?" Delmar questioned. "You would use him as a weapon against the Domineers? See him trained to fight?"

Matheus hesitated for a second. That was the same concern he had shared with Rowan when she first pitched the idea to him.

"Not necessarily," he clarified. "Simply learn what we can from him. We should have him tell us all about the ways of the outsiders. Haven't we established already that he is neither with us nor against us? Actually, I take that back; he seems to be on our side more than that of his own kind."

Delmar took a quick glance outward from the tower. This was somewhat out of place for the Matheus he knew.

"It's interesting," he muttered. "And this was your idea?"

Once again, Matheus was found to be hesitating, as if searching his thoughts carefully.

"Y-yes," he stammered. "My idea. In fact, I've already learned more than enough from talking to him to convince me that there are ways that he can help us in our dire time of need-"

"Then why don't you just follow him out into the world while you're at it!" A loud voice stormed the atmosphere from behind Matheus. He turned around abruptly to see Malachai returning to the top of the tower. He appeared to be quite exhausted from training in the arena; he was breathing heavily and his hair was soaked with sweat. This was surely a confrontation that Matheus was hoping to avoid.

Malachai pointed at Matheus the wooden training sword that he still held in his hand.

"I never would have expected that sort of thinking from you, Matheus!"

"Maybe it's because you still have a great deal to learn about me," Matheus responded hotly, "Malachai."

Malachai's attention suddenly moved past Matheus and right to Delmar.

"How can you be considering this?" he asked in a tone that was almost panicky. "It was a grave mistake to ever bring that scum into the Citadel. If it was me who found him alone out in our territory I would have done away with him like *he* should have!"

"He was not alone, Malachai!" Matheus interjected.

Both of their tempers were undoubtedly rising. Malachai nodded arrogantly.

"Of course he wasn't. Where you found him you found the Domineers also. How in your wildest dreams did you come to the conclusion that the boy did not belong to them?"

"Because they did not know who he was either!" Matheus yelled at his accuser. "He's too young to be one of their fighters.

"Dammit, Matheus!" Malachai was enraged. "The attack on Ravenna was five years ago; many of the Domineers involved were almost just as young. But you wouldn't know that because you weren't there!"

"I know the juvenile well enough to know when they're telling the truth!"

"ENOUGH! Both of you!" Delmar shouted. Most of the time, Delmar was no stranger to keeping his emotions in check, but he efficiently silenced the two of them with such a thunderous roar of authority. Both Matheus and Malachai froze and silently gazed at Delmar like children in the presence of their angry parents. "This bickering is pointless! Do not allow the presence of one boy to consume you," he looked past Matheus in particular. "Especially you, Malachai!"

Malachai seemed as though he wanted to open his mouth to defend himself, but suddenly fell silent and lowered his head. Even now, he was feeling anything but a sense of humility. For a brief second he almost felt the thought rush through him that Delmar may have trusted this treacherous outsider over his own closest friend. However, he quickly expelled that idea, knowing very well that Delmar never put the wellbeing of their people second to anyone else.

Matheus turned his attention away from Malachai and back to their leader.

"What do we plan to do about him then? If you don't mind me asking."

Delmar paused and seemed to be thinking deeply about the situation. He gave a quiet sigh and looked outward again.

"You shouldn't let Rowan's feelings get the better of you, my friend."

Matheus' eyes widened.

"Rowan's feelings?" he stammered. "No, I-"

"Matheus," Delmar cut him off. "I think I know my sister well enough to recognize her words."

Now he too was lost for words. Thoughts were suddenly running through Matheus' head, things that he had not contemplated before now; what was Rowan's purpose for making this request to him? Why were her feelings so strong for the outsider, despite all the loathing she harbored inside because of what they had done to them? He was beginning to question Rowan's motives, even though he still found himself agreeing with her; the boy could be useful.

"Exactly my point," Malachai interjected. "That Outsider is already taking advantage of the minds of our youth! Rowan is too young to consider what is best for our people. She should never be exposed to his kind!"

"Do you hear yourself right now?" Matheus shook his head in disbelief.

Malachai tried to ignore his comment.

"What would your father do about this were he here to understand our situation?" he asked Delmar.

Keeping his cool was beginning to become difficult, as even his closest friend was starting to pull his trigger.

"Malachai!" Delmar responded harshly. "Let my father rest. He's already seen more than enough and paid the price for it."

Malachai lowered his head, realizing just how far his words were going.

"I'm-" he breathed roughly, "I'm sorry."

"That's a first," Matheus mocked under his breath.

Delmar sighed and approached the two of them.

"I think you both know that arguing amongst ourselves is not going to solve any of these issues."

"Well, what do you believe about the boy?" Matheus asked intently.

"Personally," Delmar thought for a moment, "I think it's clear that he certainly poses no visible threat to us. He learned that firsthand when he first tried to run," he said, referring to Alex's previous reckless attempt to escape his captors.

"That only tells me that he would try it again," Malachai argued, "and if we're not careful, he could run to the Domineers and tell them everything he's seen here. If that were to happen then our final refuge would be compromised. How long do you think we could hold against the entirety of Moreno's retribution?"

"That is not going to happen," Delmar replied confidently. "Look, it is still far too early to know for sure what our best course of action is regarding the outsider. In truth, and I cannot believe I am saying this, I agree with Matheus," he said, gesturing his hand toward him.

Malachai's jaw dropped.

"You what?" he breathed, shocked by Delmar's apparent stance. "How can you say that? You want to make use of that boy?"

"I don't know!" Delmar retorted. "All I'm saying is that all this stress is meaningless right now. If we allow ourselves to become so consumed by the idea of this one boy entering into our plight then we risk our people as a whole failing to fear and concern. For the time being, I think it wise to simply let the boy be. Let him rest and gather his thoughts, the same goes for us as well. I agree with Matheus when I say that if Alex Lee is allowed to feel comfortable, then the more he may be inclined to cooperate and the less we will have to deal with insecurity. Is that understood?"

Malachai was still heated up inside, that much certain. Both Delmar and Matheus knew that there was hardly any chance that his mood toward Alex would ever change. If that was to be the case then all Delmar was requiring of him was that he maintain his distance from the boy keep his volatile, hostile resentments to himself. Of course, despite all of the angry thoughts which Malachai felt the right to have toward all outsiders, his loyalty to the chief still came first, as he lowered his head again in reluctant compliance.

"I understand," he muttered just loud enough to be heard.

Delmar nodded in approval as he turned his attention back to Matheus.

"I've already given him quarter," anticipating Delmar's thoughts, Matheus referred to the tent-like structure where he had left Alex and Rowan. "I thought it best to allow him solitude so as to keep him distant from the others while still under our watchful security."

"Very good," Delmar replied. He reached over and placed a hand on his shoulder. "I know I've been asking a lot from you, Matheus, but I want to keep an eye on the boy. Stay near to him. If he should have any questions, any concerns, be there to answer. I'll be counting on you to make sure he does not feel unwelcome as long as he remains here."

Matheus nodded his head, but even he was still unsure about the future.

"I'll do what I can."

Malachai just grunted in disbelief. Not wanting to be a part of this conversation any longer, he turned and stormed off. Delmar knew that the next few days would be trying, as he attempted to juggle the needs of his people with securing their future, if they had a future at all. Only time would tell for sure, and until then he knew that he had to keep his eyes open at all times; focused intently on the boy, on Ranger, and most of all, on his sister.

Interlogue -
Alex and Rowan

What am I doing?

The day wore on and night came with the warm, soothing breeze of the zephyrs from the west. Alex struggled to drift off to sleep on his roughly sewn mattress, covered by a single thin sheet, in the personal confines Matheus had given him. The Citadel had grown quiet and all Alex could hear before was the soft chirping of crickets in the distance. This was the most peace he had been allowed to have in the past thirty hours, yet it seemed like more than an eternity.

He still had no idea what sort of fate lay in store for him here, but bigger questions remained on his mind. Though he couldn't sleep, Alex closed his eyes and allowed his mind to wander. He did not know what to think of these people. No one had yet given him an actual explanation of their seemingly dire situation, but Alex could see just from looking around how devastating an effect it was having on them. He remembered his first encounter with Matheus; an expert swordsman swooping down from the trees and laying waste to several adversaries at once. He hardly showed them any respect.

Though Matheus seemed to lighten up toward Alex significantly, there was Malachai on the other end of the spectrum. It did not take much observation to understand that Malachai absolutely despised Alex. He had never done anything to wrong him, and therefore nothing to instigate such hatred. It only made Alex question the nature of their enemies even more, these "Domineers". Who were they? Where did they come from? Why were they here?

Balancing the views both Malachai and Matheus had toward Alex, Delmar appeared to show no real concern for him. It was Alex's understanding that Delmar was the leader of these people. However, it was quite obvious that that title went far deeper than a simple position of authority. In all his life he had never seen people as loyal and dedicated to a leading figure than this man. True it was that Delmar was prepared to put anything and everything second to protecting the people who looked to him for leadership. That would earn him a great deal of respect from Alex.

Rowan; she was different. Alex did not know what it was, but she had been the one to look at him differently than anyone else he had met here so far. While some looked at him with interest and curiosity, others would stare him down with looks of hate and suspicion. It was almost as if these people were split in their views of him by those of Malachai and Matheus; those who were fascinated by him, and those who would probably like to see him dead.

Yet then there was Rowan. Personifying neither the end point of either perception of Alex nor the fulcrum balancing the two, Rowan seemed to have something else on her mind. When she looked at him, it was as if she was looking past him, like she was peering into his soul. Not in an intimidating or threatening manner, but rather like was searching for something within him, but what did she see? She was the younger sister of Delmar; fourteen-years-old, just like Alex. An instant compare and contrast had hit Alex: he had a younger sister of his own, but the difference was that Delmar showed unending desire to keep his sister safe from harm in their darkest hour, and Alex realized all of the recent years he had spent practically neglecting his only sister. Above all, that was something he desperately wanted to change, if he ever got out of here in one piece.

He was so deep in sleep now, having strange dreams flashing through his mind of the 18th century ancestors of Rowan's people. He never registered the soft sound of the tent's cloth flap moving away, nor did he hear the light footsteps approaching his side. His subconscious mind began to warn him that someone was near, but before he could react any further he felt a hand cover his mouth and he froze.

"*Shhhhh,*" a soft voice quietly urged him to remain silent and calm. The hand was slowly removed from over his mouth. As his eyes began to adjust to the darkness he was eventually able to make out the outline of a female figure kneeling next to him.

"R-Rowan?" he muttered tiredly. He could barely see her, but he knew he somehow recognized the soft tone of her voice.

"I'm sorry," Rowan whispered, "I didn't mean to wake you."

"No it's fine," Alex replied, rubbing his eyes. "What is it? Is something wrong?"

"No," was Rowan's simple response. Alex was a little confused as to why she was here right now. "Are you comfortable?"

Alex hesitated briefly. "Yes," he answered plainly, "thanks."

"Glad to hear it," Rowan responded ever so casually. She made a quick glance back toward the tent flap. "Come with me."

Alex raised his eyebrows.

"What?"

"I need to talk to you," she explained. "Please, we have to hurry."

Before Alex could answer, Rowan stood up and exited his tent. For a moment, Alex was not sure if he wanted to move or if he should do as she said. Rubbing his eyes once more, he pulled himself to his feet. He was a bit dazed at first, and his eyesight was bouncing in and out of focus in the darkness, but eventually he composed himself and headed outside.

Rowan stood just outside of the tent flap and was staring toward the outer wall. She seemed to wait for a moment before acknowledging Alex's presence.

"What are we doing?" Alex asked, almost impatiently.

"You'll see," Rowan gave yet another vacant response. "We have to be quick. Come on!" Without another moment's pause, Rowan grabbed Alex's hand and ushered him away from his tent. At first, Alex thought she was preparing to lead him out toward the Citadel's gate, but to his surprise she instead turned around and quickly made for the smaller wall which surrounded the tower.

Alex saw no other option but to simply follow her. She was moving fast, but Alex quickly caught up with her. Rowan glanced back at him.

"Stay low, Alex," she whispered, gesturing for him to keep his head down so as to avoid drawing attention. "There are guards on the walls."

Heeding her advice, Alex lowered his stature. Even in the darkness it would amazing if anybody were to see them at first glance. However, Alex was very careful to keep her strides from becoming too loud and distinguishable, but the deathly silence of the night only made it all the more difficult. Rowan, on the other hand, moved ever so swiftly and stealthy like a deer.

The two of them continued until they reached the base of the wall. Rowan stood with her back up against it and Alex did the same. Looking up above him, he realized that in this position it would be improbable for anyone atop the wall or farther up the tower to see them. His mouth hung open, allowing him to gather his breath as quietly as possible. Rowan was as calm and confident as ever. Whatever it was that they were doing, she must have done it quite often.

Rowan signaled for Alex to keep following her as she made her way alongside the wall. It was not long before they suddenly came to an opening in the wall; the large archway which led to the base of the tower structure. Unlike the outer wall of the plateau, there was no gate here. Rowan halted and carefully peered around the corner. Immediately after she quickly crept to the other side of the gateway and was gesturing for Alex move quickly. He hesitated as he also peaked around the corner cautiously.

"Come on!" Rowan breathed impatiently. Forcing himself to throw aside his worry, Alex rushed across the opening, hoping nobody saw him in the process. Where was she taking him that she was in such a hurry and so careful not to be detected? Alex continued asking himself this as they moved forward along the wall. As it continued to curve around the tower, Rowan began glancing back up to the top of the wall. Certain that no one was around this part of the wall to spot them she swiftly made a quiet run for the outer wall now. At this point they had traveled nearly halfway to the back of the tower and the distance between the two walls was significantly shorter. As Alex followed he looked around at the wall behind. Sure enough there no guards of any sort keeping an eye around this area. To him that seemed like something of an oversight. What if by some chance their enemies scaled the walls at the blind sides? They would never see it coming.

As they reached the outer wall, Rowan knelt down before it. Alex was quite certain that here there was absolutely no chance anyone would be able to spot their dark figures splotched against the shadow of the walls and shielded by the shroud of night. He knelt down near Rowan to see what it was she was doing. Propped carefully up against the wall were two large slabs of rock. They leaned there casually, but as Rowan slowly moved them both to the side they revealed behind them a small opening broken into the wall. Alex peered over her shoulder to get a glimpse of the hole, and it did not take long for him to realize that she was sneaking them outside of the fortress.

"Rowan?" he muttered to her in a soft tone. She looked around at him. "What are we doing?"

"I told you already," she replied with a grin, "you will see." The hole went at a downward angle and Rowan turned herself around and began lowering herself into it. "Just do me a favor and move those rocks back in place as best you can once you get in here." Without waiting for him to answer, Rowan continued backing into the hole.

Alex shook his head, still unsure about what was really going on. Once Rowan was out of the way he too lowered himself into the hole. When he was in far enough he reached out and pulled one of the large rock slabs over the entrance. They were certainly heavier than they looked, but Alex was able to slide them back into place. It almost made him wonder how a fourteen-year-old girl was able to do this so easily. Just when he thought it couldn't get any darker than the night, his vision inside the hole was reduced to nothing once the rocks were covering the mouth again. He slowly backed his way through the narrow confines of the tunnel. He wanted to be careful not to run into Rowan, but for all he knew she was probably out on the other side by now. The intense darkness of the tunnel was not so bad, at least not when Alex felt his feet coming out the other side. As he back his way out, he started to stand himself up once outside. He looked up in front of him and sure enough they had come out just on the other side of the wall. They were outside of the Citadel.

Alex backed up a step and turned around. He let out a loud gasp as he saw what was now right in front of him, and he realized now that there was absolutely no chance any of their enemies could ever breach the Citadel's wall here. Just in front of him the ground suddenly dropped away into a steep cliffside. The cliff dropped so far down that Alex could not see the bottom in the middle of the night. One more step back and he would have fallen right down into the abyss below him. The sudden sight scared him so much that could feel his balance faltering.

A hand quickly pressed against his chest and pushed him back against the wall. Alex caught his breath and saw Rowan just beside him, holding him back. He looked over at her with wide eyes which displayed a significant amount of shock as he breathed heavily.

Rowan stared back into his eyes.

"Watch your step," she said calmly.

Alex was completely baffled by her strange sense of humor.

"Thank you!" he muttered sarcastically.

"Did you put the stones back?" she asked, ignoring his astonishment. Without waiting for him to give an answer, she continued, "then we won't be followed." She then turned to walk off. The strip of cliffside that they were now standing on sloped down around the tall body of the mountain plateau, almost like a natural staircase eroded into the rock. Alex was utterly amazed by all that he had seen in this place. However, at this point he was not sure he wanted to know where this girl was taking him.

She led him down the narrow slope around the plateau. Alex could still barely see in the dark, but he kept his back against the mountainside and tried his best not to look down again. "I'm not so sure about this." He stammered, trying to avoid hyperventilating.

"Relax," Rowan replied ever so coolly. "This is how I sneak out of the Citadel."

That was not so reassuring to Alex.

"I hope you don't come back up the same way."

"Of course not! I come back through the front door, usually after the sun rises."

"Uh-huh," Alex mumbled under his breath. As they continued winding around the cliffside, Alex looked up and could vaguely make out the natural land bridge far above them which connected the fortress to the surrounding mountains. When they were almost directly under the land strait, the narrow slope suddenly opened into a hillside which formed the base of the mountain. Feeling much better now that they were practically on the ground again, Alex caught his breath. "But why do you want to sneak out? I don't understand."

Rowan leaped from the slope and onto the hillside, stumbling slightly as she steadied herself. "Because my brother does not allow anyone to leave the Citadel without his permission. But he never lets me leave anyway. This is the only way I get to roam the home that used to be a part of my life before it was taken from me."

Alex continued to follow her, as usual. Her sentiment had once again hit him in the deepest chambers of his heart, even though he still nothing because nobody would share the information with him. At this point he was just going along for the ride. Or maybe there was a reason she refused to speak to him about it.

"Then is that why we snuck out in the middle of the night?" he asked, hoping this would go somewhere.

"Of course not," Rowan bluntly answered. "That would be against Delmar's command; you're not to be set loose into the wild until further notice."

Alex abruptly stopped in his tracks.

"Well, that just- what?" He was more than utterly perplexed by Rowan's words. Here he thought for a moment that, while he was trapped in unknown territory, nearly losing his mind in the process, Rowan would be sneaking him to the edge of their borders so he could finally get out of these God-forsaken mountains; but did she just blatantly tell him that she could not let him go because it would go against their leader's will, at the same time she was currently breaking them both out regardless? The logic had blown Alex's mind so much that he just could not keep it to himself. "What kind of hypocrisy is that?" he blurted out. "How can you say that?"

Rowan too stopped where she was and turned around to face Alex. She slowly stepped toward him, staring him the eyes the whole time.

"Because, Alex," she began in a serious tone, "there are two kinds of people up there in that tower: there is Delmar, our new chief, the one who led us from chaos in our darkest hour and built a new life for us in the Citadel, and he deserves all of our respect and loyalty. And then there is my brother, and my brother is not my keeper."

Alex tried to think of a proper response, but that short speech traveled right into his head and began to overcome him.

"What's the difference?" he muttered roughly.

For a brief second, Rowan glanced away, as though she was being made to consider Alex's statement, but she was quick to return her gaze to him.

"The light," she whispered her response. Without another word, she turned to head deeper into the woods. Alex quickly followed, not wanting to find himself lost in the nighttime mountains at any given moment.

His eyesight had greatly improved after about a half hour of hiking through the woods again. Despite that, walking around the mountains at night was absolutely terrifying, but it was at a little bit better tonight since he was with someone. Alex's eyes were darting back and forth at the darkness as if he was expecting to see something truly horrifying, but Rowan hiked serene and completely unfazed by the dark.

Alex caught up to her and walked by her side as best he could.

"Rowan, we've been walking forever now. I thought you said you needed to talk to me. Why couldn't we do this back up at the Citadel?"

Rowan just continued to lead him down the mountain paths. Her ability to navigate the mountain paths was absolutely flawless.

"Not exactly," she replied. "To be honest, I want to teach you something."

He was not quite sure what to make of that statement.

"What is it, Rowan?" he persisted. "Please, talk to me! What are you trying to do?"

Rowan put her hand up to silence him.

"We're close," she said under her breath.

"Close to what?" As they reached the lowlands of the mountains, Alex began looking around. He noticed the area they were coming to was becoming cluttered with mountain laurel and rhododendron bushes. Their thick, wavy branches were numerous and allowed the bushes to stand up so tall that it would have been nearly impossible to see through them. The canopy of the tree tops was starting to break apart and the faint light of the moon and the stars began penetrating through to the ground. It made Alex's surroundings much more visible, and he was feeling a little less anxious of the dark of night.

"I think you're gonna like this place, Alex," Rowan said as they began zigzagging through the clusters of the mountain brush. "No outsider has ever seen it in our lifetime."

"Why is that, I wonder?" Alex asked, mainly to himself. As the two of them wound throughout the brush, he was absolutely amazed by Rowan's seemingly photographic knowledge of these lands. Alex would have gotten himself lost in seconds, but she navigated so flawlessly. And where the hell was she taking him? He did not know whether he should be worried or if he could remain calm.

Rowan rounded a corner on the thin path through the brush and stopped where she was. She stared out for a brief moment and then turned toward Alex and smiled. "Because outsiders cannot find this place on their own." With that, she stepped aside and allowed Alex to come forward. The brush suddenly opened up and separated, and Alex's eyes adjusted even more he gasped when he saw the sight before him.

"Holy God..." he muttered, his mouth hanging open. The sight he saw before him looked like something that could only come from some sort of fictional story. Previously, the two of them had hiked down into a low trough between the mountains. At this point, just passed the large cluster brushes, the trough had suddenly opened up into a natural basin of some sort. Alex had never seen anything like it before. The large opening at the tree canopy level allowed the light of the moon and the stars to just pour into the area. The effect this change of light had Alex's eyes made his surroundings appear much brighter and he could examine this basin very clearly.

Two small, river-like tributaries flowed from the walls of the encircling hills like a spring; one poured forth from Alex's left, the other at the side of the basin opposite from where he stood, and the two of them flowed downward and met at the center before falling over the edge of a great cliff which overlooked the mountain ranges in the distance. They flowed rather rapidly, and the nighttime light shined off of them remarkably, as it also reflected off of the abundant plant life surrounding the area. It was truly a beautiful sight that filled Alex with a wondrous sense of serenity and peace. The sound of the water was so calming, even in the chilling dark of night.

Sitting just next to the eroded point where the rushing streams intertwined was a very peculiar looking tree...or trees? Alex examined it with interest; the tree began with a single trunk at its base, but it seemed to split only about six inches above the ground into four separate trees which appeared to wind around each other as they rose up high. It only added to the strange but remarkable beauty of the plant life all around the area. The moonlight shining off the water also reflected around the variety of flora in such a mesmerizing manner that the entire basin almost appeared to display a hint of bioluminescence. Alex knew that had to be impossible. Bioluminescence did not exist in any form of plant life in the Appalachian Mountains. Whatever Rowan's secret place was, it had an impressive effect on Alex's mind.

Rowan took a few steps into the area.

"Our ancestors called it the Oasis," she said to Alex as he followed. "A secret place. I used to come here all the time as a young child; sometimes just to get away, other times when the summer days were hot." She knelt down and put her hand in the stream, allowing the water to rush around it. "I love the water."

Alex stepped up beside her at the edge of the water. He inhaled the fresh air around him as the soft, cool spray of the rushing streams hit his skin. The great feeling of tranquility, he had never felt anything like it before. In truth, it felt like more than mere peace of mind. There was something else.

"You feel it, too?" Rowan interrupted his thoughts. "It's

almost like there's a...presence; something in the air that makes you feel like there's nothing to truly be afraid of."

Opening his eyes, Alex knew exactly what she meant. It was like the two of them were not really alone here. He nodded to himself.

"What is it?" he asked her.

Rowan took a quick glance over at the strange tree near the center of the Oasis.

"I'll show you," she got up and headed light-footed across the damp river rock surface and over to the winding tree cluster. Alex followed and began examining the tree up and down.

"This is one of the strangest trees I've ever seen," he muttered as he placed a hand on it. The bark was wet from the constant spray of the streams.

"Most of us call it the Twisted Oak," Rowan responded to him. "Its growth pattern was altered by the waters that sprung from the mountains into the Oasis. But look more closely." Rowan guided Alex's attention with her hand to the space between the trees. As he looked around he noticed that there was something carved into all four trees. On two of the twisting oak trees positioned opposite from each other a series of small circles were carved into the bark. Each tree had six circles cut away in a hexagonal formation. On the other two adjacent trees were six more circles carved in the same manner, except these shapes appeared to be painted black.

Alex was unable to understand any meaning behind this.

"Is this what you wanted to show me?"

Rowan turned and walked back toward the edge of the water and knelt down again.

"Alex," she began, now in a serious tone, "my people have always been very intuitive of the beliefs of our ancestors. Everything I know of where we came from I learned from my grandmother, the one who made this necklace for me. Though I don't know everything, there are two divine figures that appeared in the old stories that she told me as a child," Rowan looked back at Alex. "The Twins, they were called in the common tongue; represented by the markings on those trees."

Her statements made Alex take another look at the symbols on the Twisted Oak. They appeared to be the exactly the same, but with one key difference: one series was darker than the other. He thought for a moment as the understanding was coming to him.

"So, they're opposites or something?" He said aloud.

Rowan smiled.

"You're very smart."

Alex approached Rowan and sat down beside her by the waterside. Somehow, he was finding himself interested.

"If they're opposites," he began, "what do they balance between each other?"

Rowan seemed to ponder his question for a moment. She cupped her hands and gathered a handful of water from the stream. Small droplets escaped from between her fingers. All of the water around him was beginning to induce thirst in Alex, as Rowan had been leading him around the mountains all night. Seeing her do this, Alex reached down and gathered water in his own hands and brought it to his mouth to drink. Though, most of it had fallen through his hands, the water was cold and tasted absolutely refreshing.

"Wow!" he exclaimed. "That's the best water I've ever tasted!" Rowan grinned and then released the water in her hands.

"In part of the beliefs of our people," Rowan began again, "the Twins were two of the most revered spirits of our great ancestors, the Seluitah."

"Seluitah?" Alex cut in, surprised by her claim. "That sounds almost Native American to me. Are your ancestors Native American?"

"In part," Rowan shrugged. "Our culture was forged from not just the people of the Seluitah tribes but also the white men who came from the east."

White men who came from the east, as she had put it. As

if Alex wasn't more than bewildered already, Rowan really did have such a minimum knowledge of the world outside the walls of these mountains for her to use such a politically incorrect term. Not that it bothered him in the least.

"The Twins," she continued, as she stood up and began walking elsewhere again and Alex followed, "were spirits that were born from the great deity of the sky; the Sky Woman, as my grandmother called her. The first spirit was born normally, but the second killed the Sky Woman when he burst out from her side."

"Well, that sounds gruesome," Alex muttered to himself. Rowan ignored his comment.

"The Twins' true names have long since been lost to us. The first born was a divine being of light. In particular, my people revered him as the personification of the moon; shining its light down on us when the sun could not shroud the Earth from the darkness. He was the one who aided the power of Mother Earth to give life; empowering us with energy and happiness."

As much as Alex was finding himself even more intrigued by these people he never even knew existed two days ago, this story of ancient gods and spirits was not exactly sitting right with him.

"No offense, Rowan," he spoke up, "but I hardly believe in religion."

Rowan stopped to look him back in the eyes.

"And I'm not trying to tell you what to believe," Alex suddenly felt a bit guilty of the way he had shut Rowan down just then. She turned and continued to lead him away again, but where was she taking him this time? "Besides, I don't think it's my place to make you believe any differently."

Alex followed her to the far side of the Oasis, where the second of the two springs flowed out of the mountainside opposite from where they had come.

"What do you mean by that?" he asked, regarding her previous comment. She seemed to ignore him, and soon became aware of where they were heading. Next to the spring, the hillside had actually split apart and revealed a crevice in the rock just wide enough for a single person to pass through. The passage was so inconspicuous that it could not possibly be seen in the dark except by those who already knew where it was.

Rowan passed through first, disappearing instantly from Alex's sight as she was shrouded by the darkness. Alex quickly followed, not caring where they went as long as he still had her company. As he entered, the light of the nighttime sky and the unnatural reflections of the Oasis' environment quickly evaporated from Alex's peripheral vision. He could barely see his hand in front of his own face. Looking up, the immense clusters of mountain laurel were so cluttered that they formed a natural roof over the small, rocky passageway which completely blocked out the light. Alex was growing increasingly uncomfortable as he stared as hard as he could into the darkness trying to find his guide.

He followed the narrow path for over a minute and soon the rock had expanded away from him and he realized that he was now outside of the Oasis, but the trees and plant life around him were so dense that his sight was still reduced to nearly nothing. And worst of all, Rowan was nowhere to be seen.

"Rowan?" Alex quietly called out as anxiety began to grip him. There was no answer. He had had about enough of this now, and he was starting to feel excessively drowsy, almost like he was hypnotized. "Rowan! Where are you?" He took each step very carefully, as he could hardly see the ground as well. Still she did not respond. "Come on! This isn't funny. I can't see a thing!"

"Don't be a fool, Alex," Rowan suddenly replied from out of the dark.

Alex jumped as he heard her voice. She sounded so close, but he could not tell from which direction her voice had come from. His heart was racing.

"Where are you?"

"You may not be one of us, but even you should know

that wherever there is light, there is also darkness."

He was beginning to feel a sense of nausea well up in his throat.

"I've heard enough of this! Let me out of here!"

"Don't you know where to go?" she responded, confusing Alex even more. "You will if you would just focus."

"What?" he breathed. "What are you talking about?" Alex was not even sure which direction he was facing anymore. He did not know how to get back to the rugged passageway which would lead into the Oasis. He was completely lost in the darkness.

As if that was not bad enough, the sharp sound of a twig breaking behind him made him jump out of his skin. At first he thought it was Rowan, finally showing herself again. Alex whipped around to face the source of the noise, but what he saw before him caused all the blood to drain from his face.

In the brush, no more than twenty feet away from him, Alex found himself staring into a pair of pale, yellow eyes. Alex's jaw dropped and he could hardly breathe. There was nothing else there that he could see, just the eyes suspended above the dark-shrouded ground, like two yellow orbs staring him down.

"Oh my God..." he uttered under his breath.

There was no sound to be heard; just the sound of his quiet, heavy breathing and the rustling of tree leaves. Alex felt as though he were trapped here, just staring back into this frightening sight as the goosebumps completely covered his body. When panic finally gripped him, Alex nearly lost his mind and turned and rushed off into the darkness, his hands out in front of him as he still could barely see a thing. He just had to get away, but he did know where to go. However, that experience did not compare to what he ran into next.

The light improved as the cluster of leaves and branches above him began to slightly recede, but once it illuminated the sight which lie before him, Alex froze in his tracks. From out of the darkness, Alex found himself standing in an open space surrounded by the immense brush. Spread out around the area, Alex was staring at a series of elongated stones standing up out of the ground. The stones appeared to be sorted in a circle pattern, with three larger slabs standing outside of the pattern at the 2 o'clock, 6 o'clock, and 10 o'clock positions. What was even more unnerving was the markings engraved on each of the large stone slabs. Alex recognized the style of the symbols he had previously seen carved into Rowan's locket, as the same were embedded on the surface of each of these stones as well, except these were much more elaborate. Each hexagonal symbol contained an extensive amount of lines and markings covering the space within the shapes' perimeters.

Alex was extremely uncomfortable now. He could not move, he had been so petrified so fast. However, his nerves were slightly calmed by the sound of Rowan's voice speaking up from behind him.

"Relax," she said softly. "It's nothing anymore, just some of the preserved remnants of my ancestors. There's nothing to be afraid of."

Trying to compose himself once again, Alex breathed as lightly as he could.

"What is this place?" he asked in a hushed tone.

"It was once believed to have been an old shrine intended to sate the wrath of the second twin, the darkness." Alex was completely overshadowed by her words now. It all would have sounded completely ridiculous under normal circumstances; hell, it would have been more believable if it had come straight from a public school history book, but Rowan must have been playing with his mind somehow. Her knowledge of these mysterious territories, along with everything she knew about her ancestors who lived so long ago, made this experience all the more terrifying and, dare he believe, real. "Contrast to its counterpart of light," Rowan continued from behind him. "The darkness has been known by my people to do two things whenever it chose to reveal itself: take a life by its own hand, and spare one."

As her voice got closer, Alex quickly spun around to face Rowan, who was now standing before him.

"Why are you telling me this?"

Rowan inched close to Alex, looking right in the eyes the whole time.

"Because," she began, and Alex could see tears starting to build up in her eyes, "the darkness is already upon us. But the light is coming back, too."

The goosebumps covering Alex's flesh did not retreat, but he felt that they were no longer there as a result of fear and anxiety. Rather, he now felt a sense of pity and compassion, and looking into Rowan's eyes made this feeling exponentially strong. Here, standing in front of him, was the image of an innocent culture ravaged and decimated, but she was desperately trying to tell him that there was still hope. Did she want his help? If so, what did she want him to do?

Alex was speechless for a while, but he managed to summon the words from his throat.

"I don't know what you're expecting of me," he said roughly, as he was trying to hold back the tears from filling his own eyes. "You don't know who I am. You don't know the life I've lived up until now. I'm not strong like you, I don't have that kind of good in me."

Suddenly, Rowan did something that Alex never thought he see: she released a single tear from eye and allowed to drop down along her face.

"That's not true, and you know that," she whispered in low tone. "Everyone has both light and dark inside of them; everyone has good and evil," She reached up and placed her hand over Alex's heart, "but all it really takes is one's ability and willingness to find the light within them."

Alex now could no longer resist the tears that were trying to flow from his eyes. He no idea who this girl was to offer him such redemption. He realized he had spent far too many years caring about nothing other than himself, and completely disregarding the lives of those around him, especially his own sister, Nickole. And here he was now, thrown into the most unlikely scenario imaginable; stuck outside of his own life and tossed into the middle of the struggle of Rowan's people. He was having mixed feelings surging through his mind that he had hardly felt before this experience, almost as if there had been something in the water. Despite all of that, Alex was more than overcome. Rowan had found in him a sense of warmth and compassion that he had never felt before. Maybe she was right, this was the time to redeem himself once and for all.

Alex placed his hand over Rowan's, which was still against his heart. He looked her back in the eyes as more tears rolled down his cheeks.

"I found my light," he muttered quietly and placidly. The moonlight helped his eyesight adjust much better now. The two of them seemed to gaze into each other's souls for a while. The darkness that Alex had been forced to endure just moments ago was dissipating from his mind, and they both leaned in and rested their heads against each other's.

Alex closed his eyes, as the drowsiness was the only thing that had not left his system.

"I'm kind of tired," he whispered in his growing exhaustion. As it began to take him over completely, the last thing Alex remembered was standing within the brush, Rowan standing before him, embraced in friendship with the moonlight shining faintly down upon them. It was the greatest sense Alex had ever felt in his life.

CHAPTER FOURTEEN

When Alex opened his eyes, he realized that he was exactly where he had been that night; lying on his patched mattress in his oversized tent structure. The events and images of that night were the first things to begin flashing through his waking mind. He remembered exactly where he was now, in the middle of the Citadel; a mountaintop fortress built and protected by these people who called themselves the Ravennites, after several years of some sort of dire oppression. Though he woke in the same place in which he had fallen asleep just the evening before, it felt like he had been away from here for an eternity.

What happened last night? Alex could recall Rowan disturbing his attempts to fall asleep and sneaking him outside of the Citadel walls. As soon as she had taken him off of the high plateau, Alex had felt as though he were walking into yet another world, seemingly separate from the real world around him. Right now it felt like an elaborate dream that he had woken from. Maybe it was a dream? Alex hazily remembered everything that Rowan had led him into last night; from his astonishing close call on the cliffside just outside of the Citadel's wall, to the peculiar environment of the spring hole called the Oasis, leading up to his alarming experience in the darkness. No matter how hard he thought about it, hardly anything about that night felt real enough to convince him that it had really happened. The number one question on his mind was how, if it were real, he managed to end up back in the Citadel exactly where he had apparently left with Rowan. The last thing he remembered was just moments after Rowan tricked him into getting lost within the vast brush of mountain plant life, at which point she pulled out of him a great sense of emotion that had, up until then, been all but unknown to him in the past.

That was the only thing that contrasted with his idea that it had all been a dream; just the day before, when she had spoken to him by the lakeside here in the Citadel, Alex recalled feeling a strange attraction which he described to himself as, 'no romantic attraction, but instead a sort of pull that he simply could not explain.' Whether it was a dream or not, there was one element which remained with him as he woke now this morning: everything he felt toward Rowan just before his mind had gone blank stayed with him now.

It was true. Upon waking up Alex still felt the sensation of the tears in his system, as he sensed his attraction to Rowan had substantially increased to levels he could barely comprehend; now, he was feeling fueled up with a love for Rowan as a true friend, and not just her but all of her people as well and for this whole new world he had never seen before. What it was he intended to do was still uncertain to him. These past two nights were the longest that he had ever endured in his life.

Alex had no notion of what time it might have been. His typical sleep cycle had been seriously altered; ordinarily he would have woken in his own bedroom moments before the rise of the sun whose red rays would peer in through his window. Here within his shabby tent in the Citadel a faint, white light leaked in through the walls, and Alex lied still and gazed into it. Like a powerful drug, the atmosphere penetrated his being with such wonder and tranquility. Alex pulled himself to his feet. He groaned as he stood up, his legs were so stiff and exhausted from all he had gone through. He took a few deep breaths and stepped outside of his tent.

It seemed like it was really early in the morning. The Citadel was dark with the shade of the mountains surrounding it. The morning fog was much lighter today than it had been before, and looking past the outer walls and into the trees Alex could make out the soft glow of the rising sun, which told him that it could not be much later than dawn. He could see the puffs of his breath as he exhaled and his fingertips were freezing, but Alex felt quite warm and soothed by the balmy spring air. He felt free; as though his mind had been able to start releasing the years of stress and confusion which he had kept piled up inside. Each breath was so fluid and brimming with serenity. Alex's gaze wandered aimlessly as he just stood still and listened to his surroundings; the soft sounds of birds in the distance and the flimsy gusts of the springtime breeze fluttering through the trees, and even the sound of someone gently playing some sort of stringed instrument. All of this was enough for Alex; he closed his eyes and managed a slight smile.

He was so distracted right now, but at the same time he was beginning to know his surroundings very well; well enough that even in his trance Alex was aware of someone heading quietly his way. He did not want to open his eyes just yet, and at first he thought it was Rowan who approached him. Upon reawakening he looked over to see Matheus coming to stand at his side.

Neither one of them spoke for a brief moment, as if the both of them were trying to appreciate the serene atmosphere. Matheus then gave a deep breath and spoke.

"You look well rested."

Alex was still busy feeling the cool gusts of the breeze as they passed by.

"I feel it," he nodded. "I feel so much better." However, it was now that part of him wanted to tell Matheus of his mysterious experience last night but part of him also thought it best to keep it to himself, and yet another part wondered if Matheus had known about it. He was looking at Alex a bit differently today than he had before. Alex looked into his dark eyes and recognized it to be similar to the way Rowan had changed the way she looked at him; before last night Rowan would gaze at him with endless curiosity, but then it would change into a look of pure hope and trust. Now Matheus was giving him a strong look of trial, as if he really wanted to see what lied within the depths of Alex's heart.

Alex could feel his own mood shifting from the mixed feelings he had been enduring for a long time to a new sense of willingness, although he still did not know what sort of future he was truly in for. He turned toward Matheus and the only thing he found himself able to do was repeat himself.

"I am rested," he said a low voice.

Matheus gave a quick nod.

"I imagine you must be hungry, too."

When he said those words Alex immediately felt the returning, intense pangs of hunger, realizing it had been nearly two days since he had eaten anything at all. His body suddenly felt weak and withered as he nodded sheepishly.

"Yes I am," he replied below his breath.

"You'll get used to it," Matheus responded amusingly, patting Alex on the shoulder. "But I understand how you feel, so follow me."

The sun ever so slowly continued to climb over the mountainsides. Alex looked around at the people of the Citadel as he followed Matheus away from his tent; dozens of people going about their business with the walls. There were many fire pits set up in different areas around the plateau, several of which were burning with people gathered around. Just like the day before, many people stopped to take looks at Alex, and again some stared at him with fascination, others with contempt and even potential hate. He almost felt as though he wanted to remain as close to Matheus as possible.

The two of them made their way over to one of the burning pits. More heads rose and turned to look at Alex. Matheus approached one of the men around fire and muttered something to him in the language Alex had heard him use before. The man gave him a quick nod and then turned to reach down at a small, black pan sitting on a rock just behind him. Piled into the pan were a couple dozen loaves of bread. He pulled one of the breads out and handed it to Matheus. He shook the man's hand and then turned back to Alex. The bread loaf was slightly larger than the palm of

Matheus' hand. He gracefully tore it in half and handed one of the pieces to Alex. Again realizing just how hungry he was, Alex grasped the loaf and took a large bite out of it.

Matheus smiled and took a carefully measured bite out of his own.

"Make it last," he said once he swallowed. "We have to keep tight rations."

Alex snickered to himself. He then took a vacant look around the Citadel and at the tower.

"Where's Rowan?" he asked casually.

Matheus seemed to follow his gaze briefly and hesitated to respond for a second.

"She has her own business to tend to."

Feeling a little bit awkward for asking, Alex sat down on the grass near the fire pit and continued to eat his ration. He certainly still had a lot of things on his mind; everything from where he even was right now, to why the people of the Citadel were so afraid and oppressed. Alex hoped that today he might actually be able to learn some valuable information that would make him feel better about remaining stuck here until further notice. An even bigger concern growing in his mind was that, the longer he was here, the more he found himself developing an unexplained motivation to learn everything he could about these people, and to maybe even help them if he could.

A sudden voice spoke up and interrupted Alex's thoughts.

"Are you really from the Outside?"

Alex looked over at the small group of people around the fire pit. One of the people nearest to him had looked over and spoken to him. He appeared to be just a young boy, around several years younger than Alex, dressed just as similarly to everyone else and had long, dark, scruffy hair.

He was just about to answer the boy until a woman sitting next to him reached over and attempted to redirect his attention away. She muttered something in their language, and Alex was quite sure it was meant to deter the boy's own thoughts about him. Although common sense told him to keep quiet and remember his place, he could not help but feel compelled to respond.

"Yes, I am."

The boy's head jolted back toward Alex, his eyes glowing with fascination. The woman beside the boy, whom Alex assumed to be his mother, simply glared in his direction.

"My father says you come from a violent world, and that you don't belong here," the boy replied bluntly.

Alex was actually quite shocked and little bit hurt by the comment. He got the hint from Malachai yesterday that there might be some people here who would not like him, and now here was a young child given the impression that Alex was some sort of dangerous animal. Of course, he knew in his heart that he would never say or do anything to harm these people. How could he possibly make them understand this?

Matheus put a hand down on Alex's shoulder.

"If you're about done, why don't we move on?" Wanting to avoid any more awkwardness, Alex stood up to follow Matheus away from the fire pit. Even as he walked away the little boy's eyes continued to follow him.

When he was sure they were out of earshot, Alex asked Matheus, "What was that about?"

Matheus did not even turn around to acknowledge what Alex had been referring to.

"I told you before," was his response, "you're not going to be well liked by many here."

"But why?" Alex persisted. "If you're not going to let me leave here then I should know."

In a motion that caught him off guard, Matheus halted, turned and planted his hand against Alex's chest. Alex froze and gazed at Matheus' eyes which look as though he was prepared to blast him for being so persistent. However, he surprised Alex when he seemed to immediately calm down.

Letting out a brief exhale, he said, "You really want to know?"

"I want to know why I'm here," Alex replied sternly. "I

want to know what is really going on."

Matheus sighed to himself, a look of deep thought traveling through his eyes.

"Later, Alex."

He was really starting to feel like they were trying to keep something from him. Sure, Matheus had seemed to open up to him a little, even after almost killing him. There was no doubt Rowan was more fond of him at this point than anyone, and her brother, Delmar, clearly trusted him enough to allow him to be walking freely. It was those under the mindset of Malachai which left Alex feeling unnerved; the idea that many within these walls would not care if he lived or died, and not knowing why only made matters more uncomfortable for him.

"Well," Matheus continued, "how about we see what you're made of?"

"What do you mean?"

"Come on," Matheus gestured for Alex to follow him. As they had been walking, he did not realize that Matheus had been leading down toward the large, corral-like area where he had seen Malachai honing his impressive swordsmanship the day before. At his time of day there appeared to be no one training in there, and it was clear that Matheus was interested in observing Alex's own fighting skills, but Alex knew that he was no warrior.

Matheus led him within the fencing of the training corral.

"Matheus, I'm really not a fighter, if that's what you want me to show you."

"Really?" Matheus responded casually as he walked over to a small rack against one of the fenced boundaries and picked up a carved, wood object shaped as a sword. "That's what I said once." He threw the training sword over to Alex. He made a quick attempt to catch it but dropped it clumsily. Matheus snickered and shook his head.

Alex picked up the wooden sword. It was rather light and felt really smooth in his hand. He was impressed, whoever crafted it had really taken great care in their work. Alex gripped the sword in his hands to get a good feel for it. Despite always being one to avoid confrontations, it felt rather empowering to hold a weapon in his hands, even if it were nothing but makeshift trainer hardly capable of inflicting a head wound.

Matheus observed with interest, though it was obvious that he thought Alex to be his inferior by far.

"Do you know how to use one of those?"

Alex pondered briefly.

"What is there to know? You swing it," he joked as he made a swinging gesture with the wooden weapon.

"Is that right?" Matheus jeered. He picked up a training sword for himself and held it before him. "Then why don't you try to strike me?"

"What?"

Without a second's hesitation, Matheus made a swift swing at Alex's sword, knocking it clear out of his hands with little effort. In the same movement he swung his sword around again and stopped it to rest against Alex's throat. Alex's jaw was wide open in shock and his arms surged with goosebumps. He was just thankful there was no actual bladed edge.

"That hesitation killed you, Alex," Matheus scolded him. "Remember what happened to those Domineers?"

Alex composed himself, pushing the sword away from his neck.

"Okay," he replied, heading over to pick up his makeshift trainer, "what do you say we try that again?"

"Agreed. But this time you make the first move."

Alex gripped his sword tight and breathed deeply. He moved in to attack Matheus' sword, but again, in a matter of a few seconds, Matheus effortlessly seized control of the duel. This time he ducked below Alex' attack, and then snatched him by the arm and spun him around to hold him in a complete death grip, again pressing the sword's wooden edge against his throat.

"You're dead again," Matheus whispered in his ear. He

then released him and tripped him intentionally. Alex grunted as he hit the dirt ground. "Do not fall in a fight, Alex," Matheus continued to mock him. "I'm counting that as a third kill."

"Ha-ha," Alex muttered back. He knew he was up against a far superior fighter, but somewhere in his mind he was not going to accept humiliation that easily. Feeling as though he could get the hang of this, Alex jumped to his feet and attempted to charge his opponent. Of course, he knew he should have seen a surprise coming, and it did. Matheus blocked his sword swing without releasing a single breath. He allowed Alex to make another attempt to strike him, and when he parried it away he quickly poised himself and swung his foot up hard into Alex's groin. Alex froze, opening his mouth to cry out but could make no sound. Matheus back away as Alex crumpled to the ground, clutching his aching testicles. Matheus just stood there and watched as Alex was left lying on the ground and moaning in pain, and over his suffering he could hear a girl laughing nearby.

"That's not how you're supposed to fight!" Rowan playfully taunted from the other side of the fence.

Alex pulled himself up to a kneeling position, still holding himself and breathing slowly.

"That was a cheap shot, Rowan."

"No!" Matheus declared, pointing his sword down at him. "There is no such thing as a cheap shot in a fight. There is only resourcefulness. You need to know how to employ it."

Alex glared up at him.

"I have never fought a day in my life," he retorted. He then looked past him and pointed to Rowan. "Why don't we switch this up and give her a shot?"

Rowan raised her eyebrows. Without waiting for Matheus to answer, she quickly vaulted over the railing and into the corral. Matheus said nothing, but a slick grin grew on his face as he took a step back and tossed his wooden sword to Rowan.

To be honest, Alex was not sure that Matheus would even

allow Rowan to engage in such an activity. In fact, he was only partially serious when he opened his mouth. The first thing he found himself thinking was that he really would not have wanted to strike a girl with a weapon, real or fake. As soon as that thought passed he immediately cursed himself for thinking it. Was that really his mental go-to; that just because she was a girl Rowan would not put up enough of a fight? He tried not to show any hint of shame or hesitation as he stood back on his feet, and Rowan twirled her sword around in her hand a couple times.

Alex had already somewhat seen what Rowan could do with a bow, but not with a close combat weapon.

"Why don't you go first?" he said, trying to regain his full composure after the blow he had received from Matheus.

Rowan raised her sword up, pointing it toward Alex. She made a quick thrust toward him with the weapon. For once, Alex found himself prepared as he managed to block the attack with his sword. Rowan moved significantly slower than Matheus had, it was clear to Alex that she must have simply been toying with him. She made a few more attacks, all of which Alex met with a single parry, however, it was not until he made his own attacks that she began to reveal her ability to fight.

Where Matheus had instantly turned Alex's assaults against him, ending the fighting sequence in seconds, Rowan continued to fool with him by deflecting his attacks away and swiftly dodging his swings, forcing him to keep rapidly tracking her down, but she was always one step ahead of him. With each gesture Alex was growing more tired, trying to catch his breath while simultaneously attempting to get ahead of Rowan, but she was too clever. When she had ultimately deemed him exhausted enough she finally made her move. Rowan quickly wound up her arm and swung her sword down against the back of Alex's knee, effectively crippling his balance. This was all she needed to make her killing blow, by regaining her stance and driving the wooden sword at Alex's side.

The point sent a quick jolt through his body.

"Dammit Rowan, that hurt!" he gasped.

"Of course it hurt," Rowan said back in a mocking tone. "I killed you."

Matheus was shaking his head in slight disapproval as Alex stood back up.

"I told you," Alex said with a sigh, tossing his wooden sword to the ground. "I'm not a fighter. I can't just hurt people."

Matheus gave him a hard look, adding to his disapproval.

"Well you better learn. We did not survive these years of hardship by trying to make our aggressors feel 'comfortable'." Alex did not know what to say. He looked over at Rowan, whose expression had gone from one like a child at play to a look of bitter grief.

Alex was lost in a world he had never seen before, being constantly bombarded by mixed feelings and emotions not akin to any circumstances he had ever experienced. He could only look at this girl standing beside him and question the life he had lived so far. She had to be the same age as him, forced to grow up too soon by some devastating element that invaded their lives. With all of these factors surrounding and engulfing him, he seemed to be stuck with the same thought that he felt he needed to answer: what was he meant to do about this plight?

It was such a long day, just as the previous day had been, but Alex was just thankful to be in decent company, so to speak. Together, Matheus and Rowan led Alex around the Citadel, familiarizing him with his new surroundings, and engaging him in different sorts of basic fighting techniques. A training sword was simple enough, but when Matheus had handed him a real one Alex felt a much different sensation. It was crafted from stone, well cared for and chiseled to a fine, sharp edge. It felt significantly heavier in hand than the wooden one he had previously used, and it strained his muscles as he waved it around.

Perhaps the hardest thing he tried today was archery. Rowan took Alex to an open area designated for shooting bows. Shabby targets held together by sticks and branches were set up at different ranges, all displaying a great number of piercings which told Alex that they had been used many times. Rowan had fetched Alex one of the many bows stored in the area that were used for target practice. It was made of a light and flexible strand of yew wood; the string of the bow was tied firm, and the handle was crafted into basic dimensions with a gripping section carved away in the middle. Alex had never held one before. Rowan was armed with her own personal bow. Unlike the trainer Alex held, Rowan's bow was beautifully carved and painted dark, and lined up and down the handle elegant sequential patterns were etched. She had fired each arrow with such proficiency and hit her targets with remarkable precision. Alex was more than amazed, as it was obvious that she had honed such skills for years. He felt as though it had put his own young life to shame, and it only made it worse when he miserably failed to hit a single target with a quiver of a dozen arrows. In fact, it took him several tries to even successfully fire a shot.

At the end of the day, once the sun had set and Alex was quite exhausted again, Matheus led him to another fire pit. This particular site was much smaller and sat nearby the edge of the plateau lake. Rowan still accompanied them as she had all day. The dusk sky glowed a faint red shade as the sun was nearly gone and stars began to appear. Matheus kneeled down by the pit and stacked a small pile of wood and twigs to make a fire. He then took a small chunk of flint from his pocket and struck against a stone he had picked up to spark a flame into the pit. By the time the fire was lit and roaring the sky was dark with night. Matheus sat down across the fire from Alex, with Rowan just beside him. The air was growing cooler at a rapid rate, and Alex moved in close to the fire.

Alex was growing rather tired as he gazed dazedly into the fire. For once, after the day he had, he was beginning to feel that might actually sleep peacefully tonight.

Rowan sat across the fire just beside Matheus. She looked over at Alex, watching the light of the flames dance off of his hard, gray eyes, and wondered what thoughts were really going through his mind in this inordinately decisive moment for him.

Matheus, as he poked around the base of the fire a few times, knew that he was running low on his ability to withhold the truth from Alex. He watched him stare blankly into the fire, and Rowan looked back to him as if she was thinking exactly as he was. Matheus sighed under his breath.

"Do you know why I brought you here?" he asked.

Alex looked up and shook his head.

"No."

The fire was stable and roaring strong. Matheus sat back and positioned himself for the tale he knew he was about to tell.

"You want to know why you're still here?" he said in a tone just over a whisper. "You want to know what's really going on?"

Rowan's attention was shifting between the two of them. Alex briefly caught her eyes and could see that she knew what he was about to be told, and he nodded his head.

"Yes, I do."

Matheus tried to think of the best way to begin.

"I'm not entirely sure where to start."

"Why is it so dangerous for me to leave?" Alex responded. "Tell me that. Tell me what is really out there."

"Your kind," Rowan muttered. Alex's eyes darted to her with a look of inquisitiveness. Rowan glanced up and met his gaze. "Outsiders."

"I know that already," Alex looked back at Matheus. "I want to know what that has to do with me."

"They're the reason why I warned you that so many within these walls are going to hate you," Matheus poised himself for a lengthy speech. "Do you know who we are?" he asked. "Do you know anything about us?"

Alex shook his head.

"I didn't even know anyone existed up here."

This hardly fazed Matheus.

"Our people have lived here in these mountains for many generations. Our ancestors built hidden communities here with the last of the native tribes of the region in the hope of escaping the feared onslaught of the war."

"War?" Alex repeated to himself. He thought for a moment with what Matheus had just told him. "The Revolution?"

Matheus and Rowan briefly exchanged hazy looks.

"Over the years our two societies have made a point of remaining separate from each other. That's probably why you've never heard of us before. We used to have a shaky relationship with the Outside; the vast world beyond our own borders, but we've recently ended that relationship for good."

"Why?" Alex cut in. "What happened between you- or, us?"

"Your governments are greedy and power hungry, that's what happened," Matheus answered rather bluntly. "Whatever their thought process, they did not want us to remain separate from them any longer. They wanted us to assimilate with them, to share with them everything we worked so hard for. You can imagine that did not sit right with us. Our chief, who at the time was Rowan's grandfather, officially stopped the struggle by severing all ties with the Outside once and for all. As of then our people were forbidden from ever being accommodated by the Outside, and vice-versa, of course. This way we remain separate, for the good of both our peoples. Unfortunately, that did not last as long as we had hoped."

"What happened after that?" Alex asked, listening intently.

Matheus leaned down and readjusted the fire again.

"For well over a decade we were at peace without the Outside world interfering with our lives. They held true to their word all that time, and we destroyed all roads and paths leading in and out of our borders. However, about five years ago two young outsiders learned about us, managed to get around the obstructions we created and found the Chief's village of Ravenna, in a great valley in the northeastern region of our territories."

"Two outsiders?" Alex interjected again. "Who are they?"

"Their names," Matheus began to answer as Rowan turned her head to look away. "Are Ramon Moreno, and his younger brother Robert."

Alex observed Rowan's diversion of attention at the sound of their names.

"And they did all of this to you?"

"Actually," Matheus replied, "they were much like you. That's why I told you that you would be looked on with contempt."

Alex shook his head. "I still don't understand. What did they do?'

"At the time," Matheus continued his story, "they were just wanderers from the Outside. They told us of how their world had turned its back on them, and that they had searched us out and were willing to offer their services to us in exchange for one thing-"

"A home," Alex finished for him, speaking on the one thing that came to mind, "a place to sleep, I could imagine."

"That's exactly what they wanted," Matheus nodded. "It was a sad story. Naturally, we could not accept it."

"Why?" Alex did not understand. "If they offered to work just to stay somewhere why would you turn them down?"

"Our laws, Alex," was Matheus' blunt answer. "I told you already, ever since we broke our relationship with the Outside neither of us is permitted to seek refuge with the other. I don't know about the world you came from, Alex, but here our people hold to our commitments with unrivaled devotion. Look, that's not to say that many of us were against welcoming the brothers. I for one thought it would have been a compassionate decision, if my thought would have counted."

"What do you mean? Why didn't it?"

"Because I'm not from the valley village of Ravenna, Alex, unlike Rowan. I was born in the highlands of the south regions led by Darowe, but in my youth I travelled north to the communities near Ravenna. That's where I met Delmar and Rowan, and it's where I spent much of my time after that.

"But that's beside the point," Matheus continued. "The fact is that our newly implemented laws forced us to refuse refuge for the Morenos. The last anyone really saw of them they left the village quiet and disdainfully. Where they went after, I don't know. However, several months later, at the dawn of winter, I woke in the middle of the night to learn that Ravenna had been attacked."

Alex's eyes widened. Rowan looked back over at him and he was shocked to see tears beginning to well up in her eyes.

"Attacked," Alex repeated under his breath. "Are you serious?"

Matheus took a deep breath.

"I saw it," he hissed the words. "Not the event itself, but I saw Ravenna burning that night from atop the vistas. My first thought was the Outside government. However, when we finally rescued Delmar and the remnants of the survivors he informed us that the Moreno brothers had returned with an army." He leaned in closer to the fire. "When we turned them away, Ramon went back to the Outside and gathered some sort of following to help him march back in and take Ravenna by force. And not only the valley; in time they chased us up into the mountains, continued to burn our villages and forced us westward. Eventually, Delmar took his position as Chief and found us sanctuary at the peak of this very plateau."

"Delmar is your leader now," Alex said. "What happened to the Chief before him, his father?"

"No..." Rowan gasped quietly. Alex felt a cold wave rush up his body as he suddenly knew the answer to his thoughtless question.

Matheus and Rowan locked eyes for a moment. She knew that he was preparing delve deeper into the story and cause her to relive the pain it had heaped upon her, but in a way she knew there would be no avoiding it, so she lowered her head into her arms.

Hesitating for a brief moment, Matheus said quietly, "Not everyone managed to escape the burning of Ravenna, Alex. I was not there, but I know that when the attack began only a handful were able to take up what arms they had and fight back. Delmar sent Rowan away to the mountains and joined his father in rushing to defend what was left of the valley, and not only him, but Malachai was there to.

"Within the hour the fight was over, and Ravenna was lost. The Chief fell fighting beside his son. When Delmar tried to avenge him, he was wounded, taking with him a scar which still marks the left side of his face. The last few defenders of Ravenna standing fought desperately to protect Delmar and pull him away from the chaos, and in the end only Malachai was left to help him escape into the mountains."

"And Malachai despises me because I'm an Outsider to you," Alex said.

Matheus had to nod his head in affirmation, knowing it to be true.

"To this day, Malachai remains the only other person alive to have seen the battle that took place in Ravenna. It is because of that experience he has it in his head that all outsiders are evil, whether it's true or not."

Alex wanted to protest such a claim. Though he could not argue with the notion that such evil existed in the world, because it existed everywhere, that did not mean everyone from beyond these boundaries shared the same sort of cruelty. He knew that he could never be capable of inflicting such harm on anyone, but at the same time he could sense it would be a lost cause trying to convince these people of that.

"So they're still here then?" Alex asked over the silence.

Matheus nodded.

"For five years, yes. The Morenos and their mindless followers have completely dominated our territories in the east and they've been slowly attempting to push us out for good. Ever since then we've branded those aggressors as 'Domineers.'"

"Domineers". The word echoed in Alex's head. Now he knew what Matheus had really meant when he ruthlessly slayed the lot of them by the creekside.

"They don't know you're here?" he asked.

"No," Matheus answered. "At least, not that we know. We've been very careful to construct this fortress to be as impenetrable as possible should the time come that Ramon would learn of this location. There is only one way in or out, and that is over the cliffside which forms a bridge between the plateau and the surrounding mountains. The walls around the Citadel are guarded at all times, and the plateau is completely unscalable. I believe it may be our only hope to fight back a massive Domineer attack if it should ever come."

Such thoughts were so disturbing to Alex that, even in the warm company of the fire, he could feel the hairs standing up on the back of his neck. At the same time, something did not seem right about what Matheus had said regarding the Citadel being impenetrable. Just last night, he could still remember Rowan waking him and sneaking him away through a small hole leading onto the narrow cliff edges of the mountain. The thought was still fuzzy enough for Alex to almost believe it had been a dream, but when he looked at Rowan now he could feel the intense emotions that she had brought out of him rising to the surface yet again.

Rowan rubbed her hands over her eyes, and as she did the light of the fire drew Alex's attention again to the patch-like object that she bore on her left arm; on it the hatchet and the sword crossed in an X, just beneath the green arch.

"What is that?" he asked curiously, pointing to the patch.

Matheus followed his attention. Though he could not see the patch from his angle, he knew what Alex had been referring to.

"It's a symbol of hope for the people of Ravenna," he replied. "It was designed after the founding of the Citadel. It bears a tomahawk and a short sword, they were the only weapons that Delmar took with him into the attack at Ravenna. Most of our people keep it, believing that the time will come when we can finally pick up arms again and take back all that was stolen from us."

Alex sat upright as he heard the words.

"So you really do intend to fight back?"

"It's a hope, Alex, nothing more," Matheus rebuked him. "Delmar knows how risky it is. With our people divided and lost throughout the mountains the Domineers outnumber us at least five to one, and more of them are coming in all the time. And what's more is that they are far more organized and competent than you realize."

"And why is that?" Alex asked, almost afraid to know the answer.

Matheus reached into one of the folds of his outfit and pulled out a small object.

"This is why." He tossed the object over the fire to Alex.

Catching it, Alex realized it was another patch. He held it near the light of the fire to examine it. This one was nothing like the one on Rowan's arm. It was a simple design, but it sent a quick chill down Alex's spine. On the face of the patch he could make out what appeared to be some sort of bird, like an eagle or a hawk, burning in a sea of fire. Alex was left utterly speechless.

"That one I took from one of my kills when I found you," Matheus interrupted the silence, "and it's not the only one I've ever seen."

Alex looked up with a look of concern on his face.

"What is this?"

Matheus gave him a quick nod which told Alex that he should already know what it is.

"It's their mark, just like we have ours." He gestured to Rowan's patch. He looked at Alex seriously. "They've organized themselves, Alex. They're ranking each other, and taking great precautions because they are afraid of us. Ramon knows that if we fought back it would result in a devastating outcome for him so he's gone to great lengths to make the Domineers as powerful as possible. We're not ready to fight back yet, and I fear that if we can't do something soon they will eventually find us and overwhelm us. We're all afraid, Alex."

Even after all of that, Alex could not believe that this was possible.

"You can't just let them do this to you," he spoke up. "Get out of here. Take your people and run. Tell the government, my government, what's happening to you here. Tell everyone! I know my world and they would never allow this to happen to anyone!"

Matheus suddenly put his hand up to cut him off.

"We've tried, Alex," he replied. "We have honestly attempted to break our law and seek help from the Outside, but we can't make it out. There is no way out of here, since we destroyed our only paths. We're trapped in our own home. The only way I can think of to get to the Outside is the way you came in, but that's deep in Domineer territory. You only got in unseen as far as you did by sheer luck. We still don't know what would be waiting for us out there, and Delmar will not risk the lives of his people by rushing them into a trap."

Just then, Rowan looked up at Alex again. This time he could see several tear trails running down her face, and she gave him a look that almost said, *"You see? This is truly our darkest hour."*

Matheus took in a long breath.

"Alex," his voice suddenly seemed to shake a little, "this is not going to end well, I think you that. I am not supposed to do this, and I will face a heavy storm for this, but I truly do not want to see you caught up in this fight. Delmar does not want to feel responsible for anything happening to you if he let you walk away, but if you really desire it, I will personally see you out of the Citadel. I could not go with you beyond the walls, but will let you go so that you may find your way out return to the world you came from. I leave that choice up to you."

Alex never thought he would hear those words be spoken. He immediately turned and looked over to the Citadel walls where the gate stood, leading out into the mountains. It was easy now. All he had to do was say yes and Matheus would see him released, though he was not quite sure how he planned to do it. However, even if he did, Alex still did not know anything about the area or the hills surrounding it. If what Matheus said was true, that had removed all passages in and out of the mountains, then the only way out would be the way he came, but there was no way he would be able to find it again, not before he starved to death.

Despite these morbid thoughts, another came to mind which had overshadowed the rest. Alex moved his attention all around the Citadel again and pondered deeply on everything Matheus had told him. For the first time in his life, he felt a great sense of shame would come over him if he were to leave. He had never felt it before, and the more he dwelled on the thought, the more it seemed to fill him with anger. The intensity was beginning to chew him up as he gazed back into the fire. Alex closed his eyes, clenched his fists, and quietly uttered his answer, "No."

Rowan shifted suddenly. Her eyes widened as she heard an unexpected word come from Alex's mouth. Even Matheus found himself surprised to be sure, and somewhat lost for words.

"What did you say?" he muttered.

Alex looked him in the eyes from over the flames and shook his head. Though he could not find the right words to say, he thought to himself, *What are you doing, Alex?* There was nothing else he could do but stare down into the fire pit, listening to the crack of the flames and the distant sounds of coyotes deep in the mountains. He was just as lost as anyone else within the Citadel walls; lost for hope, not knowing what to do or what was going to happen. Every moment that passed by made his thoughts race ever more rapidly and chaotic, and from now on he felt as though he was reduced to instinct, and he knew what his instincts were telling him.

"I'm not going anywhere."

CHAPTER FIFTEEN

November, 2010

Seven months later

More than half a year had passed since the disappearance of her brother, and still Nickole felt herself struggling to move on. It had been the hardest summer of her life. She had been quiet most of the time, spending less time with her friends than ever and preferring to remain isolated at home with her mother as often as she could.

It was not her fault, it was not her fault; that was what everyone kept reminding her, especially her mother. Nickole had spent several days after Alex got separated from them in the abandoned clay mine trembling in her irrational, childlike fear that she would never see him again. That fear, however, was soon brought to life when the authorities were forced to call off their efforts waiting and watching for Alex to make his way out of the boundaries of the Dark Zone. Soon after that, to everyone's horror and dismay, her brother was presumed to be dead, and Nickole was never the same again.

Months had gone by, summer turned to cooler seasons, and when the month of November came around Nickole could feel herself returning to a state of anguish when thinking about her lost brother. It was the middle of the afternoon, on a Sunday, and Nickole was sitting alone out on her front doorstep staring out into the distance. The air was cold and the wind was bitter with the oncoming spell of winter. From her position Nickole could see the face of the lake, its surface painted with a freezing, ice cold cover of blue, the same blue that she once saw in her brother's eyes before they dimmed to gray. The cold, stinging breeze against her face forced Nickole to shed tears from her eyes. Today, of all days, was one that she would have preferred to ignore. November 21, 2010; it would have been Alex's fifteenth birthday.

Nickole had never imagined she would see the day that her brother was no longer with them to celebrate his birthday. As if the feeling had not already consumed her, today only made Nickole realize once and for all that her older brother was gone. First her father whom she never knew, and now Alex. All she had left in her family was her mother. Now she felt truly alone.

The front door behind her opened up abruptly, as Eira looked out at her young daughter sitting alone in the cold.

"Nickole, please come in," she said in a serious tone. "I don't want you getting sick." Nickole only turned her head slightly, not wanting to show her mother her tears. Hesitating for a moment, she stood up and headed into the house, holding her head low.

The warmth of her home was still not soothing to Nickole, as it never had been ever since the incident. There was not much left today for her to do except retreat to her room and wait out the rest of the day until nightfall, and return to school the next day. Though she tried to be quiet while slipping away, her mother suddenly put a hand on her shoulder and stopped her.

"Nickole, wait," Eira began. "Where are you going?"

Hesitating briefly, she replied, "I just want to be alone."

Eira sighed.

"Look, I know it hurts. I really do, and I wish he was still here today more than anything. But you can't keep isolating yourself like you have-"

"No, you don't." Nickole interrupted, pushing her mother's hand off of her shoulder.

Eira stopped her words in their tracks and look at Nickole in astonishment.

"What did you say?"

Nickole did not look directly at her mother.

"You don't know how it feels."

"How could you say that?" Eira was growing increasingly upset. "You are not the only one who cared about him."

"Then why don't you ever think about him anymore?" Nickole fought back.

Eira's jaw dropped.

"I do think about him, all the time! He was my son."

"No you don't! I never hear you talk about him anymore. I think about him all the time and all you do is shame me when I would rather be left alone. You're just trying to forget about him, like you did our father!"

Eira was appalled.

"How dare you!" she breathed shakily. "What is the matter with you?" Nickole felt herself on the verge of losing control, and she quickly retreated up the stairs to her room. Her mother, however, was not willing to simply let her go. "Don't you dare walk away from me, young lady!"

"Just leave me alone!" Nickole called back. She slipped into her bedroom and slammed the door, immediately switching the lock in place.

Eira followed and grabbed hold of the doorknob, but it would not turn.

"Nickole!" she yelled out. "You can be angry with me all me want but you will not treat me in such a way!"

On the other side, Nickole stood firmly against the door. She did not respond nor move a muscle, but just stood there trying desperately to hold back the torrid tears of anger. She never thought that this was how she would spend her brother's first birthday out of her life.

"Nickole," Eira's voice spoke again, this time much calmer, and from what Nickole could hear it sounded as though she was also on the verge of tears, "I'm sorry. I really am." Nickole felt the intense anger beginning to fade away as her mother continued to speak through the door. "Please don't do this to me. The last thing I want is to lose you, too."

Nickole was having trouble breathing properly. She had no

idea what could have possessed her to grow as angry as she did. She was at a total loss for words. Not knowing how to respond, Nickole felt her nerves take over as she turned and shakily opened the door. Though she dreaded the sensation, Nickole found herself locking watery eyes with her mother, and she immediately broke down, lumbered forward and wrapped her arms around her.

Eira embraced her daughter as well. Nickole trembled as she sobbed, until she finally found the strength to speak.

"I'm sorry, Mom," she managed to say.

"No," Eira replied quietly, "it's not your fault, Nikki."

"That's not true," Nickole muttered in response.

Hearing the words, Eira released Nickole and looked her in the eyes, both hands on her shoulders.

"What are you talking about?"

Nickole reached up and rubbed her eyes.

"I-" She stammered weakly, "I never went to my friend's house that day."

Eira thought for a moment to remember what it was she was referring to.

"What?" she said, rather confused. "Yes you did, I picked you up there."

"No, Hetrick took me there later. I lied when I told you where I was going." Nickole could almost feel herself choking on her own words, but she had to let this come out once and for all. "I knew where they were going, Alex and his friends. I knew they were going up into the mountains, and I begged them to let me come along. If I had told you from the start then you would have stopped him from ever going. If it wasn't for me he'd still be here. It is my fault."

Eira had fallen deathly silent. Nickole knew she had planted the nail in the coffin, and she braced herself for what she expected to come next. She knew that she deserved it.

Instead, her mother put her arm around her and pulled her close again.

"Thank you for telling me the truth," she whispered to

her daughter. "I love you, Nikki, and I know you loved him. Please, don't let anyone make you believe that it was your fault."

Miles away, deep within the borders of the Dark Zone in the Adirondacks, the mountains had grown cold with the changing of the seasons and a layer of snow had begun to make its way beneath the tree lines.

Alex Lee was hiking up the wooded hillsides. Seven months had passed since his accidental arrival in the Dark Zone and he had come a long way. He had long since repressed his desire to leave these territories. So many things happened to him over the course of the most extraordinary summer of his life. After his fireside night with Matheus and Rowan, Alex willfully complied with Delmar's refusal to let him go and spent the next few days working on his basic swordsmanship. Though he never managed to hold his own in a friendly duel against Matheus, he certainly improved well enough to earn his respect.

His first few weeks among the Ravennites in the Citadel were rough. Many of these people still looked on him with a harsh mix of fear, contempt and hate. Malachai did his best to avoid Alex as much as he could, but would still give him a loathing death glare whenever he saw him. It was clear that Delmar's command for his people to leave Alex untouched was effective enough. Eventually Alex shed his old, grimy clothes which he had worn since he arrived and was given his own leather garments to wear, and it was after that many of the negative attitudes toward him began to lift. So many things changed the longer Alex remained in these mountains. His fighting abilities continued to strengthen and eventually Matheus helped him to forge his own personal sword, and all the while Rowan tried to pass on her archery skills to him but Alex proved to be particularly weak in that area.

Weeks soon turned to months, and Alex felt a great deal of change come over him. He grew stronger and taller, and his hair also became longer and his eyes slowly regained their pleasant blueish color. He was feeling healthier than he had in years, and this brand new environment was beginning to put the memories of his old home deep within the dormant sections of his mind. Many nights went by when he lied awake at night and thought about the life he was leaving behind. He thought about his sister, Nickole, and how she must have been dealing with his absence. Despite the homesickness he endured in the beginning, Alex grew even more attached this place the longer he stayed, and the longer he remained there the more it became clear that he was not going to be leaving for a while; and he willingly accepted that.

Now it was the middle of November. The trees were totally shed of all of their leaves and the once green and luscious summer hills had become a beautiful snow laden wilderness. Alex was captivated by the elegance of the wintertime mountains as he walked. During the early weeks of autumn, as Alex had become increasingly loyal to his new, temporary haven, the Ravennites also began to feel their spirits lift, as though they could sense a growing rise of hope. It was at this time that Delmar cautiously agreed to open the Citadel gates and begin expanding reconnaissance efforts around the area. With every day that passed the Ravennite scouts went further away from the Citadel. At first they found no signs of any Domineer activity around their proximity, which gave the Ravennites a much needed sense of relief. However, as they started scouting many miles out they began to come across several small Domineer parties patrolling the north. By Delmar's command, the Ravennites were instructed to keep the slaughtering to a minimum out of fear of a possible direct retaliation from the Moreno brothers. Eventually, they managed to clear all of the Domineer spies within a ten mile radius of the Citadel.

With hope and morale quickly beginning to rise, Malachai sought approval from Delmar to establish a small outpost near the borders of the mountains which directly surrounded the Citadel. By doing this, it was his hope to continue to expand their resources throughout the Dark Zone and eventually flush out the Domineer forces in the northern territories, wherever they might be hiding. It was now time to fight back.

In time, Alex had finally been trusted well enough by the Ravennites to be allowed to assist his companions beyond the Citadel walls, much to Malachai's loathsome disapproval. When Alex arrived at the outpost it had already been constructed; it sat within a large open clear cut surrounded by the trees, with a small stone wall built around it which stood only about four feet high and was still being secured. Many tents and shelters were erected within the walls and campfires were set up all around the area just like they had been back in the Citadel. At this point, the outpost was occupied by several dozen armed Ravennites, with more preparing to arrive in the near future. Alex was thoroughly impressed by their efforts to finally start making a stand against the outsiders who had oppressed them for all this time.

Alex had made himself at home in the small Ravennite camp and spent the first few days sticking close and continuing to practice with his own personal stone sword. Today, however, was no ordinary day. The Ravennites employed the same Gregorian calendar that most of the world in the Outside used, and Alex knew today to be his fifteenth birthday. For some time now there had been no suspicious activity of any kind to report around the outpost, so Alex decided he wanted to simply slip away for the afternoon just to be by himself and gather his thoughts.

It was a cold, autumn day as Alex hiked around the snowy hills between the Ravennite outpost and the Citadel, but the sun still felt warm and inviting as it dominated the cloudless, blue sky. He spent about a little over two hours wandering in and out of the trees, stopping only to rest and to admire his elegant surroundings. With the exception of the conflict with the Domineers, which he was still being introduced to, Alex felt as though he were at peace here in these mountains, with a people that he could almost call family more and more with each day that passed.

As he neared the peak of the hillside on which he had been rambling, Alex stopped for a moment and leaned back against a tree to catch his breath. He could feel the stress of the cold air within his throat and the exercise was really warming him up. Alex closed his eyes for a second and continued to breathe deeply, but a sudden, quiet sound in the near distance caught his attention. Reacting purely on the instincts he had been learning, Alex reached for his stone sword which sat in a scabbard on his back and swiftly spun around to point it downhill at the source of the sound.

A figure had been following Alex's footsteps in the snow, dressed as another Ravennite. The character stood about thirty feet away from Alex, resting their shoulder against a small tree and simply looked back at him. Around the neck, the stranger wore dark gray, silk scarf which also extended up into a hood over their head. Alex smiled, though, as he could clearly see who it was that had joined him out here.

"Take it easy, Alex," Rowan laughed as she reached up and pulled her hood back.

Alex regained his composure.

"I'm just working with what you've all been teaching me, that's all," he replied calmly, returning his sword to its sheath. "What are you doing out here?"

Rowan smiled and walked casually over to Alex.

"My brother has gained a bit more peace of mind lately ever since we've claimed a stronger foothold around the Citadel. Now he's finally letting me wander beyond the walls, you know, without me having to sneak out, of course."

Alex laughed to himself.

"So you came looking for me?"

"Sort of," Rowan shrugged, "I just wanted to see how you've been doing out here, make sure everything is okay. I know Malachai is still not quite fond of you."

"You can say that again," Alex huffed. "I do my best to avoid him when I can. I'm sure he's got his own problems to deal with, like keeping the campsite together."

Rowan nodded in agreement. As they talked she took her chance to get a good look at Alex now, and realized just how far he had come since his first days being stuck inside the Citadel walls. He finally looked as though he belonged, and not just physically but she could also see in his eyes how much he was becoming acclimated to this sort of life which he had never known before.

"Can I see your sword?" Rowan asked. "Just for a moment?"

"Sure," Alex unhesitantly removed his sword again and handed it to Rowan. She held the sword by the hilt with both of her hands and scanned her eyes over it very thoroughly. She then ran her hand ever so lightly up and down the stone blade.

"This is a very good sword," she said to herself, handing it back to its owner. "You're taking great care of it."

Her comment made Alex admire the weapon even more.

"It's really all I have out here." He gripped it in his grasp, which always gave him a great sense of strength. "I practice with it every day now, or whenever I get the chance."

Rowan grinned in approval, but not long before her look shifted to one like that of a mischievous child. She took a few steps back and then she swiftly produced the stone sword which hung in a sheath at her side. Alex jolted as his attention was drawn to her. Rowan stared him down, the sword she held sturdy between the gazes of her hard, green eyes.

"Why don't you show me then?" she taunted him.

Alex glanced from Rowan to the sword in his hand, and then back to Rowan.

"You mean with real swords?" he questioned. "You can't be serious!"

"What's the matter?" Rowan teased. "Afraid I can still kill you?"

"Yes! That's exactly what I'm afraid of!" Alex responded. However, he was not nearly as fearful of Rowan now as he had been when they first met.

By the time he finished his response, Rowan quickly raised her sword over her head and swung it down at Alex, and it was now that Alex was able to witness the true merits of his practice. Without thinking, he brought his sword up just as fast to block Rowan's strike. The two blades made a loud clanging sound as they clashed. It was the first time Alex had ever heard it come from his own sword. Despite feeling immensely shocked that he had actually crossed blades with Rowan, the sense of a dormant warrior within him rising to the surface was far stronger than anything he had ever felt before.

Rowan laughed to herself.

"Good block!" Alex leveled himself and forced Rowan off of his sword, shoving her lightly back a few steps. "Come on!" she called out exuberantly. "I wanna see what you can do now!"

Alex felt a heated rush overcome him. He grasped his sword firmly and smiled back with a playful, malicious grin.

"Alright then. Don't hold back!"

"I don't intend to," Rowan declared. She began by making another swift attacking movement toward Alex which he easily deflected. The rush of the action felt strong to Alex as they winded their way around the trees and up the hill.

Rowan was a fine fighter as she certainly kept him on his toes. Alex had been taught by Matheus as well as many other Ravennite swordsmen that his weapon was more or less an extension of his reach, and he learned best to hone his skills by employing brute force and attack combinations intended to overwhelm his opponent. Rowan, on the other hand, moved fast and elegantly, using her blade to attack only when she had pinpointed the best opportunity to strike. Not only that, but she was also in perfect harmony with her surroundings; knowing exactly where to step and using all obstacles to her advantage. It certainly showed Alex how much he still had to learn, but he managed to keep up with his opponent nonetheless.

The two of them continued to dance around each other, clashing blades and stopping only to catch their breath while eyeing each other like hawks to their prey. As they neared the snowy hilltop, Alex did his best to gain a stronger footing against Rowan. Seeking his opportunity, he unleashed a flurry of attacks at Rowan's sword and managed to carry it out of her direct range of motion until she was finally forced to release her grip. The stone sword was thrown from her hand and went through the snow, piercing its way into the ground.

Rowan's jaw dropped as she watched her weapon abandon her and Alex pointed his directly at her. She turned and looked at Alex over the point of his sword, an expression of astonishment and utter defeat on her face. Neither of them moved, but Rowan quickly grew a wide smile and the two of them soon began to laugh.

"You actually beat me!" Rowan gleefully exclaimed. "I can't believe it!"

Alex lowered his sword and lifted his eyes as though he was trying to think of something to say.

"Ve'su-" he began thoughtfully, speaking the Ravennites' tongue, "ah'galast mahki." He was certain that what he had just said translated closest to, "You are a worthy adversary."

"Asoh've!" (Thank you!), Rowan replied, as she touched her hand to her forehead and then down to her heart, which Alex learned was a form of salute to the Ravennites. "And I'm glad to see how much you've improved with our language."

Over the course of the summer, Rowan took it upon herself to teach Alex what she could of the language of her people. It was more than difficult at first, but Rowan was able to force repetition into Alex until he caught on to the basic grammar of the language. The Ravennite's tongue, he learned, was formed by their ancestors as a means of secret communication when the American colonists attempted to hide in the mountains from the war. It was sparsely used by the Ravennites up until the point that the Domineers made their unwelcome arrival, and the language had been revived.

After their friendly duel had ended, Alex and Rowan stowed their swords away and walked along the hillsides for a while longer. The sun reached its peak in the blue, cloudless autumn sky and cast a bright light all along the surface of the snow. As they came to the top of the hill, Alex took the time to gaze out in awe and admire the incredible view. He was looking out the great series of large, snowy mountain ranges in the distance, and a freezing, azure river rushing down from the hills and into the valleys below. Rowan had told him once that the mountains which he was looking at were part of a sort of boundary which divided the northern regions of the Dark Zone from the southern, as well as separating the Ravennites under Delmar's family line from their brothers on the other side.

"What exactly is on the other side of the mountains, Rowan?" Alex asked curiously.

Rowan walked over to a nearby tree and pulled herself up to sit on one of its low branches.

"I've never been down there before," Rowan replied. "All I know of it is what Matheus told me. He says those lands were much like our own, before the Domineers came, of course. Darowe's people were much more conformed warriors than my people ever were, though I never thought they would ever need to be."

"I have definitely seen a warrior in Matheus," Alex laughed lightly. "Do you think anything happened to them?"

Rowan shook her head.

"We lost all contact with Darowe shortly after Ravenna was taken. Some of us thought he had forsaken us when the Domineers attacked. When we gathered the remains of our scattered people behind the walls of the Citadel, however, we learned that Ramon Moreno and his brother, Robert, had split up, with Robert staying in the north. Delmar believes that Ramon went south to try to finish of Darowe." She looked out at the mountains and snickered to herself. "Good luck."

Alex leaned against the tree and looked up at Rowan.

"You know what Darowe was like?"

Rowan thought for a moment.

"I met him once, when I was a small child. He and my father shared a circle of friendship. I daresay Darowe was an even greater man than my father. When I first saw him I remember shaking in fear after seeing how big he was. My mother had to pull me away to comfort me. He would typically travel up to Ravenna to join my father whenever they went out hunting bears in the mountains, along with Caine's father as well."

Alex winced as the name Caine suddenly sounded familiar to him. In the months he had been here he never heard Rowan or anyone else speak the name, but when he heard it just now he specifically remembered that moment by the creekside just before Matheus had found him. The Domineers had got there first and were soon joined by a young man whom they named as Caine. Alex recalled the group of Domineers being dressed in the very filthy clothes which they had presumably entered the Dark Zone wearing, but Caine was wearing an outfit very similar to those which the Ravennites wore; similar even to what he himself was now wearing. It was a curious thought to Alex.

"Who is Caine?" he asked casually.

Rowan took a deep breath.

"He lived in the valley. His father was more or less a right hand man to the Chief; actually Delmar tells me that Caine's father was among the few who were directly opposed to separating from the Outside, and Caine shared his views. I remember him being there when the Moreno brothers first came to the valley."

Alex took all of this in with interest.

"So if he lived in Ravenna, where is he now?"

Rowan shrugged her shoulders.

"They say he must have died in the attack on Ravenna."

Died? That did not sound right to Alex. He was fairly certain he had seen him before, and he doubted that it was a different Caine; that did not sound like a very common name. What concerned Alex the most, however, was why this Caine would have been around the Domineers, the enemy of the Ravennites. And Rowan believed him to be dead? It sounded to him as though there was something else that he was not being told, but more than ever he just wanted to shrug it off. Right now the Ravennites were experiencing a great increase of hope and confidence, and even though Alex was doing everything he could to prepare himself if the worst of this conflict should come, whatever form the worst might take, he still found himself hoping that the need to use his sword for its intended purpose would never cross his path.

CHAPTER SIXTEEN

Later that night, after the sun had long set and the woods had fallen dark, the Domineer camp at the Iron Furnace was in a state of unrest. For weeks their attempts to push westward into the Ravennites' territory had been met by resistance much more extreme than it had ever been. Many of the outsiders known as the Domineers under the leadership of Robert Moreno were growing increasingly paranoid and worried.

Robert sat alone in his personal quarters. Along the wall which skirted the hillside a long, choppy structure had been built to border the inside of the wall and surround the tall, stone furnace like a crescent. Near the center of the mediocre architecture a short tower-like extension was supported upward by the framework. It was in the small, dim lit chamber within this precarious extension that Robert called his own quarters. There was a wide opening in the wall at the far end of the room which formed a broad window looking out at the large campsite and the old furnace which stood off to the side.

Robert glanced out of the opening. The enclosed site was dark with the nightfall but wide awake as Robert's subordinates were struggling to recover from the latest encounters they had experienced with the Ravennite aggressors. Robert knew they had every reason to be worried, for he was growing uneasy himself but he refused to allow the others to see it in him. The Ravennites had been stepping up their game severely, and he knew it had to be because they had finally been pushed into a corner and were fighting back like animals being pursued by hunters.

Still, Robert believed he had no real reason to worry, but

at the same time he was not so sure. His older brother Ramon was certainly much stronger and a better leader than he was, even he could not deny that. Robert Moreno was only eighteen when they first left the valley of Ravenna after being turned away by its inhabitants, and at that time he was afraid; he was afraid that he and his brother would be forced to return to the world beyond these isolated mountains and live off the streets once more. Ramon, however, assured him that they would never live such a lowly life again, and Robert never knew if he was doing this for the both of them or only for himself.

The two of them had spent all of their time over the following months trying to gather everyone they could, mostly the homeless and those far too poor to live out in the real world, to the seemingly noble cause of taking what they needed to survive. They would march into the isolated, unprotected territory of the great Adirondack Mountains, known as the Dark Zone, chase out the current inhabitants and take over their very way of life. Robert could tell that Ramon almost felt that it was owed to them. He did not join Ramon when he fought to take the valley, as he did not feel that he was up to the fight that the Ravennites would give.

The Morenos were forced to split up and divide their followers in order to keep spreading throughout the Dark Zone, and Robert took to the north. Ever since then he thought that he had been given an opportunity to prove himself to Ramon, and he did indeed prove a competent leader as he managed to force the Ravennites further west and establish a forward camp at the Iron Furnace. Robert's penchant for his task soon began to skyrocket when his brother sent Caine to aid him in his efforts.

Caine. Robert could hardly stand the sight of him. The young man was not one of Ramon's vast following. He was the very Ravennite whom had greeted their arrival in the valley and had defected to Ramon when they returned with their ragged army. Ever since then, Caine remained close to Ramon and fed him all of the information he could to help them take total control of the Dark Zone. Robert did not know if this was out of fear or pure betrayal of his people, but either way he still despised him.

Caine claimed to have been sent north by Ramon to advise Robert with all of the information and wisdom he had given him, but Robert had a feeling it was because his brother did not trust his ability to succeed. This thought only fueled Robert with an envious desire to prove his point to Ramon. Now that he believed he had his enemies cornered, Robert was growing increasingly anxious to move in and deliver the killing blow, but these new attacks on his scouting parties were threatening to tear his plans, and his leadership, apart, and Caine was just as insubordinate as he was arrogant. Robert felt that he did not need his advice to finish the Ravennites once and for all, but he was beginning to worry that soon he might need a new plan or else everything would be ruined.

Robert heard the sound of someone knocking against the wooden beams that formed an open door frame at the other end of the room. He turned to see someone standing in the doorway. Robert was hardly in the mood right now to deal with any sort of bad news.

"What is it?" he growled in a tired voice.

The man in the small archway seemed to swallow slightly before he answered.

"It's Caine," he muttered. "He wants to speak to you outside."

That name was the last thing he wanted to hear at this point. What could Caine possibly want now? Perhaps he wished to gloat at his apparent failure to hold his ground against these Ravennite raids, or maybe he might actually like to offer some sound advice for a change. Whatever the case, Robert felt his subconscious urging him to follow this messenger out his quarters and down through the structure's dark corridors. This life had been just as difficult and miserable as his life on the streets, but Robert tried his best convince himself that it would all be worth it in the end, when they would be able to seize total control of the Dark Zone and start anew without any of the oppression of the Outside, as these people had seemingly done so for generations.

The cold air hit Robert as soon as he stepped outside, the gust gnawing at the flesh of his face. This is what the cold seasons felt like every year in these dreary hills, but he was no stranger to it anymore. Caine was already waiting for him outside of the structure, just as his messenger had said. Robert just glared at him through the columns of breath that escaped his nostrils. Caine absorbed his look and shot it right back at him. He opened his mouth to speak but was suddenly cut off when Robert put his hand up.

"Don't," he snarled at Caine. "If you're just going to try to give me another pointless lecture then you can leave now."

Caine narrowed his eyes at his ignorance.

"I'm not here for myself," he gave a sharp response. "I have more news from your brother."

Robert closed his eyes and clenched his fists. He knew what that had to mean; that Ramon intended to interfere with his hopes to finish off the Ravennites himself, or that this was yet another scam by Caine to gain Ramon's favor.

"What is it this time?"

Taking a step forward, Caine locked eyes with Robert harshly.

"You think I don't know what you're trying to do?" he said under his breath. "Well, I do, and you have no idea what sort of mess you're getting yourself into."

"You don't know anything, highlander," Robert lashed back defensively.

Caine raised an eyebrow.

"Don't I?" he sneered. "Am I wrong in stating that you believe you have the remainder of my people in the farthest corners of our lands and that you intend to attack them and finish them off for good? Don't deny what is very clear to me."

Robert felt a heated rush sweep through his system. He hated the arrogance of this man, and tried to think of a way to counter Caine's words.

"That's not true," Robert replied hotly. "If I could attack them don't you think I would have done that already? We're stuck in a stalemate right now because we don't know exactly where the Ravennites have dug in, and we can't get close because they keep assaulting my scouts." He reached up and jabbed his finger into Caine's chest. "But aren't you supposed to be the fine line between us? Aren't you supposed to be telling me everything you know about these territories? That's what Ramon sent you up here to do! So tell me, why aren't the maps drawn yet?"

Caine held his composure and simply started to laugh at his desperation.

"If I knew, wouldn't I have told you already?" he mocked. "You think I enjoy seeing you fail so miserably?"

"Yes, I do!" Robert fired back. "You're not telling everything you know like you're supposed to be doing, and you're doing it on purpose to humiliate me!"

Caine shrugged his shoulders.

"It is quite amusing, actually," he continued to jeer, "watching you think you could just blindly stand a chance against my people. You know what the difference is between you and them? You're fighting to take something from them, and they're trying to defend it. Your problem is that you don't know anything about my people."

"What should I know?" Robert was getting irritated.

"The new Chief," Caine replied, "Delmar is his name. I knew him well in Ravenna. He'll have the absolute loyalty of the people. They'll be rallied under his name. They'll fight to the death for him. I know, I saw it myself. You might have my people pinned in a corner and you might not, but even if you did I assure you that you would not able to defeat them in a fight without the perfect advantage. I'm warning you right now not to do something that you'll regret."

"Enough!" Robert huffed. "If you are so sure of this then

why don't you make yourself useful and tell me what advantage I need to end this insufferable conflict? Or don't you know anything, as usual?"

Caine continued to glower with his arrogant gaze.

"Of course I don't know any more than you do! I don't know where exactly the remnants of my people are hiding, or how fortified they might be. I think you're starting to realize how inefficient your current tactics are becoming, am I right?"

Robert shook his head in frustration.

"The only thing inefficient around here is you! I've yet to hear you offer any solutions. Do you mean to try to tell me that there's no way to crush those animals? I highly doubt that they're that perfectly protected."

"As a matter of fact," Caine lifted his eyes, "we might have a solution. Well, not a solution per se, but I know how we can work closer to one. That's why I called you out here."

Robert's eyebrows rose.

"What are you talking about? What solution?"

Caine turned and pointed over toward the furnace tower.

"You see those men?" Robert followed his direction and could see a group of about a dozen men hanging around the furnace. Some of them were standing around and talking to each other. One of them sat on the edge of the base of the furnace. He was a grim looking man, his hair was buzzed short and his face was roughly shaven. On his lap he was holding his own stone sword and sharpening it with a small rock. All of these men seemed to make a point of standing out from the rest within the walls of the Iron Furnace. To Robert, they looked very firm in appearance, as if they were completely unfazed by fear or by a sense of hopelessness. Whoever they were, they had a seriously hardened atmosphere about them. As Caine pointed, he signaled for the man sharpening his sword to come over to them.

"Who are they?" Robert asked.

Caine seemed to examine the group of roughnecks again.

"Just a few newcomers according to Ramon. Word got

down to him of the Ravennites' new resistance efforts and he sent them up here to aid you. He thinks you could make good use of their strengths."

Robert gave a brief nod. "What kind of strengths?"

"The kind that get the job done," a deep, cold voice spoke up. The man whom Caine had beckoned over came to stand next to him, the sword still in his hand. Even Robert had to hide a slight feeling of intimidation. He stared at this man with a vacant look.

"Who are you?" Robert asked sternly, trying not to lose his composure in this man's presence.

"The name's Wilson," he replied. His voice was almost cold and unfeeling. "We've seen action with these savages already," he boasted, stroking his blade.

Robert gave Caine a curious look.

"You mean to tell me that Ramon has already engaged the inhabitants in the south?"

"Not exactly," Caine shook his head, "but Darowe's people are tougher and far more capable fighters than Delmar's, and these boys formed the tip of the spear in pushing them deeper into the mountains. Ramon says they are about as tough as they come. I believe we can make effective use of their abilities."

"How?" Robert snickered. "My entire company has not been able to make a dent in the Ravennites' protective circles. The cowards refuse to show themselves properly; they stalk us and attack during the night."

"Well, maybe that's the best time to attack then," Caine cut in.

Robert put his hand up to silence him.

"Even if we could create a new strategy, it would be pointless to go after the Ravennites without knowing their exact location."

"Have you tried capturing any of them?" Wilson jumped in. "Interrogating them?"

"Yes, we've tried it in the past," Robert was getting frustrated. "It doesn't work. They refuse to say a word and we can't break them."

"You mean *you* can't break them," Wilson mocked him. "Our methods might be a little more...convincing."

Robert glanced down at Wilson's sword as he said this. Shaking his head, he said, "It's still too risky. We don't know for certain what would even happen if we stepped foot into their guarded territory again."

"Maybe," Caine responded, "but there might be another way to go."

Both Robert and Wilson stared at Caine as he spoke.

"What do you mean?" Robert asked.

"I agree," Caine continued, "you would be playing a difficult game trying to make any one of my people talk once you get ahold of them. But there's someone else with them who might be a little less challenging."

The other two exchanged looks of confusion as well as interest.

"Someone?" Robert uttered. "Who?"

"He's no Ravennite," Caine droned on. "He's an Outsider, and a rather young one at that."

"What?" Robert was quite surprised. "What do you mean an Outsider? Is he one of ours?"

Caine laughed as he shook his head.

"No. Months ago a young boy from the Outside wandered unknowingly into our territories. We found him first, but the scouting party you had patrolling the area was incompetent and got themselves killed when the Ravennites attacked, then they took the boy with them."

"How can you be sure those beasts did not kill the boy as well?" Wilson questioned.

"Because I saw him again recently," Caine answered as Robert glared at him with a look of disbelief. "He was with them when they began expanding their territories. I would not have believed it if I did not see it with my own eyes. My people molded him into one of them, and now he fights for the Ravennites."

There was a brief, awkward pause. Robert Moreno stared

at Caine perplexingly. He could not believe what he had just heard.

"You knew a stranger from the Outside was taken in by the Ravennites all this time and you never thought it wise to inform me about it?"

Caine looked back with a blank gaze.

"Consider it an oversight."

Robert's jaw dropped.

"An oversight? Are you kidding me!? If the boy has sided with the Ravennites, then just imagine what kind of information he might be willing to give them, you incompetent idiot!"

"Exactly," Caine muttered in response. "Think about what he might be able to tell you, too, with the right persuasion. He would be much weaker than my people, I can promise you that."

Robert opened his mouth to give an arrogant response, but Caine's idea suddenly swarmed in his mind. He had an excellent point, but Robert could not help but detect a great many flaws.

"How exactly would you propose we get ahold of this boy?"

"That's why we're here," Wilson cut in again. "If Caine knows what the boy looks like then he can lead us to him."

"Don't you understand?" Robert interjected. "All of our efforts to stop the Ravennites' resistances over the past several weeks have failed. Why should this time be any different?"

"Because I'm here now," Wilson replied confidently. "Caine will track down the Ravennites' campsite and lead us to it, we will lead the rest of our boys into the fray and capture the boy and not stop until we have him."

"That is still a poorly conceived plan," Robert responded.

Caine shook his head angrily.

"There is nothing more you can do at this point. Face it, you've pushed my people too far and now they're pushing back. It's time for you to either take a great risk or wait for them to grow bolder than you. So tell me, Robert, what is your next plan?"

Robert turned around and groaned to himself. He put his hands against his face and desperately tried to think of the best answer to give. The Ravennites had been forced into a corner, that much was clear, and now they were risking everything to fight back. As much as he hated to admit it, Caine must have been right for once.

He closed his eyes and took a deep breath.

"Caine," he began as he turned back to face them, "lead the men to the Ravennite camp. Wilson, bring me this boy." With that final command, Robert began to head back to the structure and his personal quarters. "And bring him alive."

"Yes, sir," Wilson muttered to himself. He gestured for Caine to follow him back to the furnace.

As Robert made his way back to his quarters, he could not help but feel anxious about the near future. The Ravennites had never put up much of a fight in all the time he had spent chasing them throughout the Dark Zone. So why now? Surely it must have had something to do with this boy from the Outside. Who was he, and what was he doing here? Robert was certain that he had no connection to the Ravennites, or to him and Ramon. He knew that Caine had to be right, however, that if they managed to capture this boy and bring him back to the Iron Furnace then there was a much better chance that he could be interrogated than any of the Ravennites. He tried to convince himself to have faith that Caine and this new arrival, Wilson, could accomplish this risky task. In truth, he had no faith in Caine whatsoever.

It only took minutes for Wilson to rouse his men for the mission Robert Moreno had given him. Caine made a point of gathering nearly half of the Domineers within the walls and arming them. Most were significantly terrified to go back out into hostile territory so soon after their most recent encounters, but not until Wilson gave them a short and rather harsh speech and headed straight for the large campsite's gate. As he walked with confident composure toward the gate one of the men in his gang caught up with him.

"Hey, Wilson," he said, walking by his side, "do you really think these scrubs can handle this job?"

"They better," Wilson replied condescendingly. "They're gonna need to learn to man up if they want any hope of surviving this conflict."

The other man snickered to himself at his ringleader's comment.

"There's one problem though," he continued. "Caine might know what this boy looks like, but how are we supposed to properly identify and take him during the skirmish?"

Wilson never stopped walking, but suddenly grew a malevolent grin on his face.

"Simple," he uttered his answer, "we take them all!"

CHAPTER SEVENTEEN

Alex and Rowan had returned to the Ravennites' camp just before the sun had set. The temperature, though cold enough during the day, had dropped significantly. The Ravennites within the walls of their outpost were gathered by the firesides. Several were armed and guarding around the wall on all sides. Alex had gone over to one of the large fire pits near the center of the campsite, where the Ravennites were preparing and cooking the meat of the game they hunted, which mainly consisted of deer. Alex collected two thin slabs of deer meat and then headed to the small campfire that he had set up nearby the wall. Rowan was sitting alone by the fire and looking down at her wooden pendant again. As Alex approached, he glanced down at the charm. As usual, the first thing that caught his eye was the strange, red symbol at the top of the charm's face which Rowan apparently could not see.

Alex went to sit down next to Rowan.

"Here you go," he said, handing one of the meat pieces to her.

Rowan put her necklace away and took the deer meat.

"Thank you!" she said as she chewed into it.

The two sat together by the warmth of the fire. Alex took a bite of the tough deer meat in his hand. It was what made up most of his diet here in these mountains. Until then, he had never eaten deer before, and the tough texture of it took him a little bit to get used to.

"You know," he began as he swallowed, "I never thought I'd get so accustomed to deer."

Rowan giggled to herself.

"We didn't always have to ration our food so accordingly.

We lost all of our livestock when Ravenna was taken."

Alex winced slightly, as he knew that Rowan always hated to talk about what happened in Ravenna. Despite that, he noticed that she had grown much less sensitive over past few months. He guessed that must have had something to do with how much time she spent teaching him about her people. If anything, she certainly seemed to be happier than she had been when he first met her.

Sighing quietly, Alex gazed into the fire.

"Sometimes I still wonder what is happening outside of here."

Rowan looked over at Alex. She knew exactly what he must have been feeling inside.

"Today is your birthday, isn't it?" she asked.

Nodding his head, Alex replied, "Yeah, it is." Then he smiled and looked back at Rowan. "You remembered?" Since the Ravennites still employed the same calendar used by the Outside, he was able to keep track of his birthday, and he was pleasantly surprised to see that Rowan had as well. Alex had turned fifteen today, but the months that he had long endured made him feel much older and far more mature than ever. Rowan was about the same age as Alex. She had turned fifteen herself back in June, but for some reason never told Alex about it until long after it had passed. She seemed to be rather modest about her birthday, almost as though she wished to avoid it.

"Of course I remembered!" she said cheerily. At that point, Rowan reached down into a small backpack at her feet which she had brought out with her. "I actually had something made for you."

Alex was quite taken aback. He naturally did not expect anything for his birthday. By the light of the fire, he saw Rowan pull a folded cloth-like object from her bag. She handed it to Alex and he unfolded it and held it in front of him. It appeared to be a scarf, made from the same material as Rowan's gray hood. Even in the faint firelight, Alex could see that the scarf showed off a beautiful dark blue color.

Alex's eyes widened as he held the scarf in front of him. It was such a simple gift, yet Alex was overwhelmed by it.

"Do you like it?" Rowan broke the silence.

Alex realized how long he had been gazing at the scarf.

"You made this?" he stammered.

Rowan nodded her head casually.

"I had a little help with it." She reached over and pointed to one of the ends of the scarf. "This I made myself."

Alex looked at where she was pointing. He held the scarf's end closer to the fire. Sewn into the silk-like material was an image of Delmar's symbol of the Ravennites, the same which Rowan bore on her left arm. The stone sword and the hatchet crossed in an X-shape, the green arch which underlapped them both, and just below the symbol Alex was able to make out a single word written in the tongue of the Ravennites which read, *"Arrun."* Alex was learned well enough in their esoteric speech to know exactly what it said: ***"Honor."***

Completely awestruck, Alex felt warmer inside than he had in a long time, despite the cold, nighttime atmosphere. There was no debating it in his mind, this was the greatest gift anyone had ever given him. Alex let out an exhale of glee.

"Thank you, Rowan!" he breathed. He carefully put the soft, blue scarf around his neck. It felt very warm and comfortable. "I really do like it!"

"I'm glad you do," Rowan beamed. "You've earned it," she said, referring to the Ravennite mark designed into it.

Alex held the tail of the scarf in his hand and stared into the fire. A lot of feelings were going through his mind. He looked over at Rowan and thought of what to say.

"Why?" he said quietly.

Rowan looked a bit confused by the question.

"Why what?"

Alex closed his eyes briefly.

"What are you so...so good to me?"

Rowan stared somewhat blankly back at Alex. She looked

at him as though she expected him to know the answer. In the midst of the silence, she put her hand up on Alex's shoulder and gazed into his blue eyes.

"You're my friend," she answered softly.

Her words hit Alex directly in his heart, so powerfully that he could feel the light trauma in his chest and warm tears forming in his eyes.

"Rowan..." Alex murmured. The moments were becoming more delicate as each one passed. The two of them never looked away from each other's eyes. Every minute felt like a long hour and the warmth of the fire continue to lick the side of Alex's face. The moment was abruptly killed, however, when a sudden sound like a rustling off in the woods drew their attention.

Alex and Rowan both jumped to their feet and looked out by one of the small openings in the wall toward the source of the noise.

"Did you hear that?" Alex whispered.

"I did hear it," Rowan uttered as she turned and gave Alex a serious look. "That was not an animal."

Alex swallowed roughly, worried that the Domineers were sneaking around their territories again.

"What do we do?" he asked cautiously.

"We have to alert Malachai," Rowan said as she prepared to move toward the wall's opening, but Alex quickly reached forward and grabbed her arm.

"Wait!" he breathed. "Maybe you should be the one to alert Malachai."

Rowan just stared back, but then she soon recalled that Malachai was still held a heavy disdain for Alex.

"You're probably right," she nodded. Rowan turned and headed quickly toward the center of the campsite. Alex picked up his sword scabbard up from the ground as Rowan called back to him. "Whatever you do, don't leave the wall, Alex." And then she turned and hurried off.

Alex tied the belt attached to his scabbard around his waist and crept up to the opening in the wall. It was impossible to see much of anything past the first line of the trees in the darkness. He kneeled down and leaned against the short stone wall, trying to keep as quiet as possible. If the Domineers really were attempting to spy on them then he needed to know for sure. Despite how far they had come over these previous months, Alex was more than unsure as to how the future was going to play out. Both the Ravennites and the Domineers were at rising odds with each other and it was only a matter of time before one of them was forced to make a daring move, and that was precisely what Alex feared the most.

Feeling himself beginning to grow slightly paranoid, Alex groaned quietly and glanced back into the outpost. "What's taking you so long, Rowan?" To his surprise, as soon as he had looked away, Alex heard another rustling sound amongst the trees, this one much closer than the first one. He jolted his attention back toward the tree lines, breathing roughly. It took a few seconds for his sight to properly readjust, and Alex blinked his eyes a couple times to be sure that he was seeing this right: someone was standing at the edge of the trees, and they were looking right at him.

The dark figure was tall and broad shouldered, standing absolutely motionless. Alex felt himself become just as still as he stared right back at the figure. It seemed like the environment all around him had gone completely silent; so silent that he could clearly hear his own low breathing.

"Who-" Alex stammered, half-afraid to speak, "who's there?" The figure did not respond, but instead it slowly turned and began to slip off into the woods. "Hey!" Alex called out quietly but assertively. Whoever was sneaking around on the borders of the campsite, Alex did not feel that he could simply let him walk away. Just now, from far behind him it sounded as though Malachai had finally been alerted to the strange presence around the outpost. He could hear many of the Ravennites rushing around and calling out in their secret tongue.

By now the mysterious figure had already disappeared

into the woods, and Alex was simply not willing to wait for anyone else to join him. He knew it was very dangerous to leave the campsite. He was breathing heavily and skin was almost crawling, but Alex felt his nerves take over as he slowly stood up, removed the sword from its sheath, and crept off toward the tree line.

The Ravennites were dispersing into the surrounding territory in search of any signs of intruders. Alex could hear them growing more distant as he continued through the woods in search of the figure he had seen. He tried to follow the footsteps which had been left in the snow, but as he tracked them further in the darkness began to diminish his ability to make them out. Several minutes had passed as he wandered, and he was starting to think it was all in vain. More than anything he was terrified that, if the Domineers were really out here, that one of them might reveal themselves in a hostile manner at any time. He had no way of knowing if the figure he saw was in fact one of them or not. At this point he knew that he had made a terrible mistake leaving the outpost after Rowan had warned him not to.

Alex was preparing to retreat back to the campsite until he suddenly heard the sound of footsteps rapidly approaching his location. Alex jumped in shock, and then he realized that the footsteps were actually coming from the campsite. Before he could decide what to do, the shadowy figure of a man wielding a bow ran out from within the trees. He turned his head and looked directly at Alex, swiftly arming his bow with an arrow from his back. Alex instinctively threw his hands up into the air, trying not to panic.

"Don't shoot!" he yelled out. "Ravennite! I'm a Ravennite!" Although he knew that was not exactly true, of course, he had to assure this man that he was friendly.

To his great relief, the man immediately lowered his weapon. "Sorry," he breathed. The man sounded rather young, around his early twenties. He took a few steps toward Alex to get a better look at him, and it was at this point that he seemed to recognize him. "Wait a minute," he said with a hint of surprise. "You're that Outsider! Alex Lee," he continued, trying to remember his name.

It was sort of interesting to see this young man actually recognize Alex for who he was, in addition to not showing any sort of contempt or hostility as an outsider. Alex nodded his head to him.

"Yeah, that's right," he replied. "What's your name?"

The man regained his composure, putting the arrow back into his quiver.

"It's Zak," he answered.

Alex nodded again in approval.

"Well, good to meet you, Zak," he then immediately recalled what he was doing out here. "Hey," he whispered to the man called Zak. "Have you seen anybody wandering around out here?"

"No," Zak shook his head, "not yet. Malachai has sent half of the camp out to sweep the area."

"How far out?" Alex asked.

"About a half-mile radius. He wants to run the Domineers down before they can get away."

Alex glanced back off into the dark woods.

"I don't know if they are Domineers."

Zak gave Alex a curious look.

"What do you mean? Do you think someone else is out here with us?"

"Well, I didn't mean to say it like that," Alex responded, trying to keep his thoughts in line. "They could be out here, the Domineers, but I saw someone near the edge of the woods earlier that did not look like one of them. I was trying to follow but I lost them. That was when we ran into each other."

Zak was about to speak again, but the two of them were suddenly interrupted when yet another rustling noise rose up again, this time louder and closer. Both of them fell deathly silent, and Zak stepped carefully forward, staring like a hawk into the trees.

Alex shifted his attention back and forth between his companion and the trees, waiting for something to happen.

"What is it?" he whispered very quietly. "What do you see?"

Zak remained motionless for a brief second, but then he took a step back and appeared to be much more anxious.

"Hide," he uttered quickly.

"What?" Alex hectically responded.

"Now!" Zak did not hesitate to duck down and disappear behind a large tree to hide himself. Feeling his blood beginning to rush, Alex quickly scanned around him for a place to hide. Now he could hear the footsteps of several people approaching them. Trying not to panic, Alex slipped himself behind a tree in the other direction. Planting his back up against the tree, waiting for something to happen, he suddenly heard something that completely wracked his nerves.

"Alex."

A hoarse, male voice suddenly rang out in his head, and it was definitely not his mind's voice. Alex's eyes flew open, and as soon as they did he found himself staring out at the same dark, mysterious figure he had originally seen before, and once again they were standing motionless and looking right at him. At this point, Alex was certain that there were Domineers in the area, but this was someone else. Who was it?

Just like before, the figure turned and walked off again. Alex hissed under his breath.

"Not this time!" he muttered. Completely disregarding the approaching footsteps in the near distance, Alex pushed off from the tree and began to chase the dark stranger. He had only been running for about ten seconds before he suddenly felt a strange sensation like a force of air sweeping against his shins. The strange force was so strong that it caused him to trip and fall to the ground. He accidentally released his grip on his sword and it was thrown down several feet away from him. Alex hit the ground and realized that he had landed inside the tight space of a frozen, rotting log. He groaned loudly as the impact nearly knocked the wind out of him.

Before he could even move to get up to his feet, Alex suddenly heard the running footsteps close in on his current location. Part of him just wanted to stand up and keep running, but he then heard a voice speak up very close to him. "I thought I heard something over here!"

Alex quickly turned himself onto his back inside the hollow log. The footsteps were getting even closer, and he made a risky move by swiftly reaching up and pulling his blue scarf over his face so as to help him camouflage better. Seconds later, the figure of a person emerged from the shadows of the woods and was walking slowly toward where Alex was lying.

Alex held his breath desperately. Just looking at this person with the very limited amount of light he could tell without a doubt that this was indeed a Domineer scout. He did not seem to take notice to Alex's presence, but he continued to walk closer to him, scoping out the area around him. To Alex's great horror, the Domineer came to stand directly over top of him, with one foot on either side of the dead log. Alex tried his best not to move a single muscle, still holding his breath and praying that this man did not look directly down.

Just then, another voice rose up from nearby.

"What is it?" someone called out.

Alex saw the man above him shake his head.

"Nothing," he growled. "There's no one here." He then stepped off of the log and walked back toward the second voice.

Still holding his breath and feeling his lungs strain painfully, Alex listened in on the brief conversation.

"We better head the other way now," one of the men said, "toward the Ravennites' camp. Wilson wants us to take as many alive as possible and take them back to the furnace."

Alex's eyes widened when he heard this.

The other scout replied, "All of this just for one boy? I don't understand that logic."

"We don't know what he looks like. Caine will know for sure if we manage to capture him. Plus, Robert believes capturing as many of these animals as possible will deal them a serious blow."

Alex listened intently until the two voices eventually faded away into the distance, and then he finally released his restraint and sucked in a great wave of breath. When he was sure that he was alone, Alex sat up in the log. His clothes were damp now and his body was freezing, but his heart was racing in response to what he had just heard. It was clear that the Domineers were not on some random scouting job this time. From what he heard it was apparent that they were preparing to assault the Ravennites' outpost, and if they intended to take as many of them prisoner as possible, then it sounded like there were a lot of them. He knew he had to get back quickly to warn Malachai himself.

It was at that moment that his thoughts were interrupted by a disturbing sound; the sudden uproar of many people shouting in the near distance. He was too late. The Domineers were already attacking.

"Oh my God," he breathed in panic. "Rowan!" He quickly jumped to his feet, snatched up his sword from the snow and ran toward what he believed to be the direction of the campsite.

There was no sign of Zak or anyone else. Suddenly, he heard the same mysterious voice ring out his head again, *"No!"* it echoed in his mind. Alex had so much going through his head right now that he tried to blot it out completely, but just then he heard the voice shout again, only this time he heard it come from somewhere to his right. *"They can't have you!"*

Alex never even had a chance to look around. He heard a loud swishing sound and a bright red light like a burst of fire appeared in his peripheral vision. His eyesight suddenly began to flash rapidly and, to his horror, he could have sworn he saw the same mysterious, red symbol from Rowan's locket appear in his eyesight and disappear as if in the blink of an eye. An instant later, he lost his balance in his legs completely and everything around him went black.

Alex never felt himself hit the ground. Soon after his eyes had gone black he regained his sight, but to his great confusion he could not remember where he had been before he was suddenly knocked out. Alex could not remember much of anything right now, but when he opened his eyes he found himself gazing at some sort of vision.

Nothing about his current surroundings felt real. Alex's eyes were burning and his sight was slightly blurred. He was not at all sure where he was. The only thing he found himself looking at was a man standing a few yards away with his back turned to him. The man did not move, and Alex was completely unable to make out any of his features as well as anything in the distance, as his entire vision was cloaked by a bright light. The only thing he could see was that this man was holding something in his right hand. The object looked like a large sword, but instead of a blade there were a series of blade-like appendages protruding up from the hilt and encircling each other as they extended to form the vague shape of a sword. As Alex continued to register all of this, he heard a hoarse, male voice speak and resonate all around him, and he could have sworn it was originating from the light-shrouded man standing before him.

"Who are you?"

Before Alex could even attempt to give an answer, the bright light covering the distance flashed intensely and Alex's eyes went dark once again as he felt himself drift into sleep.

Upon being knocked unconscious Alex toppled forward and face planted into the snow. At that point, the mysterious dark figure whom Alex had been pursuing stepped out from the trees, holding his large, bronze-colored relic sword in hand.

Ranger gave an exhausted sigh. He set his sword down and gently picked up the limp body of the boy lying before. The temperature was far too cold to simply leave him until he regained consciousness. Ranger carried him over to a large, dying tree nearby. The trunk of the old tree had fallen apart and opened up a small alcove in its base which was just large enough for a single person to fit into. Ranger eased Alex into the rotting slot of the tree trunk to try to keep him as hidden as possible.

"I'm sorry I knocked you out, boy," Ranger said quietly to himself as he picked up his oversized sword. "I had no choice."

... ...

"I couldn't let their enemies find him. I was right; they were after him in particular, not the Ravennites." The noise of the chaos continued to ensue in the distance. Ranger's spine tingled as he heard the occasional sound of blades clashing.

... ...

Ranger rubbed his face with his hands.

"Why? I don't understand! If the boy is so important then why must I be forced to avoid any kind of contact with him?"

... ...

"I really hope you know what you're doing," Ranger sighed deeply, "because this entire venture has cost me everything, and everyone I love, and now that I am this close to my old life again, how can I possibly restrain myself from interfering with the flow of events?"

... ...

Ranger suddenly shifted uncomfortably as he glanced back over his shoulder.

"I know! I can sense it." He took in a long, cautious inhale. "They're here."

More footsteps could heard approaching from behind Ranger, but he remained as still as possibly so as not to draw attention to himself. Within seconds a small party emerged from the trees, all armed with crafted weapons. From the corner of his eye it was clear to Ranger that these were not Ravennites.

One of the men in the group quickly spotted Ranger and raised his stone sword in caution. The rest of the party came to his side and pointed their weapons at him.

"Easy," the first man said anxiously, his extended arm shaking slightly. "Turn around now."

Ranger turned slowly and glared at the group of armed, young men menacingly. One of the other Domineers narrowed his eyes curiously.

"He's not a Ravennite," he exclaimed.

"Not he's not," the man in the center replied. "Who are you?" Ranger did not respond, but only tensed his stance. The Domineer then looked past him and spotted the dark, unconscious form of Alex Lee shoved into the rotting tree trunk. "What about him?" he said, pointing his sword toward Alex.

"He looks young," another of the party observed what he could in the dark of the night. "He might fit the description of the boy we're after."

"Agreed," the group's leader said in affirmation. "Step aside, we have no quarrel with you."

Ranger just shook his head in refusal.

"I don't think so," he growled.

"You don't think so?" the leader snickered and the rest of the Domineers laughed along with him. He gave a head nod to the man at the far right of the lineup, who nodded back and then produced a very strange looking gun-like object from his back above his waist. Ranger observed as he appeared to take from his belt an object which vaguely resembled a drum magazine and fitted it firmly at the back of the weapon's body, pointing it directly at Ranger. The leader of the group continued to mock him. "There's five of us and only one of you, and we're armed to the teeth."

At that point, Ranger raised his oversized, brass-colored

sword relic in front of him, grasping it tight with both hands. The Domineer group's ringleader only gazed at it nervously. He swallowed and continued to threaten the mysterious man before them.

"I'm warning you! Step aside and give us the boy!" he said angrily, his voice almost shaking. "Don't make us kill you."

Ranger was not at all fazed by his threats. He grew a sinister grin on his face. He twitched his thumb along the side of the large hilt and in the blink of an eye the relic's protruding structure was suddenly engulfed in a piercing red flame which formed the shape of a great blade. The flame roared powerfully as it sustained itself, and the Domineers were awestruck and quaking with fear.

The group's leader struggled desperately to find his voice.

"What are doing?" he called to his cohort holding the strange gun. "Shoot him! Shoot him now!"

The gunman unhesitantly pulled the weapon's trigger and five small, ballistic projectiles shot forward from the gun and soared at their target. Ranger simply held his flaming sword in front of him in a defensive position. When the projectiles reached him the red fire cloaking the blade suddenly produced a series of shocking flares which lashed out and vaporized every one of the makeshift bullets, leaving Ranger completely unharmed, and worse, unafraid.

The Domineers were now backing up in complete terror.

"Who-" their leader choked on his words, "who are you?"

Ranger remained motionless, staring them down past the fire of his magnificent weapon, and in a cold, malevolent tone he declared, "I am the man who has fought with gods!"

Even with the clamor of the ambush continuing to ensue in the near distance, nothing could have masked the horrible sound of this party of Domineers screaming in terror as Ranger mercilessly struck them all down.

CHAPTER EIGHTEEN

Alex suddenly jolted awake, gasping in shock. Someone had blindsided him and knocked him out, he could instantly remember. He recalled a strange red light, but never felt anything hit him. He figured the Domineers had captured him as he tried to hurry back to the campsite.

Alex tried to move but realized that he was wedged into a tight alcove in the side of a dead tree. A quick look around revealed to him that he had not been taken anywhere after he was knocked unconscious. He was still out in the woods bordering the outpost, but someone must have placed in this tree. Who and why, he had no idea. As his senses quickly started returning to him he soon became cold, as he had been lying out here for who knows how long. It was still nighttime, but the sound of the chaos ringing up from the campsite was gone which told him that the fight was over.

Regaining full control of himself, Alex pried his way out of the tree. He scrambled to find his sword, which he fortunately found a few feet away lying half-buried in the snow. Alex picked it up and brushed it off. He cringed as the snow was chilling him to the bone, but it did not bother him. He had to get back to the campsite as quick as he could. A fight had taken place and Alex felt as though he had abandoned the Ravennites. Whatever had ensued at the outpost it was now over. Alex tried to regain his coordination and quickly lumbered off.

There was no easy way of knowing whether or not he was going the right way, as the light of the campfires that had been lit was gone. He was running blind, but at least there was no sign of any more Domineers in the immediate area. That either meant that they had all be killed in the skirmish or, Alex winced at the thought of the possibility, the other way around.

"No," Alex mumbled anxiously as he ran through the woods. The thought was unbearable. He knew he would simply have to find his way back to know for sure. Looking around, his surroundings were soon becoming a bit more familiar. He could sense that he was approaching the campsite, and soon Alex broke the tree line and found himself finally coming upon the Ravennites' outpost. However, it was precisely the familiar sight before him that disturbed him the most.

Alex froze in his tracks and held at his breath. The large campsite was now completely deserted. The short, stone wall surrounding the area was broken in many places, and the tents which had been erected were torn down. Alex made his way into the campsite and looked around somberly. There was absolutely no one around, Ravennites or Domineers alike.

"Rowan!" Alex called out. There was no response, exactly as he feared. "Malachai!" This was not at all good. Everyone was gone. Alex scanned around the campsite and to his horror, by the faint light of the moon and the stars, several bodies lying here and there. He gasped to himself. So there really was a fight, and clearly it had ended with casualties. Alex examined a few of the bodies and found both Domineers and Ravennites among the dead. It was sickening to look at, but the question which concerned him even more was where were the rest of the Ravennites?

Fearing the worst, Alex took time to thoroughly search all of the bodies around the site. He was thankful that there were not very many of them, and even more so to find that Rowan was not among them. Alex dropped himself down against the haphazard post of one of the destroyed tents and tried to clear his head. Only a percentage of the Ravennites sent out here had been killed it seemed, and yet the rest were now gone. Alex tried to think about everything that had happen tonight. He and Rowan had heard something moving in the woods nearby and Alex had gone to investigate, during which he found himself pursuing a dark figure whom he never managed to catch. Out in the woods, however, he had overheard a couple of Domineers conversing on their plan of action. What was it exactly that he had heard? They said that they were looking for a boy, obviously belonging with the Ravennites. Alex had a disturbing feeling in his gut which told him that the boy they were looking for was him. What could the Domineers possibly want with him?

Alex needed to think of something, but his mind was racing too fast. He had no way of knowing whether the surviving Ravennites managed to escape or if they were taken by the Domineers, and if they were he had no idea where. Right now he was alone and it appeared that this outpost was all but lost. Alex wondered if his best option was to head for the Citadel. If none of the others made it back then it would be up to him to warn Delmar of what had occurred. However, his spirits suddenly sank when another thought invaded his mind; if the Ravennites had really been captured by their enemies and he returned to the Citadel alone, how could he possibly explain to Delmar that Rowan, his sister whom he was determined to protect from the conflict attacking their home, was taken by their enemies? Alex felt sick to his stomach. He felt as though he had failed the accord. The Ravennites were attacked and he had unknowingly vacated himself from area where the fight had taken place. Just hours before he was happier than he had been in a long time while in the presence of good friend, and now, just like that, she was gone. There was so much doubt in his mind that he might ever see her again. He was alone out here now, slumped down in the ravaged remains of the campsite. He was tempted now more than ever to simply slip away and run; to find his own way out of the Dark Zone once and for all. Could he live with himself if he ran now? Alex was beginning to remember that this was not the world he came from, and hardly the one he was meant to be a part of.

Alex jerked his attention as he thought he heard a faint

sound coming from somewhere around the wall. He cautiously stood to his feet, gripping his sword firmly in hand, and scanned diligently around for any source of noise. His mind was so wracked right now that he was not sure he could handle any more surprises from the Domineers. Alex slowly approached the ravaged wall and scoped around. Sure enough, he could hear a muffled sound like a moaning around one of the areas where the stone wall had collapsed. The realization struck him that there may have been someone buried under the rocks. Alex dropped his sword, ran over and began carefully shifting the rocks around. It did not take long for him to uncover the barely conscious body of a single Ravennite. He was face down under the pile of stones with a splotch of dried blood covering the side of his head. Alex would not be able to identify who it was until he could pull him free of the collapsed wall.

It was harder than it looked, but at last Alex managed to heave the rest of the rocks off of the downed Ravennite. He was very careful as he pulled the limp body from the rubble. Alex took a few deep breaths and then turned the Ravennite onto his back, and gasped as he recognized his face.

"Malachai!" he mumbled.

He was completely unconscious now. Somehow he must have gotten trapped under the rubble when the wall fell over. If the Domineers were taking captives then they must not have ever found him. Alex placed two of his fingers against Malachai's neck, and to his relief he detected a slow pulse. He was still alive, but he could not get him to wake up. Not sure what to do, Alex dragged the limp form of Malachai over toward a nearby tent which had managed to stay partially standing. Alex ripped the leathering covering from the tent and set it over Malachai to keep him warm as best as he could.

Alex rested himself against the post of the damaged tent. He felt as though his options were very few. Much of him wanted to simply vanish now while he had the chance, especially with the faint, would-be warrior lying next to him who never ceased to hate Alex's guts. Still, it seemed the right thing to do to wait for Malachai to regain consciousness and find out what he knew, if he even knew anything at all. Alex wondered what he had been doing to get himself trapped under the fallen stone wall in the first place. Whatever the case may be, Alex knew for sure that the future ahead of him was going to be very decisive. He had no idea right now how near it was to dawn, and more than anything he hoped that, while he stayed here by Malachai's side, that the Domineers would not return to the fallen campsite, for he would be completely unprepared.

Several miles away, at the Domineers' fortress at the Iron Furnace, Caine was isolated in his private quarters, which was hardly more than a large tent he had built adjacent to the furnace tower. It was dimly lit by a single torch which stood on the ground near the back of the tent. Caine was standing in front of a single shelf which hung suspended on one of the beams supporting the tent's frame; on it sat several old-looking wine bottles, all of which were filled with the clear-colored alcoholic drink.

Caine poured the wine from one of the bottles into an old, aluminum cup and drank from it, wincing as he did so. One thing he had learned from these outsiders when they established themselves in his territories was how to make wine for himself, which he had done over the course of the summer for when the colder months arrived. Though he had never quite grown accustomed to the taste, in the back of his mind he felt a very distant sense of remorse for the way he had been turning his back on his own people. However, more than that he believed his actions were verily justified, but either way the effects of the alcohol helped to relieve him of the conflict within himself for however brief a time. He figured now was as good a time as any after they had let loose some of Ramon Moreno's best fighters upon his people. Within hours they had returned, bringing with them a few dozen of the Ravennites that they managed to subdue and take captive. That was Wilson's idea of getting the job done, even though their objective was to simply capture one boy; the outsider whom had foolishly aligned himself with the Delmar.

From just outside of his personal quarters, Caine could hear a slight commotion.

"Keep moving!" a harsh voice spoke in a commanding tone.

"Get your hands off me!" came the response of a female voice. "I know how to walk.

Out of the corner of his eye, Caine saw the flap of his tent open as a couple of young Domineers pushed a young girl into his presence. She tripped as she was forced in and fell down onto her knees.

"This is the one you wanted," one of the men said as Caine put his hand up to signal them to leave him.

Once the tent's flap had been closed, Caine turned his attention to the girl before him. He took a deep, anxious breath and another quick sip of his wine.

"Hello, Rowan."

The girl looked up as her name was spoken. Her dark hair was ragged and a single line of blood had run down from her nose and over her lips. It was clear that should must have put up an effortful fight when the Ravennites were overtaken. She glared up at the man she had been brought before, but her expression suddenly became one of astonishment when she realized that it was no Domineer.

"C-Caine?" Rowan stammered, narrowing her eyes in the dark lit room. "Is that you?" She did know what to think of this circumstance. She was still in a slight state of shock after her people were suddenly confronted by the Domineers. Caine seemed to ignore her for a moment, as he took another small, metal cup and filled it with his fermented beverage. "What are you doing here?" she asked persistently.

Caine sighed to himself, as he sipped his wine yet again.

"It's been a long time, Rowan," he spoke in an almost

hoarse tone of voice. "You've really grown a lot."

Rowan pulled herself to her feet. Caine had still yet to answer her question.

"I-" she began, trying to calm her thoughts, "I thought you were dead."

"I'm fine," Caine replied bluntly, "fine as I've ever been." He slowly walked over to stand in front of Rowan, holding the second aluminum cup in hand. "Here," he said, holding it out for Rowan.

She just looked down at the clear substance with a puzzled expression.

"What is it?" she asked as she looked up into Caine's eyes. Something about him did not seem right to her, but she was not sure what it was.

"Just take it," Caine gave a stern response. "It will settle your nerves."

Something was not right about him at all. Rowan shook her head.

"I'm not drinking that."

Caine did not respond, but simply gave a brief exhale as he slowly reached his hand up and smoothly wiped the short streak of blood from Rowan's face. She barely flinched, but Rowan could tell that was something seriously off about Caine. Many questions were rolling through her mind, like why was he here among their enemies, and why did he want to see her personally?

Caine walked back over to the shelf and set the cup down, wiping Rowan's blood off on his clothing.

"I'm sorry for your suffering," he muttered back to her.

Rowan never took her eyes off of him.

"What are you talking about?"

"Everything," Caine muttered. He felt his heart beating harder than usual. "The loss of our home in the valley all those years ago still haunts me to this day. All the violence, all the destruction, and what happened to your father that night was the most tragic event of all."

Rowan shuddered. Whatever Caine was trying to

accomplish here right now, it had gotten her guard down.

"You know about my father?" she said in a high voice. "Were you also there when it happened?"

"I take it Delmar doesn't speak much of it?" Caine said in response. Rowan's eyes went down and he felt as though he needed to choose his words wisely. "I was there," he said, as Rowan's eyes jumped back up. "I saw what happened when your father fell."

Feeling it difficult to keep her cool, Rowan was desperate for more information.

"What happened?" she pleaded. "Tell me, please. All these years Delmar left me in the dark. I've been up most nights wondering if he at least died with honor and nobody will tell me anything. It's not fair to me!"

Caine put his hand up and quietly gestured for her to remain calm.

"I understand how you feel, Rowan, I really do, but I'm not here to talk about the Chief. What I know, however, is that he chose his own fate."

Rowan's breath suddenly stopped and her blood ran cold.

"What did you say?"

"Let me speak again," Caine replied. "The fight that took place in Ravenna that night, all of our people who died there, it could have been prevented. And if it had been, much would be different right now."

"And you just gave up," Rowan interjected. "You turned yourself over to the Domineers? How could you do that?" She waited for Caine to answer her, but he seemed to be growing colder with every minute that passed throughout this troublesome conversation. Rowan took a quick glance back toward the tent flap to make sure that no one was there, and then she moved in closer to Caine. "Come back with me," she whispered.

Caine looked her in the eyes with a serious expression.

"What?"

"You don't have to do this," Rowan continued. "You don't have to remain trapped her with our enemies. Help us get out of here. We'll take you to the stronghold we've built. Delmar will forgive you, I know he will." There was a long, awkward silence as he neither one of them spoke for a moment. Caine's eyes were looking this way and that, and Rowan's were fixated upon him, waiting for him to give her a sensible answer. "Please," she uttered desperately.

"Enough!" Caine screeched in frustration, clutching his head with his hand. Rowan had fallen silent with astonishment. As Caine glanced from the wine bottle on his shelf back to Rowan, his expression was becoming darker as each moment passed. "There is an outsider amongst you, isn't there?" Rowan's eyes widened at the mention of it, and Caine grew a slight, malevolent grin on his face. "I thought so."

"How do you know about Alex?" she asked impatiently.

"You saw all of those men out there, from the Outside?" Caine replied, pointing toward the entrance of the tent. "You remember the ones who brought you here? They are more steps ahead of you than you realize. We know everything, and anything we don't know we will learn soon enough, this I promise you. I've been here since the beginning of this unfortunate conflict. You are a fool if you think you can stand against Ramon Moreno and his followers. They will discover the location of your final hiding place and they will burn it to the ground, crushing all who resist. But I brought you here to offer you a chance to escape that inevitable outcome."

Rowan was shaking her head in utter disbelief.

"Inevitable outcome? How could you do this to your own people?"

"Do you think I had a choice?" Caine snapped back. "I told you already, it is a lost cause to resist Ramon's efforts, and I care too much to ever let you leave here and put yourself in danger. I know how you can help make this agony go away as soon as possible: you can tell me where the others are hiding. Tell me now, and I can guarantee no harm will come to you."

Rowan was struggling to maintain a calm demeanor. She

was starting to feel hot in the eyes and her muscles were tensing up as her gaze turned into a glare.

"I will never tell you anything!"

The atmosphere had fallen deathly silent. The two of them were locked in a glowering stare down. Deep inside, Caine had a strong feeling that Rowan would refuse what he believed to be reason. He was hardly surprised. For a moment he thought he could save her from an impending conflict; but the way he saw it now, she was still the young, naive, little child that he remembered before the fall of Ravenna.

"Fine," Caine snapped his fingers and the same two Domineers who had escorted Rowan to his quarters returned and seized hold of her arms. "Either way, I'm keeping you safe here, and I promise you this: we will learn where Delmar has dug in." Rowan struggled uselessly against her captors' grips as Caine continued to taunt her. "The outsider will tell us everything we need to know."

Rowan clenched her teeth in anger.

"Alex will tell you nothing!"

Caine snickered maliciously. He took a step forward and swiftly ripped Rowan's wooden pendant from her neck. She gasped as the thin, leather band snapped along the flesh of her neck.

"Oh, I think he will," Caine responded, pocketing the charm.

"Give that back to me!" Rowan squealed helplessly. "Please! It's all I have!"

Caine turned his head and waved for the Domineers to leave.

"Get her out of here," he commanded them as they began to force Rowan from the tent.

"YOU TRAITOR!" she screamed back at him.

"Delmar has chosen his fate," Caine spat back, almost choking on his words, "and I will do what he could not; I will keep you safe from harm."

Rowan continued to struggle against the Domineers' grip

on her as they carted her away. Caine stepped outside of his quarters into the cold, dreary environment and watched as she was taken. Wilson passed by as he approached Caine's tent. He looked from Caine to Rowan and back to him as if he was trying to analyze the situation. He stopped before Caine and waited for him to speak.

Caine first let out a brief sigh of exhaustion.

"What do you have to say?" he muttered.

"We've finished rounding up the Ravennite captives and placed them into holding cells," Wilson replied.

"Alright," Caine said back, seeming rather impatient, "but you know what I'm going to ask."

"Yes," Wilson nodded his head. "We've interrogated the prisoners one by one to attempt to identify the boy we're looking for-"

"And?" Caine cut him off.

Wilson swallowed. It seemed to him already knew the answer that he was about to deliver.

"Most of them refused to give us their names despite our best efforts. Those who did, however, do not have me convinced that they came from the Outside. Of course, this is extremely difficult nonetheless without knowing the boy's name or physical appearance."

"The boy's name is Alex," Caine answered almost instantly.

Wilson was slightly speechless.

"How do you-," he stammered, and then he remembered seeing Rowan being taken away from his quarters. "That girl told you his name? Who is she?"

"It doesn't matter," Caine said in frustration. "All that matters is that we get what we went out there for. You told me your men could get the job done, isn't that what you said?"

"You didn't give us anything to work with, you idiot!" Wilson snapped back. "But in case you haven't noticed, we brought back with his over two dozen Ravennite captives, something not even the Morenos could do in one night."

"But did you acquire the boy?" Caine was growing tired of hearing excuses. "I gave you his name, so I suggest you go back and try your interrogation methods over again."

Wilson narrowed his eyes.

"Watch who you're giving orders to, Ravennite. I'll take mine directly from Ramon Moreno, not you. My men and I are only here to share our abilities with you, not submit. We will proceed as we see fit."

"Don't test me, outsider!" Caine was feeling the excessive effects of the alcohol take hold of him. "As far as I'm concerned, you're as incompetent as those worthless fools who failed to capture that boy the first time!"

"You're drunk!" Wilson shook his head in disapproval. "Look at you, you're falling apart already!"

"Shut up!" Caine clutched his head in his hands. "For both our sakes, just get Robert what he asked for. I need time to think."

Wilson angrily restrained himself from responding. Instead, he turned around and stormed back toward the large, shabby structure lined around the wall. He had more work to do before he knew for sure if this boy called Alex was among the captives or not. If so, then he could be the key to discovering the location of the Ravennites' last hiding place, as well as what steps may need to be taken to run them down for good.

Inside the structure, the Domineers were guiding Rowan through one of the small, dim lit corridors. On one side the hallway was line with narrow, wooden doors, each roughly ten feet apart from each other. All of them were closed, but as they passed by Rowan could occasionally hear someone shuffling around on the inside and knocking against the doors. This was where the Domineers were keeping their prisoners, she was sure of it. At the end of the corridor there was one door that was open, which seemed to be precisely where they were taking her.

As they reached the open doorway, the Domineers

forcefully shoved Rowan inside. She found herself lying on the floor of a small, dark room hardly any bigger than a large closet. Realizing that this was meant to be her own personal cage, Rowan stood to her feet and stared at the two Domineers with as much intimidation as she could muster.

"You won't win!" she growled. "You hear me?" Her captors did not respond. One of them reached over and pulled down on a small lever which jutted precariously out of the wall beside the doorway, and instantly a wooden door slid quickly across the opening and sealed her cell.

Once the door had closed the small holding cell became pitch dark. Rowan began breathing rapidly as she instinctively knocked against the door, but it felt way too sturdy for her to ever break down. She scrambled along the surface to find the place where the door had met its frame when it shut, hoping to be able to pry it open, but there was nothing. There was nowhere to grab onto to gain any sort of leverage. It did not take Rowan long to realize that she was hopelessly trapped in this freezing box of pure darkness. Feeling the energy drain out of her system, she leaned forward and rested her head against the cell's door. "Alex," she whispered as she closed her eyes, "where have you gone?"

CHAPTER NINETEEN

Less than an hour had gone by since Alex had recovered Malachai from the debris. He had still not woken up, and the nighttime sky did not lighten up at all. Alex's sense of time had been completely disoriented since he was knocked out himself. All this time he spent stealthily patrolling the shattered remains of the outpost, hoping that the Domineers in the area would not be coming back to scavenge the campsite, or that the Ravennites from the Citadel might come to his aid.

Despite enduring the mountains' winter weather for weeks now, Alex was feeling colder than ever; not just on the outside but in his mind and heart as well. In the span of less than a single night it seemed that all of the efforts his Ravennite friends had made in the sparse name of hope had been all but ripped away. Everyone whom had occupied the outpost was now gone; either captured or killed, and only Malachai now remained. Rowan was gone, and he blamed himself. He abandoned his post, and for all he knew he left the rest of them open for a surprise attack. He had a strong feeling in his gut that if, by some miracle, he ever saw Rowan again that she might see him just as guilty as he currently saw himself.

As Alex completed yet another round along the outpost's broken walls, he headed back to the center of the site where he had left Malachai's unconscious husk. He was shivering consistently as the ice cold breeze gnawed at his face. It made him feel very grateful for the gift Rowan had given to him earlier which was wrapped around his neck, but at the same time it filled him with just as much guilt. Alex sat down near Malachai and gazed off into space. He started trying to imagine what the Domineers might have in store for their captives. Where did they come from, and where had they taken the Ravennites?

With a loud, disturbing gasp, Malachai suddenly regain his consciousness. Alex jumped as he looked over to see Malachai thrash about as he clambered to his feet and rapidly scanned around in all directions, grunting menacingly. Soon he managed to calm down a notch and looked directly at Alex, still breathing heavily. Alex was motionless as he stared back blankly, awkwardly positioning himself to grab his sword in case he needed it.

"You!" Malachai screeched hoarsely. He glanced around again at the destroyed campsite. "What happened? Where are the others?"

"Captured," Alex caught his breath, "I think."

"You think?" Malachai was still panicking. "The Domineers closed in, I saw it! We tried to fight but I went dark!" He set his attention on Alex once again. "Why are you still here?"

"Malachai, relax," Alex stood up and tried to calm him down.

"I can't relax! My people are in danger, and they'll be back I just know it! What happened to you? Answer me that!"

Alex gathered his thoughts as quickly as he could.

"I was knocked out while searching the borders. When I woke up the fight was already over and everyone was gone."

Malachai scanned the area again.

"And the dead?"

"Very few," Alex answered, hoping that it might be enough to cool Malachai's hysteria. "I searched already. That was when I found you buried under the rubble of the wall."

No such thanks ever came from Malachai for digging him out, as Alex expected. He simply turned his back on him and tried to take in his surroundings.

"Where have they gone then?" he muttered to himself before glancing back at Alex. "Back to the Citadel?"

"I don't think so," Alex replied grimly. "I told you, I have reason to believe they've been captured."

"What reason?" Malachai hissed. "I can't believe that all of my people here could be taken so easily. What makes you think otherwise?"

Alex took a deep breath before answering.

"Earlier, while I was scouting the woods, I overheard a couple of Domineers talking about their mission. I heard them say that they were to capture as many of us alive as possible." Alex managed to stop himself there. Something in his head told him that it might not be wise to tell Malachai that he believed the Domineers were specifically looking for him. Surely Malachai would not hesitate to hand Alex over to them in exchange for the rest of the Ravennites.

"You heard them say that?" Malachai was in a state of total disbelief. "Where did they go?"

"I-" Alex began. Did Malachai not realize that Alex was just as lost as he was? "I don't know. I told you everything I heard them say. They said something about a furnace but they left before I could hear anything else." Malachai turned his back again, and Alex could see that he was clenching his fists in frustration. Alex did not want to see the atmosphere become too heated so he continued to speak what he could. "I doubt they could have gone too far. They must have been near enough in order to stage an assault like they did."

Malachai suddenly whipped around and pointed at Alex.

"You said a furnace?"

Alex looked up and could see a serious look in his eyes.

"I did. At least that's what I heard." He nodded his head.

His expression turning somewhat blank, Malachai seemed to be thinking deeply. Alex held his breath, waiting for him to say something. Eventually, he could see the light bulb going off in his head.

"By the moon!" Malachai exclaimed. "The Iron Furnace! It must be!"

Alex was confused.

"What? What is that?"

Malachai shook his head.

"You're as ignorant as the lot of them," he sneered

disrespectfully. "Don't worry about it."

"Don't worry about it?" Alex said in frustration. "Our- I mean, your people are in trouble. We both need to share everything we know with one another, it's the only way."

"You've done enough already," Malachai hissed. As he turned his back once again he sighed to himself, and Alex was pleasantly surprised to hear him answer his previous question in a low tone. "The Iron Furnace is a location in these mountains which was once used by our ancestors for firing clay and other precious resources extracted from the vast mines below. It was abandoned years ago, but if what you heard is correct, then I'd be willing to bet my life that the Domineer scum have set up camp there all along."

Alex found himself rather impressed with Malachai's reckoning. He had never heard of this Iron Furnace before, but it sounded as though it might be possible that Malachai's words were true.

"Where is this place?" he asked urgently. "How far away?"

"Several miles east at most," Malachai immediately answered. "It makes sense now; it would make an excellent foothold while trying to keep us pinned down." He clenched his fists again, and soon began to march away toward the stone wall.

Alex stood up and alert.

"Wait, where are you going?"

"To rescue my brothers!" Malachai declared confidently. "The ones that are still alive."

"Alone?" Alex exclaimed in astonishment. "Wouldn't it be wiser to go back to the Citadel and get help? The Domineers' numbers must be huge."

"You go back," Malachai grunted as he walked. "I, on the other hand, will not leave my people to suffer and die at the hands of your kind."

His words were offensive to Alex. Quickly trying to make a decision of his own, he began to follow Malachai out of the campsite and into the woods.

"You can't go out there alone! It's too dangerous!"

"Don't tell me what I can and cannot do in my own homeland, Outsider," Malachai fired back. "I told you to go back to the Citadel. This does not concern you."

It was becoming more apparent that Malachai was not willing to sit down and compromise with reason, so Alex stopped and called out desperately, "They've taken Rowan."

Just as he thought, Malachai halted in his tracks and stared back at Alex.

"What did you say?"

"You heard me," Alex replied daringly. "I don't want harm to come to her any more than you do. This situation is way too serious for you to handle on your own, don't you see that? We need to get help from Delmar."

Malachai was stuck in a brief silence. He seemed to be struggling to make his decision, and for once Alex could sense a state of fear rising up in him.

"I can't," he shook his head. "If the Domineers have hostile intentions in store for my people then I can't afford to waste any time. I have to try. I have to do something." With that, he began walking away again.

Frustrated as he was, Alex had to admit that, for the first time, he and Malachai were sharing a mutual idea. Knowing this, Alex composed himself and proceeded to catch up with Malachai.

"Then I'm coming with you."

"What?" Malachai responded in disbelief. "I don't want you with me. Don't you know that?"

"But you need me. You can't do this by yourself."

"You really think I need you?" Malachai snickered. "The Ravennites have gotten along perfectly fine without you here, and especially without the scum that came before you."

Alex was on the verge of snapping. It was so sick and tired of Malachai's attitude toward him.

"Stop blaming me for what the Morenos did to you. I am nothing like them."

Malachai froze again, and for a moment Alex thought he was preparing to start a quarrel with him. However, he saw that Malachai was staring off into the trees like a hawk.

"Shut up!" he commanded in a whisper. Alex listened intently. "Someone's coming!"

He was right. Soon Alex could hear footsteps quickly approaching. Malachai had already gone for his sword and wielded it out in front of him. It was clear that he was not going to go down with a fight. Holding his breath, Alex held tight to his sword and waited for the Domineers to break the tree line.

Suddenly, a figure emerged from the darkness before them, looking around frantically before finally seeing the two sword bearers. Alex gasped out loud and Malachai made a threatening gesture. However, when their potential foe quickly armed a bow and pointed it at them, Alex's sight adjusted well enough to identify who it was.

"Zak!" Alex exclaimed. "Is that you?"

Turning his arrow toward Alex, Zak then lowered it when he finally recognized the two of them. "Alex," he sighed with relief, "Malachai! Is it really you? What happened?"

Malachai lowered his sword and let out a sigh of relief.

"The outpost is lost," he answered somberly. "Those Domineer cowards ambushed us. Were you with the outpost as well?"

Zak nodded in response.

"Yes I was. I ran into Alex Lee searching the surrounding woods just before the fight began, but we got separated while hiding from a party of scouts."

"What happened to you?" Alex asked him. "Why didn't you make your way back to the campsite?"

"At first I tried looking for you after the Domineers headed away from us, but I couldn't find where you had gone. Shortly after the fighting started at the outpost. I headed back to it as fast as I could but when I got there the Domineers had already overwhelmed those who were still inside the walls. It was then that I realized what they had done; they somehow knew that they could draw us out into the trees and cut our strength by separating us. I regret to admit that I hid when I saw that it was hopeless. The battle was over in minutes, and the majority of our brothers were captured and taken. I tried to stalk them back to where they had come from but, their footprints were many and too difficult to follow. On was finally on my way back to the remains of our outpost when I ran into you two."

Malachai and Alex exchanged looks of concern. It seemed that, given what Zak had witnessed, their enemies were much smarter and stronger than they had originally thought. Malachai could not help but feel angry with himself for failing to defeat their attackers. In a way, he must have felt that rescuing the captive Ravennites was his burden to redeem himself.

Alex stowed his sword back into its scabbard.

"Malachai thinks that the Domineers may have made a command post in a place called the Iron Furnace."

Zak's eyebrows rose at the sound of the name. He looked over at Malachai.

"The Iron Furnace? Do you really think it's possible? How could we not have known?"

"I don't know," Malachai replied bluntly. "The only lead I have is what this wretch here thinks he heard from the Domineers." Alex glared at Malachai behind his back for continuing to disrespect him. "The furnace is not far from here. We'll have to search the area to know for sure. Ravennite lives are at stake."

"Then I'm with you!" Zak said proudly. "We will not abandon our people to suffer and die, or we will die trying."

For a brief second, Alex could have sworn he saw Malachai manage a slight smile. However, another thought was coming to his mind.

"Wait a minute," Alex interjected. "Wouldn't it make more sense for at least one of us to go back to the Citadel and send for help?"

"Listen to me, boy!" Malachai clenched his teeth. "We've

already been over this, the Citadel is too far away and my people need help now. If you want to run then be my guest, then maybe I can finally be rid of your worthlessness."

Alex was so tired of dealing with Malachai's insults at this point that he was beginning to let his frustration get the better of him.

"Worthlessness? I saved you from freezing to death under that pile of rocks. You're welcome," he fired back.

"I don't need your help!" Malachai stubbornly retorted. "Don't forget that the only reason you're still here is because Delmar has ordered that not a hand be laid on you."

Alex's jaw dropped at the sound of what seemed to be an apparent threat. Zak was watching the argument with growing concern. He stepped closer to the two of them.

"Malachai, we need to hold ourselves together if we're going to have a chance of helping our people."

"Yes, he's right," Alex was trying to relieve his tension. "This arguing is pointless. We need to save our energy for the Domineers. I have a feeling we'll need it."

"Is this coming from two cravens who separated from the company at the time that the Domineers attacked?" Malachai responded condescendingly.

Upon hearing this comment, Zak lowered his head in shame. Alex, on the other hand, was growing angrier and less patient with Malachai's attitude.

"We were doing what we could to seek out the Domineer scouts," Alex said in defense. "We had no idea that they intended to launch a full scale assault on the campsite itself. None of us did, not even you."

"Watch your mouth, Outsider!" Malachai growled. "I don't need you here anymore than I needed you at the outpost."

"And I'm not here for you," Alex spat back. "You may not like it, but I'm here to help my friends the same way you are, especially Rowan, because you and I both know that Delmar would be devastated if anything ever happened to her."

Malachai glared at Alex.

"You stay away from Rowan, you understand me? I don't trust you not to harm her the same way I don't trust the other Outsiders."

"How dare you!?" Alex cried out with wide eyes. "How dare you compare me to the Domineers? You don't know anything about me. You never bothered to learn about me like she has. That is why she's my friend!"

Zak was feeling uncomfortable as the tensions were continuing to escalate. Malachai was breathing irregularly and angrily, giving Alex his death stare.

"You brainwashed her!" he hissed at him. "Just like you brainwashed Matheus and all the others. Even Delmar is falling for your ruse. But you won't fool me! I've seen what the savages of the Outside are capable of, and as far as I'm concerned you are all evil! You all deserve to die!"

As Zak continued to watch with growing uneasiness, Alex felt his anger causing him to becoming increasingly aggressive inside.

"Is that a threat, Malachai?"

Swishing his sword briefly in front of him, Malachai was losing control of his leading composure.

"Know this; only Delmar has been protecting you from the Ravennites giving you what you deserve. If it weren't for our loyalty to him you'd be long dead already!"

Alex quickly lost his grip on his calm demeanor. He swiftly drew his sword once again.

"You've wanted this for a long time, haven't you?" he stood his ground as best he could. "To challenge me?"

"To challenge you?" Malachai responded with something between a snicker and growl. "You're hardly as skilled at fighting as a newborn a wolf pup. I will crush you right here and right now, and nobody will ever know!" He grew a very angry grin on his face.

Alex did his best to stand as intimidating as possible. The conscience in his mind was trying to tell him that this was a very foolish thing to do. He only recently became skilled enough with his sword to defeat Rowan in a duel but had never even been able to overcome Matheus' abilities. There was absolutely no way he would stand a chance against the rage of Malachai, but his own anger with him was blotting his common sense out completely. His judgment and his eyesight were becoming hazy.

"Your trouble is that you think you're the only person in the world who has problems. Your anger and your hate stretches farther than your ability to think."

"Shut up! You've never fought a day in your life the way we have been forced to!"

"Oh, really?" Alex mocked. "For what are fighting? You have no home, no allies, and not a hope in hell. You have nothing to fight for."

"We do," Malachai said, his restraint almost depleted, "it's called honor, something you Outsiders know nothing about!"

Alex's muscles were so tense now that he was not sure how much longer it would be before the two of them lost all control.

"If honor is all you have left," he muttered to Malachai, "then you're as good as dead."

"Stop!" Zak shouted at them, anticipating the impending battle. It was too late, however. Malachai's eyes burst wide open as he cried out and lunged at Alex with a sword attack. Shocked, but prepared nonetheless, Alex quickly managed deflected his attack. However, as soon as he did Malachai snatched hold of his blue scarf and threw him aside. Alex tumbled onto the ground but quickly leaped back onto his feet. He hissed with every breath as he squared his shoulders and prepared for another clash with Malachai. The two of them moved against each other again and again, all the while Zak was shouting at them to stop what they were doing before one of them was killed, or worse, both of them.

Alex tried to hold his ground against his opponent, but unlike Rowan and even Matheus, Malachai was a fiercely powerful combatant. He applied so much force behind each swing of his blade that Alex could feel himself struggling to not fall down on his back every time their swords collided. His grunts were terrifying and full of hate. Alex did not want to kill him, but it was obvious that Malachai did not share that thought. He was trying to find the best opportunity to disarm Malachai but he was just too strong.

As Alex grew more exhausted from the fight, Malachai built up his ground and unleashed a powerful front kick against him that completely threw him off of his feet. The wind was knocked out of him as he hit the ground, and Malachai was circling around him like a predatory shark.

"You're weak," he taunted Alex on the ground, "just like all of the other Outsiders, and I'll prove it when I rescue my brethren from your kind of scum." Alex was hissing angrily as he attempted to get up to his feet, but Malachai pointed his sword back down at him. "You get up, you die."

Alex's anger had become so critical that his mind was going completely blank. He felt his head beginning to ache. He had felt the same aching sensation before; many months ago when he was stuck in the abandoned clay mine after it collapsed on him. There was something very unusual about the feeling. It made him feel...powerful. Tears were being forced out of the corners of his eyes by the intense cold. He sturdily brought himself to his feet and met Malachai's gaze. Malachai raised his sword up, and Alex stared back at him, feeling a level of anger that he had never experienced before. For a second, he did not even know if he was in control of his own actions, for he suddenly released a long and loud cry as he swung his sword at Malachai's. As their blades clashed again, Alex hit it with such incredible force that it instantly shattered Malachai's sword.

Malachai's eyes widened immensely and his jaw dropped as the powerful impact forced him back. It was the first time he had ever truly been shocked. Alex, however, released his grip on his sword as an intense, sharp pain suddenly engulfed his head, emanating in rapid waves from his forehead outward. The unknown red symbol was flashing in his sight again. Alex screamed so frighteningly that it disturbed Zak and even Malachai as they watched as he clutched at his forehead and writhed violently before collapsing unconscious onto the ground.

Sensing that he had been knocked unconscious once again, Alex opened his burning eyes. He was staring at the same mysterious vision he had seen before, but his mind was so dazed that he could not think anything of it. Just as before, he was looking at the shrouded figure of a man cloaked by a bright light in the distance. The man was holding the massive sword-like object, just like the last time. Alex remained motionless with a mixture of fear and curiosity running through his head as the vision seemed to repeat itself.

"Who are you?" The echoing voice of the man spoke up again.

This time the vision did not end and allow Alex to wake up. At first he thought the man was speaking to him, but suddenly he heard the sound of woman's voice respond to him.

"My grandfather's grandfather was called Janus," Alex listened to the female voice speak, but no one else appeared in his vision. He narrowed his eyes at the sound of it. The woman's voice sounded so familiar, but Alex's mind was too clouded to recognize it. He could suddenly sense the vision coming to an end as the light in the distance began to glow brighter and engulf his surroundings once again, but this time, as the vision faded away, he could faintly hear the woman's voice finish speaking, "He is not of this world."

Malachai was back up against a tree in shock at what had just happened. Alex was lying on the ground, out cold. Looking at the remains of his sword, Malachai was utterly speechless as he stared down at the hilt with nothing more than a couple inches of the blade shards still attached to it. Against what he could have ever imagined, Alex somehow managed to muster enough strength to break his sword, leaving nothing but many pieces of the stone blade scattered around on the ground. Malachai was more than confused by what happened to Alex after the dramatic incident. He acted so erratically before he finally passed out in the snow, and the two of them did not know what to make of it.

"What just happened?" Zak exclaimed with a tone of astonishment.

Malachai stepped forward and picked Alex's sword off of the ground.

"That boy is a freak," he mumbled. Malachai stroked Alex's blade a few times, a look of contempt on his face as he stared down at the limp boy before him. "I will end him right now."

"What?" Zak gasped out loud. "Malachai, stop this now! This has gone too far already."

Malachai only turned his glare to Zak.

"I blame Matheus for this. I intend to do right now what he should have done months ago. I will end this here and now and be done with it, and then we will rescue the others."

"You can't, Malachai!" Zak persisted. "Delmar has commanded that Alex not be harmed by our own hands. Would you really go behind Delmar's back and disobey his authority?"

Malachai was taking deep breaths. He could not admit that there was truth in what Zak was saying. He was just as angry with this boy as he was every outsider he had encountered in the past. In the back of his mind he knew that he was afraid; afraid that his anger might be so strong that it would actually interfere with his unshakable loyalty to his oldest friend, Delmar. No, that could not be true. He needed to do this. It just had to be done.

"Stay out of this, Zak!" he growled instead. "This does not concern you." Malachai raised a shaky arm, preparing to strike Alex's unconscious body with his own sword.

"Malachai!" Zak quickly fetched an arrow from his quiver and pointed his bow at him. "You will not kill that boy!"

Malachai froze and turned his head to stare at Zak in surprise. He was speechless to see that his own ally seemed to be turning on him.

"You dare turn your weapon on me? Me!?"

"Look at yourself!" Zak fought back. "You have so much hate for the outsiders that you've allowed it to blind your judgment. Alex Lee has never meant any harm to us and you know that, and now he's spent all this time trying to help us in any way he can. I can see that, why can't you?"

"We don't need his help!" Malachai yelled at him. "You don't understand! He's an outsider, he's no different the rest of them. I've seen what they can do!"

"Delmar has ordered his protection!"

"Delmar is wrong!"

Zak was shocked by the words that he just heard. He was beginning to believe that there was no hope for Malachai to let go of his hatred. His arms were beginning to shake unstably, but he managed to maintain hold of his bow.

"Malachai," he said with a strong tone of voice, "if you lay a hand on the boy then I swear on the grave of the Chief I will shoot you!"

For a moment which felt like an eternity the two of them were locked in a tense stare down. Malachai still held the sword above his head, and Zak was aiming his arrow directly at Malachai's heart. Both of them were waiting for the other to make a decisive move. Malachai started breathing heavily again. Zak braced himself, trying to hold tight to the string of the bow. Suddenly, Malachai let out a loud roar of anger, and he threw Alex's sword down into the snow.

Zak was surprised by his action. He lowered his bow cautiously. Malachai shot him a deathly look, and then he turned and stormed off into the dark woods.

"Malachai!" Zak called after him. "Where are you going?" Malachai did not answer, and just disappeared into the darkness.

Zak did not know what to think. Was Malachai abandoning them? He was walking in neither the direction of the Citadel or the Iron Furnace. Zak was just as lost on what to do. He could not leave Alex alone, unconscious in the snow, but he did not know what Malachai was going to do. For a moment, it seemed to him that their efforts to save the Ravennites captured by the Domineers had all been in vain. Zak sat down against a tree and put his head in his hands. After all the hope their people had built up in the past weeks alone, this single night seemed to bring them all back down to their knees.

Malachai hiked aimlessly through the woods for several minutes. He was so angry that he felt the endless urge to punch every tree that he saw. That boy deserved to die and his own cultural brother had deliberately stood in his way; someone who had been enduring everything that he had, and he was defending the outsider with his life. As far as Malachai was concerned, that was treason, pure and simple.

He knew exactly what had happened. Zak was trying to manipulate him by using Delmar's words against him. That is what he felt inside. Malachai never understood it. Why would Delmar command his people not to lay a hand on an outsider who just willfully walked into their territory? Why would he afford him the freedom to walk among the Ravennites as if he was one of them? This was all so incredibly frustrating to him. They spent years preparing to combat these bloodthirsty outsiders and now they were harboring one and teaching him to fight like one of them, and somehow he had proved strong enough to break Malachai's own sword. Who knew what else he would be capable of?

It was not fair! More and more he felt as though he was the only one left with his grip on the real world. With everyone now trying to protect this boy as much as they were protecting what was left of their ravaged home, Malachai was beginning to feel like everybody was turning on him. He could not stand to see the way Delmar, Matheus, even Rowan seemed to trust the outsider with their lives. Why should he do the same? Outsiders were responsible for stealing their homeland with no remorse. He had killed many of them that day, and he knew what they were capable of. So why was this one any different?

Malachai felt like he was losing his mind. Could it be possible that Delmar really did know what he was doing? And what about Rowan? He could not stand to see how close she had become to Alex. Malachai cared about Rowan's safety just as much as Delmar did. He knew that he would have done everything in his power to keep Rowan out of the evil hands of the outsiders, but it was undeniable that she was now happier than she had been in years whenever she was around this particular one. Now, to Malachai's greatest fear, it appeared that Rowan had been taken away by the Domineers along with several dozen of his friends and brothers. A sudden realization was invading his mind; the realization that Alex was trying to do everything he could to help rescue them, especially Rowan. More than that, Alex had returned to the outpost after the attack and pulled him out from under the rocks of the fallen wall. Malachai could not believe this. When the boy could have taken his perfect chance to run away and never come back, he actually came to his rescue. Alex had come to his rescue, even after the terrible way he had treated him ever since he first arrived, and now it seemed that he wanted to help them all more than anything.

The constant struggle within Malachai's mind was almost too much for him to endure. He had trained himself for years to unfairly judge all outsiders by the way he had seen the actions of some of them. His intense anger which still flowed inside him was quickly turning against him. Malachai tried desperately to gather his thoughts, but they were racing too fast for him to control. It did not matter, though, and he knew it. He knew in his heart what the real answer was. Malachai dropped down into the snow and leaned back against a tree. Shaking and breathing rapidly, he tried hard to control himself, but to no avail. He soon broke down in tears, resting his head in his hands.

Malachai spent several minutes pouring the intense emotions out through his eyes before he finally looked up at the sky. To his surprise, he found himself looking up through the tree canopy at a clear opening in the nighttime sky. He could see the full moon surrounded by countless stars. It looked so beautiful to him and, for once in his life, the cold, autumnal air felt quite soothing to him. It almost felt like something was trying to help guide him to do what he knew was the right thing to do.

"Delmar," Malachai whispered as he continued to gaze up at the moon, tears still flowing out of his eyes, "I am so sorry."

CHAPTER TWENTY

Zak never moved from his spot. With Alex unconscious and Malachai gone, he had no choice but wait for him to wake up. What it was that they were going to do after that was unclear. If the Domineers really were at the Iron Furnace, then there was no way they could save their friends without Malachai's help. Zak wanted all of this to end just as soon as the rest of them did.

To his surprise, Alex woke up sooner than he expected. For a while, Zak was contemplating picking him up and trying to hike all the way back to the Citadel. Alex had woken with a brief panic episode. He quickly sat up on the ground and looked around hastily for Malachai before he realized that he was gone. Alex caught his breath and saw Zak sitting against a tree adjacent to him, looking back at him silently.

"What happened?" Alex asked, catching his breath and putting a hand to his forehead, which was still aching a little bit.

"I'm not sure," Zak shook his head. "Your fight with Malachai did not end well."

"Where is he?" Alex said, looking around for him again. "I didn't kill him, did I?"

"No," Zak replied. "You destroy his sword somehow. I've never seen anything like it before. You looked like you were in a great deal of pain and then you passed out completely."

"I remember," Alex muttered. This night had proven to be the strangest he had ever been through by far.

"Malachai," Zak began with a brief stammer, "he tried to kill you after you fell, but I stopped him."

Alex was having mixed feelings coursing through his mind. "Where did he go?"

"I don't know," Zak replied, glancing down. "He stormed off in anger. I didn't know what else to do so I stayed here with you, waiting for you to wake up.

"Well, then," Alex sighed, pulling himself up to his feet, "we'll have to find the Domineers' camp without him." He began searching around the woods to figure out which way they would need to go.

"Wait, what?" Zak jumped to his feet. "Alex, we can't do this by ourselves. We wouldn't have a chance without the rest of the Ravennites, let alone without Malachai."

"What would you propose we do, then?" Alex retorted, still glancing this way and that. "You'll have to lead on, Zak, I don't know the way to the Iron Furnace."

"Alex, you're not listening to me!" Zak tried to get his attention. "We cannot march in there completely outnumbered. I don't think there is anything we can do right now."

"I don't care!" Alex shook his head. "Rowan is being held there and it's all my fault, I left my post at the campsite. I don't care what happens out there, I'm getting Rowan out of there, or I'll die trying."

Zak was utterly speechless. Malachai was gone, and now it seemed that he was not going to be able to get through to Alex either.

"But..." he began, but was suddenly interrupted by an unexpected entrance.

"Count me in," Malachai suddenly took over the atmosphere as he returned from out of the dark tree line. Zak and Alex both stared as Malachai reappeared. The last time Alex had seen him they were both locked in an epic duel. Upon seeing him, he quickly realized that he had never picked his sword back up.

"Malachai," Zak began, but Malachai quickly put his hand up to silence him as he walked past him and toward Alex. As he approached him, Alex found himself instinctively backing up as Malachai walked toward him. He accidently tripped back over a log buried in the snow and fell onto his back.

Malachai headed over and stopped before Alex, looking down on him. Zak stood by, holding his breath and waiting for Malachai to start another violent confrontation.

Alex lied on his back in the snow and stared up into his eyes. Malachai took a deep breath and closed his eyes.

"Alex," he breathed, "forgive me."

Narrowing his eyes cautiously, Alex was not sure what to think of this.

"What?"

Malachai outstretched his hand. It seemed that he wanted to help Alex up off of the ground. Reaching up and taking hold his hand, Malachai then pulled Alex to his feet. The two managed to lock eyes again, but this time, for the first time, they were not looking at each other like hated enemies.

"I am sorry," Malachai began to apologize quietly. "I am sorry for all of the hostility I showed toward you all these months. It was not fair. You must understand, I've seen the outsiders at their worst. I saw what they did to my innocent people in the valley. From then on I was led to believe that you were all the same." He looked Alex in the eyes once again, giving a serious look but also an apologetic one. "I was so wrong, but I think I've known that for a while now. Rowan saw something in you. I don't know what, but thanks to you she was able to show many of the Ravennites that they need not be afraid of all of your kind."

Zak could not believe what he was hearing come out of Malachai's mouth. Alex felt exactly the same way, but only a small part of him was cautious about what he was saying. Most of him knew that Malachai was being sincere.

"You know I really meant it when I said that I would help you take back what was stolen from you in any way I could, you know that right?"

"Yes, I do," Malachai muttered in response, "but for the longest time I did not want to believe it. I just wanted a reason to believe that you would cause harm to my people, and for that I am truly sorry."

Alex looked past Malachai at Zak. He could see that Zak was more than moved by Malachai's sudden change of heart. Just by looking into his eyes, Alex could see that Zak was once again prepared to do what they had come out here to do. Alex put a hand on Malachai's shoulder.

"Do you still have anger in you?" he asked. Malachai looked at him curiously. "Good," Alex continued. "Let's show it to the Domineers. We've got friends and family to save."

Just then, Alex saw something that never thought was possible up until now: Malachai grew a smile on his face. Not an evil or malicious smile, for once, but a smile of confidence in a new friend. Zak approached the two of them and joined the group.

"Malachai," Alex began again, "you know the way to the Iron Furnace, right?"

"That's right," Malachai answered with a nod.

"Good," Alex replied. "Lead us there. Together we'll find our captive comrades and bust them out of there."

It took little more than an hour for the party of three to hike through the snowy hills. They followed Malachai's lead as he seemed to know exactly where he was going like the back of his hand. He was constantly signaling behind him for Alex and Zak to stay low or to get out of sight, just in case Domineers may have been patrolling the area.

It was strange, but Alex seemed to be feeling colder now than he did during his previous battle with Malachai. Maybe it was because of the freezing breeze which occasionally picked up and rushed through the trees, or maybe it was because he was feeling more than anxious about what they were about to do. If the Domineers were numerous and cunning enough to take the majority of the Ravennites from the outpost, then how could the three of them possibly hope to be able to free them. The truth was that he had absolutely no idea what they were going to do. He was just as scared as they were.

Eventually, Malachai brought the small company to a halt

at the base of a medium sized hill. After asking what it was, he informed them that the Iron Furnace lied in a small valley just on the other side of the hill. He told them to keep quiet and listen, and sure enough Alex could hear the sounds of multiple voices ringing up in the near distance. There was no question anymore, the Domineers had set up camp at the Iron Furnace. Malachai and Zak knew about the location, but Alex had never seen it before. Alex looked up at the sky. It had still not lightened up any, but he knew that it to be at least close to dawn, which meant that they would soon run out of the cover of darkness. So they had to make this quick, whatever it was that they intended to do.

The three of them quickly hiked up the hill, staying low and using the trees for cover, which grew more and more sparse as they neared the top. At the peak of the low hill, Malachai suddenly told the others to drop down immediately. Alex and Zak did as they were told. Dropping down into the snow, the three of them crawled through the cold, white substance until at least they could see what they had come for.

Malachai had told Alex that the Iron Furnace lied on the other side of the hill, but he did not expect it to be so literal. They had crawled through the snow to the edge of a sudden drop almost steep enough to be a cliff. The drop descended about thirty feet, and just at the bottom they could see the beginning of a wooden wall, built about a dozen feet high and wrapping around the valley in a huge circle, similar to the way their own outpost had been constructed. However, something told Alex that the Domineers had been here a lot longer.

Alex examined the Domineers' fortified camp. It was at least three times the size of the Ravennites' destroyed outpost. There were torches lined all along the wall, just like the walls at the Citadel. Looking out, near the center and toward the left, Alex could see the large, rock tower which he assumed to be the Iron Furnace. Dozens of people could be seen walking all around the fortress. Along the wall which bordered the hillside a large structure was built that stretched halfway around the wall, and a short tower was standing up near its middle. Alex was amazed by how much the Domineers had managed to accomplish on their own. It was obvious, however, that the Ravennites' Citadel was much larger and far more fortified, but the very sight of this fortress was a testament to just how crafty their enemies really were, and there was no doubt anymore that this must have been where the Ravennite prisoners were being held. The question was: how were they going to get in? And how were they going to free their friends?

"Hey," Zak whispered in a low voice, "look over there." He pointed toward the wall to their right. "I think I can see a gate. That must be how they get in and out."

Malachai examined what he was pointing out and shook his head.

"That won't be any good to us," he rebuked. "There's no way we could make it past it."

"He's right," Alex agreed. "We need to find a way to make it in unseen while we still have the dark to cover us. If we're caught then it's all over. Look down there," Alex himself was now directing their attention toward the structure along the wall. "I'd be willing to bet that they're keeping their prisoners somewhere within that building. It doesn't look like it would be too difficult to search, that is depending on how many Domineers are in there."

Malachai nodded.

"You're probably right. The hard part is still getting in. I propose we make it down the hill, for starters. It doesn't look like they're guarding the rear walls as heavily. Maybe we could find a way to scale it and sneak in without them seeing us."

"Yeah, I'd like to see you try."

The three of them quickly exchanged brief looks of confusion, and then they leaped to their feet only to come face to face with a small party of Domineer scouts who had snuck up behind them. At the same time, about a dozen more of them emerged out of the darkness, all pointing swords and strange looking gun-like weapons at them.

"No," Alex gasped under his breath. "No!" By instinct he put his hands in the air, but Zak and Malachai stood their ground and stared at the Domineers with hate. As the Domineers approached them, the one in the center of the party, presumably the one who had spoken, was eyeing the three Ravennites heavily. What seemed to catch his eye was the contrast in the way they had reacted when they realized that they were cornered. Two of them stood still and glared angrily, but only one of them had put his hands up, just like an outsider might.

"Caine's prediction was right," the man presumed to be leading the squad spoke again. "He warned us that any straggling Ravennites would attempt to follow us in the hopes of saving their friends." He walked slowly in front of each of them as if to taunt them. "This must be the last of them." He signaled for his comrades to approach. "Take their weapons and bind their hands, then take them all to a cell. Robert will figure out what to do with them when we're finished with the others."

Malachai held his expression firm, but his mind lit up at the Domineer's words. The rest of the Ravennites really were here, and it seemed Robert Moreno was spearheading the fortress. However, none of that mattered anymore. He could not believe how quickly and easily they had been captured. The Domineers had tricked them, and he was more than enraged at the thought of letting them win.

As the Domineers were binding Malachai's hands together with a dingy rope, Zak was looking over at them as if he was expecting some sort of backup plan. Malachai was continued to give them all his loathsome glare. Alex, as much as he felt in his gut to remain silent, could not help but blurt out. "Where is Rowan!?"

All of the Domineers suddenly stopped and stared at Alex. The leader grew a very curious expression about his face as he approached Alex and stood directly in front of him. He was close enough to Alex to feel the light tips of his breath. Alex stared back into his eyes for a second, but could not help but look away due to the pressure. The man continued to stare him down intensely. As Alex looked away, the man uttered one simple word in a tone as low as a whisper, "The Outsider?"

At the sound of the buzz word, Alex suddenly looked back up at him in reaction. It was not long before he realized he had made a terrible mistake when the Domineer began to grow an awestruck expression. "Change of plans," he muttered to his cohorts. "Take the other two to a cell. This one comes with me."

Alex's eyes widened as he glanced at Zak and Malachai. The two of them were concerned but confused at the same time, but Alex knew what was really going on. It all made sense; the point of the Domineers' attack on the outpost was to try to find him and bring him here, and they took as many of the Ravennites prisoner as they could. Now, against his better judgment, he unwittingly revealed to them by his own hand who he was, and he hated himself for it. As Malachai and Zak were bound and the three of them were taken back down the hill and toward the fortress' gate, Alex could not help but feel that, despite their best efforts, the Domineers had just won.

As the Domineer party led them to the gate, they signaled for it to be opened up and they took the three of them inside. While leading them toward the structure at the other end of the wall, Alex looked around at the Iron Furnace fortress. All of the Domineers that they passed gave them looks of triumph. It seemed to Alex that they also believed they had won. He did not know what lied in store for them now. Just as he had heard, the other two were going to be put in cells, which must have been what they were keeping the other Ravennites in this whole time, but where was he being taken? He certainly did not have a good feeling about it whatsoever.

Soon they had entered into the structure. It was dark

inside, lit only by a small torch on the walls here and there. Malachai and Zak were immediately told to turn and head down a long corridor to the right. As they turned, Alex tried to call out to them. "Malachai!" his voice reverberated throughout the corridor.

Malachai made a quick glance back at Alex and gave him a look that almost said, "Don't worry about me."

"Move!" The party's leader nudged at Alex's back and urged him to head up a short flight of steps at the opposite wall of the hallway. Halfway up the staircase opened up into a whole new hallway which would have run parallel to the first level. Alex's captors urged him to instead turn right as the staircase continued up several more steps and revealed a separate corridor which they had entered. The Domineers guided him down the narrow hall until, to their right, there was an opening in the wall with a couple of steps leading up to wooden doorway. One of the Domineers stepped forward and grabbed hold of a small handle on the door and slid it out of the way. "In, now!" The man who opened the door grabbed hold of Alex's arm and forced him through the doorway. He then slid the door shut behind him.

Alex turned and tried to examine the dark lit room that he was now it. It was small, and he immediately saw a young man standing with his back turned to him and looking out of a long window cut out of the far wall which overlooked the Domineers' fortress.

"Where am I?" Alex demanded to know.

"At last," the man said in a low voice before turning around to face Alex. He was just as filthy as the rest of the Domineers, but he carried with him a great stature and a sense of leadership which told Alex that this was the man he had been informed was commanding the Domineers in the northern regions of the Dark Zone; the younger brother of Ramon Moreno. "The boy I've been hearing about," the man continued to speak. "Hello, Alex."

Alex's jaw dropped at the sound of his name mentioned among the enemy. He had a sick feeling in his gut about the reason that they had been searching for him. There was only one thing that came to mind: they wanted him to betray the Ravennites.

On the level just below him, Malachai and Zak were still being led down the corridor by a small company of Domineers, both of their hands bound behind their backs. The whole time, Malachai was wiggling his arms around very slightly, hoping that their captors would not notice. Zak was looking around and observing his surroundings. As he looked up at the ceiling of the hallway he noticed something that caught his eye. Along the left wall, just under the ceiling, Zak thought he was looking a long, thin rope suspended all the way down the corridor. He narrowed his eyes, wondering what it must have been for.

The Domineers took them to the end of the hallway until they arrived at a closed sliding down which was guarded by two more men armed with swords. The Domineers escorting the two of them told the guards that they were taking them to their prison hold. As Malachai continued to subtly move his arms around, he heard the Domineers tell them that they had found the outsider that they were looking for. He and Zak exchanged looks of curiosity. It must have been why they singled Alex out from the rest of them, but where had they taken him? Malachai could sense that they were preparing to open the wood door and taken them to a cell where they would hold the two of them prisoner. By his life, he was not going to allow that. Wiggling his arms a little harder, a small, stone shard suddenly fell down his sleeve and he managed to catch it in his hand. In fact, it was one of the shards of his old sword which Alex had shattered. He had picked it up before they continued their search for the Iron Furnace. Using all of the strength that he could muster, Malachai used the shard to cut his way through his bonds.

At last, the rope was torn and fell from his arms. The Domineers were completely unaware. That is until Malachai grabbed hold of the nearest one and swiped the stone sword from the sheath at his side. Both of the guards saw his quick action and cried out, raising their own swords. Malachai took the sword and swiftly ran it through the guard nearest to him. He gasped for hopelessly for breath and dropped his sword. The second guard prepared to attack him. Thinking quickly on his feet, Zak charged himself head first into the Domineer guard and rammed him into the wall. Malachai pulled the sword out of the guard's lifeless husk and swung the blade across the next Domineer's throat. He clutched at his neck, but not before it had already started gushing blood, and he fell to the ground.

This left two more men for Malachai to contend with. One of them raised a sword in defense and prepared to engage him. However, Malachai saw the Domineer behind him take out another one of those strange looking guns and point right at him. Without thinking, Malachai quickly charged the swordsman and snatched him by the collar. He managed to spin him around just before the Domineer behind him fired his weapon. Malachai saw several small arrowhead projectiles fly from the weapon straight at him, but an instant later they dug their way into the swordsman's abdomen which Malachai had taken as a human shield. He threw the Domineer swordsman aside and mercilessly charged his sword into the last remaining Domineer.

"Malachai!" Zak called out from the corner here was trying to tackle the last remaining guard which his hands tied behind his back. "I could use a little help here!" The guard finally managed to throw Zak off of him, but not before Malachai was already upon him, pointing his sword at his face.

"Get clear, Zak!" Malachai urged him to get out of the way. "This one we're keeping alive." While keeping a close eye on the guard on the ground, Malachai quickly cut Zak's own bonds and he picked up a sword of his own. As he did, Zak's attention was suddenly brought to the unknown weapon that one of the Domineers had dropped when Malachai had killed him. He picked it up and turned it over in his hands.

"Hey, Malachai," he called for his attention. "What do you make of this?"

Malachai shrugged his shoulders and turned to the Domineer guard again.

"What kind of weapon is that?"

"Wouldn't you like to know?" he taunted him from the ground. "Highlander scum!"

Malachai reached forward and touched the point of his blade to the man's throat.

"Where are the prisoners?" he demanded. "They're through that door, aren't they?"

"Oh, of course they are," the Domineer answered with a sneer. "If you want to go in there, then be my guest. You'll find yourselves severely outnumbered and outmatched. You would never be able to free your animal friends."

"Is that right?" Zak said as he approached him. "What is that up there?" He pointed up to the rope running just below the ceiling.

"How should I know?" the Domineer responded in resistance.

Malachai began to press the blade harder against the man's neck. He started gasping for air as a small streak of blood flowed down his neck.

"How about I make you know?" Malachai threatened.

Choking on his breath, the Domineer struggled to squeak the words, "It's a wire system!"

Zak and Malachai looked at each other.

"What is that?" Malachai asked. He slightly released the pressure he was placing on the man's throat.

The Domineer had become significantly more compliant with a sword pointed against him.

"It's rigged throughout the whole structure. We use it to keep our prison cells secure."

"How is that even possible?" Zak asked with fascination.

"Answer him," Malachai jabbed at the Domineer again. "How do we cut it off?"

"Ah!" he gasped against the force of the blade tip.

"There's a central hub here where we can control the entire system!"

"Malachai," Zak said, "this might be our chance to actually pull this off. We can save our people."

Malachai nodded in approval.

"Get up!" He ushered the Domineer guard to his feet and continued to hold him at sword point. "Take us to it, now!"

Meanwhile, in Robert's personal quarters, Alex had found himself finally face to face with Robert Moreno himself.

"Hello, Alex," he said with a sly grin upon his face. "The name is Robert Moreno."

Alex felt instantly cautious around this man.

"How do you know my name?"

"We know everything, Alex," Robert responded with a hint of intimidation. "You should know by now that I have endless resources all over these mountains. How do you think we found your pathetic excuse for a campsite?"

Alex gritted his teeth. Although, he quickly realized how important it would be to maintain his composure now that he had an audience with the enemy's leader. He took a deep breath and tried to remain calm.

"Why are you doing this?" he breathed. "How could you do all of this to these innocent people?"

Robert took a step closer to Alex with a serious look on his face.

"Innocent, you think? Believe me, nothing about these mountain savages is innocent. They are nothing but a bunch of heartless liars and killers, I've seen it firsthand."

"I wonder why that might be!" Alex retorted angrily. "I know that you and your brother started this conflict. You brought a cataclysm upon these people and now they're fighting back! You deserve what they have coming to you!"

Robert began snickering at Alex's rant.

"You really think you can believe a word those animals say?"

Alex was trying to ignore this man's lies. Nothing that he

was saying about the Ravennites was true, it simply couldn't be.

"I know that you were looking for me when you attacked the Ravennites' outpost," he began, trying to steer their tense conversation back on topic, "and I know what it is you want from me; you want me to talk, but I'll never tell you anything!"

"Oh, is that what you think?" Robert responded arrogantly. "I already told you that the Ravennites are nothing but a race of liars."

Alex raised his eyebrows.

"What are you talking about?"

"What if I told you," Robert began, taking on a calmer demeanor, "that I wanted to bring you here in order to help you?"

Alex could not believe what he was hearing.

"What do you mean help me?"

"It's no secret, Alex, that the only reason you were forced to align yourself with the Ravennites is because they refused to release you. You, an innocent outsider who accidentally wandered into the wrong world and wanted nothing more than to find his way back out again. Isn't that what you wanted?" Alex could not find the proper words to respond with. Robert continued to walk toward him, growing more serious as he spoke. "You don't belong here, Alex," he uttered in a low tone. "You don't belong in this world. I understand how you must feel. You spent many months trapped among a race of savages who would have sooner killed you than simply release you back where you belong. That just doesn't seem right to me at all. But you're here now, away from that kind of oppression. I'm not like them. I can offer you what you've been waiting for all this time. So why don't you pick up your ass, right now, and just go home." He pointed out the wide window of his quarters. "It's waiting for you. This is not your war."

The words hit Alex like a powerful, speeding train. As much as he hated to admit it, he was starting to remember his first days among the Ravennites at the Citadel. He remembered being so homesick and wishing that they would just let him go and allow him to risk being caught by the Domineers on his own terms. Here he was now, in the midst of the very enemies that Delmar and Matheus and Rowan had constantly warned him about, and it sounded as though their leader, Robert Moreno, the younger brother of Ramon, was actually offering him what Delmar refused to give him. The common sense to accept was gnawing at him so sharply.

Something else, however, was poking at his mind as well. He was suddenly able to recall all of the bonds he had made within the walls of the Citadel. The very people whom he himself first believed to be just as savage as Robert was now accusing, he had come to see them as not only friends but family as well. There was one of them whom Alex had grown particularly close to, and that was Rowan. Suddenly, he remembered why he was here again. He, Malachai and Zak had come to rescue Rowan and the rest of the Ravennites taken captive by the dangerous Domineers. The thought of these people holding them hostage only enraged Alex, so much that he now found himself glaring out at Robert. He stood his ground and, with a voice full of pride and confidence, he declared, "This is my home!"

Robert barely reacted, though it seemed to Alex that he was trying to hide his true emotions from him. Robert turned and walked away toward the window, looking out of it.

"Well, then," he said, "I tried to offer what I could, but I thought that it was going to come to this regardless." Facing Alex once more, now with a much more stern face, he said, "You're right, my men were in fact searching for you. It's because you're going to tell me something. You see, for the past few years we've captured more than a few Ravennite fighters and have tried to get them to spill where the last remnants of their societies have gathered, but none of our interrogation tactics have worked. However, when we learned that an outsider had foolishly joined the ranks of the Ravennites, we believed that he might be significantly easier to crack, and now that you're here that is exactly what we intend to do."

"I knew it," Alex glowered at him. "I knew you were lying to me this whole time."

"Oh, no, Alex. I was sincere before, but you refused to accept the easy way out. Now we can do this the easy way or the hard way," he stepped forward and got in Alex's face. "All you need to do is tell me one thing, and I will not ask it a second time: where have the Ravennites gathered? Where is their final hiding place?"

Alex did nothing but shake his head and laugh to himself.

"If you really think that you can break me then you're the fool. I've decided a long time ago that I will never betray my friends, the brave Ravennites. I will never talk, and you have nothing that will make me talk!"

Robert did not respond. Instead, he raised an eyebrow and walked over to a shelf hanging on the wall adjacent to the window. Alex was more than certain that he could withstand whatever measly questioning methods Robert could throw at him, that is until he saw what method Robert was preparing to exploit. He picked a small object off of the shelf, turned back toward Alex and held it up in front of him.

"We have this."

It took Alex a second to identify the object in the faint light of the room, but when he realized what exactly it was he gasped in horror. Clasped in his grip, Robert was holding up Rowan's wooden pendant, the one that her grandmother had made for her. The first thing that caught his eye was the strange, red symbol at the top of its face. So he was right all along; they really had captured Rowan, and they had stolen her most cherished possession. Alex was left utterly speechless, but Robert saw the expression on his face and was able to read his mind from there.

"Ah, you recognize it," he jeered at him, "and no doubt you know who it belonged to."

Alex was only becoming increasingly angry, his breathing turning more into hissing.

"Where is she?" he snarled at Robert. "What have you done to her!?"

"Oh, nothing yet," Robert replied with an arrogant smirk. "Don't worry, she's safely locked away in her own personal cage like the animal she is." Robert walked slowly and menacingly over to stand in Alex's face once again, holding the pendant up in the air the entire time. "I've tried being nice, but you've chosen to play this the hard way. I told you that I would not ask a second time, so I'll make it quite simple for you." His voice suddenly changed to a cold, sadistic tone as he delivered a bone-chilling threat to Alex. "Tell me where the Ravennites are hiding," he began, "or you can watch her die." Alex's blood had run completely cold. He could not believe what he was hearing. "And don't think that we're afraid to do it."

His heart was racing now. This fiendish man was threatening him now with the unthinkable. Alex's mind was rushing through too many thoughts to keep track of. He was completely lost on what to do. For months he had trained himself to maintain his loyalty to the Ravennite cause, but he could never forgive himself if any such harm came to the best friend he'd ever had. Robert Moreno had truly been lying to him from the start; the Domineers were the evil ones here, not the Ravennites.

Robert had taken a step back, and was obviously enjoying watching Alex's inner torment.

"Tick tock, Alex. Tick tock."

CHAPTER TWENTY-ONE

Malachai continued to hold the Domineer guard at the point of his sword as he forced him to lead him and Zak through the complex. Through quick and convincing interrogation, they had learned from the guard that the Domineers managed to rig an impressive system formed by a series of rope tracks running throughout the structure. Along the way, the guard told them that the system was primarily used in their designated prison hold area to help keep the makeshift cells' doors tightly secured so that their prisoners could not break out on their own. He proceeded to mention that their standard method of controlling the cell doors was by use of a lever planted beside each cell, but that they had also constructed a sort of central hub where all of the rope systems in the structure met and could be controlled from one place. That was where Malachai and Zak were forcing him to take them to.

Though the two Ravennites were at a total loss for understanding of this seemingly advanced system, they intended to have their captive do the work for them. The guard led them up the same flight of steps which Alex had been taken. They followed the Domineer into the first corridor. Midway down the hall was another door built into the wall. Malachai was cautious, keeping his eyes pinned to the guard like a hawk. The Domineer stopped the group in front of the door.

"Where are we?" Malachai demanded. "Is this it?"

"Yes," the Domineer replied through clenched teeth. "This room controls every wire system in the building. Go in and see for yourself."

Malachai and Zak looked at each other suspiciously.

"Why?" Zak asked, narrowing his eyes. "What's waiting on the other side?"

The guard turned around and faced his captors with a sly grin on his face.

"More than enough armed adversaries who would be more than happy to see you. You didn't seriously think you could infiltrate our own base and free your filthy pets so easily, did you? You can't. It's impossible."

"Enough!" Malachai wound up and knocked the outsider over the head with the hilt of his sword. He grunted upon impact and fell to the dirty, wooden floor, knocked out. "I don't know what's on the other side of that door," Malachai said to Zak as he regained his grip on his sword, "but I'm not willing to abandon our people when we're this close to saving them, are you? We're going in, and we're going to kill!"

"I'm with you," Zak breathed nervously but confidently. "This is for everything they've done!"

"This is for Ravenna!" Malachai grabbed hold of the door's handle and quickly pulled it open. The two of them charged in, crying out passionately.

Upon entering the room, Malachai targeted the first person he saw. The Domineer closest to him had his back turned and Malachai did not stop charging until he had run him through with his sword. He gasped futilely for breath as Zak made for his own target. Another Domineer had been standing just inside the door. Zak turned his attention to him, quickly jabbed him in the face with his fist and then made a swift sword motion across his throat.

The room was suddenly filled with the sound of the Domineer sounding off in surprise. Malachai and Zak quickly observed their surroundings. They were standing in a chamber about the size of Delmar's map room, and they were face to face with over a dozen Domineer fighters, all of which were reaching for their swords. It was clear to them now that the guard who had escorted them here knew that they would be significantly outnumbered.

This grave disadvantage, however, hardly phased Malachai

at all. He took a few deep breaths as he stared down all of his opponents. The Domineers, as he observed, appeared to be noticeably afraid, despite their numbers. There were a series of murmurs going around amongst them, such as, "Who are they?" and, "How did they get in here?" With their weapons raised, they made an effort to form a semicircle around the two Ravennites.

Zak was a little less confident than Malachai right now, but like him he could also sense the fear in their adversaries.

"What are we going to do now?" he whispered to his ally.

Malachai strained his eyebrows as stared at them all with so much deserved loathing.

"We fight," Malachai hissed, more at the Domineers than to Zak. "We kill them all, or we go down fighting!" Hearing his sentiment, the Domineers did not seem to know if they should laugh at the Ravennites' disadvantage, or to be terrified of the rage which they intended to unleash upon them all. Malachai increased his breathing rate, before finally shouting in their tongue, *"Seeta'hai Ravenna!"* (Vengeance for Ravenna!) He gave a shrill battle cry and charged valiantly at his foes, followed almost immediately by Zak.

Malachai had shifted to pure, combat instinct by charging at the Domineers. Zak, however, could not help but expect them to immediately strike back and defeat them effortlessly, as there were only two of them and about fifteen of their enemies. Incredibly, his morale spiked when more than half of the Domineers suddenly backed away in total fear, some of them even losing their grips on their swords. Malachai attacked several foes at once, all which had their swords raised and ready for battle. It was now, for the first time in a long time, that he was once again introduced to the bloody ferocity of battle. He used sheer force and his almost animal-like viciousness to overwhelm his opponents, slaying them quickly and mercilessly. Zak was a less experienced warrior and did his best to engage one opponent at a time. However, with the incredible prowess of Malachai by his side, he found himself fighting with a force of will that he had never felt before, all the while he thought of Alex and how he had witnessed the way the boy brought a new feeling of hope to the struggling lives of his people. The two brave Ravennites knew it now more than ever: this would be the day when their savage oppressors realized that the war for their homeland had truly begun.

By the time the two of them had finished off the Domineers who had foolishly stood their ground, Malachai lumbered over to the others. Seeing their brutally slaughtered comrades before them, the remaining Domineers had all but fallen to their knees, begging for mercy. Zak had lowered his guard, feeling almost sorry for them now, but to his great shock Malachai had started going around to each and every one of them, killing them all quickly and completely ignoring their pleas.

When it was over, Zak caught his breath and spoke up,

"Malachai?" he tried to get his attention. "Forgive my impudence, but was that really necessary? I've never seen them attempt to surrender before."

Malachai stared at him with sweat running down his face, and trying to catch his own breath.

"Oh please, they deserved it." Although he strongly believed it to be true, Malachai's head suddenly lowered and he closed his eyes. "Yet, I do understand now that not all outsiders have such evil and cruelty in their hearts. I understand now that these men made their own choices, and tonight they paid for them." He looked over at Zak, whose eyes revealed an astonished sense of admiration at Malachai's words. "I only hope that those not so much like them would find it in their hearts to forgive us."

Zak managed a smile. He never thought he would see the day when Malachai uttered words of respect for the lives of the good Outsiders. They existed, sure enough. They saw it every day in Alex Lee. Coming back to his senses, Zak looked around at the chamber they were in for the first time. At the end of the room, where Malachai had slayed the scared

Domineers, there was a large panel that extended the entire width of the chamber. Just above it was a window, just as wide as the panel. Zak looked out of it and found himself looking down on an unfamiliar corridor. This one had at least twice as many Domineers standing guard. Most of them were looking up at the window, as they could hear all of the ruckus that he and Malachai had just made.

"There they are!" One of the yelled out, pointing his sword up at the window. "The Ravennites are here!"

At the far end of the corridor, in a locked cell built into the side of the wall, Rowan had been sitting against the back of her pitch dark cage, her eyes closed and her arms around her knees. However, her attention suddenly sprung to life when she heard the muffled sound of one of the guards shouting something. It was difficult to hear, but she could have sworn that she heard the word Ravennites. Thinking with both logic and hope, she found herself coming to the conclusion that the rest of the Ravennites had come to save them, and in the midst of the pure darkness, she finally managed a wide smile.

Meanwhile, up in the control hub, Malachai flinched as he thought he heard the sound of running footsteps approaching just outside.

"Oh, no!"

"What is it?" Zak responded alertly.

Malachai ran over to the open door. Just before he got there, a couple of Domineers came bursting in, swords in hand. Unfortunately, they had no time to think or react as Malachai instantly overtook them, throwing their lifeless husks on the floor.

"Do something!" Malachai yelled at Zak.

"What do you want me to do?" Zak replied, confused by the panel before him.

"Figure out it! I'll hold them off!" Sure enough, more Domineers were attempting to flood the control room, only to be brought down by Malachai.

Zak rushed to examine the panel. There was a whole

series of large levers scattered around the surface. He remembered what the Domineer guard had told them, that they used levers to open and close their holding cells. He was quick to understand that these must be how they control their wire systems all throughout the structure. Taking a closer look, he could see that each lever had a mark next to it carved into the wooden surface. Examining the marks, each lever appeared to be labeled by either one or two letters. The first one that caught his eye was a lever right in front of him, the mark which read, "CH." Without thinking, he pulled back on it, and an instant later a door on the opposite of the room from where they had entered suddenly slid open. Zak realized that the letters CH must have stood for Central Hub, as the guard had referred to it.

Dropping yet another charging guard, Malachai whipped around at the sound of the door opening.

"What did you do?" he cried out. "You're supposed to be finding a way to open their prison cells!" He turned back around just in time to catch two more Domineers rushing into the chamber.

"I'm sorry!" Zak yelled back. Realizing the concept, he began searching for a mark that might give him a clue as to what lever he was looking for. Behind him, Malachai had taken out one of his new foes, but he second had whipped out another makeshift gun and pointed it right at Zak, firing it immediately. Due to his lack of time to aim properly, most of the projectiles shot missed, but one of them had hit Zak in the right shoulder and another buried its way into his leg. Zak cried out in pain and collapsed down on one knee, hissing in restraint.

Malachai was quick to end the shooter's life.

"Are you alright?"

Zak pulled himself back up to his feet.

"I'm fine!" he growled. It was then, to his surprise, he suddenly noticed another lever which was marked with the label PC. While simultaneously trying to suppress the pain of being shot, he was not entirely sure what it could stand for.

However, the first thing that came to mind when he saw the letter P was, "Prison." Biting his lip, Zak pulled the lever and held his breath.

Indeed, the mark stood for Prison Corridor. Down in the hall just below, the doors of the many cells suddenly sprung open. The guards shifted their attention from the window above them to the cells which were now all open.

Inside one of the cells, which was holding two Ravennites, they raised their arms to block the sudden change of light. Looking out of the dark cage at the Domineers standing guard, one of the Ravennites gasped at the realization of what had just happened.

"We're free?" he muttered under his breath. The Domineers began reaching for their swords when they too understood the situation that they were now in. The two Ravennites sharing the cell jumped to their feet. "We're free!" Before the guards nearest them could retrieve their weapons, the Ravennites charged from their cell and tackled them into the wall. It was not long before the rest of the Ravennite prisoners quickly fled their own cells and attacked the guards, with only a few of them being killed by the Domineers. They were being overcome by fear very fast as the Ravennites broke out of their hold.

As Rowan's cell had opened up at the far end, she too jumped to her feet and cautiously headed outside of it. Her fellow prisoners had already taken care of the guards in the immediate area, but more were beginning to flood it from outside. Seeing her come out, one of the Ravennites picked a sword up from a fallen guard and handed it to her.

At the other side of the hallway, the Domineers were storming the cell block. Evenly numbered now, the Ravennites were able to fight them off with relative ease. As a few Domineers managed to penetrate into the corridor, one of the unarmed prisoners began grabbing hold of them as they came and throwing them hard into one of the posts helping to support the great frame of the structure. After several impacts, the vertical support beam began to give, causing a chain reaction with slightly damaged the frame in its area.

Above the post, in Robert Moreno's personal quarters, the entire room began to shift and tilt slightly forward off its supports. Robert and Alex struggled to keep their balance and fell to the floor as the room shifted to angle leaning down toward the way of the wide window. Alex looked from the window back over at Robert. He had taken a solid fall to his stomach, and Alex seized his opportunity.

He jumped up, ran over and snatched Rowan's necklet out of his hand.

"Thanks!" he called out and then ran for the window. He ducked and blindly vaulted himself out through it. With the new angle of Robert's quarters, Alex found himself falling a little over fifteen feet and landing roughly in the snow below. He grunted harshly as he landed on his back and the wind was briefly knocked out of him. He pulled himself up and looked around to see many of the Domineers rushing into the structure from the end at which he and the others had originally been escorted. They must have been heading for the holding cells. He had definitely heard the fight begin within the corridors beneath Robert's chamber, just before it had tilted over.

Alex was trying to quickly gather his thoughts until he heard a quiet voice speak up from behind him.

"Stay there," a man's voice said. Alex spun around to see a single Domineer by the structure's wall, standing beside a stacked cord of chopped wood. He did not seem to be talking to Alex, but noticed him just as quickly as he did. The man looked a couple years older than Robert.

Alex realized now that he was still unarmed, and the Domineer realized it too, as he pulled out his stone sword and charged at Alex with a battle cry. Alex leaped backward as his attacker made a slashing motion at his abdomen. He fell onto his back and managed to roll to the side just in time as the Domineer's sword nearly came down on top of him. Alex jumped to his feet as fast as he could and backed up the way his attacker had charged from. The man was breathing erratically with a raw killer's demeanor. He rushed Alex again, and he successfully dodged a couple more blade swipes before managing to snatch hold of the Domineer's sword arm. The two of them struggled around each other briefly before the man was able to throw Alex off of him and onto the ground beside the woodpile. He walked toward him with malicious intent. Alex backed up on the ground until he his hand come across a large, splintered wood fragment buried beneath the snow. The Domineer was still coming at him. Without thinking or hesitating, Alex pulled up the object in his grasp and swiftly thrusted it upward as the man charged him one last time, his sword raised high. The two of them cried out at the same time. Alex closed his eyes and clenched his teeth. Waiting for the worst, he suddenly heard a bloodcurdling sound that made his stomach roll.

Upon opening his eyes, Alex looked up and saw that the Domineer had inadvertently charged right into the pointed, splintered post which Alex had drawn from the snow. It impaled his abdomen, and the man dropped his sword and began choking on his blood. Alex used the post to steer him over to the side and allowed him to collapse onto the ground, the piece of wood still stuck in his body.

Alex shakily stood back on his feet. He reached down and picked up the Domineer's sword, and looked at him as he slowly died. He could hardly believe it; it was his first kill and it already made him feel a little sick inside, but he tried to remind himself that it needed to be done.

A sudden sound of movement behind him made him jump. Alex spun and pointed his sword at the stockpile behind him, but he did not expect to see what he was now face to face with. There, hiding within a small crevice in the cords of wood, Alex was pointing his sword not at a Domineer per se, but a young child; a girl with ragged, dark blonde hair and a terrified expression upon her face. She could not have been any more than eight or nine-years-old. She raised her hands up as if to beg Alex not to hurt her. No thoughts were going through Alex's mind as he stared at this girl. Suddenly, he could hear the Ravennite prisoners breaking out of the complex from the opposite end which he and the others were originally taken. As he looked around he could see another wave of armed Domineers rushing toward the structure from the furnace tower. Alex immediately disregarded the little girl and hurried over to join his Ravennite friends before, hopefully before the Domineers reached them.

Back up at the complex's control hub, Malachai had finished off the remainder of the guards attempting to run them down. Zak sat himself down on the floor and against the large panel. He reached around and painfully pried the ballistic pieces from his leg and his shoulder, gasping out loud as he did so. He examined them and they appeared to be shaped like small arrowheads. Zak was intrigued by the Domineers' apparent innovation with their weaponry.

Malachai checked his surroundings and then walked over to his ally.

"Are you okay?" he asked with concern. "Can you walk? Can you fight?"

"I- I think so," Zak stammered. He carefully climbed up to his feet, trying to suppress the pain. The wound in his leg had reduced him to a slight limp, but Zak did his best to walk it off. "I can still fight."

Malachai nodded in approval but concerned about the nature of his condition as well.

"That's good. Come on, we have to get down there to help lead our brothers to safety!"

"Right!" Zak stretched out his hurt sword arm. "What about Alex?"

Malachai stopped and tried to think about what happened to Alex in all the time that they were busy here.

"We can only hope that he can manage to find his own way out of here. We don't have time to go looking for him."

Zak nodded hesitantly.

"Yes, you're right. Come on, let's go!" It took him a few more steps to suppress his limp as best he could, and the two of them quickly headed out of the chamber to make their way back outside. Their decisive battle for freedom had already begun.

Rowan twirled her sword in her hands a few times as the Domineers reached them. The area suddenly rang up with the sound of clashing blades as the Ravennites were quick to gain the upper hand against the fear-stricken Domineers. Even the Ravennites who were unarmed rushed into the fray, attacking their enemies together and seizing their weapons. Rowan engaged the nearest Domineer to her. He attempted to make a powerful swipe at her head, but it was no challenge for Rowan; she swiftly ducked under the sword's path, spinning around as she did and slashed at the Domineer's hip. He cried out and fell to ground, writhing and clutching his side, but such a sight did not hinder Rowan from driving her sword through his abdomen to finish him off. This was her first kill, but it did not phase her at all, for she believed that she was doing it for the cause of her people. She did not manage to kill any of their enemies back at the outpost, as they had been discoordinated and captured too quickly. She looked all around at as her Ravennite brothers continued to storm the area, bringing down all enemies in their path. The only thing that truly concerned her was how they were going to escape from the Iron Furnace, especially because they were vastly outnumbered. Her attention was suddenly drawn away by the sound of a familiar voice calling her name.

"Rowan!" Alex called out as loud as he could, throwing himself amongst the great brawl. One of the Domineers suddenly locked eyes with him. Alex was still a little bit shaken after his first kill against the man who attacked him after he leaped out of Robert's quarters. The Domineer made an attempt to engage him. Alex stood his ground and, using every technique and discipline which Matheus and Rowan had taught him, he was able to deflect his attacks with relative ease and run him through with his sword. As the fallen Domineer hit the ground, Alex tried to ease the tension in his muscles. "I think I'm getting the hang of this," he breathed.

He scoped around the ensuing battle again, looking for his friend. "Rowan!"

Rowan had just finished off another adversary when she heard her name called a second time.

"Alex!" she responded.

Overjoyed to hear the reaction that he was hoping for, Alex hurried through the skirmish toward Rowan's voice. He ruthlessly cut down another opponent before at last he was able to spot the elegant, fighting form of Rowan among the chaos. As he made his way over to her, she suddenly turned around and spotted Alex fighting through the crowd. She smiled brightly and cried out with spirit as she struck down another Domineer.

Before long, the two of them finally met on the battlefield. They gazed at each other briefly, and Rowan could not hold back her happiness to see him.

"Alex!" she exclaimed again.

"Good to see you, Rowan," Alex responded with a laugh. "Here," he said, reaching down at his belt and retrieving the pendant. "This belongs to you."

Rowan's jaw dropped as she took the charm from Alex with a shaky hand.

"Thank you!" she gasped, full of emotion. "Thank you so much!" She quickly put her pendant back around her neck where it belonged and tucked it underneath her clothes. The last of the wave of Domineers had were turning tail and running back toward the gate of the Iron Furnace camp. The Ravennites were now taking this opportunity to regroup themselves. They were still trapped; the Domineers continued to stand between them and their only way out of the fortress, and they were still currently outnumbered.

Rowan turned her attention back to Alex, looking at him like a long-lost friend.

"I didn't know what happened to you," she said quietly. "I didn't know where you went. But you came back!"

Just hearing her voice again made Alex's head rush. He realized that, while she was being held prisoner here, Rowan must have been reeling off the idea that he may have abandoned them, abandoned her. He knew that he could never do that.

"Of course, I did," he replied, looking her in her green eyes and saying the first thing that came to his mind, "We're friends."

Rowan looked from his eyes down to the scarf around his neck that she had given him. She was beginning to realize every time she looked at Alex that she was seeing him as more of a friend than before. Every moment they shared, from the day they met at the point of her bow to their talks on the tower overlook and by the lake on the plateau. From every day she helped train him to fight and taught him their language to their duel on the snowy hilltop. Now they were fighting side by side against their common enemy; fighting to save her people from the thieves of the Outside.

"The Domineers!" one of the Ravennites called out, pointing toward the gate. "They're regrouping!"

"How do we get out of here?" asked another.

Alex stepped forward and tried to get their attention.

"They're protecting the gate," he spoke up, "because it's the only way to get out. We have no other choice, we have to fight our way out of here!"

"We're outnumbered!" another Ravennite pointed out. "Can we really win this fight?"

"Yes we can!" Alex responded sternly. He did not notice, but behind him Rowan was staring at him with a strong sense of admiration and reverence. The Ravennites were strong fighters but filled with doubt in this seemingly dire situation, yet Alex was stepping forward to fill them all with the spirit, morale, and hope that they needed to survive this fight. To Rowan, he had the heart of a true Ravennite. "We can win! We can beat them because they're afraid of you, afraid of us, afraid of what we can do! It's finally time to stand and fight! Let's show them what happens when you mess with the Ravennites! Let's crush them now, and go home!" His brief speech was instantly followed by a great roar of battle cries and cheers. Alex was hardly thinking straight as he spoke, but he could feel the waves of goosebumps surge over his body and he knew that he was doing the right thing. The Ravennites were turning now to face their enemies across the site and crying out threateningly.

"Yes!" Rowan exclaimed, feeling pumped by Alex's speech. "I'm ready! I'm ready to fight!"

"No, you're not!"

Rowan suddenly felt a powerful grip steal the sword right out of her grasp from behind.

"Hey!" she shouted and turned to see that Malachai and Zak had joined the rest of them, and Malachai had just taken her weapon. "I need that!"

"No, Rowan," Malachai rebuked, putting his hand up to silence her. "You've been through enough trouble already. By my life, I will not allow any more harm to come to you before you get back to your brother, and I refuse to risk it by letting you fight."

"What!?" Rowan was glancing from him to Alex. "Malachai, the time to fight is now! I've trained for this for years!"

"Rowan, enough," Malachai bluntly responded. "Today is not the day. Please, keep low and stay behind us." He then shifted his attention to Alex, and Alex could have sworn he saw him nod to him. "We're getting out of here now." Malachai, now wielding two swords, marched forward to the head of the pack of Ravennites. "Come on! For Delmar! For Ravenna!"

The Ravennites were crying out now louder than ever, and they followed Malachai in a charge toward the gate. Alex looked out and saw the Domineers at the other side begin to charge toward them as well. They were preparing to clash. Alex turned to Rowan and could see a look of pure disappointment in her eyes. He knew that she wanted this more than ever, to fight and avenge her fallen friends and family, but now he had to agree with Malachai. It was important now that they get out in one piece and make for the Citadel. As he looked at Rowan, he did not know what to say, so he simply nodded his head and began to make for the battle.

"Alex!" Rowan suddenly reached out and grabbed hold of his free hand.

Surprised, he turned and faced her again.

"What is it?" he asked urgently. Rowan looked as though she wanted to say something but found the words unable to come out. She said nothing, and for a sudden second Alex saw a look in her eyes that he had never seen before. For months, she had always looked at him like a friend, but not this time; this time her gaze appeared to be much stronger. She looked past him briefly at the charging Ravennites as if to see who was around them right now. Alex could feel the seconds flying by quickly and intensely, his sight was still locked on hers, and felt as though he knew what was coming.

Rowan said nothing. Her actions spoke much louder. She reached up and grabbed hold of Alex's garment, pulled him close, and kissed him.

Alex was taken completely by surprise, but he immediately surrendered to it. He did not let go of his sword, but he felt his free hand move to her side. It did not last for more than a few seconds, but it felt like an eternity before they pulled apart. They looked into each other's eyes, only inches away from each other; Alex's ice cold blue eyes and Rowan's emerald eyes which gave off the soothing warmth of spring. He was utterly speechless as he stared back at her, and in the tone of a low whisper, she said with a slight stammer, "It could be the only time."

Alex had no idea how to respond. It was only now that he remembered the decisive fight that was ensuing ahead of them. He gave Rowan a slight head nod and muttered, "Stay close to us." Alex turned and hurried off toward the battle. Rowan exhaled awkwardly. She did not think that was the response she was hoping to hear, but then again she hardly knew what she was even doing anymore. Now was not the time, however. With Alex heading off into the fray, she hurried to catch up with him.

About two and a half dozen Ravennites charged into battle, but still the Domineers outnumbered them almost two to one. If it were not for the fighting skills honed by the Ravennites then they would have stood no chance against their enemies. As Alex reached the chaos, he observed the others fighting with intense ferocity, and every minute that passed the Domineers seemed to grow ever more demoralized. He managed to spot Malachai in the center of the skirmish fighting off foes by the waves with both of his swords. He fought so mercilessly, shouting with fierce hate and slaying all in his path. The Domineers were dropping like flies and they knew it. From what Alex could see, only a handful of them were truly fighting back. These few appeared to be bigger and much more proficient fighters than the rest of them, so much in fact that he watched them start killing Ravennites almost as fast as Malachai was slaughtering their own, but it was not long before they were forced to retreat back due to the incompetence of the rest of the Domineers.

Alex fought his way closer to Malachai, feeling more capable with every life he took. The Ravennites pushed nearer and nearer to the fortress' gate. With the gate practically unguarded now, Rowan slipped through the violent discord and headed over to it. She pushed against it and tried to force it open, but it did not budge. A few of her fellow warriors attempted to aid her effort but to no avail.

"We can't get the gate open!" she called out, continuing to push against it in vain. "Something has it locked closed!"

Alex heard what she said. He turned and quickly scanned around the gate and its frame. It did not take him long to see the problem as well as the solution. At the top of the wall, just beside the gate's frame, Alex could see a large wheel with a long rope wrapped around its edges, feeding the rope into the frame itself like the chain on a bicycle. It was obvious, the Domineers were quick to anchor the rope so that the gate could not be opened and the prisoners could not escape, until now.

"It's the rope!" Alex responded, pointing up at the wheel. "It's holding the gate closed. We need to break it!"

Malachai seemed to be on top of it. He grunted loudly as he ran closer to the wall. Eyeing the rope closely which Alex had pointed out, he took aim and threw one of his swords up at it. The sword spun through the air for a second and, to Alex's amazement, it sliced right through the tight rope like a buzz saw. The torn rope recoiled with incredible speed. Rowan and the other Ravennites suddenly felt the gate release its sturdiness and they pushed it open.

Rowan could hardly breathe as she realized they had just secured their escape. It was obvious that the Domineers realized it too, as the survivors began trying to escape the losing battle. Alex looked up at the sky. He could see the dim blue shade of the first moments of dawn. The sun was finally beginning to rise, and it seemed to mark the end of the struggle. The Domineers were running for their lives deeper into the fortress as Malachai called and signaled for the Ravennites to follow him out of the gate and back into the dense woods. Alex ran by Rowan's side as they all hurried to make their way back to the Citadel, and most importantly ensuring that the Domineers did not follow.

Nearly an hour later, Robert Moreno came out of hiding from his half-broken quarters. He walked slowly around the remains of his fortress, glowering with raw anger and hatred for the damage that the Ravennites had caused, and the death they had wrought upon his men. The muscles in his fists were sore from clenching them so much, and his teeth were aching from grinding them anxiously. More than sixty Domineers he commanded from the Iron Furnace alone, and now more than half of them were killed, and the rest were all but drained of their willpower. Only Wilson and his gang seemed to hold onto their firmness.

Robert stopped before the gate of the fortress, which was still left wide open after the Ravennites' escape, and stared out and into the woods.

"ALEX!" he screamed at the top of his lungs. Many of the Domineers around him froze and looked at him nervously. "You filthy, meddling child! I will make you pay for humiliating me!" He looked back at the others around him, and they quickly went back to their own business so as not to meet his pissed off gaze. There was one, however, who was much bolder even at a time like this, and he walked over to stand before Robert.

Caine made no gesture as he stared right at Robert, but it was clear that he was giving him a look of disappointment and even arrogance. Robert was growing angrier by the second.

"I am in no goddamn mood, Caine!" he screeched in frustration. "Look around you! This is all on you! We brought those savages behind our walls and they destroyed us from within!"

"I blame your men," Caine calmly responded.

Robert's eyes widened.

"What did you just say?"

"I mean, I would be willing to imagine that they would fight with much more determination and strength if they actually believed that they were fighting for something. What have you got them fighting for, Robert? All of this death and destruction and you've learned absolutely nothing of value."

Robert took a few slow, menacing steps toward him. Caine firmly stood his ground, and it appeared for a moment that Robert might start an ugly confrontation with him.

"I would be about two seconds from being all over you right now, if it weren't for the fact that you're wrong."

Caine was taken aback by his comment. Surprise was not something that he expressed very often.

"I'm afraid I don't understand."

Robert put his hand up in his face and walked by him.

"This is not a defeat," he said confidently, "not by a longshot. We may have been knocked down but it's time to get our asses back on our feet."

"What do you mean?" Caine asked skeptically. "You really think you can rebuild what you just lost?"

"No," Robert answered bluntly. "That is not the plan." He faced Caine again and gave him a serious look. "For once, I need you for something. Take a squad, go back throughout our territories and bring every single man and weapon under my watch back here and prepare them for battle."

Caine narrowed his eyes at Robert.

"What are you talking about?" In his head, he knew what it was that Robert wanted to attempt, but it was unbelievable, even to him. "You want to attack the Ravennites' at their heart, don't you? How do you even know where they are?"

No response came from Robert. Instead, he looked over his shoulder back at his lopsided private quarters and smiled evilly.

CHAPTER TWENTY-TWO

Although the sun would take some time to crest over the tree canopies as usual, it was shining with the red light of morning by the time the Ravennites finally made it back to the Citadel. The gates were pulled open fast as they passed over the natural bridge leading to the great plateau, and upon entering they were greeted by nearly all of their people within the Citadel's walls.

Alex immediately collapsed to his knees and struggled to catch his breath from all of the running. They had run for miles to make it back to the Citadel, breaking only a few times to breathe and for only seconds at a time. He was totally exhausted, on account that he had gotten no sleep last night with the exception of falling unconscious twice, as well as enduring the extreme stress of trying to coordinate a blind rescue mission. He was just more than happy that it worked with minimum casualties. Nevertheless, Alex still felt himself mourning over the few Ravennites that they did lose over the course of the night. They fought bravely and if it were not for the evil of the Domineers they would never have been placed in that dire situation at all. He knew, with solemn heart, that he was on the right side and was not prepared to leave until the conflict was done. That is, if he managed to survive it.

Word reached Delmar like lightning of their return, and he hurried out of the tower and down to the gates to meet them. When he saw Rowan, he seemed to lose his cool for once as he rushed forward and embraced her in his arms.

"Thank the light, you're safe!" he breathed rapidly and kissed her lightly on the head.

Rowan held him tight, her face leaning against his.

"I'm alright, brother." They released their embrace and looked at each other with teary eyes.

"What happened out there?" Delmar addressed his people. "I demand to know!"

"The Domineers assaulted our campsite in the middle of the night," Malachai stepped forward and answered him, at the same time giving Delmar the salute. "They deceived us, they scattered us apart from each other before attacking and capturing the majority of us. What prisoners they claimed they took back to a fortress they built at the Iron Furnace."

Rowan looked her brother seriously in the eyes.

"Delmar," she added worriedly. "Caine is alive. He was there, among the enemy. He is helping them to oppose us!" She anticipated a concerning response from Delmar, but to her shock he and Malachai only exchanged glances of disappointment. Rowan quickly caught on to their thoughts, as her eyes widened with a revelation. "You knew?" she breathed awkwardly. "All this time, you knew Caine had betrayed us?"

A series of murmurs rose up among the crowd.

"The Iron Furnace, you say?" Delmar said with growing concern, as if he was trying to distract from the news Rowan had tried to bring up.

"Yes," Malachai nodded. "We managed to break out and cripple the fortress, killing more than half of them in the process. We made our way back here as fast as we could."

"How did you break free?" Matheus joined the conversation, feeling quite intrigued.

Malachai opened his mouth but hesitated to respond. When Rowan saw this, she answered for him.

"It was thanks to Alex," she said proudly. Everyone immediately stared over at the weary, slumped form of their precious outsider kneeling on the ground, still taking his much needed breather. He looked up at them, not knowing if he should say anything back. To Delmar's great surprise, he saw Malachai lower his head and give a sheepish nod of agreement. Rowan continued to tell the story. "He, Malachai,

321

and Zak over there were the only ones to avoid capture. Alex and Malachai forsaked their bitter rivalry in order to save us all from the Domineers."

"It's true." Malachai stood straight up, bearing an impression of newfound humility. "In fact, he did much more than I did for our people. I don't know what he was doing out in the woods after the attack, but I do know that when he could have turned tail and fled like a coward and a traitor, he instead came back and rescued me from the crumbling remains of our camp. I never thought that I would ever say it, but he showed me the dedication of a Ravennite to save them from our enemies."

Such a sentiment was all but unheard of coming from a stone cold loather of outsiders like Malachai. Everyone who heard was left speechless and awestruck. Alex finally stood up and nodded to Malachai with respect, and he gave a nod right back to him. Matheus' mouth was hanging wide open. He never thought that he would see the day when Malachai let go of his unfair hate for all outsiders. Rowan was leaking more tears with the same thought, but at the same time she was still having mixed feelings about what she had done last night back at the Iron Furnace. Although almost everyone had come to see Alex as a friend and an ally now, she would not dare tell anyone about their kiss. She was trying to remember what thoughts were going through her mind when she did it, but all that she found was a disoriented sense of delirium mainly due to her exhaustion and fear.

The Ravennites were now dispersing throughout the Citadel again, retiring to get some much needed rest after their experience. Delmar walked over and stood in front of Alex. He still feared the great stature of the Ravennite chief, but Alex stood tall and looked him back in the eyes. Delmar held his hand in front of him.

"Thank you, Alex,"

Alex reached up and clasped his hand firmly.

"I did what I thought was right."

Delmar smiled.

"You went out of your way to help my people, and I am especially grateful for the safety of my sister. You are a good man, Alex."

He felt overwhelmed by the compliments of Delmar. They made his eyes water with emotion.

"I'm just a boy," he said quietly.

"But you have the heart and the honor of a man and a Ravennite," Delmar replied. "You've truly come a long way from the lost little boy I met all those months ago. I know that it was unfair of me to keep you here against your will, but I could not be more proud and thankful for the decisions that you made for us."

Alex found himself managing a laugh of glee, but he soon turned quiet as a dark realization occurred to him. With a serious expression, he addressed Delmar again.

"Listen," he began, "there's something we need to discuss, all of us. It's important."

"What is it?" Delmar asked curiously.

"Can we go to the map room?" Alex responded. "I think the Domineers might be coming to attack the Citadel."

Rowan had urged Alex during the whole trip up the tower to get some rest. He was extremely tired, everyone could see it, but Alex kept assuring her that there was an imminent threat from the Domineers.

At the peak of the tower, Delmar, Malachai, Matheus and Alex all gathered inside the dim map room. The walls were still covered all over with handmade maps of varying scales and sizes showing different areas of the Dark Zone territories. Delmar told Rowan to leave and get some rest herself, but she stubbornly insisted that it was her right to be a part of their meeting.

"Are you certain of this?" Delmar asked Alex. "That is a very serious presumption."

"I agree," Malachai said, looking over at Alex. "The Domineers, whether under the leadership of Robert Moreno, or even Ramon himself, would be fools to stage an attack on the Citadel. We've spent years fortifying it to be all but impenetrable, and after what we did to them last night, I wouldn't be surprised if they had the will to fight completely drained out of them."

"I understand that," Alex replied, trying to maintain his composure, "but when we were captured by the Domineers and separated, they took me right to the presence of Robert Moreno."

A wave of curiosity infiltrated the atmosphere.

"You really had an audience with Moreno?" Matheus said with growing interest. "Incredible! Why would he want you?"

"Because I think they were searching for me specifically when they attacked our outpost," Alex answered.

Rowan tilted her head curiously.

"You? I don't understand."

"I do," Alex was quick to explain. "He told me himself that he wanted to find me because-" he suddenly hesitated, as he became afraid of telling the complete truth of what happened during his audience with the enemy's leader, "-because he wanted to get me out of the way."

The others were exchanging looks of confusion. "What are you talking about, Alex?" Rowan asked apprehensively.

Alex took a deep breath as he tried to gather his thoughts. "He tried to offer me a chance to leave these mountains once and for all, promising to set me free of the conflict between you. I refused immediately. I told him that I would never abandon the Ravennite cause."

Rowan smiled at the sound of his words. Matheus, however, was still not convinced.

"But what makes you believe that Robert would be on his way here to attack us?" he asked, trying to steer the conversation back to the central topic. "They don't even know the location of the Citadel, let alone how to penetrate our defenses." He seemed confident at first, but then he glanced around at the rest of the company with growing concern. "Do they?"

The memories of Alex's audience with Robert were fast returning to him, and he felt cold and anxious. Malachai looked over at him and could see that he was thinking deeply.

"How do you know, Alex?" he asked him. "What did you learn from Robert?"

Alex was almost choking on his words.

"I-" he stammered roughly. The others eagerly awaited him to answer. "I saw a map in Robert's chamber, just like the ones in this very room. It was already drawn out, and I could see the plateau's location marked on the map. I think they already know where the Citadel is."

He held his breath nervously as the information was being processed by the others. Rowan looked shocked by the thought of the secret of their last hiding place being revealed. Malachai's eyes suddenly lit up.

"It makes sense, then," he said in response. "It might explain why the Domineers were so desperate to capture us out there if they wanted to thin our numbers even further."

The murmuring among the group had ascended to debate as they seemed to try to figure out what their responsive action to this news should be. Alex had completely tuned out what they were saying. He felt himself being chewed up inside by guilt. Although he was certain the Robert Moreno was planning to stage a full scale attack on the Citadel, he knew that the nature of his knowledge of this place, the way Robert was able to learn of its location and its vulnerabilities, was very different than the lie he had just told them. He was there with Robert, he knew what really happened, and it was haunting him already.

Alex's mind was flashing back to his decisive meeting with Robert only mere hours before. He recalled the sadistic and perverse manner in which Robert had intended to get the information that he needed from Alex. He could still hear that chilling threat replaying in his head.

"Tick tock, Alex," the voice of Robert Moreno echoed in his memories. He could see him holding Rowan's pendant up in front of him. "Tell me where the Ravennites are hiding, or you can watch her die."

Alex was trembling as Robert's ultimatum was gnawing at his mind ever so sharply. He felt as though he was all alone now, with Malachai and Zak having been taken to a cell only moments before. Now, more than ever, he did not what to do. He was torn between his loyalty to Rowan's people and her very life. He despised this man for holding him by the throat with such blatant cruelty.

Robert shrugged his shoulders arrogantly.

"Alright then. That's yet another chance you've let slip by. Let's see how your little friend feels about your choice."

Alex's eyes shot wide open. He lashed out at Robert in raw anger, intending to beat the bastard to death if need be. Unfortunately, Robert had anticipated such a gesture, and he swiftly pulled a sword from one of the shelves hanging on the wall and pointed it toward Alex. It was a rather short sword, and it had a curved blade, but it made Alex freeze in his tracks just the same as any other weapon.

"I don't think so!" Robert taunted him. "You're neck deep in my territory now, and you'll play by my rules. Since you've already refused to abide by my terms, somebody has to pay the price for your insolence, and it looks like it has to be the girl."

Breathing heavily and shaking uncontrollably, Alex suddenly lost his grip.

"Wait, wait!" he blurted out.

Robert locked his eyes on Alex, waiting to hear what he now had to say.

"Yes?"

Alex took a long, deep inhale to gather his thoughts. He tried to convince himself that he was doing this for the right reason; for Rowan's immediate safety.

"There's a plateau," he began, looking down at the floor, "in the far western corner of these territories. That's where the Ravennites have gathered."

Robert looked on him with a quick smile of cooperation. He never set his sword down, but he walked over to another shelf and pulled a large, filthy, rolled up object with a thick, paper-like surface. He unraveled it on a small table in the corner of the room and told Alex to approach it. Upon examining it, he could see that it was a map of the Dark Zone, similar to the ones Delmar kept in the tower, but this one appeared to be much plainer, and it was not even completely finished. Alex noticed a large chunk of information was not drawn in around the map's western portions. Clearly, this was all they needed to discover before they mapped out nearly all of the Dark Zone and its territories, and Robert wanted Alex to give it to him.

"Show me where," Robert demanded, allowing Alex to take a close look at the map.

"It's difficult to say, looking at what you've got here," Alex replied, narrowing his eyes at the map.

"Then you better make it a little less difficult," was Robert's condescending response, "for your friend's sake."

"You don't have any knowledge of these areas," Alex said back, running his hand over the empty portion of the map. "I can't give you an accurate location with this limited amount of information."

"You can give us an estimate," Robert was getting frustrated. "We'll know how to pinpoint their exact location, believe me. Now get to it."

Alex sighed to himself. He studied the map again as best he could. Finally, he took a shot in the dark and pointed down to the general area where the Citadel should have been located.

"It will be around here," he began, the words tasting horribly as they came out, "anywhere from ten to fifteen miles from your fortress. They call it the Citadel."

Robert nodded slightly.

"Tell me about the environment."

He was not sure how much more he could reveal before he would hardly be able to live with himself anymore.

"The mountains in the area become taller and much more difficult to navigate as you get closer. The plateau itself stands alone and is encircled by the surrounding mountain ranges. The only way to get in and out of it is over a single narrow bridge formed between the plateau and the ranges around it."

"Is that right?" Robert said with interest. "If that's true, then it sounds like it would be the perfect place for the Ravennites to dig in. What about their fortifications? How heavily protected are they?"

He really did not want to say any more than he already had, but suddenly, Alex felt a thought forming in his head that he hoped might ease the pain of his unintentional betrayal. He stood up more firmly and proceeded to tell Robert what he now wanted to know.

"They are far more protected than you understand," he said confidently.

Robert stood up and stared out at him again.

"Give me details."

"The suspended land bridge is the only way to get into the Citadel, and they know it. The area between the mountains is nothing but a deep abyss running the whole perimeter of the plateau and it is completely unscalable. The Ravennites have built a wall around the edge of the Citadel where they have a perfect vantage point over the bridge and enough archers to hold back an entire invasion. Even with all the numbers you could muster, you would never be able to reach the walls."

It was obvious that Robert was not fully satisfied with what he was hearing.

"What if attacking them is not our intention?" he played with Alex's mind again. "It sounds to me like the Ravennites are cornered. What if we simply sieged them in and waited for them to starve and die out?"

Alex shook his head.

"Not at all likely. The Ravennites are farming within the walls of the Citadel. They would be more than prepared to outlast a siege. Take my word for it, there is nothing you can do to destroy them."

Robert took a few steps forward. He picked Rowan's pendant back up and dangled it for Alex to see again.

"Oh, we'll see about that, my friend."

Alex was about to respond, but suddenly a loud uproar rang up from below them. He did not know what to make of it for a moment, but Robert's expression suddenly shifted to anger and disbelief.

"No!" he gasped. "The prisoners!"

Shortly after, the two of them felt something heavy slamming against the supports holding up Robert's quarters and eventually it began to give away. At this point, the Ravennites had broken free and the battle for their escape had begun. Alex had managed to snatch up Rowan's necklet and escape through the window of Robert's chamber, which was now awkwardly angled downward.

Back in the map room, Alex swallowed painfully as he thought about the previous night. He knew exactly what he did, he failed to live up to the unshakable loyalty to these people that he thought he had developed. He betrayed their location to the Domineers, but at the same time he did his best to boast the Citadel's invulnerability. Alex was absolutely certain that this fortress' defenses and physical features would prove to be impenetrable against a Domineer attack, and he hoped that what he told Robert would be enough to keep him away but somehow he seriously doubted it. Robert Moreno had an unusually dangerous boldness about him. It was obvious to Alex that, given any faint light of chance, Robert would rally all those who could to storm against the Citadel.

"It doesn't matter if the Domineers would be stupid enough to attack us here," Malachai spoke up over all of the noise. "It would be a useless gesture. We'll crush them all with our superior fighting abilities and impervious defenses!"

"It should not have to come to that," Matheus argued. "The purpose of the Citadel has always been to protect the remainder of our people. We've never had to defend it against an invasion before."

"And it looks like that time may finally be upon us," Malachai said back. "Given what Alex saw, I'd say the Domineers have been planning for this for a long time, and we need to be ready for it when they come."

"Listen," Delmar stepped up, "we don't know what is going to happen. We don't know if Robert means to march against the Citadel or if he intends to rally with Ramon in the south."

"I have to agree with Malachai," Alex responded. "I think it might be wise to check our defenses, cover up any possible weaknesses that might be exposed. We should open up the armory so we can arm ourselves at a moment's notice."

"We have archers posted around the walls at all times," Delmar replied.

Alex continued to speak his mind.

"I think we should also send scouts around the area to keep eyes out for the Domineers. If they come fully armed and ready, then we need to be ready ourselves."

"It's too dangerous," Malachai said. "The fact is that the Domineers are far more bold and cunning than we ever realized." Just then, he picked up a small sack that he had brought up with him and walked forward to the table in the center of the room. He pulled a strange object from the sack, the strange, gun-like weapon which one of the Domineers had attempted to use against him, and dropped it down on the table. It hit the surface with a solid thud.

Everyone stared at the object with a mix of confusion and fascination. Delmar, Rowan and Matheus had no idea what to make of it.

"What is that thing?" Delmar asked anxiously.

"I don't know," Malachai answered. "Some sort of weapon. We picked this off of one of the Domineers in the Iron Furnace. I think they use it as some sort of ranged weapon."

"Yeah, you're right," Alex agreed, stepping forward to pick up the weapon. "It definitely resembles a gun."

The word almost reverberated throughout the room. Before the Domineer invasion, the Ravennites' people had never employed the use of guns. However, their former relationship with the Outside had provided them with a basic knowledge of guns. Even Delmar winced slightly at the sound of it.

"What's a gun?" Rowan asked, sounding afraid of it already.

"It's a deadly weapon from the Outside world," Delmar answered her grimly.

"Consider it a highly advanced bow," Alex added to help her better understand. "A weapon capable of firing at high speeds in order to kill."

"The Domineers are getting craftier," Malachai cut in. "During the escape at the Iron Furnace, Zak was shot by one of these things. I watched it, and he was hit multiple times at once by some sort of arrowheads."

Alex nodded his head as he examined the gun more closely.

"He's right," Alex said quietly. "It's much more primitive, but if I'm looking at this right, it almost has the qualities of a shotgun. I think they're using weapons like these to fire several shots at once." A sudden chill went down his spine. It certainly seemed that the Domineers were not lacking creativity.

"Well, I'm definitely glad that you're here to tell us these things," Matheus said in a joking tone.

Alex was trying to remain serious.

"Look, all this tells me is that the Domineers truly believe that they're capable of taking over the Citadel. I don't know about the rest of you, but I'd be willing to stage my life on the chance that they're going to be coming. We need to be ready."

Delmar turned around and buried his face in his hands. So far, Alex had not done anything to let them down, or to make him believe that he would ever bring harm to his people. They were in a very dark time right now; they were nowhere near prepared to stand up and fight against the Domineers, but even he had to admit that, while they had spent all of this time sheltering behind their high walls, it was all too likely that their enemies had been preparing for a well-coordinated assault.

"Well, then," Delmar took a deep breath and spoke again, "what is your suggestion, Alex?"

A little taken aback by the question directed at him, Alex was not sure what to say.

"Why are you asking me?"

Delmar stared right at him with a gaze that both disturbed Alex and made him feel rather dignified.

"Because I trust you," he said openly. "I trust your judgment."

"I doubt that we could hold back the entire Domineer army with just bows and arrows," Matheus put in. "If they overrun our immediate defenses and manage to breach the walls, then I don't know how long we could last."

Alex bit his lip as he tried to take everything into account. They had learned firsthand that the Domineers' numbers were far greater than theirs. Granted, the Ravennites were much stronger fighters and definitely possessed greater convictions, he doubted that it would be enough. He thought as hard as he could, as everyone's eyes were upon him. It was then that a sudden realization came back to him; something that he had noticed back in the spring when Matheus first showed him around the Citadel.

"Wait a minute," he muttered as he thought hard. "The bridge!" He suddenly turned and quickly headed outside.

"Where are you going?" Rowan asked. He ignored her and the others followed him outside of the map room to see what it was that he was thinking about.

Alex walked over to the lookout point. He looked down at the many bridge-like appendages spanning from the tower to the outer wall. Beyond the walls he stared out at the natural land bridge connecting the plateau to the mountains surrounding it. Alex nodded his head as he continued to formulate his idea.

"What is it?" Matheus asked impatiently, trying to look where Alex was looking. "What are you thinking about?"

"Matheus," Alex put his hand on Matheus' shoulder. "Do you remember what I told you on my first day here, when you were introducing me to the Citadel?"

He tried to think about what Alex was referring to but his question was far too vague.

"Not really, no."

"Look out there," Alex directed their attention to the bridge beyond the wall. "When I first saw that bridge, Matheus, I told you what I knew about the story of the 300 Spartans."

It took him a moment, but Matheus' eyes suddenly lit up as he recalled what Alex was talking about.

"What is that?" Malachai questioned. "And how exactly does that help us?"

When he spoke, Alex felt the gears turn in his head which made him realize that Malachai might be perfect for what he had in mind. He turned and started speaking to him now.

"Malachai, you're a strong and brave warrior. If you could rally a group of Ravennites of your caliber then we might be able to implement a formidable defense against the Domineers."

"How so?" Delmar joined in. "What exactly do you have in mind?"

Alex prepared himself to retell the story that he had originally told Malachai.

"Alright, it's like this: there's an old legend from the Outside that 300 men, the Spartans, were able to fend off an enemy army of thousands. They fought in a narrow passage called the Hot Gates to rob the enemy of their advantage of numbers, using their superior combat skills to hold them back for three days. If we gathered our strongest fighters to take up the same formation out on the bridge, along with the archers defending from afar, then I believe that the Domineers would not stand a chance in Hell."

Both Malachai and Matheus were looking at each other with expressions of admiration for Alex right now. Even Delmar was fascinated by his idea. That is, until Rowan finally spoke up.

"Wait, Alex, I thought you said that those 300 men lost the battle?"

Just then, the others' expressions had changed from admiration to curiosity and slight distaste. Alex raised his hands to keep them all calm.

"No, no," he assured them, "they lost because the enemy managed to find a pathway which led behind them, rendering their strategy useless. But we know for a fact that there is absolutely no possible way for the Domineers to do the same here. I've seen it myself. You guys built this place for that exact purpose. There is no other way to get in here except over that bridge."

"Supposing we agreed to do this," Malachai began, "how do we do it? What sort of techniques and strategies do we use?"

Alex thought about it briefly. "Shields," he answered plainly. "Shields and spears. It's called a phalanx formation; we create a wall of shields for the Domineers to smash against, and use the spears to kill them as they come. Combine that with wave after wave of arrows from the wall and the Domineers will finally see the futility of their actions, and we live to fight another day."

No one was questioning Alex's idea any further, but Delmar still had a few things to say.

"A well-conceived plan, but somehow I'm just not convinced that Robert Moreno would be outwitted so easily."

Alex did not understand his skepticism.

"There would literally be nothing else for him to do. If there are any flaws about the Citadel, any other weaknesses that could possibly be exploited, please tell me."

Delmar had nothing to say, but he still maintained a concerned look on his face. Malachai nodded his head and grinned.

"I think Alex may be right. Delmar, you and I both know that we built the Citadel to be as impenetrable as possible, but that won't work if we do not apply the proper defensive strategies." Delmar stared out past the walls and looked like he was lost in deep thought. Malachai spoke again. "I'm willing to do my part, Delmar. I'll gather the strongest Ravennites I can find, Alex and I will train them to work this formation, just in case the time does come that we need to use it. I do fear that it may be soon."

Matheus stepped forward as well.

"I can head around the wall and ensure that the archers are stocked and ready."

"And we need to send scouts to patrol our perimeters," Alex added. "We would need as much of a heads-up as possible to prepare."

Delmar was not ignoring them, but the immense stress of trying to lead his people and protect them at all costs was still gnawing at his mind. Rowan walked over beside him and grabbed hold of his hand.

"Delmar," she tried to get his attention and he looked down at her. "We can do this. You said that you trust Alex's judgment. We can't hide behind these walls anymore. It's time to stand and fight."

Delmar let out a deep sigh. He knew that his sister was absolutely right. In the days that were sure to come it was obvious that there would be no more hiding and waiting behind the walls of the Citadel. For now, he agreed that it was time to do everything in their power to defend it. He glanced around at his friends and allies and nodded in affirmation.

"Let's do it," he said positively. "I will rally the Ravennites and we'll prepare them for the worst. It's time to fight for what's ours once again."

Later that night, at the remains of the Iron Furnace, Robert had returned to his private quarters, ignoring the fact that it was now slightly lopsided. He was staring out of the wide window in the wall and down at the broken fortress. At dawn that morning, he had sent Caine and several other messengers all across the northern regions of the Dark Zone to rally all Domineers under his command. By now, most of his messengers had returned, including Caine, and the fortress was now overflowing with hundreds of men and women prepared to fight against their enemies of these mountains. Not only were they within the walls of the Iron Furnace, but there were a great many Domineers outside of the fortress as well, all being armed and specifically informed of the job which they had been summoned to take part.

Caine headed up into the structure to meet with Robert. Their attitudes toward each other had improved slightly, mainly due to Robert's vision of a Domineer victory finally being on the verge of realization. He was so confident about his superiority that Caine could not help but feel impressed by it, but at the same time he had a strong feeling in his gut that Robert was on the path to meeting a very tragic end if he attacked the Ravennites at their heart.

"Have the rest of our emissaries returned yet?" Robert asked as he heard Caine enter the room.

"Not yet, but soon," Caine answered straightforward. "I have to admit that your numbers are very impressive."

Robert turned around to face him.

"Yes, and this is why I have no doubt that my men can accomplish this task."

Caine shook his head.

"Are you certain that you've learned everything you need to know in order to stage such an attack?"

"Let's go over this one more time," Robert responded bluntly. He walked out of the small chamber and signaled for Caine to follow. "You are going to lead our forces to the Ravennites' hiding place, this Citadel. I will coordinate the rest from there."

As they headed down the structure and made their way back outside, Caine had more questions to ask.

"You know, you are only basing this strategy off of what that Outsider told you. How, if I may ask, can you be sure that he told you the truth? And even if he did, what exactly is your plan of action to get into the walls of their fortress?"

"What we know, from what the boy told us, is that the only way to reach the fortress on the plateau is to cross a narrow bridge connecting the mountains. That will be easy enough to identify."

"But surely you can't think that it would be easy, or even possible?" Caine interrupted. "They'll be defending the bridge heavily with archers, that much is entirely predictable. Whether you have the numbers or not, you'll lose all your men's will to fight if too many of them get themselves needlessly killed trying to take the bridge."

"And that, my naive friend," Robert teased him, "is why crossing the bridge will only be half the objective. Because I agree, it won't be easy. That's why we'll need to utilize a secondary route inside."

Caine shook his head.

"You heard what he said, there is nothing else connecting the mountains to the Citadel, and the plateau is too steep to be scaled. I know he told you the truth about that because he does not want you to attack them. How do you expect to overcome their defenses?"

"I will leave that to Wilson and his men," Robert answered with confidence. As he said it, the two of them had approached Wilson's gang once again sitting around the old furnace. Robert directed Caine's attention to them so that he could observe what they were doing.

Wilson and his men were tinkering around with a strange contraption which Caine had never seen before. From what he could observe with his seemingly primitive mind, it looked just like an oversized bow, its body about ten feet long. It took two people to hold sideways, and a third person was pulling back on a rope connecting each end of its narrow body, and Caine could see that it definitely had the distinct qualities of a standard bow, but much, much larger.

Behind them, another Domineer was standing what appeared to be oversized arrows against the furnace. They were not like any arrows Caine had ever seen. They were approximately two feet long from tail to tip and were made completely from stone like their swords. The point, however, was not shaped like a normal arrowhead. It was actually formed like a large grappling hook. From the tail, an exceedingly long rope was attached and coiled on the ground. The tail rope had been given a stone, chain-like covering as well. Wilson had gathered a team of Domineers to gather all the resources they could and spent the entire day crafting these interesting weapons. He knew that they would need every effort that they could muster, and Caine was more than impressed.

"What will you accomplish with these, I wonder?" Caine asked Wilson, who was sitting back against the furnace tower and watching his men finish sorting out their instruments.

"You leave that to me," he replied with a deathly grin. "We'll get inside those walls. Mark my words."

Caine nodded casually. Turning to Robert, he asked, "When do you intend to make your move against the Ravennites' fortress?"

Robert looked him dead in the eyes with a hint of impatience.

"As soon as the last of our reinforcements arrive and are armed and briefed. Soon, we will bring the last of the Ravennite savages to their knees. I will gain my brother's complete respect, and then we'll help him to finish off Darowe in the south."

Before, Caine would have liked more than anything to see Robert crash and burn due to his arrogant ambitions. Now, however, he did not care what the outcome of the future battle would be, but he certainly that there were only two possibilities: either Robert would miraculously succeed in capturing the Citadel, or he would meet his untimely doom. Only time would tell what would become of the Domineer cause.

CHAPTER TWENTY-THREE

The day had turned into night, and the night back into day without any signs of a Domineer presence approaching the Citadel. The Ravennites were able to breathe a sigh of relief for the moment, but after getting a brief, but needed respite in order to rest and regain their strength, Alex and the others spent almost all of their time preparing the Ravennites for an impending battle. At Alex's request, scouts had indeed been sent out to keep an eye on the perimeters around the front of the plateau, switching in and out consistently. He also took time to teach Malachai and his chosen team of warriors how to execute a phalanx formation. It did not take long for the Ravennite crafters to make sufficient shields and spears as Alex had requested. They were not exactly iron forged, but they would work, and they practiced the powerful defensive line out on the land bridge several times. It took some getting used to, but Malachai's men proved capable of creating a violently hostile formation that even scared Alex for a moment.

Matheus informed the archers along the walls of Delmar's new orders. They retrieved as many stores of arrows as they could and stocked them all over the wall. Many of the archers spent time in their training areas and even just outside of the Citadel practicing their skills. Alex found Rowan out on the archery fields practicing herself. When the Domineers had attacked their outpost the other night, she watched as her beautifully crafted bow was taken from her and snapped in half. Now she had claimed a bow from the tower's armory as her replacement. The loss of her personal bow had saddened her greatly, but she made the best of what she had. Alex stood by and watched her hit each of her targets with pinpoint accuracy as usual. It still amazed him to this day. If anything, she was one incredibly talented archer. Alex often wondered if the Native American blood in their ancestry actually contributed to their skills. It sounded somewhat absurd, but it would not have surprised him.

When Rowan ran out of arrows in her quiver, Alex walked over to her side to congratulate her on her precision, but to his surprise she had lowered her head.

"What's the matter?" he asked caringly. "I'm sorry about your old bow, but you're still just as amazing as ever."

"It's not that," Rowan sighed. "It's just that, even though I've prepared for this day for years, I cannot deny that I'm a little bit..." She suddenly dropped off.

Alex looked a little concerned.

"What?" he asked, putting a hand on her shoulder. "You're a little bit what?"

She looked him in the eyes as she swallowed and then finished her sentence with a single word, "Scared."

Alex's eyes widened. Not because he was surprised to hear such a word come from her mouth, which he was, but because it suddenly made him realize that neither was he completely unafraid of the battle that they were preparing for. It was coming, he just knew it in his heart, and he wanted his friends to be prepared to fight.

He tried to keep cool, and then he brought his hand down to rest against the patch on Rowan's arm.

"If you ever feel like you're losing faith, Rowan," he said softly, "have faith in this, as you always have."

His words made Rowan feel warm and safe. To her, it was something only a true friend would say. She glanced down at the tail of Alex's blue scarf where the same insignia of his own was knitted into it along with the Ravennite-tongue word for honor. He had truly earned the right to be called honorable, as well as the best friend she ever had.

"*Vah'Seluitah maso per'ne si yom,*" (The Light shines

upon us this day) Rowan said to her friend, *"re'tenn."* (I know it.)

Alex nodded and smiled as he replied to her sentiment, *"arrun'ai te seeta'hai,"* (For honor and for vengeance), *"in vah'morah."* (To the death.)

Despite their readiness, the both of them still understood that there was no way of knowing yet if the Domineers were even coming to start a fight. The day dragged on with nothing to report. The scouts switched out their duties once again as the sun began its final descent for the evening. The clouds had started to roll overhead and snow began to fall. Most of the Ravennites unable to fight had gather in and around the tower, awaiting their young chief to tell them to take cover or that there was no threat to fear.

As the sun had finally set and the sky had gone dark, Alex and Rowan retreated to his own personal tent for a moment to relax. A second day had passed without any sign of the Domineers. Alex was starting to think that maybe Robert Moreno had heeded his warning against attacking the Citadel. Or maybe he was out seeking help from his older brother, the true leader of the Domineers. Alex did not know what Ramon was like, but for someone who boldly led a merciless attack on an innocent society, he was sure that he himself was a force to be reckoned with.

With some free time to themselves, Rowan asked Alex to tell her about the Outside some more. He began by telling her about his family again; his younger sister, Nickole, who had always looked up to him, his mother who had raised them both on her own, and the mysterious father who had walked out on them when he was very young. Rowan liked hearing about his family, and said that she wondered what it would be like to meet one from the Outside. She seemed to be growing more and more fascinated by his world all the time, and Alex thought it to be rather ironic but flattering.

They continued to talk in Alex's tent quite some time. Alex felt himself starting to get a little tired as he yawned against his restraint, and Rowan could help but yawn as well.

Eventually, she knew that she was going to have to return to the tower for the night and let Alex get some sleep. The two of them had gotten so deep into each other's company that they almost forgot what was going on outside of the tent, and it took them a brief moment to react to a new sound that had started to rise up around the area. The two of them stared toward the tent flap as the terrifying and foreboding sound of the people yelling and running around outside sent chills up their spines.

Alex jumped up and headed outside to see what all the commotion was, followed closely by Rowan. The remaining Ravennites began flooding into the tower as the fighters were hurrying to gather near the Citadel's gate. Alex looked and Rowan, whose eyes were displaying a sense of worry.

"This can't be good," Alex said as they ran to join the Ravennites at the gate.

Delmar and Malachai were rallying the warriors in their tongue. Alex headed over to them.

"What is it?" he asked, catching his breath. "What's going on?"

"You were right!" Malachai answered him intensely. "The Domineers were spotted approaching the Citadel from the east, about three miles away."

Alex suddenly felt his muscles go tense. He was deathly afraid that this hour would come.

"How many?"

Delmar stepped over, and Alex could see that he looked a little bit worried himself, which was never a good thing.

"Numbers in the hundreds," he breathed in a dire tone, "and armed for war."

To Alex's surprise, he saw Rowan's expression become confident and eager for battle. He wished that he could muster some form of bravado for himself when he needed it most.

"Are the archers getting into position?" he asked.

Delmar nodded and pointed up at the platform at the top of the wall.

"Matheus is rallying them now."

"Right then," Alex said. He looked over at Malachai, "get your team ready. The phalanx needs to be firm and unmovable." Malachai nodded his head to him and began calling his men to him. With the rest of the archers lining all along the wall, Alex also saw a secondary line of them, as well as Ravennite swordsmen, positioning themselves on the bridges behind the wall. "What should I do?" he asked Delmar. He had never actually thought about his own role in the fight until now. "Where do you want me to be?"

Delmar looked around briefly, and then pointed up at the wall again.

"Up there," he ordered. "Help Matheus to command the defenses along the walls. I will be down here to maintain authority among the rest of our warriors."

Alex nodded in agreement. Inside, he shivered slightly at the idea of Delmar asking him to command his own people in their darkest hour. It certainly made him realize just how much he had proven himself to be trusted by the Ravennites, and it was an amazing feeling.

"You're a good leader," Rowan complimented him as he started to make for the nearest ladder going up the side of the wall. "I'll be proud to fight by your side!"

Alex felt honored to hear Rowan say that, but he realized that he failed to anticipate Delmar's sudden response to her words.

"What do you think you're doing, Rowan?"

She froze in her tracks and stared at her brother. Before, she had always been sadly shocked and disappointed when someone had prevented her from being able to fight for her people, but this time she was giving Delmar a look which spelled out reluctant compliance. It was apparent to Alex that she knew there was not going to be any arguing with her brother.

"Why?" she muttered dismally. "How many times must I train for nothing? Why can't I fight for what was stolen from me the same as you?"

Delmar look at her not with stern authority, but with an expression of protective love.

"Because I almost lost you out there, and I just got you back." He placed both of his hands on her shoulders and she looked away from him. "You are the only family that I have left. I don't want to lose you."

Alex looked on them and believed he was seeing a very similar character of his own family in the Outside. He started to realize that the one blessing of a small, close-knit family was that the love for one another was all the more powerful. For once, he truly agreed that Rowan would be better off if she did not partake in this battle. Eventually, she seemed to accept her brother's will. She knew that Delmar, despite how stubborn and overprotective he could be, always put her wellbeing first. Rowan stepped forward and embraced her brother. She looked at Alex briefly and smiled to him as a friend before turning and leaving for the tower.

Soon after she had retreated to the tower, Delmar suddenly spoke up with a loud voice of authority.

"My brothers and sisters of Ravenna!" he began as he looked around. "We are standing today face to face with perhaps our darkest hour to come. It has been a great honor of mine to lead you as best as I could, and not a day has gone by where I don't thank each and every one of you for your loyalty and your devotion to our home and our great ancestors. The outsiders on our doorstep think that they can take whatever they want from us. Well, tonight we are going to show them the error of their ways, and we will show them the true resolve of the Ravennites cause! We will never surrender! We will fight to the bitter end to reclaim what is ours! Fight with me now, my brothers and sisters! Fight with the power of our great ancestors, the Seluitah!"

All of the Ravennites were facing their young chief as he delivered his blood-rushing speech, and they cheered thunderously as Alex could feel the morale of the warriors around him soaring to unprecedented levels. Like all the rest of them, he was ready to fight for future of their people.

Alex climbed the ladder and up onto the wall. He met up with Matheus, who was more than happy to have him by his side.

"Do you think these guys can handle this?" Alex asked as they walked along the wall and past the long line of archers. "They need to provide effective cover for Malachai."

"They'll do their job well," Matheus answered. He was quite confident and Alex could only hope that it wasn't misplaced. "I truly have no doubt that we can win the day."

"Well, I hope you're right." Alex was quite sure of it himself. He was just extremely on edge. Though he had been training for months, he hand not fought the Domineers before the other night at the Iron Furnace, and he was sure that the battle which took place there was hardly going to pale in comparison to the action that would soon ensue. It made him really nervous to think about it. It felt a little shameful to him, but Alex was a bit thankful that he would only practically be watching the battle rather than actually participating. That was certainly a thought that he intended to keep to himself. He looked down over the wall as the gates were opened up and Malachai's team headed out onto the land bridge, shield and spear in hand. He took with him exactly thirty-five of the strongest warriors that he could find. They formed their phalanx with four rows of nine, with Malachai front and center.

Alex stared out curiously as he thought he saw Malachai and his front line burying their shields underneath the snow. He called for Matheus' attention.

"What are they doing? They need to have their shields ready!"

"Don't worry," Matheus replied to his concern, "Malachai told me they wanted to have a little surprise ready if the Domineers tried to charge them."

Alex wanted to know exactly what it was Malachai intended to do to fight their attackers. This was bound to be a very decisive battle, there would be no room for mistakes. He took a long look around. Malachai's phalanx line was in place, the wall was armed to the teeth with defensive archers, and several dozen swordsman stood on the ground below under Delmar's direct command. Finally, he looked out at the tower and wondered if Rowan could watch the battle from where she was, wherever she was. The sooner that this was over, the better.

The tree lines began to lighten up before soon breaking apart completely as the Domineers closed in on the Citadel. The snow was still falling lightly and they were quite cold, but more than that most of them found themselves to be itching for their scrape against the savage Ravennites. Robert Moreno had them all convinced that this would be the day that they crushed them once and for all. He told them that they would avenge all of those they lost at the Iron Furnace, and he told them, most importantly, that they would be taking no prisoners this time. There would be no room for such an extra effort when they knew that were going to be outmatched in their skills. They were going to have to rely on their vast advantage of numbers. Attrition was going to be the name of the game tonight.

The light of the torches all around the Citadel gave it away as the Domineers finished their approach and stopped several yards before the natural land bridge which Alex had described. Robert perched himself on top of a small rise of land at the edge of the tree line, joined by Caine and a small personal guard consisting of four other men. Here they had a perfect view of the bridge. Robert examined the setting that stood before his army. At the top of the wall which lined the edge of the plateau, as predicted by Caine, there were a great many archers perched in defensive positions. To his surprise, however, he saw a group of Ravennites standing out on the bridge as if they were protecting it themselves. Robert and Caine exchanged glances of interest, and Robert gestured for him and the Domineers accompanying him to follow him out toward the bridge.

The group passed through the army of Domineers and

slowly and cautiously headed out onto the land bridge. Robert raised his hands up for a moment in order to send a signal to the Ravennites that he was not currently approaching them with hostile intent.

Malachai narrowed his eyes at the Domineers as they came closer. He certainly did not trust them in the slightest. He glanced up at Alex and Matheus. Up on the wall, Matheus was just as confused as Malachai was, but Alex leaned over to him and explained that he believed Robert was seeking an audience with them before the fighting started.

It seemed that he was right when the Domineers stopped halfway across the bridge and Caine spoke up when he saw Malachai at the front of the line of defenders.

"Malachai!" he called out. "May we have a word with you?"

Malachai did not want to let his guard down in the presence of their enemies, but he knew that if the Domineers were deceiving them they would be instantly rained upon by a wave of arrows. He signaled for his front line to join him. They carefully stepped over the spot in the snow where their shields were buried and walked slowly out to meet the Domineers.

As they stopped before them, Malachai shot Caine a deathly stare that even made him look away. Robert took a deep breath before calmly beginning to speak.

"So, you must be Malachai, then," he said to the Ravennite in the center with the ill-favored look about him. "The one responsible for ransacking my fortress and killing a great deal of my men."

Malachai shook his head in disbelief.

"And I'll gladly do it again, right here and now, to avenge all of those you murderers have slaughtered!"

Robert snickered haughtily. He was surprisingly confident in the presence of the Ravennites.

"Look around you!" he stretched his arms outward to signify the vastness of his Domineers compared to their number of defenders. "I've brought all of the brave men under my command to your doorstep. There is nowhere for you to go and you know it. You can stand and fight all you want, but nothing will stop us from overrunning your defenses in the end, believe me. After what you did at the Iron Furnace, well, let's just say that I'm not exactly in a mood for mercy, but why don't tell Delmar that if he would simply surrender this fortress right now, then I'll let Ramon decide what to do with you, and you can only hope at that point that he might be more merciful than me."

They had been talking just loud enough for Alex and Matheus to hear them from the wall. Alex looked at Matheus for his thoughts on the matter. He just shook his head angrily at the sick words that were coming from Robert Moreno's mouth.

"Do not speak to me with such threats," Malachai spat back, "you filthy Outside scum!"

Robert did not seem interested in giving them a chance to reconsider his offer.

"If you want to sign your own death warrants, that's fine with me. I'm not going to lose any sleep over burning every single one of your dead carcasses when this is over."

"I've heard enough!" Matheus hissed from atop the wall. He reached over and took the bow from an archer standing beside him and an arrow from his quiver. He quickly aimed a precise shot and released the string. Even in the dark of night, Matheus' aim was remarkable. Nobody even saw the arrow as it soared through the air and directly into the chest of one of the Domineers standing just behind Robert himself. He grunted painfully and collapsed back onto the ground.

Robert spun his attention to his fallen guard and then back up at the wall. Malachai was just as surprised as he was as he tried to figure out who shot the arrow. Robert's jaw hung wide open in complete shock.

"You savage sons of bitches!" he cried out it. He and the remainder of his guard were quickly backing up to get out of range of the archers. "You've chosen death, you ignorant fools, and that's exactly what you're going to get!"

Malachai called for his own men to hurry back to their positions amongst the phalanx. Matheus gave the archer back his bow and began shouting out commands and words of morale in Ravennite-tongue. Alex was trying to regulate his breath as it had become absolutely clear that the battle for the Citadel had already begun.

As Robert and Caine returned to the Domineer army waiting for their commands, Robert began issuing them as he retreated back to his lookout point on the small hill.

"The treacherous beasts fired first!" he shouted as loud as he could. "Kill them all! Show them no mercy! Show them who the new rulers of these lands are!" While they headed back through the huge crowd of armed Domineers, there rang up a great roar of battle cries, and it could even be heard all around the Citadel. From the overlook at the peak of the tower, Rowan trembled as she looked out on the massive enemy force on their doorstep.

Malachai remained a calm composure. He noticed that the light snowfall had ceased, and suddenly he felt a faint ray of light shine down on them from above. He looked up at the sky and saw the clouds breaking apart, revealing the starry sky and the magnificent full moon casting its light upon the eventual battlefield. The Domineers were still making an uproar on the other side. As Malachai felt the light of the moon peering down on him, he could feel a great surge of energy and rage coursing through his being. He did not intend to hold anything back, and he released a powerful battle cry of his own which was instantly followed by the rest of the men in his formation, and soon by the archers on the wall and all of the Ravennites among the Citadel.

Alex raised his fist high in the air and shouted along with the outcry. The Domineers all cried out for a full minute as Robert and Caine returned to their perch to watch the battle. At that point, the Domineers in the front lines raised their swords and began to charge toward the bridge, with every line of fighters behind the first following closely after them.

Malachai shouted in their tongue, and he and the front line of the phalanx held their spears out in front of them and waited for the Domineers to start rushing across the land bridge. As they reached it, the Domineers quickly realized that they needed to greatly compress their lines together in order to get them all charging over the bridge and at their enemies. They were nearing closer, shouting fiercely all the way, and suddenly Malachai called out another command and the entire front line quickly dropped down to their hands and knees. The secondary line just behind him was prepared for this, each of them wielding a single stone tomahawk in hand. When the front line dropped out of their way, they all wound up and threw their tomahawks directly at the charging Domineers. Each one of them hurled through the air and found a random, unfortunate target. There was a quick series of sickening cries as the struck Domineers collapsed and were mistakenly run over by those following behind them. A few of them had tripped over the bodies, and even one of the targets near the edge of the land bridge had fallen over it and down into the dark abyss between the mountains. This all had sparked a slight decline in their morale, but the Domineers still never stopped charging.

Down in the snow, Malachai commanded his men again, and they leaped back to their feet, pulling their snowy shields up with them and engaging their defensive phalanx positions. As the Domineers fast approached. Matheus ordered a quick volley from the archers on the wall. A great many arrows suddenly soared out from the Citadel and hit their enemies like a firestorm. It had certainly slowed them down at the last second, but still not stop the charge. The roar of the Domineers grew louder as they drew closer. Malachai and his Ravennites stood firm and braced themselves, and at last the Domineers smashed into their shields.

The impact of countless lines of charging Domineers was great, but the support of the phalanx managed to hold them back as best as they could. Alex watched from the wall, praying that Malachai could keep the formation strong. One wrong move and he knew that it would shatter into ruin.

The Domineers pushed hard against the wall of shields, and the lines behind them also pushed as hard as they could. Malachai's resistance was strong, but to his fear he soon felt his footing begin to loosen. The front line of the phalanx tried desperately to hold their ground, but eventually they were forced to take a step back, as the force of the Domineers ahead of them was becoming too powerful. One step at a time they were being pushed back further and further.

"Come on," Alex breathed through clenched teeth. "Come on! You can do it!"

Malachai gave a quick head nod to the warriors on either side of him, and they passed it down the line to the end. Slowly, the ends of each line of the formation began to back up one step at a time. Each Ravennite in all four lines followed in the same pattern until they had formed the phalanx formation into a chevron shape, with Malachai forming the point. As soon as they were all in position, Malachai prepared himself and then shouted out again, "NOW!"

An instant later, the front line of the phalanx thrust their spears into the Domineers pushing against their shields. As they did, they could feel a significant relief of pressure coming from their attackers. The Ravennites seized their chance to begin pushing back, and thrust the spears again at the next line of Domineers as they continued stepping forward again. With every line they stuck with their spears, the Ravennites began forcing them down along the edge of their chevron formation until they started pushing them off of the edge of the bridge one by one. Up on the Citadel's wall, the Ravennites erupted in an uproar of cheering as Malachai's warriors began to take control of the battle on the bridge.

Alex was reeling with energy at the sight of it all. He looked around the archers on both sides of him.

"What are you waiting for?" he shouted over the cries. "Rain fire on them!" The Ravennite archers were quick to arm their bows and unleash more waves of arrows into the offensive lines of their enemies below.

Robert and Caine continued to watch from their lookout point. Caine was shaking his head as he witnessed the Domineers beginning to falter.

"Are you seeing this?" he questioned Robert. "Your assault is failing, Moreno! Whatever you're planning to do to counter them, you better do it quickly! I don't know how much longer they could last out there."

"I told you not to worry about it!" Robert replied angrily. He turned and grabbed one of his guards by the arm. "Go ensure that Wilson and his men are in position, and then give him the green light!" The man nodded and quickly sped off into the woods around the bulk of Roberts's army. Robert himself turned and went back to watching the fight. Caine may have already been succumbing to a loss of hope for this battle, and Robert found it to be quite amusing, but he had a devastating trick up his sleeve which the Ravennites would never see coming, let alone be able to repel. He smiled maliciously. It would be all be over soon.

CHAPTER TWENTY-FOUR

The battle had begun below. Wilson knelt by the cliffside of the mountain which stood up to the side of the natural land bridge which led to the Citadel. It was here, amidst the cover of the trees, that Wilson was looking out on the battle. For a while, it seemed as though they had the upper hand, but it hardly surprised him when the Ravennites defending the bridge suddenly turned the fight around, sending many of their adversaries over the edge. From the Citadel's walls, Wilson watched volley after volley of arrows raining down on the Domineers. He gritted his teeth as more and more of his allies continued to fall. If they did not switch up their strategy soon, he feared that the battle would be lost before sunrise and their whole efforts wasted.

It did not take long for the Domineers charging the land bridge began to realize their strategy's utter futility. As the Ravennites continued to spear them one after another, the Domineers started pushing back in order to get away from the impenetrable defensive line. Wilson shook his head in disappointment. The Ravennites were getting too confident up on their high walls, the cowards. He had already examined the area thoroughly when he and his men got up here. They had been sent here by Robert before the battle and told to await further instructions. For a while, Wilson had been waiting rather impatiently for his alleged instructions to come, when at last one of the men in his gang of fighters came down after him.

"Wilson!" he called to him. Wilson turned his attention to his comrade, and he continued, "We just got the go ahead from Moreno to execute our orders."

Wilson nodded his head.

"It's about damn time," he muttered in response. Standing up, he followed the other man back up the hill and toward an adjacent cliffside which faced toward the wall of the Citadel. "Is everyone in position?" he asked as they hiked.

"Yes, the grapples are armed and ready. The ropes should be long enough to outstretch the gap between the mountains."

"They will be," Wilson assured him.

As they neared the other side, the came upon an entire detachment of Domineers which Wilson had taken under his command for this objective. Like Malachai on the bridge below, he had sought out the best and most willing fighters that he could. After all, this was going to be the most important aspect of the battle in his opinion.

The Domineers had hauled the oversized bow-like instruments up the mountain. They had constructed five of them in total, and were preparing to set them up as Wilson approached. Two men to hold each bow in place as they pointed them out toward the Citadel's wall, they armed each one with one of the large grappling hook. Wilson went over to stand by the closest bow. The process would be simple as he looked out over the Citadel and ran it through his mind once more; they would launch the grappling anchors at the top of the wall and pull them tight before the Ravennites could attempt to remove them. Once hooked, they would tie off the rope as quickly and as tightly as possibly. One of the Domineers standing by handed Wilson a hook they had crafted so that would be able to zipline down to the Citadel and breach the wall. It was a longshot, as was this entire invasion, but it would be the ultimate test of the Domineers' ingenuity given their significant lack of proper resources. Wilson was more than ready to risk his life for this endeavor.

"Is everything good to go?" Wilson asked again. "Everyone ready for action?"

"Ready as we'll ever be," replied one of Wilson's subordinates. "We're not going to have a lot of time once the grappling hooks make contact. There's no doubt they're going to compromise our position as soon as they're fired. We'll have to be ready to go down there at a second's notice if we want to keep the element of surprise as fresh as possible."

"I agree," Wilson responded. He pointed out at the wall of the Citadel. "And remember, the hooks are only going to be able to anchor at the top of the wall. It's not going to be easy, but on your way down make sure you can gain enough swinging momentum to clear the top once you reach the other side, otherwise you'll be running smack into a solid wall and falling to your death down into what might as well be considered a bottomless pit." Several of the Domineers listening to his address cringed and looked over the edge at the cliff and down into the darkness. Even with the light of the moon in the sky, it was impossible to see the bottom, and no one wanted to imagine what it might be like to take a blind tumble downward. "Hey, man up, all of you!" Wilson commanded with authority. "I chose you all personally for this mission because I believed you to be the best that Robert Moreno had to offer me." He directed their attention down at the battle on the land bridge. "Everyone down there, giving their lives to put an end to these savage animals, is counting on us to get within those walls. My men and I will go first and clear a path. After that, you all need to be swinging down on each other's backs, one after the other. We need to target their archers and get that gate opened up from inside, then we can take the Ravennites on the bridge out from behind and let our entire force flood in and crush them! If we can get them inside the walls then it will be over, all thanks to you!"

The short speech had certainly gotten their blood pumping as they made their final preparations to launch the grapples. Wilson's right hand man stood up his side as they examined the Citadel one last time.

"Good speech," he said to him, "but are you sure these guys can anchor the grappling hooks successfully? That's a long shot in the dark and we'll only get one chance."

"I'm aware of that," Wilson agreed with him, "but that's why we've employed the best archers and dead-shots we have for this effort. They won't fail." He signaled for the Domineers to begin winding back the bows. "Fire away!" he commanded out loud.

In addition to requiring two men to hold a single massive bow's body still and firm, it took three more to pull the rope back far enough to provide sufficient forward thrust in order for the grapple to make it over the gap between the mountains. They pulled back as far as they could and aimed at the wall with extreme care. Holding their breath, the Domineers released the first bow and everyone watching as the grappling hook shot through the air, the wind whistling as the stone hook cut through it.

On the Citadel wall, Matheus was just about to order another volley of arrows when a sudden, mysterious sound caught his ears. He looked up to his right in time to see a dark missile soaring directly at them from the adjacent mountain. His eyes widened and he gasped out loud.

"Look out!" The Ravennites standing in the perceived impact zone looked up immediately and managed to leap out of the way just in time as the large grappling hook drilled down against the platform on the wall.

The Domineers manning the rope up on the adjacent mountain immediately heaved back on it and the large anchor managed to firmly hook against the top of the Citadel's wall. "Tie it off! Now!" Wilson yelled as he took his hook and prepared to zipline down. The Domineers quickly wrapped the rope around a nearby tree as tight as it would and put in a secure knot. Wilson observed the trajectory of the rope leading down the other side. From the angle at which they stood, it should have been level enough to keep them from travelling too fast that it became dangerous. As all of this was being done, the other four grappling slingshots fired their own hooks. Wilson had chosen his men wisely, for not one grappling hook missed its mark, and they all tied them securely as fast as possible.

"Now, let's go!" Wilson put his hook on the rope and held onto its handles as firmly as he could, and his loyal comrades did the same on the others, preparing to zipline down. "Follow us immediately! Let's finish this!" With that, he let out a powerful cry as he charged off of the cliff, followed by the others on the lines beside his. The rope proven to be so secure that it hardly moved as Wilson applied his weight to it. He briefly lost his breath as the shock of the leap took him by surprise. They were travelling downward at a moderate speed, but it would be enough to get them over the walls.

Matheus was awestruck as the last of the massive hooks anchored themselves to the wall like a bunch of parasites. The Ravennites had tried to remove the hooks manually, but they were so secure that would not budge. As Matheus saw the Domineers attempting to ride the ropes over to the wall, he pulled his sword from his scabbard.

"Cut the ropes!" he cried out. "Quickly!"

The Ravennites took out their swords and tried to find the rope in order to sever them, but to their horror the first few feet of the rope was shielded by a layer of stone and clay. It was impossible to break past it. One of the Ravennites attempted to climb up onto of the wall's edge to reach the exposed rope of Wilson's line. He was about halfway down the line when he saw this. Holding onto the hook with as much strength as he could as he reached for the makeshift gun which had secured on his back above his waist. It had already been armed and ready. Wilson aimed it down range in seconds and fired the five projectiles at the Ravennite atop the wall. A couple of the small, arrowhead missiles hit him in the chest and in the head, and he was thrown backward off of the wall.

"No!" Matheus exclaimed as he watched it in horror as the Ravennite toppled off of the platform. "Swords! Swords at the ready!"

Wilson dropped his gun down into the chasm below and began swinging himself from side to side as he swiftly approached the end. The Ravennites on the wall had all produced swords and awaited Wilson to reach the end of the line. Wilson hissed with rage as he worked up his momentum, and as he reached the end he used all of his force to swing himself up and over the wall. He heaved himself over the wall feet first and forcefully kicked one of the Ravennites off of the platform as he landed and rolled onto it.

Wilson instantly jumped up to his feet and produced his great stone sword. He noticed, predictably, that he was surrounded by Ravennites who meant hostile intent. Summoning as much as strength as he could muster, Wilson wound himself up and swung his blade, successfully slashing several surrounding Ravennites at once. At the same, time the other zipliners reached the wall themselves and immediately sprang into action attempting to push their enemies away from the grappling lines.

Alex's attention was drawn by the sudden commotion. His jaw dropped and his eyes widened in total shock. It was not possible, it couldn't be! He could see the next wave of Domineers beginning to ride down the ropes toward the wall. They had managed to breach the Citadel! As Malachai and his phalanx began to regroup below, he looked up and saw the Domineers assaulting the wall. For a moment, he almost wanted to abandon their formation and help them, but suddenly he noticed the Domineers across the bridge quickly bracing to charge again. This was all part of their plan to take the Citadel, but Malachai was not about to let them win without the fight of their lives, and he ordered his men to reform the phalanx.

Matheus called out as more Domineers were coming down. An archer by his side aimed his bow up at them and fired. He managed to hit one of the Domineers square in the chest and he began flipping downward in the dark rift below. The Ravennite archers along the wall had become utterly discoordinated by the Domineers' sneak attack. They were beginning to flood the walls now, one after another from five different tracks.

Delmar saw it all from the ground. He began commanding the Ravennite swordsmen around him to hurry up to the wall and help those in trouble. From the top of the tower, Rowan watched in horror along with several others on the over watch as the Domineers had actually managed to bring the fight inside the Citadel. Altha, Delmar's elder healer, was standing by her side as they watched the battle.

Rowan looked at her and she seemed to be genuinely worried about what was happening. Putting a hand on her shoulder, Rowan said, "They will defeat them yet."

Altha smiled at her and then gazed up at the full moon.

"I pray you are right. May the light shine upon them all."

Alex was glancing from the Malachai outside the gate to the Domineers attacking on the wall. He had to figure out his best course of action in response to this sudden change of the rules. The archers were all being distracted now by Wilson and his force of attackers and switching their bows out for their swords to engage in hand to hand combat. The Domineers were beginning to charge again. Without the Ravennite archers to support Malachai, he would be forced to hold the defensive line alone. If that was bound to be the case, then Alex's business would be best suited joining the battle within the walls.

As more Domineers were still pouring down from the adjoining cliff, the Ravennites were getting overwhelmed and being pushed back onto the bridges above the Citadel. "Come on!" Alex urged the Ravennites to follow him into the fray. They had to fight their way to the grappling hooks which the Domineers were using to invade the Citadel. Alex tried to fight through the crowd of attackers. With his allies by his side, Alex managed to slay a few enemies in his path, but when Wilson and his gang began single handedly dropping them like flies. Alex could not help but feel himself beginning to panic. These particular Domineers were far more skilled combatants than a lot of Ravennites Alex had seen. He looked around as Matheus and those with him were being pushed farther among the many branches connecting the wall to the tower. He suddenly realized that it was of utmost importance that the Domineers did not reach the tower.

"Fall back!" Alex called out. "Fall back to the bridges! Protect the tower!"

It was very difficult for the Ravennites to regroup and coordinate their efforts while they were now scattered along the many narrow overpasses. The Domineers were fighting their way after them onto the bridges. Looking around, Alex observed just how dire of a situation the Domineers had managed to put them in. He and Matheus were separated and scattered with the majority of the Ravennites at the top of the wall and were left to defend the many bridges. The remainder of the archers were being cornered on the wall while struggling to support Malachai at the same time. Outside of the gate, Malachai and his team were giving it everything they had to hold their formation as best they could, but without the full support of the archers from above there was simply no telling how much longer they could last. There were just too many of them. Delmar and his swordsmen were trying to get up onto the wall to aid the rest of their forces, but the Domineers had managed to seize control of the ladders going up the side of the wall, killing all who tried to climb them. As the Domineers were charging out onto the extended bridges, Alex realized exactly how hopeless the situation appeared to be. The Domineers had forced them all to separate and were covering any means of the Ravennites being able to regroup.

From his safe view at the edge of the tree line, Robert could not resist falling into laughter. Even Caine was quite astonished that his plan was actually working. The bulk of the Domineer force was continuing to pile the pressure on top of Malachai and his men, and Wilson's detachment had completely entered the Citadel.

"Take a good look, Caine!" Robert proclaimed triumphantly. "It won't be long before we cripple Malachai's pathetic excuse for a defensive line. Wilson seems to have the Ravennites on the run with the walls. Give it some time and those gates will be open before you know. This will all be over before sunrise!"

Caine had nothing to say to him but, to his great distaste, admit that Robert was right. By some miracle, he had managed to surpass the Ravennites' greatest fortifications and grasp them by the throat. It was apparent that they were now fighting desperately for their lives.

"You may really have done it!" Caine congratulated him in a moderately sarcastic manner. "But you would still be a fool to assume that you've already won."

Robert glared at him.

"What is wrong with you?" he roasted him. "Why can't you just face the facts; we've already won! The Ravennites are going to fall before the night is out, I will guarantee that. Accept it, Caine."

Shaking his head, Caine responded, "I certainly hope so, for your sake, Robert."

The battle inside of the Citadel had intensified. The narrow overpasses were swarming with Ravennites and Domineers clashing blades chaotically. The last of the archers remained cornered and had ceased their support for Malachai, as they had run out of arrows. A portion of the Domineers were descending to the ground level to engage Delmar and the rest of the Ravennite warriors.

Alex was being pushed closer and closer to the tower. Many of the Ravennites who had joined him on his bridge had fallen, and it was not long until Alex knew that he would be reduced to facing them by himself, or be killed.

On top of the tower, Rowan was shaking as she felt her restraint beginning to fail. She turned and ran back to Delmar's map room. Altha noticed her run off.

"Where are you going?" she asked, feeling worried for her. She could not believe how serious this plight had become. Even Delmar was struggling to defend his people against the onslaught of the Domineers. They were storming the ground and the long catwalks, and they had the Ravennites vastly outnumbered.

Altha and the others atop the over watch were very worried about the battle as the Domineers continued to overwhelm their people. Suddenly, like a blur in the corner of her eye, Altha saw Rowan rush forward and take a leap off of the side of the catwalk.

"Rowan, no!" Altha cried.

Rowan had retreated back into the map room, where she had left her bow and quiver when Delmar ordered her to take shelter. She grabbed her bow and slung her quiver full of arrows over her shoulder. Then she ran out of the map room and slipped herself down off of the lookout point. She slid down the angled side of the tower wall briefly and landed down on a platform about fifteen feet below the over watch.

Rowan composed herself upon the platform. She realized that she had an excellent vantage point over the battlefield. On the extended bridge directly below, Rowan spotted Alex and only a few Ravennites left fending off the Domineers who were coming right at them. Quickly arming an arrow in her bow, Rowan fired it down at one of the Domineers, hitting her target dead on. The Domineer collapsed and fell off of the long catwalk.

Seeing an arrow fly overhead and bury its way into one of them, Alex glanced around rapidly trying to find where it came from. He turned around and looked up at the tower. Rowan was perched on of the platforms above him. She shot another arrow toward the next bridge over from his, dropping another Domineer. Alex wanted to try to call up to her, but he was suddenly distracted when one of Wilson's skilled fighters cut their way through and began swiping at him. Alex managed to deflect and dodge his flurry of attacks, but it only made him all the more angry.

"I have had enough of you!" the aggressive Domineer screeched at him. "Now die already!" He began unleashing another barrage of attacks, which Alex was struggling to stand against.

Rowan continued to fire more arrows down on the Domineers fighting on the bridges, never missing a shot. At this point she no longer cared what Delmar said, her people needed her help now. As more Domineers were attempting to cross the bridges, one of them, wielding a bow of his own, caught a glimpse of Rowan raining arrows down on them from afar. He armed his bow and aimed long and carefully up at the platform before releasing it, as he was surely not as adept with a bow as she was. Rowan never saw it coming. She was lucky enough to shift her position after firing once again as the incoming arrow barely missed her but caught hold of her gray, silk hood and pinned her back against the wall. Rowan suddenly dropped her bow and choked slightly as the arrow-pierced hood tugged hard against her throat. Realizing what had just happened, she stared in bewilderment at the arrow which had just missed her by mere inches.

Alex was still locked in an epic one on one below. The Domineer warrior was a more than skilled fighter and he constantly kept him on his toes. Alex was trying to get the better of him somehow, but his foe was attacking with tactics of brute force, the same which Alex had always applied when he fought, and the Domineer proved to be stronger than him.

There was no way to overpower him at this rate, so Alex tried to outmaneuver him. He made an attempt to slip underneath one of his opponent's strikes, but the Domineer was ready. He turned and unleashed a powerful kick which knocked Alex onto his back, dropping his sword. The force was strong enough to make him roll off of the bridge, but Alex managed to catch hold of the edge. He gasped as he hung on tightly.

From the tower, Rowan watched as Alex had been subdued, and his adversary was walking over to where he hung. She tried to move but she was still pinned to the wall by the arrow. Her bow had been dropped several feet away and she could not reach it.

"Alex!" she cried out, watching his predicament with wide eyes.

The Domineer stood before him as he held onto the bridge. His eyes were filled with rage. He raised his sword over his head, and for a moment Alex contemplated his options; he could let go now and fall twenty to thirty feet, or wait for this furious Domineer to deliver the final, slashing blow and do it for him. There was no more time, and every inch of his mind and body had frozen as he could not help but watch in horror.

"No!" Rowan reached up and tried to pry the arrow out of the wall with all of her strength, but could not budge it. All of this was happening in the window of only a few seconds, from the time Alex had been suddenly overwhelmed, to the point that the Domineer stood over him, preparing to bring down his sword. Time was up, but Rowan still mustered all the force she had against the arrow. She cried out in frustration, and to her great surprise she pulled the arrow loose. The force of the release caused her to almost keel forward. Without thinking, and quick as lightning, she snatched up her bow, slipped the arrow in her hand in position and fired it no sooner than she had taken aim.

Alex closed his eyes and waited for the end. However, instead of feeling the edge of a blade, he heard a strange, piercing noise followed by the sound of the man before him gasping out in shock. Alex looked up and saw an arrow sticking out of his left side. The Domineer let go of his sword and dropped down to his knees. Alex seized his chance and, reaching up to grab hold his arm, he pulled him over the edge and onto the ground below. Alex heaved himself up onto the bridge. He gave a long sigh of relief and tried to catch his breath. He looked up toward the tower at Rowan, still standing on the platform with bow in hand, and she was looking back down at him. Alex smiled as he regained his breath and his strength.

"*Asoh've, Rowan,*" he said quietly. He looked around at the battle which continued to ensue. There was still no time to waste. He jumped to his feet, already feeling intensely strained, and headed out to aid his allies.

Delmar had his hands full on the ground. The Domineers who had breached the wall from across the mountain gap were flooding everywhere they could. Outside the wall, Malachai's defensive efforts had been marked by a series of charges and retreats by the Domineers, but he and his men could feel themselves growing weaker all the time without the support from above. They were not going to be able to keep this up for much longer.

Wilson had been working to clear the Citadel's wall as best he could. They had pushed the last of the archers deep into a corner. Seeing his opportunity, Wilson called for several other Domineer sword bearers to join him. They fought their way down the ladders and onto the ground. Wilson had his eyes set on the gate in the center of the wall. The primary purpose of their sudden invasion of the Citadel was to get the gate open to allow the bulk of their forces to flood in and annihilate all in their path. First, however, they were going to have to break the defensive line the Ravennites had established just outside. It was impressive, but it was not formidable enough.

Alex tried to help the Ravennite fighters around him to push back as hard as they could. They were all over the place, but the awkward battlefield on which they stood kept their numbers rather limited at a time. Alex glanced down at the ground level and, to his great horror, could spot a squad of Domineers fighting their way, nearly unopposed, to the Citadel gate.

"No!" he called out as loud as he could, fighting his way forward. If Malachai's formation was flanked then it would be all over. "The gate! Protect the gate!"

Matheus had been pushed up onto one of the higher overpasses. He heard the sound of Alex's call. Looking down at the gate, he saw that it was true, and there was no one defending it. As he was distracted, a Domineer attempted to blindside him. Matheus reacted just in time to duck, and the two of them suddenly became locked in each other's grasps. As they struggled, Matheus gave him quick, shock punch in the face and then threw him to the side and off of the bridge.

The Domineer managed to catch hold of Matheus' leg and attempted to drag him down with. Matheus was swept off his balance and scrambled to hold onto the edge of the bridge. Though he tried to get a grip on it, the weight of man holding on to his leg was too much. He lost his hold and the two of them fell straight down toward one of the lower bridges.

The long overpass was covered with Ravennites and Domineers fighting for control of it. Their landing was softened as they fell on top of the crowd. They were taken by surprise as the two men fell out from above and interrupted their fight. Matheus leaped onto his feet, picked a sword up from the ground and charged his way into the Domineers. They had been briefly disoriented and it was rather easy for Matheus to barrel through them, knocking them off and onto the ground below, one after the other.

Matheus made a beeline for the archer's platform along the wall. The Domineers with Wilson were nearing the gate, taking out anyone who stood in their way with ease. As Matheus made his way toward it as fast as he could, he jumped off of the wall and crashed down in front of the Domineers, rolling as he landed. He clambered up to his feet as fast as he could, pointing his sword at them as he now stood between the Domineers and the gate.

Wilson glared at him, and the others looked around each other curiously. Matheus knew that he was outnumbered, and possibly outmatched by at least one of them, but that had never stopped him before. He reached around his back and swiftly produced a second blade, shorter than the one his other hand, and positioned himself defensively.

"Come on!" he taunted with his teeth clenched.

The Domineers glanced at each other again and, letting out a series of cries, charged at the single Ravennite in their path. Matheus figured that the Domineers had no idea how much of a bite they were taking. Responding instantly, he swung his two blades harmoniously, managing to block every one of their many, simultaneous swipes. Matheus was not at all sure if he could defend the gate on his own or if he was going to fall trying, but either way he fought now harder than ever.

They were trying to surround him if they, but Matheus stayed close to the surface of the gate to rob them of such an advantage. Even though he was practically backed into a corner, fighting in this sort of setting was when he was at his strongest. He delivered a killing slash to one of his many adversaries whenever he got the chance.

Wilson was growing raw with frustration. Matheus managed to slay yet another one of his assailants, but this time Wilson leaped forward at him. Before he could react, Wilson grasped his face in his hand and forcefully shoved his head back against the wall. Matheus grunted and dropped his weapons. Wilson pulled him back and knocked him against it again several times before finally throwing him clear out of his way. Matheus rolled onto the ground, clutching his head as it vibrated painfully.

Wilson took a second to spit in his direction, before signaling for the remaining few Domineers by his side to join him.

"Get that gate open!" he hissed angrily. "This ends now!"

Matheus opened his eyes and looked. Through blurry vision he could see the Domineers unlatching the gate and preparing to open it up, which would allow them to crush Malachai.

"No," Matheus muttered. He tried painfully to pull himself up, but he was too weak at this point. He breathed heavily as he collapsed back down into the snow. He could not accept that it could over, but if Malachai's defenses were broken, there would be nothing left for them do. "No..."

CHAPTER TWENTY-FIVE

Rowan had nearly four dozen arrows packed into her quiver before the battle, and she had just used the last one. Although she did not miss a single shot, the Domineers numbers within the wall were too great for her to handle on her own, but with her help Alex was able to lead the Ravennites around him to stand their ground and keep their enemies away from the tower. Not knowing what else to do, Rowan decided that her best option was to make her way down to the tower armory and retrieve more arrows. The battle was not over yet.

Even from across the distance of the plateau, Rowan's attention was suddenly seized as she prepared to leave her platform by a terrifying sound that was not supposed to be made. She looked out, wide-eyed, across the battlefield and saw the Citadel's gates being opened up. She shook her head in terror, and then her arms began to shake as she grew ever more anxious. It could not true; they commandeered the gates and opened them. Now Malachai and his men would be flanked and crushed, just like the Spartans of Alex's tale. Once that happened, there would be nothing to stand in the way of the Domineers as they stormed the Citadel and slayed them all.

Before the escape from the Iron Furnace she had never seen combat with the Domineers, and now they were on their front porch with a great many of their numbers, only now they had the Ravennites cornered like cats and mice. Rowan remembered telling Alex earlier that it made her quite nervous to think about the battle that was being anticipated. Now she stared out at the open gates, frozen in her spot. The cold wind was forcing tears to flow down her face, and as she watched helplessly as total defeat became more and more imminent, she finally understood what it meant to be truly afraid.

The Domineers had fallen back across the land bridge once again and the phalanx formation repositioned themselves. Malachai's muscles were aching and straining. Whatever was happening inside the walls he hoped that Delmar and the others could finish soon. He need support before his phalanx shattered.

The sound of the gates opening up gained his attention. The Ravennites guarding the bridge all turned and looked toward the gate curiously, but they were not expecting to see what charged through it. As soon as the gap between the gates become large enough to get through, a horde of Domineers charged out at Malachai's defenders. His jaw dropped and he shouted in Ravennite-tongue. The rear lines of the phalanx whipped around and formed a wall of shields to meet their new adversaries. At the same time, the Domineers across the bridge saw what happened and charged forth again with a newfound level of morale. There was no choice, Malachai led his front two lines of Ravennites to reform their defense as the hind two attempted to hold back the others. It was a very temporary plan and they knew it, for there was no way that they would survive against the Domineers charging against them from two directions.

They braced themselves as hard as they could as the Domineers smashed into them on both sides. The impact was significantly stronger with only half the support on either side of the phalanx. It was so powerful that Malachai's defensive lines were both pushed until they were practically back to back. The Ravennites cried out intensely as they gave it everything they got to hold their attackers back. The way Malachai saw it, this would not be over until they were all dead, that was the measure of their dedication.

Delmar shouted various commands as the Domineers made their way off of the walls and attempted to pour more and more numbers out upon Malachai's men. He led the remainder of his swordsmen into the horde to try to cut them off. As they fought ferociously, fighters were dropping like flies on both sides. It was the most bloody and chaotic hour of the battle so far. In a way, the Ravennites seemed to realize that their demise was only a matter of time at this point, and that they were going to fall without putting up a fight that the Domineers would never soon forget. They shouted curses in Ravennite-tongue as fiercely as they could, and showed no mercy to their enemies as they struck them down, and the Domineers did all the same.

Matheus had blacked out briefly after Wilson knocked him around. After a few moments lying face down in the snow, he opened his eyes to see the shocking chaos all around him. The Domineers who passed by him must have thought that he was already dead. Once Matheus fully regained his consciousness, he sprung to his feet and attacked the nearest Domineer. His unfortunate prey did not see him coming, and Matheus swiftly and forcefully snapped his neck and stole his weapon. He was feeling the same "fight to the death" sensation as the rest of his brothers and sisters as he swung his sword around furiously, bringing down as many evil Domineers as he could. Several Ravennites nearby saw him appear on the field and fought their way over to help him, believing that none of their people should have to stand alone.

Many of the Domineers assaulting the bridges began falling back so that they might join the battle below in a more practical environment. Seeing now other option, Alex called for the Ravennites around him to follow him as he rushed toward the tower. When they reached the wall surrounding the base of the tower, they climbed down to the ground as fast as they could. There were countless Ravennite people hiding inside the tower who were counting on them in their darkest hour. Although it was more than apparent right now that defeat and death were upon them all, they still knew that they had to fight on to the end. There was nowhere to go, and surrender was not option as the

Domineers had come with nothing but hostile intent. Even as an outsider who had never been a part of the conflict and did not deserve to risk his life for people he never even knew existed a year ago, Alex was more than ready to die on his feet before he fell to his knees before the hateful Domineers. The feeling was shared among all who were with him, and they charged across the field to certain death, shouting out loud as they ran.

From her platform on the tower, Rowan was sitting back against the wall at this point. For years, she had dedicate all of her time to training for this day, to protect the remnants of her people from the evil brought forth by the Moreno brothers. She sought to be brave and strong like her great ancestors of the lost Seluitah tribe. She was starting to believe that she wanted to be far more than who she truly was. Rowan wanted to fight today, but as she watched from a safe distance as her people were slowly being massacred, she suddenly felt weak and powerless. Most of all, she felt shameful as she could not find the strength to move from her spot. Rowan could not help but believe that, as long as she stayed away from the battle, she had betrayed her people and her friend who she watched rush across the Citadel toward the massive onslaught.

The vast majority of the fight was now taking place on the ground inside and outside of the Citadel walls. The death toll on both sides was consistently rising, and the Ravennites knew that at this rate they would all be slaughtered in casualties hardly comparable to those of the Domineers, but they would continue to fight to the end.

Delmar was the most powerful warrior among them. He proved his mettle a thousand times over in this fight alone as he unhesitantly slayed his foes with nearly every motion that he made. Unfortunately, it was not going to be enough and he knew it. He fought desperately to defend his fellow Ravennites from harm. Eventually, he had become surrounded and overwhelmed. As he attempted to step up his game, he was suddenly slashed across the back from behind.

Delmar cried out in pain as he collapsed down onto the ground, clutching behind at his wound. The Ravennite warriors around him saw this and, as their people had done years ago in the valley, they rushed forward aggressively to protect him.

Alex found enemies on all sides of him, and they were setting their eyes on him almost as fast as he could kill them before they killed him. The clashing of countless blades all around him now was the most terrifying and traumatizing sound he had experienced in his life. He was sweating profusely even in the cold, and his throat was extremely sore. The world around him seemed to fade as all he knew right now was to fight the enemies around him until they had won or he had fallen himself. Nothing else was on his mind.

Wilson began leading the effort to thin the Ravennites numbers inside of the walls. He fought forward almost effortlessly, dropping his adversaries as they came, until he came upon the small group of Ravennites protecting a wounded and wracked Delmar. The Ravennite chief was here on the ground, his for the slaying. He knew that it was their leader by the impressive dedication fighters standing their ground to defend him. The Ravennites saw him coming and prepared to face him. Wilson was prepared; he continued to step forward and slaughtered them all with great force, knocking their lifeless husks clear out of the way until nobody remained to defend their chief. Nobody except for one.

As Wilson finally turned his attention to Delmar, who was still lying in the snow, he was suddenly interrupted by a man rushing to stand between them; except it was not a man, it was a boy. Wilson tilted his head curiously as this young sword bearer attempted to stand his ground against him, even after he had just killed several adversaries without acquiring a single scratch. This one would be no different to him.

Alex raised his sword up and pointed it threateningly toward Wilson.

"If you want him, you have to go through me!" he hissed hoarsely.

Wilson laughed out loud and shook his head.

"Are you alone, boy?" he mocked him. He looked Alex over with a sense of interest. "So you must be this Outsider I've been hearing about. They sent me out to capture you and bring you back to the Iron Furnace, but somehow you managed to evade us. And then you assisted in engineering an impressive escape. Now that I see you, I refuse to believe that your endeavors were anything else but pure luck. I was originally supposed to take you alive, but that was not our orders tonight, so I'd be more than willing to kill you right here and now!" he twirled his sword in his hands and smiled grimly.

Show no fear, Alex did his best to convince himself.

"Then you'll have to kill me before I let you touch him!"

"I'll oblige!" Wilson shouted as he charged Alex.

Anticipating that Wilson, given his impressive stature, would employ fighting tactics intended to overpower his opponents, Alex tried to use what he learned from Rowan and began by dodging Wilson's strikes. However, Wilson was ahead of him and immediately grabbed Alex by the scruff of the neck and threw him onto the ground. He quickly realized that Wilson was just as intelligent as he was formidable. Alex was almost overwhelmed by the thought that this might be a fight that he could not win.

Outside on the natural land bridge, the phalanx had all but shattered. Malachai ordered his men, or what was left of them, to break formation and engage their enemies in all-out hand to hand combat. As exhausted as they already were, this manner of fighting would only tire them twice as fast, but they would take as many murderous Domineers down with them as they could. Malachai fought with a ferocity which he had never felt before; not only slashing at the Domineers with his sword but using all appendages of his body to fight as well, and stomping their faces as they lied on the ground. If he fell tonight, he would sure as hell make sure that they remembered his fury.

Alex knew that he was at a grave disadvantage in every way against the Wilson. He was older, bigger and tougher than him and had most likely seen more action. Alex could feel his exhaustion beginning to get to him. His legs were trembling as though they could give away any moment now. He was struggling to keep his breath and he was building up a serious side cramp from all of the intense action. Wilson looked like he was thoroughly enjoying himself, and it only annoyed Alex even further. He charged at Wilson, ready to give him everything he had, but Wilson stepped out of the way immediately. He reached forward and grabbed hold of Alex's arm and pulled him inward. Wilson swiftly jabbed Alex in the face with his fist. Alex grunted as Wilson thrusted his knee up into his stomach and then threw him onto the ground next to Delmar. He cracked his neck arrogantly as he stared down at his two, helpless husks of prey.

Alex painfully regained his breath after having the wind knocked out of him. Blood was gushing from his nose where Wilson had hit him. He shifted over in the snow to face Delmar, he managed to glance over at him as well. Delmar's hair was soaked with sweat and his face displayed an expression of pain due to the massive gash in his back. Alex looked at him with a look of sorrow.

"I'm sorry," he gasped quietly.

Delmar tried to appear as serious to Alex as possible. He gathered his breath and muttered, *"Se amon ahk'arrun,"* (It was an honor.) It was not the pain or the sense of impending doom that had Alex's eyes tearing up, it was the thought of hearing Delmar speak those words to him, and if it was to be the last words that he ever heard, Alex would be happy to know that. It was all over and they knew it. Delmar had closed his eyes in helpless anticipation, and Alex did the same.

The sun was beginning to make its ascent as the sky started to lighten, and it was at that moment, when all of the Ravennite warriors were being overwhelmed by the immense loss of hope, that a great sound suddenly rang throughout the mountains and over the Citadel. It was a deep sound, loud and echoing, originating nearby from the hills south of the plateau's land bridge. Alex opened his eyes and gazed up curiously. All of the fighting had suddenly ceased everywhere, and everyone had turned their attention toward the source of the noise. There was no mistaking; it was the sound of a horn.

As it rang up, Robert and Caine looked over to their left. The sound of the horn was originating about a hundred yards away, from the hills which skirted the mountain ranges surrounding the Citadel. Caine took a step back in intimidation.

"Oh, no," he muttered, a look of genuine fear on his face.

Robert could sense his fear as they stared outward.

"What?" he slowly began to panic. "What is it!?"

Amidst the crowd of Ravennites and Domineers inside the walls, Matheus stared toward the sound of the horn. His eyes were wide as he gazed on with a look of exuberance and fascination.

"I know that horn!" he gasped.

Even the skirmish on the bridge had come to a sudden halt, with everyone looking in the same direction. Malachai's numbers had been brutally halved. His jaw hung open as he looked on with a filthy, blood-spattered face. A smile soon crept upon his expression, and he knew that if the Domineers were not already afraid, then they should have been. Malachai stood up straight and nodded his head toward the source of the horn.

"Darowe!" he breathed gleefully.

The horn rounded several times. The dim, dawn sky had lightened up just enough for the Domineers beyond the land bridge to see a second army forming over the hills nearby, and they certainly did not belong to them. The new arrivals were letting out a thunderous war cry. Alex could hear it even as he lie bleeding on the snow. It was a terrible sound capable of making even the strongest warrior tremble in despair, and it made Alex recall what Rowan had said about Darowe's people being even greater fighters than Delmar's Ravennites. He could hardly believe it, and neither could Delmar, and Matheus, and all of those around him; Darowe had come to their aid!

Alex looked up and realized that Wilson was still distracted. Seeing an opportunity, Alex attempted to swing his leg around and trip him. Unfortunately, he was currently too weak in his position to break his stance. Wilson whipped around angrily and forced his sword down at him in an impaling gesture. Alex managed to quickly roll out of the way. He stood himself up on his feet and faced his powerful foe once more. He knew that he was too weak now to pose any threat to Wilson, but that was not what he was thinking about right now.

Outside of the Citadel, Darowe's force began charging down the hills. As they came, the Domineers could see that their numbers were great enough to easily rival their own. Those making up the rear lines of Robert Moreno's invasion force made their way over and established a defensive formation, waiting timorously for the new enemy to crash into them. As Darowe's army quickly approached, the Domineers could see that they appeared to be far more aggressive and organized than even the Ravennites whom they were currently battling. The very sight of it made them flinch with terror, some of them even backing away slowly. By the time Darowe's warriors had reached their enemy's lines, it had become so weakened due to fear that they smashed right through their front lines, obliterating all that stood in their way. The Domineers made great efforts to fight back, but the power of Darowe's army was too overwhelming, and their harmonious battle cries were the most threatening sounds they had ever heard.

Alex and Wilson were locked back in round two, but Wilson was already overpowering him. The battle inside the walls had resumed. As Matheus managed to gain his footing against the Domineers around him, he glanced over and saw the duel between Alex and Wilson. He could see immediately that Alex was not going to last very long with his level of exhaustion. Matheus quickly scanned around the ground at the bodies which lie scattered. He came upon a fallen Ravennite and searched his body, discovering a concealed tomahawk.

Wilson was not willing to toy around with Alex any longer. He overwhelmed him as quickly as he could, and then, snatching him by the throat, he shoved Alex back on the ground. Wilson was grunting with extreme rage.

"You filthy, meddling scum!" he hissed, spit flying from his clenched teeth. "You should have left when we gave you the goddamn chance! Now you're gonna pay for interfering once and for all!"

"Hey! Alien!" a furious voice called out.

Wilson spun around curiously. By the time he realized that his attention had been drawn by the same Ravennite whom had stood between him and the gates, his eyes picked up a small object hurling at him as fast as lightning. The tomahawk buried itself into Wilson's chest and he gasped loud and painfully, his jaw thrown wide open. The sudden force caused him to topple backward and onto the ground. Alex stood up and gazed at him in astonishment. Wilson grabbed hold of the tomahawk's handle and gasped uselessly for air. He was dead before his eyes could even shut.

Matheus and a group of Ravennites fought their way over to Alex. He pointed down at the wounded form of Delmar as they approached.

"Delmar needs attention!" Alex said to them. "Get him back to the tower, now!"

The Ravennites nodded and went over to carry their fallen chief away from the battle. Matheus walked over and put a hand on Alex's shoulder.

"Are you alright?" he asked.

"I'm fine," Alex replied, wiping the blood from his face. He made a gesture beyond the gates. "Is that what I think it is?"

Matheus' attention was drawn to the new battle which now ensued beyond the Citadel's borders.

"Darowe!" he answered enthusiastically. "He's come to our aid!"

Alex could not help but laugh with delight.

"How did he know where to find us?" he asked with fascination. "How did he know that we needed help?"

"I don't know," Matheus shook his head.

The Domineers who remained inside the walls were not sure what to do. The rest of their invasion force was being ravaged outside of the Citadel. They returned their attention to the Ravennites, but now they seemed to be significantly less determined. Their willpower was rapidly being drained and the Ravennites could sense it, especially Alex as he examined them.

He breathed intensely as he tried to regain his composure for battle. Tensing his muscles and gripping his sword tightly, he took a few confident steps forward. Matheus followed by his side and the two of them called out to their allies, rallying them to reorganize and strike back at their attackers with full force. Their steps quickly enhanced into a charge. Alex began crying out fiercely, and he was immediately joined by all of the Ravennites alongside him. The sight was causing the Domineers to grow fearful and they became powerless to stand against their wrath.

The Ravennites fought through their enemy's breaking lines easily and they pushed their way through the gates and onto the bridge to join with Malachai. Seeing this, Malachai cried out viciously and unleashed his fury upon his surrounding adversaries. The bridge was taken back by the Ravennites much easier than it had been lost, as the Domineers everywhere were beginning to break down completely. Matheus rushed forward to Malachai and the two of them clasped friendly hands.

By now, the Domineers were retreating back across the bridge. Alex, Matheus and Malachai form the Ravennites and led one final charge after them. The Domineers' attempted retreat was unfortunately hindered by their own allies who were trying to get away from Darowe's people on the other side. Malachai formed the tip of the spear in their counterattack, his shield held in front of him and his sword raised above his head, and he cried out aggressively and vigorously, "RAVENNA!"

His exclamation was instantly harmonized by the rest of the Ravennites, and they charged right into the Domineers with zero opposition. The sun was rising higher; it was a new day of the battle and the tables had incredibly been turned around. The Domineers were now fighting with minimum effort as it seemed to them that all hope of victory had been lost with the unexpected arrival of Darowe. As he fought, Alex took a moment to stop and look out at their remarkable new ally. Amidst the blitz, Alex's attention had singled out one man in particular; he was a very large man, towering over every one of the Domineers as well as his own warriors. In his hand he wielded a massive club-like instrument which knocked his targets completely off of their feet. He was shouting and cursing wildly in their language. It was obvious that, with him on their side, this battle would finally come to an end.

Robert Moreno and his personal guard stood on their hill aside the fight and looked on hopelessly. Caine was utterly afraid and seemed to know that the battle was already over. The arrival of Darowe's forces was the last thing that he had expected. He gave his leader a serious look.

"Robert!" he urged him desperately. "It's over! We need to retreat!" Robert did not respond to him. He turned his attention toward the bridge and saw Malachai and Alex fighting their way across. Suddenly, he reached over his shoulders and pulled two, curved swords from the scabbards harnessed on his back. With a furious glare on his face, he ran down the small hill and charged into the battle. Caine was shocked and bewildered by his actions. "YOU FOOL!"

Malachai had completely forgotten how tired he was. All

that mattered to him right now was finishing off their enemy. It had become entirely too easy now that the Domineers had practically given up. He was so immersed in the battle that he failed to see Robert Moreno charging directly at him. He turned his head just in time as Robert lunged at him. Malachai ducked down and forced Robert over his shoulders. Robert was very quick to regain his composure and began throwing a flurry of furious attacks with his dual-wield combinations.

His swords were small and much more maneuverable than Malachai's blade. He had managed to force Malachai to back up several steps. Even Malachai had to admit to himself that this was the most formidable opponent he had ever fought, but he was not about to let it bother him. He only saw it as more of welcome challenge.

Darowe was closing in on the last lines of the Domineers. It was at this point that they completely lost all hope and began to retreat to the trees as fast as they could. Robert had become briefly distracted by this, feeling enraged that his victory, which he had nearly accomplished, had suddenly been stolen from him.

Unfortunately, his foolish distraction had gotten the better of him, as Malachai seized his chance to overwhelm him. Robert was surprised as he tried to react in time, but he had fallen one step behind of his adversary. He attempted to block one of Malachai's powerful strikes, but he had positioned himself rather awkwardly and the sword in his right hand was knocked clear out his grip. Robert gasped and tried desperately to fight back, but to no avail. Malachai had broken his defense. He swung his sword over his head and batted away Robert's second sword. Continuing his combination, Malachai spun himself around and, repositioning his sword in his hands, he thrusted it behind him and ran Robert through.

Malachai never turned his head, but he could hear Robert clawing for breath. Without showing any sort of mercy, Malachai forcefully pulled his sword back and felt it release its hold on Robert Moreno. He now turned around and watched Robert fall to his knees, clutching at his stomach. He glanced shakily up at Malachai, taking empty breaths and looking at him with an expression of pain and hatred. Malachai only glared right back down at him and, in a matter of seconds, Robert collapsed and fell down into the snow.

For the first time since the entire battle had begun, Malachai took many deep breaths as he lowered himself down onto one knee. The last of the Domineers were retreating and the Ravennites stopped and began to roar with victory, raising their swords high into the air. Alex and Matheus were laughing joyously as they turned and put their arms around each other. It had been a very tumultuous fight, but as the sun gave off the first rays of morning, they realized that the battle for the Citadel had finally come to an end in the favor of the brave Ravennites.

The citizens of the Citadel came rushing forth from the tower, cheering and applauding for the victory of the Ravennites as they returned within the walls. They had a lost a great deal of warriors, but rejoiced the arrival of their new ally as Darowe and his people joined them inside the Citadel.

Alex lumbered tiredly into the Citadel. Rowan came running over to greet him. She gazed on him with a wide smile and tears of joy flowing from her eyes. Alex looked back casually but very happy to see her again.

"Hey, Rowan," he muttered with a very hoarse voice.

Without responding, she rushed forward and threw herself into an embrace with Alex, laughing happily.

"You did it!" she exclaimed as she stared into his blue eyes. "We won the day, thanks to you!"

Alex shook his head with a smile.

"Not because of me," he replied modestly. "We couldn't have turned the battle around without Darowe's help."

"But you fought for us until the end," Rowan said, "and for that we should be truly grateful. You are a true friend, and you have given us hope!"

The two of them embraced each other once more as Malachai and Matheus joined them. Immediately following the battle, Malachai had hurried into the tower when he heard of Delmar's injury. He stepped up to Alex now and they clasped each other's arms. For the first time ever, Malachai was smiling at him as a friend.

Alex released his arm and asked, "How is Delmar doing?"

"He's asleep right now," Malachai answered calmly, "but he'll recover in time. He is as tough as they come," he looked over at Rowan and grinned, "like his sister." Rowan stepped forward and hugged Malachai as well.

Moments later, Alex turned to see the figure of a large man approaching them. He immediately recognized him as the great club-wielding warrior from before, and he quickly felt intimidated by his presence, just like Rowan when she had first met him years ago. He appeared to be around his fifties. He was a bit heavy set, had a short, scraggly beard and dark brown eyes which were just as daunting as he was.

"Rowan!" the man called out gleefully with a rather thick accent which Alex could not quite pin down. "That you? I 'aven't seen you since you was just a little one!"

Rowan bowed her head to him.

"Hello, Darowe," she greeted him. "Thank you so much for coming! You saved our people!"

"Indeed you did," Matheus responded, "but how did you know? We had no idea that your people were still intact!"

"Aye, we've been in 'iding for a couple years, now," Darowe explained. "We did not know how to find you lot, and it was far too risky to send out any envoys. 'Thankfully, 'owever, word travelled fast of a daring rescue near the Iron Furnace. Our watchmen captured Domineer emissaries carrying a message south to that bastard, Moreno, that they were gathering to march against the last of our sister tribe. We quickly mobilized and marched north ourselves, and it was not long before we discovered the battle taking place in these hills. Glad we got 'ere when we did!" As he spoke, his attention was suddenly drawn to Alex. "And who's this young one?"

Alex swallowed and remained speechless. Rowan reached over and placed a hand on his shoulder.

"This is Alex Lee," she introduced him and Darowe raised an eyebrow at the sound of his name. Rowan nodded as she knew what he was thinking. "He is an Outsider, but he is a trusted ally and a great friend. He helped us fight to victory today."

Darowe stared down at him briefly. Alex was having a difficult time meeting this man's stern gaze, but soon Darowe laughed to himself.

"Well, then," he said as he clapped Alex on the shoulder with enough force to nearly knock him off balance, "if yer a friend of Rowan's then yer a friend of mine! Pleasure to meet ya, Alex."

Alex nodded sheepishly.

"Likewise," he said quietly. He felt that it would take some time to get used to Darowe's intimidating character.

As everyone finished pouring into the Citadel, Alex and Rowan took a moment to muse on the future. Before today, the Ravennites had certainly been struggling to endure their darkest hour. Now, Alex observed as every single one of them was looking on the future with a new vision of hope. Robert Moreno had fallen and the Domineers occupying the Northern regions of the Dark Zone had been severely crippled. Still, Alex knew in his heart that the real battle still awaited out there, for it would not take long for word to reach Ramon of his brother's devastating defeat. However, Alex truly felt confident in the Ravennite cause as this would be the beginning of a new alliance between the peoples of the mountains, and they would rise up fearlessly to combat the oppression of the Domineers. For once in his young life, Alex Lee finally felt as though he had something real to strive for.

The sun was clearing the mountains now. Ranger was sitting concealed high up in the trees near the borders of the Citadel. He had perched himself there shortly before the arrival of Darowe and watched the battle closely. He kept his eye especially on the boy, Alex Lee, as he was very interested in observing his fighting abilities.

Ranger leaned back against the tree and sighed heavily after watching the Ravennites' astonishing victory. Of course, he knew just as well as any of them that there was still much more conflict to come, but he only prayed that they might be ready for it.

"I never doubted their power for a moment," Ranger muttered to himself.

... ...

"The boy has grown strong and brave since he first arrived in these parts. I find his dedication to the Ravennites to be very admirable."

... ...

"I understand. There is still a great deal of fighting to do, and Alex will help lead them to victory, I know it."

... ...

Ranger glanced out into the distance, sensing the future that was to come.

"Something else is coming," he lowered his voice to a cautious whisper. "Something unseen. The last time I witnessed it was a long time ago; the day that I discovered you, old friend, and the day that I met my love."

... ...

"I hope you are ready, Alex Lee. The greatest challenge of your young life will soon meet you head on, it has not to do with the noble Ravennite cause, it is far greater than you can possibly imagine. I only hope that, for the sake of many people and many generations to come, you will make the right choices and continue to follow the path which has been laid before your feet."

With that final sentiment, Ranger picked himself up and took one last look at the Citadel before turning and preparing to head away through the trees.

"Farewell for now," he said softly, "my son."

"The battle is far from over..."

PART TWO

WINTER'S BANE

PROLOGUE

January, 2012

Somewhere in the north-central

Regions of the Dark Zone

Night falls early in the heart of winter, and it casts its shadow over the vast mountains with a deep blanket of darkness. To the eyes of a small child, the end of the day is terrifying and fills their young minds with nightmares of the unknown. However, there are some who have never been bothered by the dark; those who have been molded by it, and welcome the darkness each day as both an old friend and an unfeeling enemy. So it had always been to the people of the lost Seluitah tribe and their diversified descendents, the brave and passionate Ravennites.

For many generations the Ravennites' civilization had thrived in a vast, secluded territory of the Adirondack mountains known to the outside world as the Dark Zone. The name was given to the Ravennites' territories by the Outside government around the early 1990s, after the two worlds agreed to remain completely separate from one another, and it was used as a scare tactic to keep outsiders from disturbing the people of the mountains.

However, word of such developments eventually reached the ears of a large group of homeless vagabonds and wanderers, led by the brothers Ramon and Robert Moreno. Their goal was to invade the Dark Zone by their own means, as they believed that the government could not lawfully defend or interfere with the culture of the Ravennites.

In the first months of 2005, Ramon Moreno and his followers mercilessly assaulted the Ravennites' home located in a great valley called Ravenna, killing nearly all their defenders and driving them deep into the mountains. Not long after reorganizing themselves, the Morenos hunted the Ravennites throughout the mountains and destroyed the remainder of their homes and settlements. The ruthless oppression of the Moreno brothers and their mindless followers earned them the name, "Domineers."

Cornered and helpless, the people of Ravenna, led by their new chief, a strong and respected young man by the name of Delmar, gathered the remnants of his people behind the walls of a great fortress they had constructed high upon a mountain plateau called the Citadel. Soon it became clear to them that there was little to no hope of fighting back against the Domineers. However, about five years after the initial invasion in Ravenna, a young boy from the Outside named Alex Lee wandered into the regions of the Dark Zone and found himself accidentally thrust into the terrible conflict. After seeing the great suffering of these people, Alex felt that it was his moral obligation to help the Ravennites in any way he could. Although he never saw himself becoming such a thing, Alex was eventually molded into a fierce fighter for the Ravennite cause.

At first he was quite young in his mind and had much to learn, but over time he was able to grow into a strong warrior with the heart of a true Ravennite. His convictions became absolute after he helped lead the Ravennites to a decisive victory against the Domineers, led by Ramon Moreno's younger brother, Robert, when they attempted to conquer the Citadel. Alex Lee did not intend to leave the Dark Zone until the Domineers were defeated and the Ravennites had taken their homes back, if he ever intended to leave at all.

More than a year had gone by since the Battle for the Citadel. The people from the southern regions of the Dark Zone, led by the tremendous Darowe, had integrated with the remainder of the Ravennites, more than doubling their numbers, their strength, and their morale. News of the Ravennite victory and the death of Robert Moreno spread all throughout the mountains and drew the last of their people in hiding to the Citadel.

The Domineers who managed to flee the Citadel retreated south and rallied with Ramon Moreno. Over the course of the following year, Ramon moved the rest of his followers north and attempted to pick up where his fallen brother had left off, only to be met by impressive resistance with the help of Darowe's people, who had proven to be even stronger warriors than Delmar's. The newly reformed Ravennites managed to push their enemies back as they spent the majority of the spring and the summer seasons fighting for control of the Dark Zone's central territories. Although more Outsiders were pouring into the mountains every month to join Ramon's ranks, the Ravennites were able to deal them enough damage to force Ramon to retreat and remain on the defensive for the time being.

As the cold, winter season approached again and the snow began to cover the vast Adirondacks, the Ravennites took to spreading their resources as far and wide as possible and established multiple camps and outposts throughout the Dark Zone. Alex Lee, continuing to hone his skills in combat, began to train a group of young Ravennites, belonging to both Delmar and Darowe, into a team of elite fighters capable of traversing the snowy environments with speed in order to keep bringing the fight to the Domineers. This skilled team of Ravennites quickly became known by both sides for their prowess, persistence, and for being seemingly impervious to the rough terrain of the winter mountains. It was not long before this reputation earned them a name of their own: the Runners. It was simple, but more than ever it struck fear into the hearts of those among the defensive ranks of the Domineers who had yet to meet them.

Just before dawn on yet another cold morning of winter, the Ravennite girl called Rowan sat alone in the shelter she had built for herself among one of the Ravennites' camps in the northern regions of the Dark Zone. A small fire was burning weakly in a pit on the ground, and she sat back against a post supporting the frame of her quarters. Not long before, the Runners had woken early to gear up and head out to track down suspected Domineer activity nearby. Rowan had personally bid her friends farewell as they journeyed out into the cold and the snow, and now she and those who remained were left alone in the camp. Rowan felt sleepless as she gazed blankly down at the old pendant charm which her late grandmother had made for her. A very plain carving of a man was positioned in the center of the charm's face, and a series of mysterious hexagonal symbols encircled him along the edge of the surface. Although Alex claimed to notice another symbol located just above the man's head, Rowan saw nothing there but a blank space, as she had for years.

Rowan's grandmother was one of the most respected elders in the valley of Ravenna. She was a skilled healer of her people and a very wise woman as far as Rowan could remember, and she had passed away about a year before the invasion of the Domineers. It was a time of sorrow for Rowan when she lost her grandmother, but even to this day nothing haunted her more than that night seven years ago, when the men from the Outside attacked her people and changed their lives forever. Many nights she was forced to lie awake and recall the terrifying events; when she was roused and hurried from her home by her mother, watching it burn behind them as her father and older brother, Delmar, stayed to fight off their enemies. Rowan did not know anything about the fight that took place except for the limited amount of information Delmar had told her; the worst of all being that only Delmar and his trusted friend, Malachai, had escaped the conflict. Everyone else had fallen, including their father.

Seven years ago, on a cold January night, the winter wind was blowing throughout the valley village of Ravenna. It had been a long time since Rowan had been able to sleep in the bed that she knew as a young child, but she still remembered it soundly, and she remembered how much this very night had scarred her for life.

The nine-year-old Rowan was lying in her bed inside her family's cabin-like home. The window by her bed was closed tight but she could still feel the freezing wind creeping in and gnawing at her underneath her blankets. This hardly bothered her, however, as she had lived through many winters just like this one in her young life. In fact, Rowan often found the cold to be rather soothing, as it helped her to drift off to sleep, but she felt like she was having trouble closing her little eyes tonight.

Rowan sat up in her bed, keeping her blanket wrapped around her, and stared blankly around her room. It was dark, with the only source of light coming from a candle flickering somewhere outside of her room. It was quiet in their cottage, as it was every night. Being the youngest of the family, she had been put to bed first. Her older brother, she imagined, was probably sitting in their family room carving away at the spear that he was making for her from the old tree standing defiantly at the edge of the valley.

It was a quiet atmosphere. As Rowan sat over the side of her bed, she gazed around her dark room with a blank stare and listened to the sound of the winter wind racing and howling against her closed window. It sounded shrill as it continued to growl outside. However, there was something peculiar about it, as if there was another distant sound blending in with the wind. Rowan listened intently with a curious and anxious look on her face. It almost sounded as though there was some sort of shouting in the distance.

Rowan did not know what to think of all the noise she was hearing, but suddenly a figure made their way quickly into her dark room. Jumping from her brief trance, Rowan realized that her mother had hurried into her bedroom. In her hand she was holding a small, rusty lantern and she appeared to be rather anxious as she scanned around briskly. She locked eyes with her young daughter as she hurried over and roused Rowan out of her bed.

"Rowan!" her mother breathed frantically as she grabbed a firm hold of her arm. "Come on, hurry!"

"What's going on?" Rowan asked, following her mother's direction. She received no answer, but instead her mother led her quickly out of her bedroom and down the staircase of their cottage. The noises in the distance were growing louder and more clear, and Rowan knew for sure that it was the sound of many people shouting at once. She began breathing rapidly as the anxious fear of the unknown was beginning to encase her.

Upon heading down the stairs, Rowan saw that the front door was open and the freezing air was pouring inside. Looking around, Rowan saw no sign of Delmar or their father. She wrapped her arms around herself to try to keep warm as the icy wind flowed around her, and her mother quickly retrieved a small, thick coat from a rack hanging on the wall and put it on her daughter.

Just then, Rowan saw her older brother hurry through the house and toward the open door. To her astonishment, she could see him grasping a hatchet which was used for wood chopping as he leaned out of the doorway.

"Father!" Delmar called out. Rowan remained speechless and nervous as her mother placed an arm around her in an attempt to comfort her. However, looking up into her eyes, the young Rowan could see that something was very wrong.

"What is it?" Rowan muttered up to her mother.

Delmar suddenly turned his attention to his sister. He seemed to be just as uninformed as she was, but Rowan could also see that he was still very worried himself. It was at this moment that their father, the Chief in the valley village of Ravenna, rushed back into the cottage through the open door. He was a great man, standing over six feet tall, with a very stern face and a short, dark beard. He was carrying with him a couple of stone short swords. He took a brief look around the room and headed over to his wife and youngest child.

"Listen to me," he began with a powerful voice of authority, "take Rowan with you. Gather as many of the people as you can and head for the mines. You stay there until we return, understand?"

The mines. Rowan knew exactly what her father spoke of: the old clay mines that ran like veins beneath the vast mountains that they called home. Her people made use of the great clay deposits surrounding the valley for much of their resources, but the remainder of the mines were mostly stripped away and retired. Rowan shuddered, however, as she remembered learning about an old Ravennite protocol kept by the Chief which stated that her people should seek temporary haven within the mines in the unlikely event of an emergency situation in the valley, such as an attack. Rowan put the pieces together, and if she heard her father right, Ravenna must have been under attack, but by whom?

Her father turned and handed one of his stone swords to Delmar, and he gripped it anxiously. Rowan swallowed roughly as her mother began ushering her toward the back of the cottage.

"Wait!" Delmar called back at them. He hurried into the family room and fetched the spear he had been crafting himself. He stepped forward and handed it to Rowan. "Take this with you. Keep it safe for me." As Rowan took the spear from her brother, she looked up at him with wide, fearful eyes, as if she was afraid he was inferring that they might not be coming back to the valley.

There was a brief silence between them as their father called out from the doorway.

"Go! Now!"

Delmar gave them both a brief embrace.

"Be careful," his mother whispered to him shakily. Delmar nodded his head and ran off to join the Chief. Rowan could only watch him go for a second before her mother pulled her away. Young as she may have been, Rowan could clearly sense the fear that was engulfing her entire family, and a very unwelcome thought was telling her that she might never see them again.

Delmar hurried off with his father toward the eastern edges of the village. Many of their people were running the other way, carrying what little they could as they made their way toward the mountains. Those who were running with Delmar and their Chief, however, were armed with what weapons they could gather. Delmar scanned his surroundings, trying to figure exactly what was happening. He looked straight ahead to the east and, to his shock, he could see an orange light beginning to grow. His first thought was an obvious one: their attackers were trying to burn the village.

"Outsiders!" the Chief called out over the noise of the mayhem. "They're invading our lands!"

Delmar was speechless as he listened to his father's words. It was only several months before that he remembered a couple of young Outsiders arriving in Ravenna and requesting refuge among them in exchange for their labor. Knowing their laws very well, however, Delmar saw no choice but to turn them away, and they left the valley in disdain. He believed that it would be the last he ever saw of them, but perhaps he may have been wrong.

The shouting was growing louder and more menacing. Delmar's eyes widened as he suddenly saw a great horde of men charging toward them through and around the many cottages. There was no doubt that they had come from the Outside. Few of them were wielding stone swords in hand, and it was clear to Delmar that they had taken them from the hands of his own people. The rest of the Outsiders were armed with whatever makeshift weapons they could haul with them into the valley as they charged into the village in droves. Delmar was sickened by this unforeseen event.

Even his people, or those few who had stayed behind to fight their attackers, were just as unprepared and inexperienced as he was. Delmar watched around his surroundings as the charge quickly turned into a chaotic, all-out brawl, with fighters on both sides struggling to bring each other down to the ground. Delmar's attention was darting this way and that as he did not know where to go or who to help. His mind was being swarmed with mixed thoughts racing too fast to be counted.

As the Outsiders continued to flood into the village from the east, one Ravennite stood out from all of the others. He was walking into the chaos with the assailants at his side, and as his own people engaged the Outsiders in the fight he raised his sword and began to strike them down in such a manner of betrayal unforeseen by any Ravennite. This man was young; his hair was light and hung low, and about his face he attempted to hide his true emotions behind a hardened expression of malice. His name was already known to his people by his seemingly impeccable reputation, but now it would be recognized for a different reason altogether.

"CAINE!" A powerful voice roared out, instantly seizing the young man's attention. "TRAITOR!"

Caine felt very cold and hardened inside as he struck down his own people and forced himself to think nothing of it. However, he turned his attention at the sound of his name being called out and could not help but tremble in the presence of his Chief. He tensed his muscles and maintained his grip on his stone sword as Delmar's father stared him down with raw anger in the midst of the chaotic conflict.

"Where is your father?" the Ravennites' Chief growled at him. Caine did not answer, but simply raised his sword up before him in a threatening pose. He grew upon his face a look of hate which proclaimed loudly that he was betraying the Ravennites by his own choice. "What have you done!?"

the Chief roared at him once more. He marched toward Caine and the two of them plunged into a hand to hand duel.

Delmar was strong but an inexperienced fighter, as were the rest of the Ravennites. He was initially hesitant to engage their attackers until they set their eyes on him and attempted to strike him down. Despite his ineptness, Delmar was still able to wield the blade and the hatchet in his hands harmoniously as he repelled each of his assailants as they came. From out of the darkness and the discord, Delmar turned just in time to see another Outsider charging at him. Before he could react, the Outsider grabbed hold of him and tackled him to the ground. The force caused Delmar to lose his grip on his weapons, and the Outsider produced a large knife and attempted to drive down at him. Delmar quickly reached up and crossed his arms to hold back his killing gesture. His assailant was grunting menacingly as he put pressure down against Delmar's resistance.

Suddenly, out of nowhere someone charged in and carried the Outsider off of Delmar, throwing him violently onto the ground. Delmar scrambled to his feet and searched for his weapons. Once he picked them back up, Delmar turned toward his rescuer, who had just finished off the Outsider and had taken his weapon before facing him as well.

"Malachai?" Delmar breathed with relief.

"Delmar!" The man called Malachai was one of Delmar's closest friends. He was around the same age as him and was built like a warrior. He approached Delmar and placed a hand on his shoulder, looking around cautiously. "Where is the Chief?"

"I don't know!" Delmar breathed shakily, his attention darting this way and that. "I lost him in the chaos. Do you know what exactly is going on, Malachai?" As he spoke, Delmar looked over in time to see one of their many assailants turn his attention to them as he attempted to attack them. Delmar froze for a brief second in hesitation and anxiety, but suddenly Malachai leaped in between the two of them and immediately drove his blade into the

Outsider. He gave a sickly groan before Malachai pulled his sword back out and threw his lifeless form down into the snow. Delmar tried to strengthen his poise as he watched his friend boldly thrust himself at their enemies in a manner that declared, "By my life, I will protect you!"

Delmar tensed his grip on the weapons in his hands. Both Malachai and their enemies from the Outside had convinced him absolutely that there was no chance for peace in the midst of this conflict. Several more Outsiders had revealed themselves from all around the cottages, letting out such hateful cries. Delmar and Malachai engaged the fray side by side as they desperately slew all foes who approached them with hostile intent. With each opponent that they struck down with their weapons, the two of them could feel their inner warriors beginning to rise to the surface in their hour of need. The outcome of this skirmish was proving to be unpredictable, so much so that Delmar found himself wondering if his people would even make it out of the valley alive. The only thing he could focus on right now was the enemies all around him and how important it was that he do everything in his power to protect his people, just as his father would.

With that mind-rending thought, Delmar's attention was suddenly drawn toward the village square. Amidst the center of the large circle of cottages the stone pathways running throughout the village met to form a small plaza. It was here that most of the massive brawl was taking place, and to Delmar's horror he spotted his father engaged in a one on one fight. However, his eyes were drawn to his father's opponent. It was no Outsider; by the faint light of the stars and the growing fire around the village, Delmar could see that this man was wearing the garb of his own people. At that disturbing realization it did not take Delmar long to see just who it was, and his blood ran cold. It was the son of the Chief's most trusted friend and associate; Caine.

"Father!" Delmar cried out as he quickly made his way toward the village square, hopefully in time to help.

Malachai turned and spotted his friend running off into the chaotic bloodbath.

"Delmar! What are you doing!?"

Delmar hurried his way across the snowy paths riddled with blood trying to reach his father. Malachai slaughtered another adversary and attempted to catch up with him. Delmar's sight was set on the fight in the center of the plaza and he almost failed to notice several Outsiders turning their attention to him. They managed to cut him off and he and Malachai readied themselves to fight.

The Outsider engaging Delmar was not wielding any sort of sword or bladed weapon. Instead, he attacked Delmar with a long, rusty shovel. With a sharp cry, he swung the shovel at Delmar's head. Delmar managed to duck in time to feel the wind of the shovel as it passed over his head. By the time he regained his stance, the Outsider turned himself around and jabbed at Delmar's stomach with the other end of the rusty tool. Delmar grunted and mistakenly dropped his weapons again. The jab knocked him back a few steps, but Delmar managed to snatch hold of the shovel's handle. He pulled his opponent toward him and the two of them began fighting over the only weapon gripped in both of their hands. They circled around each other briefly, grunting and hissing in rage. As he held onto the shovel with both of his hands, Delmar gathered his strength and pushed the long handle toward his adversary, knocking him in the head with it. In a swift motion, Delmar suddenly reached down and swiped his hatchet from the ground. With the Outsider briefly disoriented, Delmar spun him around and then stuck his hatchet into his back. Gasping futilely for air, the man dropped his makeshift weapon and collapsed face first into the snow as Delmar removed the hatchet from his back.

With a moment to catch his breath, Delmar looked around again for his father. Glancing back out toward the square, Delmar watched in horror as his fight with Caine had suddenly turned ill. As great a man as their Chief was, it was clear that Caine's youth was beginning to get the better of him. In a matter of mere seconds, Caine swiftly shifted his position around Delmar's father and made a slash at the back of his knee. He cried out in pain and was forced drop down onto his knees.

Delmar's jaw dropped.

"Father!" he called out as the battle continued around him.

As the Chief hissed trying to suppress the pain of the slash, Caine composed himself before him. The two briefly locked eyes, and Caine repositioned his sword in his grasp so that he was holding the hilt with both of his hands and pointing it directly at his adversary. The Chief was staring up at him with pure disappointment, his eyes going bloodshot. In Caine's eyes, however, he never even showed the slightest hint of remorse for his actions, whether he was truly feeling it or not. The air had become still and cold as ever, and before he could allow any resisting thoughts to enter his mind, Caine gritted his teeth as he took a powerful step forward and drove the stone sword into his victim's heart.

Delmar felt as though everything else had frozen as he watched. His very breath had come to a halt. He did not blink, and the cold air was stinging his eyes. In the plaza, Caine pulled his sword out of the Chief's chest and he instantly collapsed forward onto the ground.

"NOOO!" Delmar cried out in utter shock and disbelief. Caine shifted his attention to him and began to back away slowly. Delmar was hissing through his clenched teeth as the hot tears were being forced from his eyes. "CAINE!" he shouted at the top of his lungs and prepared to charge in after him.

"Delmar! Watch out!" Malachai suddenly called to him.

At the sound of his friend's voice, Delmar tried to glance to the side. A sudden reflex caused him to duck his head but just then he felt a terrible, painful sensation come over him as a great gash erupted upon the left side of his face. He fell straight down to the ground and planted his hand firmly over the wound as it bled profusely. His left eye had been forced shut and he gasped painfully. He could feel his hand becoming soaked by his own blood, and beside him he could just barely make out his attacker standing over him. Delmar waited disturbingly for the killing blow to be struck.

Malachai ran as fast as he could and drove his sword through the Outsider to protect his friend. Delmar appeared to be in terrible shape as Malachai looked down at him. He was barely conscious and his hand was still covering the open wound on his face. Malachai was breathing exhaustedly as their enemies were continuing to pour into the village square and turning their attention to him. He gripped his sword tightly in a defensive position and held his breath anxiously.

The last of the Ravennites standing suddenly rallied to Malachai when they saw the son of the Chief fall in a final effort to protect him. Despite appearing to be outnumbered, they did not hesitate to engage their enemies from the Outside. The plaza was suddenly turned into a massive, bloody brawl. Malachai watched his friends and brothers drop like flies as the Outsiders' numbers quickly overwhelmed them. He growled loudly in raw anger, but as much as he knew he needed to aid his people in their final stand, Malachai instead dropped his sword, grabbed hold of Delmar and began to pull him from the fight.

Delmar was moaning subconsciously in pain. Malachai glanced up as he dragged him away, and watched the battle go seriously ill as fast as he could breathe. The cold was forcing tears from Malachai's eyes mixed with both rage and despair. He heaved Delmar carefully over his shoulders and, using the cover of the darkness as well as he could, he bolted toward the tree lines and made for the mountains.

Even in the cold of winter, Malachai was so heated up with anger. For over fifteen years they had lived with unprecedented peace after they severed all ties with the insatiable Outside. He did not know who they were, but now the hordes of the Outside were attacking them, ruthlessly killing their people, and he vowed on the grave of the Chief that he would make them pay for their sins.

Rowan's memory of that night was hazy, as all she really knew about what transpired was that which Delmar and Malachai had told them all. They were the only ones to make it out of Ravenna alive, watching it burn in ruins as they fled up the mountainside to hide with the rest of their people in the clay mines. Rowan had waited anxiously for her family to return and tell them that all was well, but she was a young and naive child then. She had held tight to Delmar's carven spear in the dim lit confines of the mine tunnels, sitting back in her mother's arms until at last Malachai had been guided into the mines with Rowan's wounded older brother. It was at this time that Malachai had shared the horrifying news with Rowan's mother, informing them that Ravenna was lost to the Outsiders and that the Chief had fallen.

For the duration of the days that the remnants of the Ravennites spent in the mines, Rowan had fallen into shock and such despair unknown to her. Only a couple of weeks later, her mother had succumbed to illness brought upon her by the sheer grief, and for a long time Rowan reeled in heartache at the terrible truth that in so short a time she had lost nearly all of her family. They had been taken from her, as had her home and her life as she had always known it.

Yet, despite all of the traumatizing pain she had endured in her young life, Rowan had grown so much and she knew it. She was sixteen-years-old now, and as she sat against the post of her quarters before the dying ember in her firepit, Rowan felt as though nearly all of the pain and sorrow engulfing her life and the lives of her people was finally dissipating. A year ago she would have only guessed at such a possibility, but today she was certain that she knew who was responsible for bringing the light to their endless nightmare; it was the boy, Alex Lee. Although, he was not so much a boy anymore, lost and afraid in a world so different than his own. He was more of a man now than ever; shaped into a strong warrior with the heart of a true Ravennite, and Rowan was proud to fight their enemies by his side. In fact, she felt happier now than she did in all these long years.

Her thoughts tonight had been constantly interrupted, however, by a strange sensation that she was picking up in the cold, winter wind. Rowan knew that she need not wonder on it, for she understood in her heart that a terrible trial was coming, and it was not of the Domineers. For the first time in years Rowan found herself shivering in the cold. She had felt the exact same sensation once before, when she was a very young child, and her grandmother had sat her down before the fireplace in their cottage as she told her of the great and mysterious folklore of their ancestors, the Seluitah. A legendary occurrence was returning to the Dark Zone, as it had for all the generations of her people, and both Ravennite and Domineer alike would have to prove their mettle if they wanted to survive it.

Discover the epic mysteries of

The Aeon
Chronologies

- First Chronology -

1. Ice Cold - Part One: The Dark Zone
2. Ice Cold - Part Two: Winter's Bane

- to be continued.

www.ingramcontent.com/pod-product-compliance
Lightning Source LLC
Chambersburg PA
CBHW051936240626
47153CB00005B/1509